And so it begins...

Braedon Gerald, the young prince of Merceria, climbed up onto the marshal's lap.

"Hey, you," said Anna. "I don't remember you being invited up."

"It's fine," replied Gerald. "He serves to remind me of what we're fighting for."

A gentle knock at the door interrupted them, and then a guard poked his head in to announce the arrival of Albreda.

The Druid swept into the room behind him, not bothering to wait for an invitation. Her face broke into a smile as she beheld the young prince ensconced on Gerald's lap, but sobered as she faced the queen. "I bring news from Hawksburg, Majesty. The recruits are now fully trained and waiting to do their duty."

"Do you speak of our warriors," asked Gerald, "or the new mages?"

"Both, although I'm afraid Edwina's repertoire of spells is limited. And they're all still weak in terms of casting power, so we shouldn't expect them to use the recall spell anytime soon."

"Excellent news," said Anna. "You had me worried there for a moment."

"I did?" replied Albreda. "Why?"

"You smiled at Braedon, then adopted a more serious demeanour when you started speaking with me."

"My apologies. I'm a little rusty when it comes to interacting with others."

"You should spend more time here in Wincaster," said Gerald. "We enjoy having you here."

"Thank you. It's kind of you to say so."

"We mean it," insisted Anna. "I know Lord Richard's death was difficult for you, but seclusion is not the answer."

"I agree," added Gerald. "If you recall, you enjoyed yourself when we travelled to Stonecastle, not to mention Weldwyn."

"I did indeed," replied Albreda. "Which is why I've decided it's time for me to take a more active part in things."

"You've hardly been inactive."

"While it's true I've been of some assistance to Merceria's efforts to repel the invaders, I could've done more. I, therefore, shall endeavour to do precisely that, starting today."

Also by Paul J Bennett

<u>**Heir to the Crown Series**</u>

Servant of the Crown

Sword of the Crown

Mercerian Tales: Stories of the Past

Heart of the Crown

Shadow of the Crown

Mercerian Tales: The Call of Magic

Fate of the Crown

Burden of the Crown

Mercerian Tales: The Making of a Man

Defender of the Crown

Fury of the Crown

Mercerian Tales: Honour Thy Ancestors

War of the Crown

Triumph of the Crown

Mercerian Tales: Into the Forge

Guardian of the Crown

Enemy of the Crown

Mercerian Tales: The Spark of Change

Peril of the Crown

Saviour of the Crown

Victory of the Crown

Power Ascending Series

Tempered Steel: Prequel

Temple Knight | Warrior Knight

Temple Captain | Warrior Lord

Temple Commander | Warrior Prince

Temple General | Warrior King

The Frozen Flame Series

Awakening - Prequels

Ashes | Embers | Flames | Inferno

Maelstrom | Vortex | Torrent | Cataclysm

The Chronicles of Cyric

Into the Maelstrom: Prequel

Midwinter Murder

The Beast of Brunhausen

A Plague on Zeiderbruch

Duality of Magic Series - Coming 2026

Voices From the Past

SAVIOUR OF THE CROWN

Heir to the Crown: Book Fourteen

PAUL J BENNETT

WARRIOR CROWN
PRESS

Dedication

To my wife, Carol.

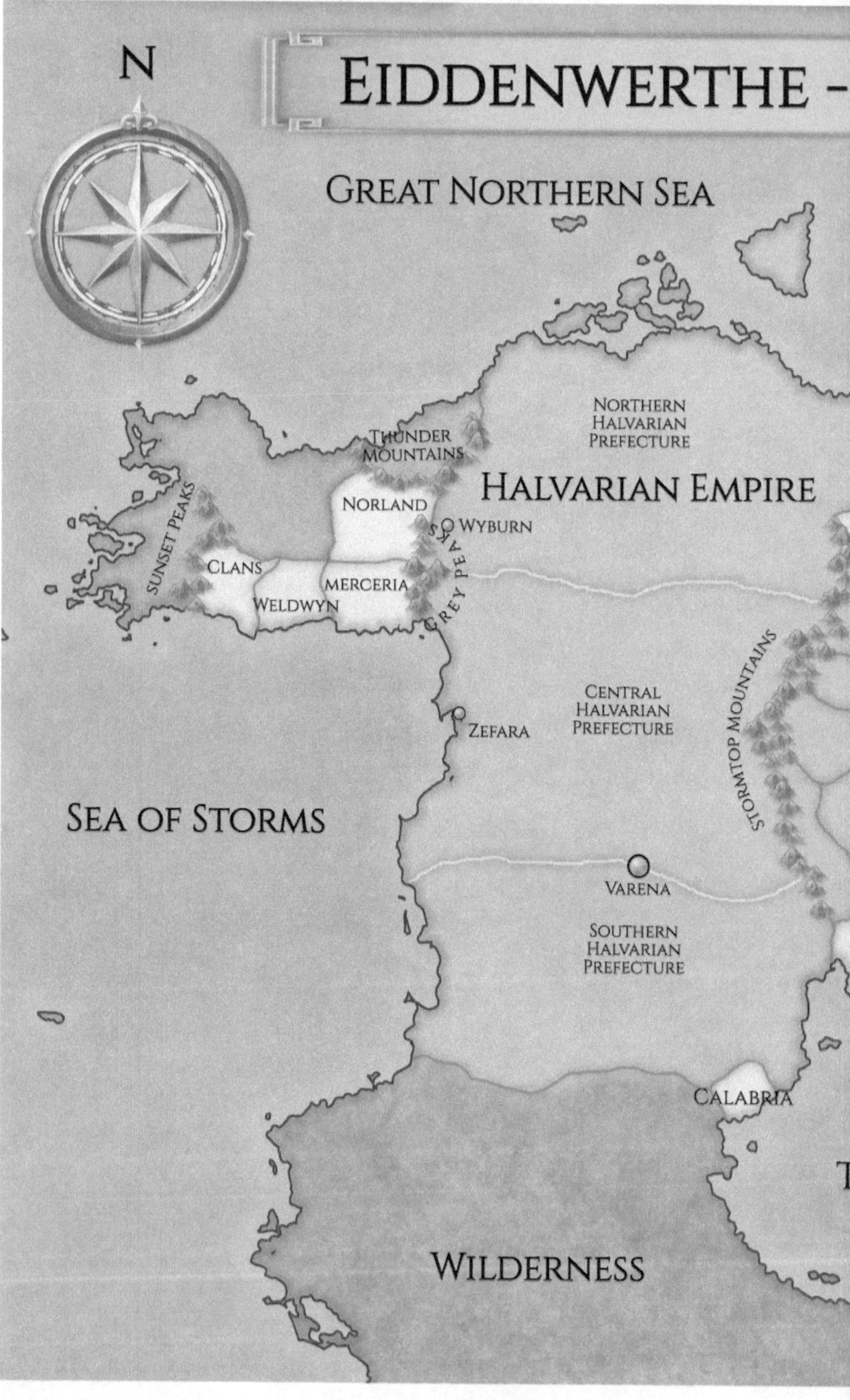

N
EIDDENWERTHE -
GREAT NORTHERN SEA
NORTHERN HALVARIAN PREFECTURE
HALVARIAN EMPIRE
THUNDER MOUNTAINS
NORLAND
WYBURN
SUNSET PEAKS
CLANS
MERCERIA
WELDWYN
GREY PEAKS
CENTRAL HALVARIAN PREFECTURE
ZEFARA
STORMTOP MOUNTAINS
SEA OF STORMS
VARENA
SOUTHERN HALVARIAN PREFECTURE
CALABRIA
WILDERNESS

68 MC/1110 SR
REINWICK
RUZHINA
ANDOVER
CARLINGEN
WILDERNESS
ARNSFELD
ERLINGEN
LUBENSTAHL
ANGVIL
OSTROVA
RUDOR
ULRICHEN
THERENGIA
ZOWENBRUCH
OTFELD
ARDOSA
ELD
GALORAN
DEISENBACH
GREY SPIRE MOUNTAINS
HADENFELD
THE WILDLANDS
CORASSUS
E SHIMMERING SEA
THE GREAT SEA

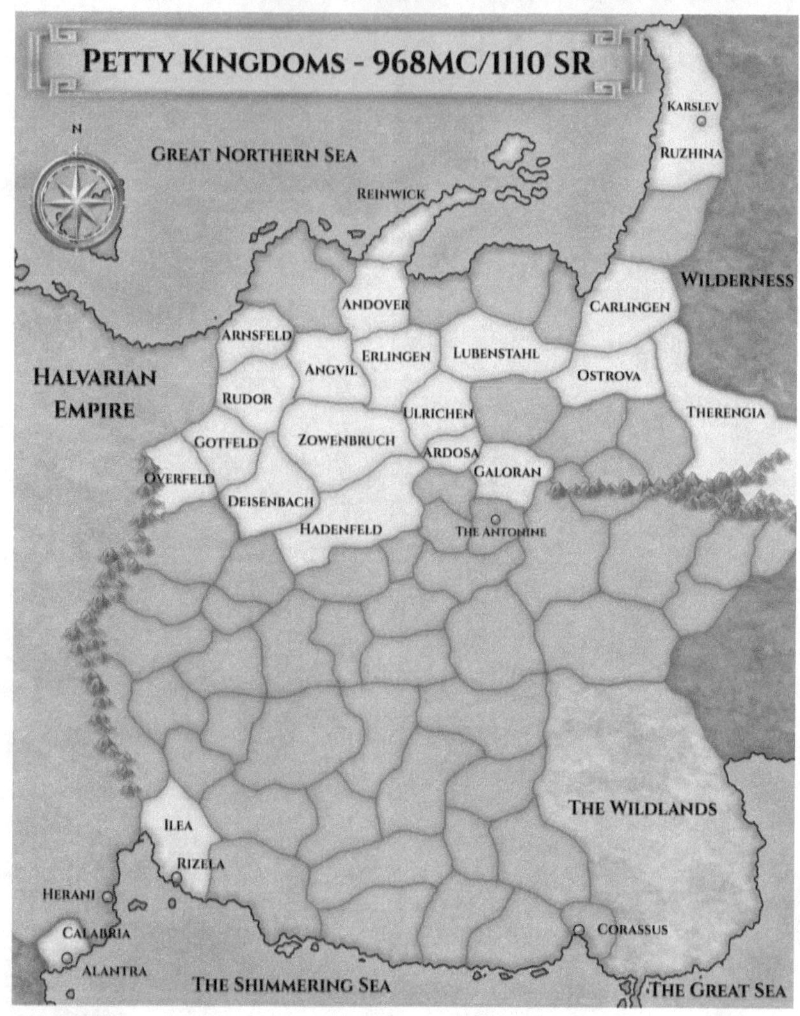

The Petty Kingdoms

ANDOVER
EIDOLON
ZURKIRK
LIESWEL
HUTFELD
ANSHLAG
CHERMINGEN
LUBENSTAHL
GROZEN
REGNITZ
TORBURG
MULSINGEN
DUCHY
OF
ERLINGEN
DUCHY
OF
ANGVIL
GALMUND
SALZING
ADELWEL
ROSENBRUCK
ZOWENBRUCH
DUCHY OF ERLINGEN
968 MC / 1110 SR
ULRICHEN

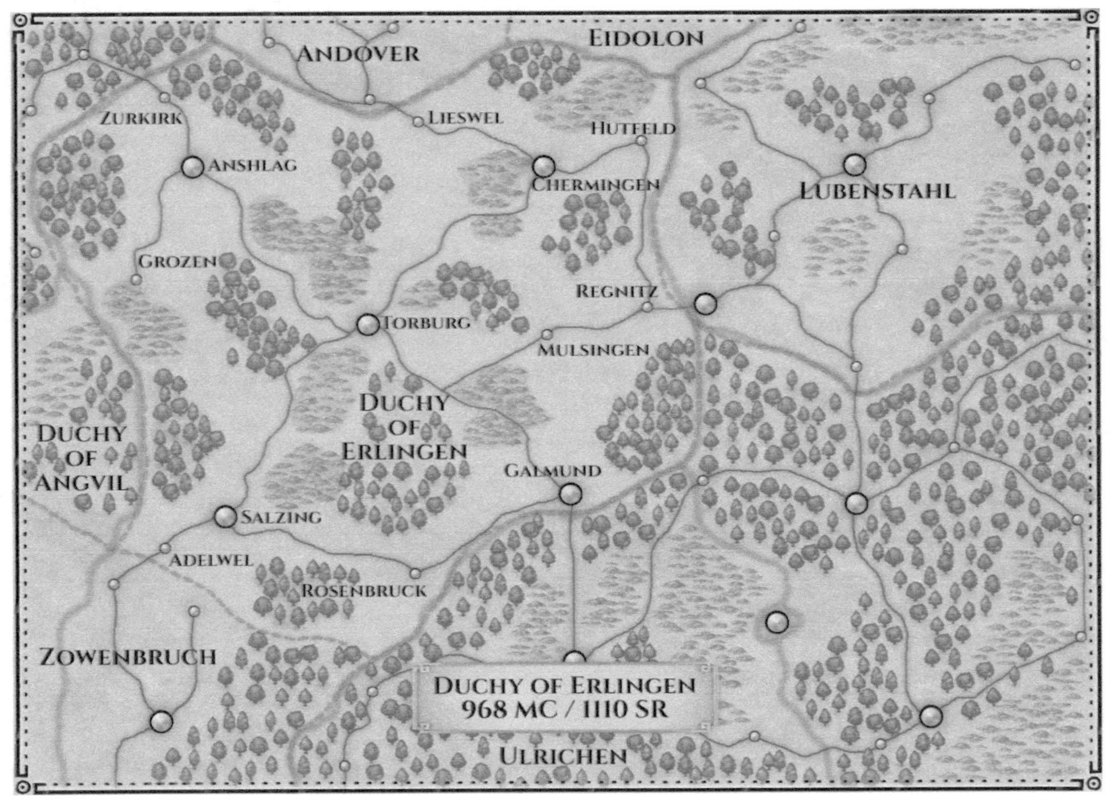

Erlingen

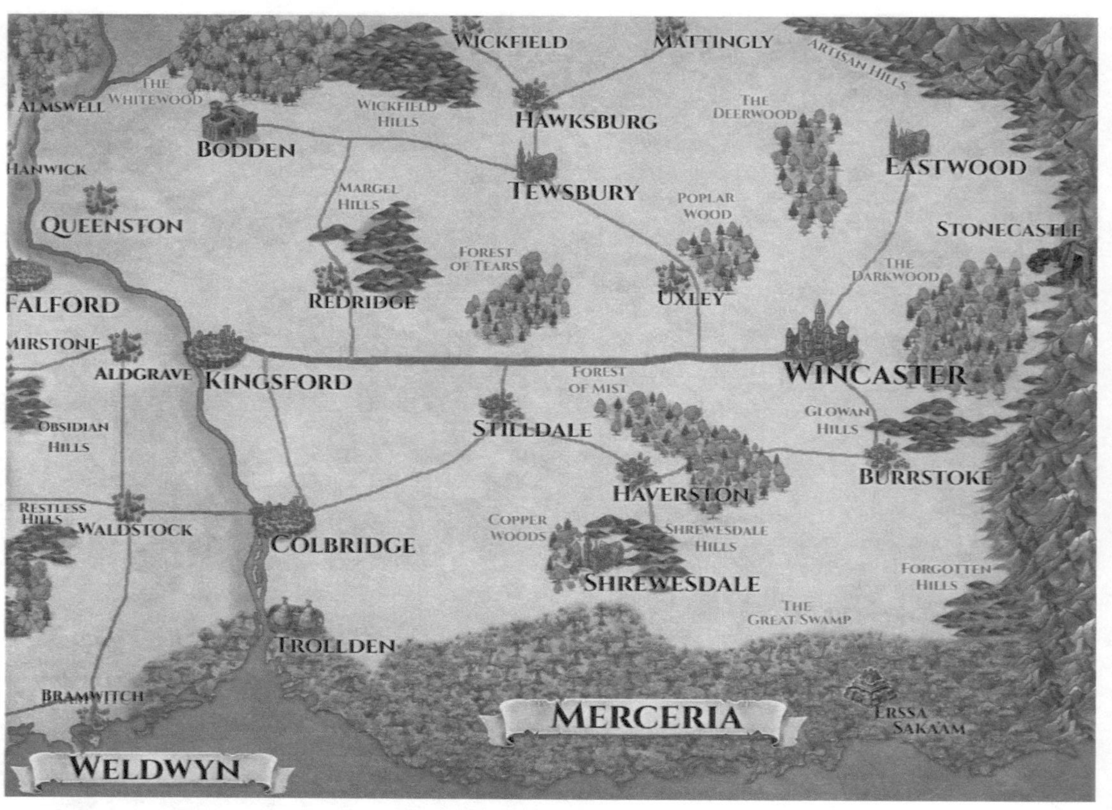

Map of Merceria

ONE

Strategy

SPRING 968 MC* (MERCERIAN CALENDAR)

Braedon Gerald, the young prince of Merceria, climbed up onto the marshal's lap.

"Hey, you," said Anna. "I don't remember you being invited up."

"It's fine," replied Gerald. "He serves to remind me of what we're fighting for."

A gentle knock at the door interrupted them, and then a guard poked his head in to announce the arrival of Albreda.

The Druid swept into the room behind him, not bothering to wait for an invitation. Her face broke into a smile as she beheld the young prince ensconced on Gerald's lap, but sobered as she faced the queen. "I bring news from Hawksburg, Majesty. The recruits are now fully trained and waiting to do their duty."

"Do you speak of our warriors," asked Gerald, "or the new mages?"

"Both, although I'm afraid Edwina's repertoire of spells is limited. And they're all still weak in terms of casting power, so we shouldn't expect them to use the recall spell anytime soon."

"Excellent news," said Anna. "You had me worried there for a moment."

"I did?" replied Albreda. "Why?"

"You smiled at Braedon, then adopted a more serious demeanour when you started speaking with me."

"My apologies. I'm a little rusty when it comes to interacting with others."

"You should spend more time here in Wincaster," said Gerald. "We enjoy having you here."

"Thank you. It's kind of you to say so."

"We mean it," insisted Anna. "I know Lord Richard's death was difficult for you, but seclusion is not the answer."

"I agree," added Gerald. "If you recall, you enjoyed yourself when we travelled to Stonecastle, not to mention Weldwyn."

"I did indeed," replied Albreda. "Which is why I've decided it's time for me to take a more active part in things."

"You've hardly been inactive."

"While it's true I've been of some assistance to Merceria's efforts to repel the invaders, I could've done more. I, therefore, shall endeavour to do precisely that, starting today."

"What did you have in mind?" Gerald asked.

"I'll travel to Ironcliff and use my magic to help end the siege."

"Is this a general statement, or do you have something particular in mind?"

"I've been pondering how to employ my magic there since we visited Stonecastle."

"And?"

"I intend to summon a deep one to use against the Halvarians."

"A deep one?" said Gerald.

"They're sometimes called earth elementals," explained Anna. "They live deep underground, where the air is foul."

"Let me guess, you read about them in a book?"

"No. From a report last summer that detailed an encounter with one in Tor-Maldrin."

"Where was this?"

"In the Clanholdings. Did I not mention it?"

"I would've remembered if you had. It's not the type of thing one forgets."

"My apologies," said Anna. "You were busy, what with the war and everything." She turned back to Albreda. "Are you confident you can control a deep one?"

"I do not control those I summon; they fight of their own free will. Having said that, I shall use everything in my power to convince it that its contribution is vital."

"How does one do that?" asked Gerald. "Do these deep ones have a language?"

"They are living, breathing creatures that inhabit the natural world. Admittedly, it's not the type of nature we're used to here in Merceria, but I'm confident my magic will allow me to communicate with them."

"Them?" said Anna. "Are you suggesting you would summon more than one?"

"I cannot answer that until I'm in Ironcliff. As I've pointed out to Gerald previously, I do not summon creatures from thin air—I call those in the vicinity. Of course, I'll first have to arrange things with the Dwarves of Ironcliff. I shouldn't like to cause them any further grief; they've suffered enough already."

"How long will it take you to arrange everything?"

"No more than a day or two, I imagine. Does that fit in with your plans?"

"We'd need time to get our new men north."

"We're also waiting on Norland," added Anna. "Lord Waverly is marching to Heward's aid at Holdcross, but he's not due to arrive for a few days yet."

"I can work with that," replied Albreda. "I'll recall to Ironcliff and determine if my idea has any merit. I can't very well summon a deep one if none are there to be called. I'll also need to coordinate things with Master Agramath, their master of rock and stone, and ensure Vard Thalgrun is amenable to the plan."

"Thank you," said Anna. "Your efforts are much appreciated."

"I'll return in a couple of days to let you know if it is even possible. Farewell, Majesty. You too, Gerald." She moved closer to Braedon and tickled his stomach. His giggles filled the room. "You be a good boy for your mother."

She paused in the doorway, glancing back. Storm raised his head and locked eyes with her. "You as well," she added before she left, closing the door quietly behind her.

"She has a soft spot for Braedon," said Anna.

"Doesn't everyone?"

"What do you make of her proposal?"

"I'll admit it sounds dangerous, but it could be just what we need to break that siege."

Gerald leaned closer, squinting at the notes scribbled all over the map of Halvaria. The immense document covered two entire tables, yet it still didn't seem big enough. "Are you certain this is accurate?" he asked.

"As accurate as it can be," replied Anna. "I collated all the information our people acquired from prisoners, then verified as much as I could."

"How does one verify an enemy's account?"

She smiled. "By only accepting details offered by two or more witnesses. As you can see, it's enabled us to build a fairly comprehensive map of the Halvarian Empire, although the south is a little under-served."

"That's putting it mildly," said Gerald. "Varena? Is that their capital?"

"Yes, and the place we'll find their emperor, who they say is a god."

"Rubbish."

"I'd tend to agree," said Anna, "but numerous accounts attest to the fact. Not that it will have any impact on our tactics going forward; even a god can't win a war without an army. Speaking of armies, have you completed your grand strategy?"

"I have," replied Gerald, "though it'll be some time before we can commence."

"Our allies are already marching into Halvarian territory."

"Only at Stonecastle. And Lord Arandil's army isn't sufficient to occupy more than a city or two, even with the Dwarves' help. No. The key to our victory lies in the north. If we successfully relieve the siege of Ironcliff, we can march our army through the Gap and into Northern Halvaria."

"Their provinces in that area are recent conquests, too," added Anna.

"Yes, and I'm hoping to capitalize on that. I plan to present ourselves as liberators rather than conquerors. Who knows? With a little luck, we might find some willing to join our cause."

"What of Trollden?"

"That remains a problem," replied Gerald. "We've contained the invasion for the moment, but their legion is still tying down our forces. If we could dislodge them, or better yet, defeat their fleet, we'd free up a lot more warriors for the push into the empire."

"We haven't the ships for that, nor does Weldwyn. I don't suppose we could employ the same tactic we used in Riversend back in sixty-one?"

"No. According to Tog's reports, the empire's fleet is larger. Oh, we might set fire to a ship or two, but I doubt it'd be enough to convince them to abandon our coast. The best we can do for now is mount an offensive that forces their legions off our land."

"Perhaps the weather will do our work for us," offered Anna. "It's not called the Sea of Storms for nothing."

"That would be nice, but the sea is not something I'd rely on to do the job."

"I understand Hayley devised a strategy to deplete the legion at Ironcliff?"

"She did, though we've yet to hear if they've fallen for the bait. If they do, Heward will march east and threaten the besieging force. However, Albreda conjuring one of those deep ones would help immensely."

Anna sat back in her chair, scratching Storm's head. "I assume you'd like to move all our newly trained warriors to Ironcliff?"

"Yes, but there's no sense in doing that until the siege is broken. Fighting in a mountain isn't exactly what our people do best, which reminds me: I've been thinking about some more reforms."

"You've been musing about those for months. You already created brigade commanders. Are you now changing your mind?"

"No, but I'm trying to standardize the size of our brigades as much as possible. Once the siege is over, I intend to organize our northern forces into three brigades under the command of Heward, Hayley, and Thalgrun."

"It won't be Thalgrun. He's already made it clear Kasri will command any forces outside Ironcliff."

"I thought she and Herdwin were still at Stonecastle?"

Anna smiled. "They returned this very afternoon, compliments of Aldus Hearn."

"I assume they'll want to go straight to Ironcliff?"

"For the counterattack, yes, but that won't be for a few days. Tell me more about these brigades of yours. How large are they to be?"

"Twelve hundred warriors for Heward and Hayley, with half of those under their command being foot. The remaining six hundred will be half archers, half cavalry. The bulk of Heward's forces will be Norland troops once Waverly arrives, but I've been assured they're up to the task. That reminds me. How did Queen Bronwyn convince the earls to help? I thought they were refusing?"

"I don't know the details, and quite frankly, I'm too afraid to ask."

Gerald chuckled. "I doubt that very much."

"True. It's simply a diplomatic way of saying that, at this point, I'm more interested in results rather than methods. It'd be different were we not battling for our very survival, but if we were under those circumstances, we wouldn't need the extra warriors in the first place."

"Typical, isn't it?" said Gerald. "We have the largest army Merceria has ever assembled, and we're forced to spread them around, piecemeal."

"Not for much longer. Thanks to Herdwin and Kasri, we've freed up our warriors in Stonecastle, releasing them for deployment elsewhere."

"That's true, but it still feels as though we're being pulled in multiple directions."

"The Halvarians have been planning this invasion for a long time."

Gerald grinned. "Perhaps, but they've badly underestimated our resolve and that of our allies."

"I've been giving that some consideration," replied Anna. "I don't believe they expected us to help the Dwarves."

"You've had time to think? I assumed the creation of this map would've consumed all your waking hours."

"Not all, merely a large portion."

The door opened to the Royal Guardsman Evard Brenton. "My apologies for the interruption, Majesty, but you have visitors—a trio of mages from Weldwyn."

"Show them in."

"Yes, Majesty." He moved aside, indicating with a wave of his hand that the guests should enter.

Aegryth Malthunen, the Weldwyn Earth Mage, led, with the Enchanter, Gretchen Harwell, following closely behind. Gerald and Anna knew them, but the third individual was a stranger.

Aegryth bowed. "Your Majesty, allow me to introduce Ekthyn Ramark, our newest Life Mage. Her intervention allowed me to survive recalling from the far north when…" She teared up. "When King Leofric was slain."

Queen Anna moved closer, taking the mage's hands in her own. "It was a terrible loss."

The Druid straightened her back, composing herself. "We've come to offer our services to the Crown."

"You have, I presume, sought permission from Alric?"

"His Majesty has gone west to Loranguard."

Anna stiffened. "This is news to me."

"He went to meet with his sister Princess Althea. I'm told he's seeking help from the Clans."

"Help?"

"Yes. Warriors to assist in repelling the enemy from Merceria. We are allies after all."

Anna looked over at Gerald. "It seems my husband can still surprise me on occasion."

"In a good way, I hope?" he replied.

"Most definitely." She turned back to the three mages. "Have we any idea how many warriors he's hoping to acquire?"

"I'm afraid he didn't confide in us, Majesty. We only received this information second-hand. With your permission, we'd like to make ourselves available wherever you deem it most helpful."

"What do you think, Gerald?"

"That Aegryth would best be employed at Trollden, where her mastery of Earth Magic would be of the greatest benefit in the swamp."

"And Gretchen?"

"I'm no expert when it comes to Enchanters. We have Kiren-Jool, but he has yet to return from Stonecastle."

"The Kurathian?" asked Gretchen.

"Yes. You know him?"

"I know of him. He served the Clans during the first invasion."

"He's a Mercerian now," declared Anna, "and I have no reason to doubt his loyalty."

"Sorry, Majesty," replied the Enchanter. "I meant no offence, but we of Weldwyn seldom interact with foreigners other than yourselves."

"You must stop thinking of them as outsiders. Doing so only perpetuates old hatreds."

"You're correct."

"Where do you feel would be the best place to employ your talents?"

"In the north," replied Gretchen. "I can use my magic in numerous ways."

"Such as?"

"As I'm certain you're aware, Enchantment spells can help protect warriors in addition to making them more lethal. I can also use my magic to scry out the enemy, which is most useful for an army."

"How far away can you scry?" asked Gerald.

"On a good day, more than a hundred miles."

"On a good day?"

"Magic is, by its very nature, complicated. Each time a spell is cast, there are… Let's call them uncertainties, any one of which can alter the spell in subtle ways, such as range or duration."

"Still, the range is impressive. Is this similar to summoning a bird?"

"No. It is more akin to using a crystal ball, if you're familiar with such stories. I gaze into a reflective surface and use my magic to project my sight to a distant location."

"And this works anywhere?"

"Not quite," said Gretchen. "I begin with a location I'm familiar with, such as the immediate surroundings. Then, as the spell progresses, I alter my point of view. The typical use for an army would be to view from high above the king's forces, searching for any signs of enemy troops."

"The Gap would be perfect for that," said Anna.

"Indeed it would."

Ekthyn Ramark finally found her voice. "Might I ask, Majesty, where I would be best employed?"

"As a Life Mage?" said Gerald. "Anywhere we risk taking casualties, which is literally everywhere. For now, however, we'll utilize you in the north, where we're due to begin our new offensive. You'll be working under the overall supervision of Kraloch, an Orc shaman. I trust that won't be an issue?"

"No, though I must confess I don't speak their language."

"He speaks ours," replied Gerald, "so there should be no problem there."

"Guardsman Brenton will see you to your rooms," added Anna.

"Someone will be in contact with you later this afternoon concerning your new assignments. Thank you for coming to our aid."

Evard Brenton cleared his throat. "This way, ladies. I'll show you to the guest quarters."

They filed out in silence.

"They're always so polite in Weldwyn," mused Gerald.

"And you think we're not here in Merceria?"

"Let's just say I'm used to our mages speaking their minds."

"That's Albreda's influence," said Anna. "She doesn't suffer fools gladly."

Gerald laughed out loud. "No. She does not. I wonder how this new Life Mage, Ekthyn, would compare to our recent graduate. What was her name?"

"Clara. I'm told she has great promise."

"Good, because we're about to go toe to toe with a Halvarian legion, and we need all the healers we can get."

"Perhaps we should rethink sending Revi to Erssa Saka'am?"

"No," replied Gerald. "Defeating the fleet at Trollden is still our main priority, and those creatures from the Sea of Storms may hold the key to destroying it. I suggest, however, that we send someone with him who can communicate using spirit talk. That way, he can recall to Wincaster if necessary."

"That's an excellent idea, but can we spare anyone?"

"With Aubrey stuck in the Petty Kingdoms, we only have four shamans at our disposal. Urgon's sister, Kurghal, is down with Tog, Rulahk is with Heward, and Kraloch is needed here to coordinate everything."

"What about Andurak of the Wolf clan?"

"I was hoping he might help with Lord Greycloak's contingent. Once they're underway, they'll need to keep in touch, which leaves no one to spare for Revi."

"We'll work around the problem, then," said Anna. "I'll give strict instructions for him to recall at the end of each week, regardless of whether he's found the answer or not. He can always return south if we don't require his aid, but at least that way, we have him here if we need him."

"Would that coincide with Lord Waverly arriving at Holdcross?"

"It would," replied Anna, "which is why I suggested it."

"Good," said Gerald. "It appears we have a time frame to launch our counterattack."

TWO

Andover

—————————

SPRING 968 MC

Sir Owen gazed skyward. "It looks as if it's going to rain."

"It will not," replied Krazuhk in the common tongue. The Orc's mastery of the Human language had grown by leaps and bounds, but she still resorted to her native tongue when dealing with complicated issues.

"Those clouds say otherwise."

Beverly smiled. "You should know better than to argue with a master of air after all this time."

They'd met Owen nine months ago when she, Aubrey, and Aldwin had been stranded in the middle of the Continent after a magical mishap left them no way to return to Merceria. They'd travelled north in hopes of finding a ship home, only to discover the Empire of Halvaria, the same realm threatening Merceria, had invaded this part of the world as well.

As fate would have it, they'd arrived in time to help the Duke of Erlingen defeat a Halvarian legion, but that only slowed the invasion. Now, they were in Andover, along with a Temple Knight of Saint Mathew and an Orc master of air they'd picked up along the way, hoping to convince another group called the Northern Alliance to come to the duke's aid.

"How much farther to the capital?" asked Aldwin.

"You mean Zienholtz?" replied Owen. "Likely another day or two."

"He is correct," offered Cyric. "I've travelled the area extensively in service to Temple Commander Roland. Our progress will depend on the weather, but if Krazuhk's forecast holds true, and I have no reason to doubt it wouldn't, we should arrive sometime tomorrow afternoon."

"What can you tell us about Andover?" asked Beverly.

"It's ruled by King Dagmar, who's sat on the Throne for several years.

He fought a war with Reinwick over a year and a half ago, which resulted in a humiliating loss at the Battle of Ebenhof, where he was captured, but the new Duke of Reinwick, Lord Fernando, offered him the hand of friendship rather than imprisoning him. Quite a remarkable turn of events, I must admit, and not something anyone expected."

"And that led to the formation of this Northern Alliance everyone keeps talking about?"

"It did. Combined, they can field an army larger than any other single Petty Kingdom, though how that fares against the Halvarian Empire remains to be seen."

"Have you met King Dagmar?"

"Only briefly. It's common practice in my order to pay proper respects to the court when visiting the realm. In my case, I was delivering correspondence to our commandery in Zienholtz."

"Was this before or after the war?"

"My last visit was just over six months ago, but other than bowing in his presence and wishing him well, I had very little interaction with the man. I am told, however, that he has changed greatly since his unfortunate capture."

"In what way?" asked Beverly.

"Prior to the war, he was obsessed with regaining the former glory of Andover. Now, he sees this Northern Alliance as a way to project power without resorting to invading his neighbours. You might say it's a reflection of the times."

"I'm not certain I understand," said Owen. "Are you suggesting he desires a war with Halvaria?"

"Nobody wants that," replied Cyric, "but Dagmar craves a place in the history books, and defeating the empire would do just that."

"That's all well and good," said Beverly, "particularly if he marches to Erlingen's aid, but who commands the alliance's army?"

"I'm afraid I am not privy to that information. I suspect the Duke of Reinwick commands his own contingent, while the same likely holds true for the King of Andover. Historically, neither side fielded much of an army, but their recent conflict changed all that. Both now realize they are better off depending on each other to keep their borders safe."

"Will they march to Erlingen's aid?"

"It would be in their best interests to do so, but I don't know either ruler well enough to judge how they'll react to the recent events. There's every chance they might remain in Andover and wait for the empire to come to them, allowing them to choose where to make a stand."

"Then we must convince them otherwise," said Aubrey. "Without their aid, Erlingen will fall, and then who else could possibly stand against the Halvarians?"

"Hadenfeld," said Owen. "Although, word is, two civil wars have weakened them significantly."

"What of Therengia?" asked Aubrey. "I hear they have a remarkable military history."

"That they have," replied Cyric, "but they lie far to the east. Geography alone dictates they will play no part in this campaign." He slowed his horse and then held his palms together in silent prayer as he looked off to a field on his right.

"Is there some significance to this area?" asked Aldwin.

"Ahead of us lies the town of Legenfeldt. That field over yonder was the scene of a great battle seventeen years ago and is where I met Temple Captain Giselle."

"Yes. You mentioned her the first time we met. She now serves in Deisenbach."

"By all rights, she should be a Temple Commander by now, but she lost her command at Legenfeldt, an unforgivable failure in the eyes of the Church. As you no doubt surmise, the Church is as much a political creature as the Petty Kingdoms. Have you such problems back where you're from?"

"To an extent," replied Aldwin. "Before our queen was crowned, we had all sorts of turmoil."

"That's putting it mildly," added Aubrey. "We had an insurrection followed by a civil war."

"Yes, but we came out on the winning side." Aldwin froze in the saddle, glancing at Aubrey, his cheeks reddening in shame. "Sorry. I didn't mean to imply all those deaths were somehow worthwhile."

"War is best avoided whenever possible," said Cyric, "but to stand back and do nothing often gives tyrants free rein."

"Wise words," replied Aubrey, "but in our case, the queen's attempts to give us peace have only resulted in more war."

"A sad state of affairs, indeed. Sometimes, I wonder if the natural state of humanity is that of total anarchy?"

"Surely not?" said Beverly. "What about all those people who want to live their lives in peace?"

"You're right. I should've said anarchy is the natural state of the nobility, at least in the Petty Kingdoms. There are exceptions, but by and large, the ruling classes are far more concerned with their influence and wealth. Andover is a prime example of that. Two wars in two decades, and they're preparing to fight yet again. I sometimes wonder if the Continent will ever truly be at peace."

"You do a lot of wondering," noted Aldwin.

"Now that you mention it, I suppose I do. I try to keep busy with my duties as a Temple Knight, but I must confess my mind tends to… well, have a mind of its own."

A fresh breeze stirred the trees, leading Owen to look westward. "It appears our Air Mage was correct. The clouds are clearing."

"So they are," agreed Beverly, "but Krazuhk is a master of air, not an Air Mage."

"Is there that much of a difference?"

Beverly was about to reply, but Aubrey beat her to it. "While it's true they both employ the same type of spells, there is a vast difference in their philosophy regarding magic."

"Which is?"

"An Air Mage tries to control the element, whereas the master of air embraces it."

"I don't see a difference."

"Do you control your horse or work with it?"

"I control it, naturally. I am a knight."

"I think I understand what my cousin is inferring," said Beverly. "Lightning and I work together."

"Yes, but surely there are times when you need to take control?"

"I guide him, but he's a Mercerian Charger and far stronger than I. If he doesn't want to ride into battle, there's little I can do to persuade him otherwise."

"Yes, but he's a living, breathing animal. Magic is something else entirely."

"Is it?" said Aubrey. "Tell me what you believe magic is?"

"Why, it's a mystical force locked within the blood of mages."

"And how does a mage harness these powers?"

"I assume the same way a warrior harnesses his strength to wield a sword."

"That's a good way of describing it," said Aubrey. "Perhaps there's hope for you yet."

Beverly laughed. "I believe she just gave you a compliment, Owen. If I were you, I'd accept it and move on to a new topic of conversation before she changes her mind."

. . .

The city of Zienholtz spread out before them as they topped a rise two days later. An impressive grey wall encircled the area, which included gleaming white spires that towered over the rest of the buildings. Hundreds of men gathered on the plains to the west, a sure sign that King Dagmar had given the order to mass his army.

"That's encouraging," noted Beverly. "There must be two thousand warriors down there."

"Indeed," said Cyric, "and their camp is much more organized than when they surrendered to Erlingen at the Battle of Legenfeldt seventeen years ago. A result, I suspect, of their recent reforms."

"Would Reinwick be responsible for that?"

"It's possible, although I believe it has more to do with the empire's attack on Arnsfeld."

"I'm not certain I follow."

"We learned a great deal about Halvarian legions after their defeat, including how they organized the forces under their control. The Temple Knights did what they could to disseminate this information to the Petty Kingdoms, but few seemed interested. Having said that, I think what we are seeing here is the Northern Alliance's attempt at creating their own version of a legion. From what I can tell, they've got about the same proportions of foot, horse, and bow."

"They've done a remarkable job of it," said Beverly. "Although I can't speak to the calibre of warriors at their disposal, they certainly appear well-armoured."

"Yes, and in that, they may find an advantage. The empire's provincial troops wear very little armour."

"Why is that?" asked Aldwin. "Do they not believe in protecting themselves?"

"I'm certain they want to," replied Cyric, "but they are recruited from the empire's subjugated territories, and the last thing the Halvarians desire is to supply possible rebels with decent armour and weapons."

"Yet they arm them with bows and mount them on horses."

"True, but the provincial horsemen are not knights. They reserve plate armour for their imperial warriors."

"And that works?" asked Aldwin.

"Over the years, it's allowed them to conquer half the Continent. If not for Arnsfeld, they'd still be considered unbeatable, at least on land."

"Not at sea?"

"No. A great sea battle off the coast of Calabria some years ago ended their dominance of the Shimmering Sea, and then there was a smaller expedition that tried to cause problems in Reinwick. In both instances, the Temple Knights were involved in their defeat."

"Very interesting," said Beverly. "However, I think it's time we sought out King Dagmar and presented him with the Duke of Erlingen's request for aid."

They were challenged upon arriving at the army camp, but then Cyric addressed the guards, quickly convincing them that the group posed no threat. Krazuhk's presence raised some eyebrows, though not nearly as many as back in Erlingen. Beverly found the difference promising and wondered if there were Orcs in Andover who might assist in the campaign. The shamans to the west had certainly helped Merceria.

Cyric stopped to ask directions and was steered towards a large pavilion guarded by a pair of warriors in plate armour.

"Knights of Valour," said Sir Owen. "The king's personal order of knighthood."

As they approached, the knights both drew their swords. "Halt," commanded the one on the right. "Identify yourselves."

"I am General Beverly Fitzwilliam, Baroness of Bodden, and have the honour of representing Duke Alain of Erlingen." She pulled a scroll case from her belt and held it out, revealing the duke's seal on the top.

The knight examined it closely before nodding towards Beverly's group. "And the rest of these individuals?"

"This is my cousin, Lady Aubrey Brandon, Baroness of Hawksburg, and my husband, Lord Aldwin Fitzwilliam. Accompanying us this day are Krazuhk, Master of Air of the Sky Singers; Sir Owen, a knight of Erlingen; and Brother Cyric, a Temple Knight of Saint Mathew. That's all of us, unless you want me to introduce our horses?"

The fellow sneered. "Wait here while I see if His Majesty will permit you an audience." He disappeared into the pavilion.

"Do they not believe in manners here in Andover?" asked Aubrey, although she clearly didn't expect an answer.

After a subdued conversation within, the knight returned. "His Majesty will meet with you, but you must surrender your weapons." He called over some guards, waiting until a trio of footmen appeared. "Take their weapons and horses."

Beverly dismounted, handing over Lightning's reins, but when a guard held out his hand for her weapon, she paused. "This is Nature's Fury. It does not leave my side."

"Then you will not meet with His Majesty," countered the knight.

Cyric took a step forward. "I think you might wish to reconsider that statement." He kept his voice low and quiet. "General Fitzwilliam recently led the Army of Erlingen to a great victory over the empire. Do you want to be the one who refused her entry to your king?"

The second knight cleared his throat. "Allow me to speak to His Majesty on their behalf, Sir Kenworth. I'm certain he can be persuaded."

Kenworth threw him a stare, but then relented. "Very well, but I'll be watching you closely—all of you."

They waited as the second knight entered the tent. The silence dragged on, save for muttered words from inside, and then the knight reappeared.

"His Majesty has graciously permitted an audience, even though you bear that weapon." He stood to one side, holding the tent flap open.

"After you, General," said Cyric.

Inside, a group of men gathered around a table covered by a map. The king was easy to spot, for even here, in what was presumably his own tent, he wore a crown, along with luxurious robes as befits a ruler of a Petty Kingdom.

"General Fitzwilliam," announced the knight.

"Thank you, Gervais," replied King Dagmar. "That will be all." He looked up from his map, staring at Beverly standing there in her armour. "By the Saints, Gervais. You didn't mention she was a woman."

"I assure you she is a skilled strategist," offered Cyric. He stepped to the forefront, his surcoat bearing the symbol of a white axe on a brown background, indicating whom he served.

"And a Temple Knight of Saint Mathew? I thought your people were ordered disbanded?"

"They were," replied Cyric, "although the order still maintains chapters in a multitude of the Petty Kingdoms. This, however, is of little importance, for General Fitzwilliam brings you urgent news from His Grace, Duke Alain of Erlingen."

"Yes, I do," added Beverly as she stepped closer, extending the scroll.

One of the king's people took it, passing it along to His Majesty. King Dagmar broke it open, reading through the enclosed letter, while the rest of the tent's occupants waited with bated breath.

Dagmar looked up from the missive. "It says here you led the Army of Erlingen to victory."

"I did," said Beverly, "though it was hard won."

"Yet the Halvarians still threaten Erlingen?"

"We inflicted a great many casualties, Majesty, but a second legion was in the area, forcing us to withdraw across the border into Erlingen. His Grace, the duke, hoped you might march to his aid."

"I must wait until the Army of Reinwick arrives. Duke Fernando promised to come to our aid should word of invasion come, but we've yet to hear a reply to our requests to join forces here in Andover."

"May I enquire when you sent your request?"

"Lorenzo?" The king addressed one of the men gathered around the map.

"The first left several weeks ago," the fellow replied, "with another, eight days later. More than enough time for a return message. I fear the duke has reconsidered his attitude towards our alliance."

"Perhaps someone intercepted these letters?" said Beverly. "Were your couriers trustworthy?"

"What kind of a question is that?" demanded Dagmar.

"You've heard nothing from them since they left, correct?"

"So Lorenzo tells me, and there's no reason to doubt his loyalty. Why? What are you hinting at?"

"I suggest," said Beverly, "your messengers are dead, most likely the victims of an ambush."

"Who'd dare do such a thing within the borders of my kingdom?"

"Who would benefit by sowing dissension between your alliance, Majesty?"

"The empire, but they bear no presence in Andover."

Cyric cleared his throat. "If I might be so bold, Majesty, I have reason to believe there may be sympathizers dwelling within some of the fighting orders."

Everyone stared at the Temple Knight.

"I don't understand," said the king.

"The Church has been in disarray for some time. They've taken great pains to hide it, but the entire organization has fractured, the results of a purge of the fighting orders."

"Purge? What in the name of the Saints are you talking about?"

"A little over three years ago, the Church ordered all the fighting orders amalgamated into the Temple Knights of Saint Cunar."

"What has that got to do with anything?"

"That order was met with heavy resistance. The Temple Knights of Saint Agnes refused entirely and fled the Antonine, while my own order splintered, with some submitting, while others, myself included, chose to continue our work of guarding the Temples of Saint Mathew. From the Church's point of view, my order no longer exists, but we Temple Knights continue our work in small numbers relative to the Cunars, meaning that we are largely ignored."

"What is your point, Brother?"

"The dissolution of the orders appears to have been orchestrated to weaken the Petty Kingdom's defences."

"But the Cunars have never fought against the empire, have they?"

"Only once, at sea, Majesty. But my own order fought in Hadenfeld, and the Agnesites held back the empire in Arnsfeld."

"If this is true, it puts us in great danger."

"Might I offer a suggestion?" Instead of waiting for a response to her question, Beverly dove in headfirst. "Allow us to travel to Reinwick on your behalf."

"And if these Cunars try to block your way?" asked Dagmar.

"Then we shall fight them."

"That would be foolish, General. They are the finest warriors on the Continent."

"I am a Mercerian, Majesty. I do not fear them."

"Nor do the rest of us," added Aubrey.

"And you are?" asked the king.

"A Life Mage of considerable power," replied Aubrey, "and a Mercerian, like my cousin."

King Dagmar stared back silently, contemplating their offer before finally nodding. "I shall arrange a new letter to Duke Fernando and entrust it into your care. How soon can you depart?"

"As soon as the ink dries."

"Then Lorenzo will draft one at once. I pray you have greater success than your predecessors."

THREE

Cataclysm

SPRING 968 MC

The servant walked down the hallway, carefully balancing a tray with a bottle of wine and a goblet, a fitting nightcap for his lord and master. He paused, holding the tray one-handed as he opened the door.

Inside, Agalix Sartellian sat in his favourite chair, warming his feet by the fire. His near-white hair, which had started turning grey years ago, matched his wrinkled countenance. He waited quietly as the servant poured the wine, then placed both the goblet and bottle on the small table beside him. Without a word, the servant left, his footsteps muffled as the door closed.

Agalix absently sipped his wine, his mind elsewhere. The invasion of the Petty Kingdoms, a campaign he'd sponsored, was not progressing as he expected, and now word had come that the attack on the Dwarven stronghold of Stonecastle had failed.

He took another sip. Even though their legion had been blunted in Angvil, it was still capable of putting up a fight, and he knew Edora would adapt to the ever-changing situation there with aplomb. He'd already heard she was moving up the other legions, and their other plans would soon bear fruit.

A knock interrupted his thoughts. A voice came through the closed door. "I'm sorry, Your Grace, but you have a visitor."

"Who is it?"

"Freya Stormwind."

Agalix put down his cup. "Tell her to come back tomorrow."

"She claims to be in great distress, Your Grace."

He let out a sigh. "Show her in, but don't encourage her to stay long, or I'll be up all night."

"Yes, Your Grace. I shall bring her here presently."

Agalix stood, stretching his back. He was getting old, a rare thing for a Fire Mage, as most ended up losing control of their magic and immolating. He'd always had a strong will and believed in moderation when it came to using his magic, which had served him well over the years, allowing him to climb to the top of the Sartellian line. True, he wasn't the grand patriarch, but he much preferred dominating others, leaving the head of the family to deal with the mundane details of overseeing such an extended organization.

He heard footsteps and turned as the door opened. Freya Stormwind's puffy, pale face was a sign she'd been crying. Freya was a woman known to have great control over her emotions, making him realize something terrible must've occurred to cause such an effect on her.

She didn't wait for the customary greeting. "The Volstrum," she said, out of breath. "It's been destroyed!"

"What do you mean, destroyed? I don't understand."

"It's gone. The building itself is nothing more than a gigantic sinkhole!"

"Come. Sit and take some time to gather your thoughts." He offered her his glass of wine, which she downed quickly. She then sat, clutching the goblet in a death grip.

"Now," said Agalix. "Tell me what you know."

"A ferocious battle transpired in Karslev," began Freya. "Somehow, an entire army made it all the way to the capital and besieged the Volstrum."

"And this army destroyed the building?"

"No. They tried taking it by force. When their attacks failed, they resorted to magic to accomplish their objectives." She set down her goblet and smoothed the front of her dress. "That renegade, Natalia, is responsible."

"I'm still not clear on how the building was destroyed," said Agalix.

"Everyone knows the Volstrum trains Water Mages, but what very few people realize is that the power of the ley lines runs directly beneath it. Over the years, we've learned to tap into that power, allowing us to train the most powerful Water Mages on the Continent."

"And you think this Natalia Stormwind somehow managed to harness that power?"

"Yes. Accounts are inconsistent, but there is speculation she used it to redirect the river lying beneath the building."

"A river and a ley line? What are the chances of that?"

"The coexistence of both is exactly why the Volstrum was built there in the first place."

"How many mages did she employ to do this?"

Freya stared back silently, mouth agape, before finally answering. "Just one."

"Do you seriously expect me to believe a single mage destroyed a building the size of the Volstrum?"

"I can only relate what I've been told. The Stormwind Matriarch, Marakhova, is presumed dead, with the rest of the family scattered. And now the King of Ruzhina has ordered all spellcasters expelled from his kingdom."

"How do you know all this?" asked Agalix.

"One of my old students, a woman named Voltana, survived the ordeal and contacted me using her magic. She and a few others are attempting to make the trip westward to Halvaria."

"This is most serious, indeed. Without the Stormwinds there, our influence amongst the courts of the Petty Kingdoms is greatly reduced right when we need them the most."

"What do we do?"

"I shall call an emergency meeting of the Inner Council first thing tomorrow. In the meantime, I suggest you get some rest. You'll be called upon to relate these facts to everyone else."

She stood, her composure now restored. "Yes, of course. I shall bid you good evening, Your Grace."

He bowed graciously, then watched her show herself out. The news from Karslev was shocking, but it weakened only the Stormwinds, which meant the time was nearing for the Sartellians to become the dominant mages of the Continent.

Agalix took his seat in the Inner Council. Under ordinary circumstances, the council contained an equal number of Stormwinds, Sartellians, and Shozarins, but the news was of such import that such limitations had been waived. All four Stormwinds were present, while his own line was reduced, thanks to Edora leading the legions off in the Petty Kingdoms. Enelle Sartellian was here, but Stalgrun had yet to be replaced, leaving the Sartellians with only two representatives.

Of the Shozarins, only Kelson was present, a definite sign they didn't consider the matter important enough to warrant a full quorum.

Fadra Stormwind stood, garnering everyone's attention. He cleared his throat. "As you've all heard the news, I shall dispense with the customary summary and get straight to the point. We've reached out to our members in the Petty Kingdoms to confirm that the Volstrum was, indeed, destroyed.

A horde of Therengians marched into Ruzhina unopposed and laid siege to the building. Our brethren within repulsed the attack and would've held out for months were it not for the interference of Natalia Stormwind."

"I know that name," said Kelson. "Wasn't she the renegade who fled the family's influence?"

"She was."

"And you maintain she used magic to destroy the Volstrum?"

"Multiple sources confirm it. Though there were no eyewitnesses to the actual attack, the victors were bold in relating the events of that day."

"That's what comes of threatening one's child," replied Kelson. "I mentioned it was a bad idea at the time, but no one listened to me."

"That was not our decision to make," said Murias. "Marakhova decided she needed to be returned to the fold, and I can't say I blame her." She took a deep breath, letting it out slowly. "Natalia Stormwind represented the pinnacle of our breeding program and was possibly the most powerful student the Volstrum ever created. Her child could've taken our magic to levels considered inconceivable a generation ago."

"You can talk all day about how things might've been, but the Volstrum's loss demonstrates how wrong Marakhova was. Now, instead of having a new, powerful ally, you've lost your home!"

"We cannot undo the past," said Agalix. "Let us try to focus on the present." He turned to face Murias. "What is the current status of the surviving Stormwinds?"

"They were given a month to leave Ruzhina. Most are seeking passage heading west, but the ship captains are charging outrageous prices for berths."

"How many survivors are there?"

"No more than two dozen, and most of those were older mages living in the city."

"And the Volstrum's students?"

"They were evacuated prior to the siege. Rumour has it they've been taken back to Therengia."

"To what end?"

"We simply don't know," said Murias.

"What of the Sartellians in Karslev?" asked Enelle.

Fadra did not try to hide his look of disgust. "They did nothing."

"Should we be worried these Therengians will come after Korascajan?"

"No," replied Agalix. "Korascajan is a fortified city under our exclusive control, a very different situation than the Volstrum."

Kestia Stormwind, who up until now had remained silent, stood. "You speak of the Volstrum but fail to mention the Baroshka."

"Which is?" said Enelle.

"A repository of immense magical knowledge that, in the wrong hands, could ruin everything."

"And where lies this Baroshka?"

"Beneath the Volstrum."

"Wouldn't it have been destroyed with the rest of the building?"

"Some believe it may have been plundered before the building collapsed."

"Let's hope that's only a rumour," said Freya. "I'd hate to think what Natalia Stormwind could do with magic like that at her disposal."

"She's still only one individual," said Agalix, "and our current strategy to conquer the Petty Kingdoms relies on armies, not mages, to accomplish its objectives."

"And if she shows up to support the Northern Alliance?"

"Why would she consider that? She has chosen to live with the Therengians, a race ostracized across the entire Continent. I can't imagine them getting involved. I'm more concerned with learning how an army of Therengians marched to Karslev without being detected."

"I have no explanation for that," replied Fadra, "nor do I expect to find one in the coming weeks now that our people are scattered."

"Could we send some ships to evacuate them?"

"With the Temple Fleet in control of the Great Northern Sea?"

"We're talking about less than thirty individuals; even one ship could carry them."

"We have no ships left in the north," announced Fadra.

Everyone fell silent.

Agalix couldn't comprehend the fellow's statement. "I understand we lost ships in the campaign in Arnsfeld, but surely we've had time to rebuild?"

"The Temple Fleet sails at will across the north. They have even, on occasion, raided our ports and put our shipbuilding facilities to the torch. Let me make this very clear: we have no warships left on our northern coast."

"Perhaps we might dispatch some ships from our fleet off the Mercerian coast?"

"That would take far too long," said Fadra, "and that part of the Continent is unexplored; we have no idea if there even IS a passage to the Great Northern Sea."

"Can any of the survivors use their magic to escape?"

"They have to target a magic circle to use a frozen arch, and those are in short supply with the Volstrum destroyed, not to mention that very few Stormwinds can actually cast the spell to begin with."

"This is all very distressing," said Agalix, "but I fear we can do nothing about it at present. We should focus on our campaign in the Petty Kingdoms. Then, once our military conquest is complete, we'll re-establish the Volstrum at our leisure."

"What should we do about Natalia Stormwind?" asked Fadra.

"What can we do? By all accounts, she has chosen to live in Therengia. I say let her remain there, where she can do no further harm."

The embers spat, sparks flying up the chimney. Agalix tossed another log into the fireplace, then waved his hand, calling on his inner Fire Magic. Flames leaped up, warming the room, while he returned to his seat. His companion downed her drink before turning to her host.

"This is an opportunity for us," she said.

Agalix chuckled. "You have a way with words, Olynia. What, in particular, are you suggesting?"

"With the Volstrum destroyed, the Stormwinds are weakened, allowing us to gain prominence."

"There is still the matter of the Shozarins."

"Agreed, yet power split two ways gives us more control than split in three."

"You make a good point, but how do you suggest we go about orchestrating this... elevation in stature? It's not as if we could kill them all off. Even with the Volstrum gone, many Stormwinds are still in Halvaria."

"We know Exalor is planning to seize control of the Gilded Throne. I suggest we leak information that the Stormwinds are plotting against him and let him take care of the details."

"Devious, but the High Strategos is no fool. He'll see through such a ploy."

"Then perhaps a more subtle approach would be preferable. A scandal would lessen the Stormwinds' influence."

"Or," said Agalix, "we let them deal with the Volstrum's loss and turn on themselves."

"Would that work?" asked Olynia.

"Providing we give them a little shove in the right direction."

"And how do we do that?"

"We cast doubt on the details concerning the Volstrum's fall. We know Therengia was somehow involved, yet no one has any idea how they got their army into Karslev. We could insinuate someone within the

Stormwinds was working with her. Natalia Stormwind was made out to be their arch-nemesis. What if others were similarly inclined?"

"A brilliant idea," said Olynia, "but it can't come from us; that's far too obvious. We need someone who can plant the concept in the minds of the Stormwinds, and then let it take root. Do we know anyone of that nature?"

"Potentially," said Agalix. "Kelson Shozarin is the High Sentinel and is bound to know someone. I can't imagine he'd be upset to see the Stormwinds fighting amongst themselves. The question is, can we trust him?"

"You trusted him with the plan to invade the Petty Kingdoms."

"True, but that only worked because he was at odds with Exalor's plot to seize the Throne. I don't know how he'll react to the idea of discrediting any of the three families. We must also consider the larger implications."

"Which are?"

"By allowing the destruction of the Stormwinds, we are announcing that a purge is considered acceptable behaviour, which could easily turn on us should he later decide we're no longer of use to him."

"Or he to us," said Olynia. "You might say it works both for and against us."

Agalix stared into the fire, chewing over the situation. Life was so much simpler when he'd first come to court. Then, the three families existed not so much in harmony but at least in balance, something he'd thought would last forever. Now, many years later, he was contemplating the ruin of the Stormwinds. It wasn't exactly a happy thought, though admittedly, it did provide him some measure of joy to see his political rivals weakened.

"All things considered," continued Olynia, "what's our next step?"

"I'll arrange a meeting with Kelson and feel out if he'd agree to such a thing. I'm not committing to the enterprise just yet, as there are far too many things to consider, but it's a first step."

"And if he's against the idea?"

"Then we look at other options."

"I know there are many people who'd like to see the Stormwinds suffer." She lifted her drink, but before she took a sip, she halted. "What if there were another way?"

"I'm open to suggestions," said Agalix. "What is it you're proposing?"

"Other mage families would be interested in filling positions of power, perhaps even some we might be able to control."

"That's a dangerous game, Olynia. It might give the other ruling families the idea to do the same, and then all we'd accomplish is diluting our own influence."

"I'm only trying to keep our options open. There's also the matter of

Exalor. We know he wants to rule Halvaria, but have we any idea when he'll begin his campaign of conquest?"

"He's got his hands full dealing with Merceria at the moment," replied Agalix, "although I hear things are not going according to plan at Stonecastle."

"Should we be worried?"

"No. Even if the Third Legion doesn't take the Dwarven fortress, they should have no problem defending the mountain passes, not to mention that gorge."

"Gorge?" said Olynia.

"Yes, Kharzun's Folly. It took everything our Earth Mages had to cross it; I can't imagine the Dwarves have anything to match that level of magic."

"It's not the Dwarves we have to worry about; it's the Mercerians."

"Let Exalor worry about the Mercerians. We need to focus our attention on things back here in Varena."

"What about the emperor?"

"I think we've reached the point where he's no longer of use to us."

FOUR

Erssa Saka'am

SPRING 968 MC

Revi Bloom stepped from the magic circle. Guards immediately entered the room, their weapons drawn, but at the sight of the Royal Life Mage, they sheathed their swords.

"Welcome back, Master Bloom," said the sergeant. "Her Majesty has been awaiting your return."

"She has? That comes as a surprise to me."

"Shall I have someone take you to her?"

"If you would be so kind."

"Harper?" called out the sergeant. "Take Master Bloom to the queen and be quick about it."

Donald Harper stepped forward. "Yes, Sergeant. If you'll follow me, sir?"

"Of course," said Revi. They exited the room and proceeded down a long hallway.

"The queen is in the map room," said Harper. "Are you familiar with it?"

"I wasn't aware we had a map room."

"It's a recent development. Her Majesty needed somewhere to lay out her map of Halvaria."

"We have a map?"

"Yes. I'm told she compiled it after reading the confessions of all those Halvarian prisoners we took at Stonecastle, along with those being held at Holdcross."

"A sensible approach," said Revi. "Is it very detailed?"

"I couldn't say, sir. My duties don't normally include access to that particular room."

.   .   .

Gerald bent over the map, squinting. "Does that say 'mind'?"

"No, mine," replied Anna. "We believe it's the primary source of iron for the empire. There's also the possibility it's an old Dwarven stronghold, perhaps even the fabled city of Dun-Galdrim."

"But we're not certain?"

"There's only so much we can glean from prisoners. It might've been a little easier had we captured any senior officers, but they've proven too fanatical to surrender."

The door opened to Revi. "I hope I'm not interrupting?" he said.

"Not at all, Master Bloom," replied the queen. "Come in. There's something I want to discuss with you."

"Of course, Majesty." The mage entered, his gaze wandering over to the map. "Has this anything to do with the situation at Ironcliff?"

"I'm afraid not. It has more to do with Trollden. What do you know of events there?"

"I understand we recently defeated the empire's attempt to march on Colbridge, but I'm afraid I know little more than that."

"Their legion was defeated," replied Gerald, "but they still maintain a presence near Trollden, as well as a fleet off the coast, and that's where you come in."

"I'm a Life Mage," replied Revi. "I can do little about enemy ships."

"Do you remember Riversend?" asked Anna.

"I could hardly forget. Why? What are you suggesting?"

"In that battle, the Kurathian fleet used large sea creatures to pull their war barges."

"If I recall correctly, we sent Lady Beverly to lead a group in amongst the fleet and set fire to their ships."

"We did, but it's those monstrously huge sea dwellers I'm interested in. If we convinced even one to join us in this war, we could break up that Halvarian fleet."

"I still don't see what this has to do with me."

"It's my belief that the Saurians may have had a way of communicating with those creatures, much as they communicate with their three-horns."

"Have you any proof to back up these beliefs?"

Anna shook her head. "No, which is where you come in. I want you to travel to Erssa Saka'am and look for evidence that might prove my theory correct."

"Why me?"

"I'd go myself, but this war demands my complete attention. You've also studied the Saurians extensively. My only concern is you'd need to employ the Saurian Gates to get there."

"I assure you there will be no trouble, Majesty. My previous exposure was all-consuming, and I have no desire to repeat it. I would, however, require some assistance. The Saurian records are extensive, and I fear it would require a great amount of effort to sift through them."

"Who do you suggest?"

Revi considered his options before replying. "I'd prefer someone with some magical training, as controlling a beast of that size would involve a spell."

"There aren't a lot of mages to choose from," said Gerald. "There is a war on, you know."

"Perhaps a student or two?"

"Have you someone particular in mind?"

"I do," replied Revi. "Princess Edwina has a good education, and Durwin has done well in his Earth Magic studies, which is likely the type of magic we'll need."

"I shall send word to them at once," said Anna.

"That's it? I was expecting an argument."

"That fleet is holding back our campaign in the north. The sooner we rid the sea of them, the better. There is, however, a slight problem."

"Ah. I knew there was something."

"There are no shamans to send with you, which means you'll be out of communication during your stay. To keep abreast of your discoveries, we'd require you to return to Wincaster on a regular basis."

"You could ask the Orcs to teach me the spell of spirit talk. I am, after all, the Royal Life Mage."

"They won't agree," said Gerald. "To them, the ability to speak with the spirit world is sacred."

"They taught Aubrey."

"That they did," said Anna, "but they've developed a very close bond with her. It'd be unfair of us to expect them to do the same with anyone else. I suppose what I mean is that we must respect their wishes in this."

"Agreed," added Gerald. "Our army relies on their shamans to coordinate our strategies. We can't risk losing that ability by sharing knowledge they don't wish others to have."

"Then I shall recall once a week," said Revi.

"Once a ten-day would be preferable," said Anna, "or you'll lose too much time. After all, your return trip south will necessitate you travelling to Uxley, wasting two days every time."

"When would you like me to leave?"

"As soon as possible."

Revi nodded. "With your permission, Majesty, I shall recall to Hawksburg and collect my new assistants."

"Thank you," said the queen. "It's greatly appreciated."

The Life Mage bowed, then turned and strode from the room.

"He's very formal of late," noted Gerald.

"He still blames himself for stranding Aubrey in the Petty Kingdoms."

"Beverly and Aldwin are there, too."

"True," replied Anna, "but Aubrey was his apprentice. Since her family's death, I think he sees it as his responsibility to look after her."

"She's a grown woman."

"And he mentored her. That's a connection not unlike the relationship you had with Beverly's father."

"I suppose it is, isn't it?" said Gerald. "I concede the point."

The runes illuminated, and then a cylinder of light shot upwards, filling the Hawksburg casting room with a brilliance that dazzled the eyes. When it faded, the form of a single individual was revealed.

"Master Bloom," said Gurza. "We weren't expecting you."

"I'm surprised to see you here," replied Revi. "I would've thought hunters more appropriate as guards."

"They are outside," replied the Orc. "I was preparing to utilize the circle to amplify a spell when you made your entrance."

"I'm sorry to interrupt you. Might I ask what spell you're trying to master?"

"Recall. I do not have the strength to travel any great distance at present, but I must start somewhere."

"Don't let me stop you."

"Might I ask why you are here?"

"I'm looking for Edwina and Durwin. I have a little trip planned, and I thought they might prove helpful."

"You will find them up at the estate."

"Not the academy?"

"With their training finished," said Gurza, "the staff returned to Wincaster until such time another group of students is identified. They now reside in the Brandon manor house, which is much closer to this circle."

"Then I shall go and find them." Revi ascended the stairs. The magic circle here had been discovered in the cellar of the old manor house, so the floor above had been removed and replaced by a ramp, allowing horses easy access to the room.

He stepped outside and drew in a breath of fresh spring air. Summer would soon be upon them, and if the empire was preparing to launch a new offensive, that is likely when they would begin, making his mission all the more critical.

He found Edwina sitting in the dining hall, sipping on a hot bowl of soup.

"Ah, there you are, Highness," said Revi.

"I'm no longer a princess," she replied. "Mages cannot rule in Weldwyn, so you must address me as you would any other mage."

He bowed. "Very well, Arcanus Edwina."

She giggled. "You make me sound powerful, yet I've not mastered any Air Magic spells."

"True, but you've proven most adept at learning those spells universal to all the schools of magic."

"That I have." She tilted her head, staring back at him. "I assume this isn't a social call?"

"It is not," he admitted. "I want you to come with me."

"Where are we going?"

"To Erssa Saka'am to do some research."

"Into what?"

"Into whether we can use magic to harness the power of sea monsters."

"Sea monsters? I'd think a Water Mage would be more suitable for something like that."

"And you'd be correct, but as we have no such individuals available to us, we must rely on those who harness the power of the earth."

"I'm assuming both Albreda and Aldus are unavailable?"

"Correct."

"Then you must choose between Gurza and Durwin."

"I've chosen Durwin," said Revi.

"Might I ask why? Gurza's magic is stronger."

"Perhaps, but our expedition will be one focused on finding information rather than employing our magic at this time. Gurza is also an Orc and is new to reading, a critical requirement for this particular task."

"But aren't we going to be looking at Saurian writings?"

"We are, but my notes are all compiled in the common tongue, and I can't spend my days explaining my findings. I'd never get anything done!"

"Ahh, I see. You'll find Durwin out back, talking to his friends."

"His friends?"

"Yes, the animals he keeps summoning. He spends so much time amongst them that it's a wonder he managed to complete his training. Let's go find him, shall we?" She pushed the bowl away. "I wasn't hungry anyway." They made their way through the manor house.

"How are you adapting to not being a royal?"

"It's been a bit of a struggle," replied Edwina. "Not that I hold any great love for people fawning all over me, but I'm treated as just another student here, which takes some getting used to."

"I can well imagine."

"If you don't mind me asking, what was your training like?"

"Mine?" said Revi. "While it's true that Master Andronicus plucked me from obscurity, he did little actual training. As a result, I've learned mostly by observation and self-study."

"Perhaps that was the intent?"

"I somehow doubt it. The truth is, in his later years, Andronicus's mind began to wander."

"Could he have suffered from studying the flames as you did?"

"We didn't even know he was aware of them, but looking back, it seems obvious. He did have a direct link to the ley lines in that hidden tower of his, the same ones that almost destroyed me."

They reached the back door, and Edwina held it open. "After you, Master Bloom."

Revi stepped through into a large open space, with multitudes of blooming flowers edging a well-maintained grass area cut relatively short. However, the most striking feature was the wildlife, for deer grazed at the far end while a wolf napped in the sun, oblivious to their presence.

In the middle of it all lay Durwin, gazing up at the sky, his tawny hair a veritable mop atop his head but cut short on the sides, giving him a top-heavy look.

"Durwin?" called out Edwina. "We have company."

The youth sat up, his freckled face beaming. "Coming," he responded, getting to his feet.

"Greetings, Master…"

"Bloom," replied Revi. "Am I truly that forgettable?"

Edwina chuckled. "He'd remember your name had you antlers."

"That's not fair," said Durwin. "You know I have trouble recognizing faces."

"You can tell all those deer apart."

"That's different. Their antlers are all unique."

"You realize you just supported my earlier statement. You'd have no problem identifying Master Bloom if he sported antlers."

Durwin chuckled. "Yes. I suppose that's true. I apologize for my behaviour." He turned to Revi. "Were you looking for me, Master Bloom?"

"I was, though I'm now wondering if that might have been a mistake."

"It's faces he has trouble with," said Edwina, "not text."

"What is it you want me for?" asked the Earth Mage.

"To come with us to Erssa Saka'am," explained Revi.

"To what end?"

"The objective is to somehow convince large aquatic creatures to attack the Halvarian fleet."

"There's no such thing as large aquatic creatures."

"What about whales?" asked Edwina.

"I meant nothing bigger than whales. It's a physical impossibility."

"Except," said Revi, "we saw them during the Siege of Riversend. How do you explain that?"

"I… can't."

"You're still young, Durwin, and there's nothing wrong with that, but you must learn to be open to new ideas. Not so long ago, mages and scholars believed it was impossible to travel great distances in an instant, but here we are using the spell of recall on a regular basis. Then there's the Saurian Gates, another relatively recent discovery."

"My apologies, Master Bloom. I see I have much to learn. Where do we go from here?"

"Gather your things and meet me in the casting circle. We shall recall to Wincaster, then make the trip overland to Uxley Hall, where the eternal flame burns."

"Flame?" said Durwin. "I don't want to get burned."

"You won't. It's only a magical flame. It looks like fire, but within its flames, it hides a gateway to a distant location."

"Is it safe?"

"Of course," said Revi. "I wouldn't suggest it if it weren't."

Three days later, they stood on the grounds of Uxley Hall, looking down into a well.

"It's down there," said Revi, "in an ancient Saurian Temple. But don't worry. Aldus Hearn gave us an easier way to enter."

"How?"

"Some years ago, he dug out a tunnel to allow horses to utilize the gate during the Norland invasion. The ramp is somewhere over there." Revi pointed to the east. "You can't see it from here, but it sits roughly two hundred paces away in a depression. Come. I'll show you what I mean."

The Life Mage led them to the entrance, which now had a double door guarding it, complete with a lock to keep out the unwanted. Revi pulled a ring of keys from his robes and then searched through them. He chose one and inserted it, twisting it until it let loose with a loud click.

"There we are," he said. "Now, let's get inside, shall we? Oh, before we do that, cast your orb of light. I assume you both know how?"

Two small spheres of light appeared in answer to his question. While Edwina's was very bright, the one Durwin created appeared more yellow and emitted less light.

"Interesting," said Revi.

"Master Hearn's is similar," said Durwin. "I think it's because it's drawing on the magic of the earth."

"Come along, then. We haven't got all day." The Life Mage took the lead once again, heading down a long ramp that gradually brought them deeper underground until it ended at a slightly larger, square room, with an eerie green light illuminating an opening to the left.

"This is it," said Revi. He advanced to the opening, the light playing across his face. "A miracle of arcane design."

In the centre of the room before him stood a small, stepped pyramid with green flames flickering on the flat top. The high, arched ceiling was supported by four walls of equal length, each no more than twenty feet.

"Behold," said Revi. "This is a Saurian Gate."

"It's a wee bit small," noted Durwin.

"That's because it hasn't been activated. Now, watch and learn." Revi moved closer, kneeling to examine the stones comprising the sides of the pyramid. "Each block contains a rune representing a letter of the magical alphabet. By pressing them in the correct order, a mage connects to a distant temple." He closed his eyes, recalling the address for the one in Erssa Saka'am. Confident he remembered it correctly, he opened his eyes once more and began pressing stones while reciting the name of the rune. Each glowed in turn, and then the flame shot up to the ceiling. Another touch and the flames widened to reveal a far-off swamp.

"There, you see?" said Revi. "Edwina, you go through first."

"Now?"

Revi held up his hand. "Just a moment." He activated the last rune, and the centre of the flame rippled. "You may proceed."

Edwina closed her eyes before stepping through, almost tripping on the stone pyramid. Her image wavered before it solidified on the distant temple in Erssa Saka'am, and then almost immediately, the flame reduced to little more than that of a candle.

"We must let it recharge," explained Revi.

"How long does that take?" asked Durwin.

"It varies with the individual's magical power." Even as he completed the sentence, the flame leaped back to its original size. "Remarkable. I've used this gate multiple times over the years, but it still surprises me from time to time."

"I thought we weren't supposed to use these gates?"

"We're not, usually, but these are dangerous times. Don't worry. The effects are easily treated."

"That doesn't make me feel any better."

Revi ignored him, once more touching the runes in the correct order. The flame increased yet again, rippling as the last rune was activated.

"Go ahead, Durwin. It's your turn."

The young Earth Mage closed his eyes and took a step towards the flames. He winced, expecting heat as he neared, but to his amazement, he felt nothing. Moments later, he touched the surface of the gate, and his body felt stretched out to eternity.

FIVE

Border Troubles

SPRING 968 MC

"Why do you think the Duke of Reinwick hasn't responded?" asked Aldwin.

"Any number of reasons," replied Beverly. She glanced over her shoulder, but the rest of her group were busy talking amongst themselves. She returned to watching the road ahead. "People at court could've opposed sending help, or a threat of some sort has forced him to keep his army close at hand."

"But if that were the case, wouldn't he have the decency to inform King Dagmar? They do have an alliance."

"You raise a good point, but this whole theory about the Temple Knights of Saint Cunar might explain things just as easily."

"But you don't think so."

"I'll admit I'm not an expert about the politics of the Petty Kingdoms," said Beverly, "but for an entire order of religious knights to suddenly serve the Halvarian cause seems a bit of a stretch."

"I'm afraid it's true," interrupted Cyric. "The rift within the Church has created havoc amongst the fighting orders."

"Can you explain what caused this rift?" asked Aldwin.

"That might prove difficult, but I shall do my best. First, you need to understand how it was organized before the split. There are, or rather, were, six orders of Temple Knights. You've already met those of Saint Agnes and Mathew, who are no longer directly controlled by the Church."

"But they're religious fighting orders, aren't they?"

"They are. Unfortunately, the Church, in its infinite wisdom, decided that all the fighting orders should be united under a common command structure, that of the Cunars. The Agnesites rebelled, fleeing the Antonine to find safety in any Petty Kingdom that would accept them."

"The missing knights," said Beverly. "Temple Commander Roland mentioned them."

"Indeed. Some disappeared, but other garrisons across the Petty Kingdoms either convinced the local ruler to accept them within their borders, or they fled to other, more welcoming realms."

"But wouldn't that incur the Church's wrath?"

"Oh, it did," replied Cyric, "but what can the Church do about it? It's not as if they can punish every realm in the Petty Kingdoms. I'm afraid the move broke the Church's influence forever, at least on the political front. People still worship the Saints, but they're a lot less accommodating when it comes to Church edicts."

"And what happened to these Cunars?"

"Just before the rift, the vast majority were recalled to the Antonine, the home city of the Church, and the place from where they rule over what's left of their organization."

"And how long ago was this?"

"Three years. The Church ordered all the archpriors to keep it quiet, but it didn't take long for the rulers of the Petty Kingdoms to realize something was amiss. And there were larger ramifications. My own order is now greatly diminished, many having handed over their armour and weapons to the Temple Knights of Saint Cunar. The rest took refuge where they might while still maintaining a semblance of order."

"Like Temple Commander Roland?"

"Precisely."

"I'm surprised rulers were so accepting," offered Owen, drawn in by the subject. "I would've thought they'd be worried about repercussions from the Church."

"These are trained Temple Knights," replied Cyric. "No ruler in their right mind will refuse the addition of such warriors to their army. The Church insisted on its members remaining neutral in the politics of the Petty Kingdoms, but recent history suggests that is a waste of resources."

"Does Reinwick have any of these Cunars within their borders?"

"They used to, but that changed when the order began pulling back from the borders. That doesn't mean they don't exist, merely that they have no official presence."

"Could there be renegades within the order?" asked Owen.

"Anything's possible, but I doubt it. Unlike my own order, Cunars are taught instant obedience, making them extremely effective warriors and also very loyal to their superiors. Some might even describe them as stubborn, but that's precisely what makes them so devastating on the battlefield."

"What are the chances we might run across some on our way to Korvoran?"

"Very low, I should think."

"That's reassuring," said Aldwin. "What do you suppose happened to the king's request for help?"

"Halvarian agents are the most probable cause. We know historically, they've used all manner of tricks against those they were preparing to attack, including infiltrating a realm's borders and promoting discontent amongst its people."

"You surprise me, Brother," said Beverly. "I would think that, as a member of a religious order, you would see the best in others."

"And ordinarily I do," Cyric replied, "but the Temple Knights were formed to protect the Church, and the greatest threat to that institution is the Halvarian Empire."

"Yet by your own admission, that very Church has abandoned your order, or at least part of it."

"I can't deny your reasoning, but the dissolution of the Church had nothing to do with the teachings of the Saints. No, it was about control. Had the Primus gotten his way, the Petty Kingdoms would've been required to pay homage to the Church."

"Don't they do that now?" asked Beverly.

"Not at all. Church law applies only to those who take Holy Orders, which is a far cry from enforcing it on people across the Continent."

"So where does that leave them?"

"The Church has splintered into localized chapters who no longer pay heed to the wishes of the Antonine."

"And what's your position on that?"

"It's complicated," replied Cyric. "This new arrangement means priors now have the freedom to customize their ceremonies to meet the requirements of those they conduct services for. Inevitably, it will lead to differences of opinion across the Petty Kingdoms. For example, the teachings of Saint Mathew in Andover may differ from those in a place like Corassus."

"Does that mean you agree with it or not?" asked Aldwin.

"It means," replied the Temple Knight, "that I'm happy to leave decisions of that nature to those higher in rank."

Upon reaching the city of Ebenhof, which was only a day away from the Reinwick border, they paused for a meal at a little tavern called the Lost

King. The locals were wary of Krazuhk but gravitated towards Brother Cyric, seeking a blessing despite his being a Temple Knight, not a lay brother. The tavern keeper chased off the locals, allowing the group to eat in peace.

"Not too long ago," began Cyric, "a great battle occurred here."

"I assume," said Beverly, "that's the one that saw the Army of Reinwick defeat Andover."

"Indeed, though some don't know that King Dagmar almost won the day. Were it not for the unexpected appearance of the Orcs, victory would have been his."

"Orcs?" said Aldwin. "What tribe?"

"I'm not entirely certain," replied Cyric. "Unfortunately, the written accounts tend to downplay their contributions, but I can read between the lines."

"It is often so," said Krazuhk. "Your scholars would see us removed from history."

"Not all of them," replied Beverly. "Queen Anna's official history of Merceria recognizes their contributions."

"Interesting," said Aldwin. "I didn't know there was an actual record."

"You know the queen insists on a written account of everything that goes on in the kingdom, which includes archiving all the army's written orders."

"Why?" asked Owen. "Who's going to read them?"

"Only someone who can read Orc," replied Aubrey. "I expect eventually some of those orders will become required study for officers of Her Majesty's army."

"What a strange notion. I very much doubt you could enforce such a requirement in the Petty Kingdoms."

"Why is that?"

"The kings are weak, at least from a political point of view. For the most part, their armies consist of warriors raised by the barons or other nobles. I can't imagine any ruler forcing all their nobles to read old accounts of battles."

"In Merceria," said Aubrey, "we have a different way of looking at things. And in any case, we don't rely on nobles to raise troops anymore."

"But Beverly is a baroness," said Owen, "and your own marshal a duke."

"True, but in the marshal's case, his title was awarded after he became marshal; he wasn't born with it."

"Tell us more about this battle," said Beverly. "How many Orcs were involved?"

"That's difficult to say," replied Cyric. "Accounts mention a Fire Mage accompanied them, but bear in mind, I haven't seen anything written by the victors, only the vanquished, who likely exaggerated the numbers to justify their defeat. I'd say two to three hundred, enough that their presence was noted, but not enough to refer to them as an actual army."

"And how did they turn the tide of battle?"

"By appearing on Andover's left flank at a crucial point during the battle. It's one of the things I'm hoping to learn more about once we reach Korvoran."

"I'd be very interested to see how they were employed," said Beverly. "In Merceria, we've integrated them fully with our army, but it sounds as though Reinwick kept them separate."

"I imagine their physical characteristics would be better suited to Reinwick's approach," said Cyric.

"We do that with our Dwarven allies, but that's only because they employ different tactics than we do. The Orcs back home have adapted to our ways when it comes to fighting."

"Fascinating."

"Perhaps one day you'll have the opportunity to see the Mercerian army in battle."

"Much as I appreciate the accomplishments of valiant warriors, I pray that such a day never becomes necessary."

"I completely understand," said Beverly.

They stopped at a roadside inn just shy of the border, setting off early the next morning, intending to cross into Reinwick before noon. As they approached the border, they noted a group of horsemen blocking the road ahead. Cyric brought his mount to a halt, still a good arrow's distance from the riders.

"Is something wrong?" asked Beverly.

"I recognize those tabards," said Cyric. "Those are Temple Knights of Saint Cunar."

"Are they likely to be hostile?"

"In theory, no, but the fact that they're blocking the road suggests otherwise. Also, there are twelve of them, which is far more than is usual to patrol roads, not to mention that they have no presence in Andover."

"It appears they're on the Reinwick side of the border," offered Aubrey. "Didn't you say they used to have a presence there?"

"I did," replied Cyric, "but that was before they withdrew to the Antonine."

"How do you want to handle this?" asked Aldwin.

"I'll talk with them," said Beverly. "Perhaps they'll see reason."

"*I shall go with you,*" offered Krazuhk in the language of her people.

"*Are you certain?*"

"*Yes. I will follow a few paces behind, the better to use my magic should it prove necessary.*"

Beverly switched back to the common tongue. "The rest of you remain here. If things go awry, I'll lead them away."

"No," said Aldwin. "Don't do that. If they attack, lead them towards us so we can help."

"I would advise otherwise," said Cyric. "I have no fear of battle, but they are the finest warriors on the Continent and would quickly overwhelm us."

Beverly grinned. "Then I'll have to convince them to let us pass." She urged Lightning forward while Krazuhk followed on foot, keeping ten paces between them.

As they neared the knights, one rode ahead, raising a hand indicating they should halt. "State your business," he called out.

Beverly stopped some thirty paces away. "I am Beverly Fitzwilliam, Baroness of Bodden. I am on my way to Korvoran."

"I didn't ask your name," the Cunar replied. "I demanded to know your business."

"You don't wear the duke's colours, so what gives you the right to demand anything of me?"

The Cunar's hand went to the hilt of his sword. "The right of the Church."

"That would be, I assume, the Church of the Saints?"

"Naturally."

"Ah. That presents a bit of a problem, then. I worship Saxnor."

"I bear no wish to fight you, heathen. Turn around and crawl back under whatever rock you came out from."

"How rude," said Beverly. "Did your mother teach you no manners?"

The Cunar stared back, making her wonder whether he was about to charge, but then he held up two fingers, beckoning to those behind him. Two of his knights rode up, taking positions on either side of him.

He placed his hand on the hilt of his sword. "We can do this the easy way or the hard way."

Beverly remained calm. All three wore full plate armour, akin to what the knights of Erlingen used. It was superior to hers, at least in theory, but that didn't take into account the power of Nature's Fury.

She sighed. "I hate to ask, but what's the hard way, Captain? I assume you are a captain?"

The knight who'd first spoken flipped down his visor, drew his sword, and dug in with his spurs, his two companions following suit, then an arc of lightning shot out from behind Beverly, striking the rider on the left, dead centre. The knight stiffened in the saddle, then toppled to one side when his horse reared, frightened by the sudden flash of light.

Beverly unslung her shield and unhooked her hammer from her belt as Lightning surged ahead, her knees guiding him. The Temple Captain held his sword point forward, aiming for Beverly's head, but at the last moment, she twisted, bringing her shield to bear the brunt of the attack. The tip scraped across metal, and then Nature's Fury swung out, colliding with the knight's shield, buckling it under the force of her hit, leaving her with the satisfaction of a grunt of pain from her foe.

Anticipating her actions, the third knight had delayed slightly and now charged, intent on getting in a flank attack. He was halfway to her when he slumped forward and fell from the saddle, a victim of Aubrey's magic.

With no time to chide her cousin for closing the range, Beverly swung her hammer again to be met by the Temple Captain's parry. A test of strength ensued, and though she was strong, it soon became abundantly clear the Cunar had the upper hand.

Lightning bit out, taking a hunk of flesh from the captain's horse. The beast let out a scream and pulled back, breaking the test of strength. The captain raised his sword, ready to attack anew, but the magic of Nature's Fury propelled Beverly to strike faster and faster. She swung out, bashing the fellow in the chest and leaving a sizable dent in his breastplate before immediately following with another strike, hitting his pauldron, the captain's left arm going limp from the force of the blow.

As Lightning drove forward, the captain's horse turned and bolted, carrying its rider to safety. Having witnessed the exchange, the remaining knights drew their swords and lowered their visors.

Beverly tensed, expecting another rush, but then Krazuhk moved up beside her, speaking words of magic as she gesticulated. The air in front of her distorted as she sent a wave of compressed air towards the knights. Three of them tried to cover their ears, a difficult task while wearing a full helm, while the remaining six charged forward.

Beverly braced herself. Half of the Cunars were out of the fight, but the rest would soon make short work of her and her compatriots, then Cyric appeared beside her, his axe out and ready for use.

The enemy had closed the range to a mere ten paces when a wall of fire erupted from the ground. Unable to stop in time, the Temple Knights kept riding, emerging from the blaze with their surcoats alight as a fiery bird flew overhead, flames dripping from its tail.

Beverly met the incoming charge with a swing of her hammer, crushing the side of a helmet. She took a quick glance at Cyric as he sank his axe into someone's leg, and then all of her attention was required to fight off a pair of knights who'd decided she was a more tempting target.

She used Nature's Fury to parry a blow, only to see the blocked sword turn red, then white as it heated up. A cry of pain escaped the Temple Knight, and then he dropped the weapon, shaking his hand.

Another bolt of lightning exploded, deafening everyone. Beverly shook her head, trying to clear her mind. She fought to make sense of why the Temple Knights were withdrawing east across the countryside instead of back into Reinwick.

"We have friends," said Krazuhk, pointing north, where a group of six Orcs walked towards them.

"*Greetings,*" Beverly called out, using their native tongue.

The Orcs halted at the Human's unexpected use of their language. An older female stepped forward.

"*Greetings,*" she replied. "*I am Marag, master of flame, and these are my fellow Ashwalkers.*" She waved her hand to indicate the others. "*It appears our arrival has proven most timely.*"

"*Thank you for your help,*" said Beverly. "*We would have surely perished without it. Might I ask what drew you here?*"

"*We came at the behest of the duke. His messengers to Andover failed to return, and he fears they have met with an untimely end. Might I ask what brought you here?*"

"*We are here on urgent business for King Dagmar of Andover. He wishes the duke to march to his aid before it's too late.*"

"*Then come. We shall escort you to Korvoran.*"

SIX

Amongst the People

SPRING 968 MC

Nevarus, God-Emperor of the Halvarian Empire, looked down at his ill-fitting clothes. The common cloth was a much rougher fabric than he was used to, but rather than complain, he chose to view it as a new experience. "Tell me again what the plan is?" he asked.

"We shall leave by the servants' entrance," replied Janek, his most devoted servant, "and then go amongst your subjects."

"What of my guards?"

"They will follow at a discreet distance, Eminence. Far enough not to draw undue attention, yet close enough to come to your aid if needed." The servant held out a small pouch.

"What's that?"

"Your purse, Eminence. If you are to pass as a commoner, you must pay for things yourself."

"Yes, of course." Nevarus took the purse. "How much is in this?"

"Twenty crowns, though we've taken the liberty of supplying most of it in silver. Too much gold would draw unwanted attention."

"You seem to have thought of everything."

Janek bowed. "I shall take that as a compliment, Eminence." He took one last look at his emperor, then moved closer, pulling on a loose thread. "There, that's better. Now, if you follow me, Eminence, I will guide you to the servants' entrance."

"Before we go, Janek, there's one more thing I need you to do for me."

The remark brought a stunned look from the servant. "Have I forgotten something? If so, I do apologize, Eminence."

The emperor held up his hand. "If I am to go amongst my people as a commoner, don't you think you should refrain from calling me Eminence?"

Janek's mouth flapped open. The thought of calling his master anything else was too foreign for him to contemplate. After a short period of silence, he finally snapped his jaw closed. "What would you have me call you, Eminence?"

"That's an excellent question. What do you think might be appropriate?"

"Perhaps, lord?"

"No," said Nevarus. "We have no nobility."

"True, but we do have influential individuals, and that term is often used to describe those who have influence."

"Lord it shall be, then."

"Have you any other questions, Eminence… I mean, Lord."

"I do, Janek. Are all commoners' clothes so coarse?"

"Yes, Lord. Only the wealthy can afford finer cloth."

"And where, exactly, are we headed?"

Janek sighed. He'd explained this several times already, but the emperor clearly hadn't been listening. "We shall be going into the streets of Varena, Lord."

"Yes, I know that," snapped the emperor. "I'm not a fool. I want to know where in the capital we're going?"

"To one of the city's many merchant squares where you can see how your subjects live and sample the delights of the stalls."

"What will they be selling?"

"Food, cloth, lanterns—all manner of merchandise. Now remember, your purpose is to observe how they live, not get embroiled in arguments over the cost."

"Is arguing common?"

"Prices have increased of late," said Janek, "which means people are struggling to feed their families. So yes, arguing has become commonplace."

"I don't understand. We are the mightiest empire to ever have existed. Why are my people struggling?"

"That is a difficult question to answer, Lord."

"Come now, be honest."

"Although the empire has great wealth, very little of it trickles down to the commoners, for those in power hoard it."

"Are you accusing me of enjoying a lavish lifestyle?"

"It is only just that someone of your prestige has wealth at their fingertips. I was referring to the three families."

"Careful now, Janek. You're treading on dangerous ground."

"You wanted me to be honest."

"Yes," replied Nevarus. "I did, didn't I? Continue with what you were telling me; I shan't hold it against you."

"Right or wrong, it's believed the three families carry the bulk of the empire's wealth in their hands. Were they to share even a minute portion, the lives of the common folk would be vastly better."

"Even I don't have the power to order that."

"I understand, Eminence. I seek only to explain the view of the common folk."

"I shall bear that in mind as we wander around. Now, let's be off. I should like to get in amongst them before it's dark."

The sights and sounds of Varena were unlike anything Nevarus had ever experienced. His imperial chambers were quiet, but here, in the heart of the merchant quarter, everyone talked at once, so much so that he found it difficult to focus. Added to that was the stench of flowers mixed in with rotting fruit and who knows what else.

The emperor focused on watching one individual at a time. First was the vendor hawking earthenware jars, who carried on three conversations at once. Then, he moved on to a group of children running through the street, chasing a chicken. Once it was cornered, they grabbed it, lifting it up by its two feet despite its protestations.

He halted at another stall, examining a basket of eggs, then looked up at a shank of hanging meat that carried a strong aroma of spices. More vendors stood nearby, selling everything from fresh fish to jars of honey, all of it adding to the explosion of smells permeating the area.

"I must apologize," said Janek, his voice loud to be heard over the crowd. "I wasn't expecting it to be so busy."

"Nonsense," replied Nevarus. "It's quite liberating, although I must admit it has a tendency to overwhelm." He was about to say more when he caught sight of a family wandering down the street. The father carried his young son on his shoulders while his wife stopped to look at a stall selling candles. The child laughed hysterically as he played with his father's hair, and for the first time in his life, the Emperor of Halvaria was overcome with jealousy. His son had been removed from his presence at an early age, while the mother of his child was spirited off to who knows where, leaving Nevarus to face a lifetime of loneliness. Despair overwhelmed him.

"I am done here," he said, his voice cracking. "It's time I return to the palace."

"Are you certain, Lord? There is much more to see."

The emperor beckoned his guards over. "We are leaving." He turned to walk away, but with a shock, realized he didn't know how to get back to the palace. He'd hoped that visiting his subjects would bring him closer to them, but instead, it only served to alienate him even more by reminding him of what had been denied him his entire life: companionship.

He straightened his back. "Lead the way, Captain."

"Yes, Eminence," replied the guard, who then threaded his way through the crowd.

A surge of panic threatened to overwhelm Nevarus. So many people were here, their unrelenting voices vying for his attention. He briefly wondered if he was suffering from some type of madness, but the fear abated when they turned down a quieter street. He looked down at his shaking hands and once again began to doubt himself. How was this possible? He was the God-Emperor, yet his mortal body betrayed him!

"The carriage is waiting nearby," said Janek, interrupting his brooding. "I thought it best to be prepared."

"You have done well," declared Nevarus. "You all have." He fell quiet, his mind whirling with activity. Memories came flooding back to him, and he picked them apart, looking at them from a different perspective. Was he truly in charge, or were others simply pretending to go along with his demands while secretly ignoring them?

His whole world was turned upside down. Was he the omnipotent ruler of the greatest empire to have ever existed, or merely a prisoner in a gilded cage, his entire existence a lie?

They turned a corner, and there stood the carriage, ready to whisk him to safety. He climbed inside without another word, waiting as Janek entered and his guards fell into place alongside them.

The carriage rolled forward, the clip-clopping of the horses' hooves falling into a steady rhythm. Janek sat opposite him, settling back into the seat.

"I trust this experience was pleasant, Eminence?"

"It has certainly given me food for thought. Is what we saw today typical?"

"Without a doubt, Eminence."

"And is it always so noisy?"

"Quietness is a rare commodity in the markets of Varena and even rarer within the housing districts."

"Why would there be noise there?"

"In a word, children," said Janek. "It is accepted practice amongst the common folk that their offspring be allowed to…" His voice trailed off.

"Go on, say it. I shan't take offence."

"I was going to say… play."

"Play?"

"Yes. The act of engaging in physical activity in the pursuit of pleasure."

"That is not a concept I am familiar with."

"But as a child—"

"I'll stop you there," said Nevarus. "I was raised to believe my entire life should be devoted to the pursuit of knowledge, not the act of seeking pleasure."

"Surely you have found happiness in something?"

His servant's words caught him by surprise. Had he found some measure of happiness? He looked forward to seeing his son, Karoulus, but was forced to admit it gave him little pleasure. Things might have been different if he'd interacted with the youth more than once a week, but his advisors all insisted he must maintain an air of indifference where his son was concerned.

"Are you feeling unwell, Eminence? You don't seem yourself."

"This experience has opened my eyes, and my mind is struggling to deal with it."

"Is there anything I can do to help?"

Nevarus stared out the window, watching the buildings as they rolled past. "Would you say I live an isolated existence?"

"You are the emperor, Eminence. You could hardly be expected to socialize with peasants."

"Yet they are my people, are they not? Would it not be appropriate for me to hear their complaints in person? Instead, I am only informed of those matters my advisors deem of consequence."

"But those advisors represent the will of the people."

"Do they, truly? Or do they simply represent their own self-interest? I have spent my life in service to this empire. I am now forced to consider that my entire existence has been nothing more than that of a figurehead, my crown a mockery of the power my ancestors once wielded."

"Might I ask what has brought on these thoughts, Eminence? Was it due to the two Mercerians?"

"They were perhaps part of it," replied Nevarus, "but I think my soul-searching began after I read the accounts from the south."

"Concerning the Orcs?"

"Yes. It wasn't that I held particularly strong feelings about them one way or the other; it was that the written reports didn't match what the Marshal of the South told me. That seed of doubt has taken root, and I find myself now questioning any piece of information brought to my attention. Whom can I trust under such circumstances?"

"You can trust me, Eminence."

Nevarus's smile hid his sadness. "Yes. In that, you speak the truth, but I fear you are the only one, which puts both of us in a dangerous situation."

"What makes you say that?"

"If I truly am a figurehead, then I remain alive only so long as I do the bidding of those in charge. Even a single misstep on my part could convince them my existence no longer offers anything of value."

"But the empire needs its emperor?"

"Does it? Or will they dispose of me and crown my son emperor in my stead? He would doubtless prove more malleable!"

"I… don't know what to say," replied Janek.

"I'm not asking you to say anything. I merely want you to understand the peril we now find ourselves in. If my reign ends, so does your influence."

"I have no influence."

"Yes, you do," replied Nevarus. "Whether you realize it or not, I value your opinions, and while I trust you implicitly, others see that as a threat to their control of the Throne. I wish it were otherwise, but I'm afraid our lives are now intertwined to such a degree that our fates are tied together."

Janek went white. "Surely you're not suggesting death is the only way this ends?"

"At present, that is only one of several possibilities, but I'd surmise it's the most probable."

"And the others are?"

"Conceivably, I might devise a way to break their control over me without bringing about my death, although I am open to suggestions about how that could be achieved."

"Have you no one else you can trust?"

"These guards," replied Nevarus, "but even then, they are being changed with an increasing regularity of late, which supports the idea that whoever is behind all this is taking great pains to keep me isolated."

"Then I suppose the question," said Janek, "is who has done this?"

"What are your thoughts on the matter?"

"The logical answer would be the three families. They hold immense power within the empire, and it's not beyond reason for them to seek even more."

"That was my thought as well."

"If that's true, what can be done about it?"

"Very little, I'm afraid."

"Perhaps the Mercerians might be of some use?"

"An interesting thought," replied Nevarus, "but they didn't come all the way to Varena of their own free will, which suggests an ulterior motive on someone's behest."

"Then wouldn't it be useful to talk to them and find out? They might have some idea who transported them here."

The emperor nodded. "Once we've returned to the palace, seek them out and bring them to me."

Arnim stood in front of the ornate door, Nikki on his left, while two guards wearing the gold armour of the emperor's personal guard waited on his right. He rapped his knuckles against the door, which was immediately swung open by the emperor's servant, Janek.

"Come in," he said. "His Eminence is expecting you."

The two Mercerians entered, but when the guards tried to follow, Janek held up his hand. "You wait out there," he said, then closed the door in their faces.

The God-Emperor sat at a table crammed with plates of food. He motioned them forward with his hand. "Come, sit. You must be hungry."

Arnim approached, eyeing the food suspiciously, while Nikki plunked down on a chair and grabbed an apple from a bowl. She took a bite, then looked at her husband. "What?"

"He could have poisoned that."

"Why would he go to such trouble? If he wanted us dead, the guards could've killed us long ago."

Arnim grumbled as he sat but refused the offer of food, instead staring at the emperor. "You summoned us?"

"I invited you here for a chat," corrected Nevarus.

"What is it you want to know?"

"I'm curious to learn who brought you here."

"Your guards," said Arnim.

"No. I mean, originally. You're a long way from Merceria."

"We were waylaid in Colbridge, one of our cities, then placed aboard a ship and taken to..." Arnim turned to Nikki. "What was the name of that place?"

"Zefara," she replied. "It's a port city on the empire's western coast."

"I know of it," said Nevarus, "but I'm interested in discovering who your captor was."

"That's easy," offered Arnim. "Your High Strategos, Exalor Shozarin, or at least that was the name he gave us."

"That would make sense, considering he's leading the campaign against Merceria, but why would he send you here to Varena."

"He didn't," said Nikki. "That is to say, he intended to, but someone else beat him to the punch—a woman named Edora Sartellian. She used some sort of fiery thing to transport us here."

Nevarus raised his eyebrow. "Edora Sartellian, you say? How curious."

"Curious how?" asked Arnim.

"That very same individual is leading the final campaign against the Petty Kingdoms. I wonder why she brought you to the capital."

"My understanding is she wanted to embarrass this Exalor fellow. They pressed us to say he was plotting treason against you. It was an obvious attempt to discredit him, but we refused."

"Might I ask why?"

"Had we done as they wished, we would've been of no further use to them."

"And they would have killed you."

"That was our fear. It was a risk, for they might've murdered us anyway, but in our opinion, they would have viewed us as a potential weapon to use later."

"Thank you for your honesty," said Nevarus. "It's refreshing to finally know the truth."

"It was never our intent to trick you, Eminence," added Nikki. "We never lied to you, if that makes any difference, but our lives were on the line."

"I appreciate that you were put in a difficult position."

"Was that why you requested our presence?" said Arnim.

"Partially. I have recently come to the realization I am sorely in need of allies."

"And you think we can fill that role?"

"It would be in your best interest to, yes."

"May I enquire what led you to that conclusion?"

"I believe my time as emperor is coming to an end, and with my removal, your own usefulness will cease, at least in the eyes of the Sartellians, or the Shozarins for that matter."

Nikki put down her apple. "What did you have in mind?"

SEVEN

Greycloak

SPRING 968 MC

Arandil Greycloak, Lord of the Darkwood, dismounted, handing the reins to a nearby forest warden. Before him stood a great chasm spanned by immense stone spikes with a series of wooden planks laid overtop.

"So, this is the fabled Kharzun's Folly. I have heard much of it of late."

The Dwarf Captain Gelion moved up beside him. "Aye, that's it. Their mages formed those spikes, then wave after wave of warriors poured across. We beat them at Stonecastle, but I doubt we'll have the same success here, as they've fortified their side of the gap."

Lord Greycloak waved his hand, and his Elven archers advanced, taking up positions behind the broken wall guarding this side of the chasm.

"The vard approaches," Gelion snapped at his warriors, who stood to attention as Lord Khazad One-Eye advanced to join his Elven ally.

"Well?" said the vard. "What do you think? Can we take them?"

"It will be difficult," replied Arandil, "but we are not without means." He turned, eyeing those massed on the road. "Shalariel, a moment, if you would be so kind?"

The Mistress of Thorolandrin dismounted, then advanced to stand between the two rulers. Her gaze swept over the magically created bridge, coming to rest on the distant tower.

"What think you?" asked Arandil.

"They have taken pains to fortify their end; a crossing will be difficult."

"Aye," added Gelion. "That tower was naught but a wooden construct when we last saw this place. It appears they've fortified it with stone."

"Earth Magic, no doubt," replied Shalariel, "and shoddily done."

"With all due respect, my lady, I don't understand why you'd say that."

"The manipulation of magic is an art. That tower should be a thing of beauty. Instead, it is an eyesore that blights the mountain paths."

"Ugly it may be, but it still represents a major obstacle."

"Not as major as you might presume."

"You have a plan?" asked Lord Arandil.

"There are several options," she replied, "but all rely on removing this abomination of a bridge."

"I brought engineers with me from Stonecastle," offered Khazad, "but it would take a tremendous effort to tear that thing down, not to mention build a new bridge. Then there's the matter of all those warriors on the other side, who I'm certain would object to us attempting such a thing."

"It was created using the magic of the earth," said Shalariel. "The same can be used to destroy it."

"Aye, that's true, but we still need to get across if we're to take the war to Halvaria."

"And cross we shall," replied Lord Arandil, "but this assault requires some careful planning. There is no point in taking that tower if we lose half our army doing so."

"Warriors we have aplenty," said Khazad. "There's twelve hundred of your Elves, and I've brought five hundred of my own, including my Vard Guard." He grimaced. "Not the best name for them, admittedly, but you get the point. Gelion here is their new commander, appointed by the guild master himself."

"I had heard you were crippled," said Arandil.

"And so I was," replied Gelion, "but the Human mage, Aldus Hearn, used his magic to transport me to Wincaster, where the Orc shaman, Kraloch, healed me." He scowled. "Unfortunately, my return trip took far longer."

"Which worked out fine for us," noted his vard. "We needed the time to ready our army to march." He noticed his Elven ally's lack of understanding. "Stonecakes take time to cook, and a Dwarf can't march on an empty stomach."

"And now we are here," said Shalariel. "Ready to fight once more." She glanced at Arandil. "I still think we should have attacked before they had time to prepare."

The Elven lord shook his head. "There is no point in attacking if we cannot follow through with the rest of the campaign. We have a large force, but to carry the fight into enemy territory, we needed even more, hence our allies."

"And what about the Mercerians?"

"Their men are being sent north," replied Khazad, "to help in the campaign to liberate Ironcliff."

"Remember," said Gelion. "Our purpose is to tie down the empire's troops, not conquer them. There's far too much land to even consider that."

"My commander is right. Our aim here is to force the empire into deploying troops against us, denying them the ability to use them in their northern campaign."

"Or their conquest of the Petty Kingdoms," added Gelion. They all looked at him, causing him to redden. "Those are the lands to the east, which the empire also invaded."

"We are aware," said Arandil. "Our expedition is an integral part of the marshal's plan to defeat them, but we can do nothing of the sort until we get across that gorge."

Khazad lifted his eyepatch, rubbing the socket before putting it back in place, staring at the tower with his good eye. "When do we start? Or should I say, how?"

"The first thing," replied Shalariel, "is to move our warriors back from this so-called bridge."

"And then?"

"Then I shall use my magic to destroy it. With that out of the way, I am freed up to create something a little more useful."

"Useful?" said the vard. "It got those Halvarians across, didn't it?"

"Admittedly, it did," she replied, "but getting their cavalry across must have been challenging. Once I am done, there shall be a bridge that will put this monstrosity to shame."

"I'll move my warriors back up the road," said Gelion. He turned, marching off, leaving the other three alone.

"He's a fighter, that one," declared Khazad. "Would that I had a hundred of him." He looked across the gap once more. "I'm curious how you intend to get away with casting your magic here. That tower is likely bristling with archers."

"The bows of our Forest Wardens far exceed the empire's range, and my archers have had centuries to perfect their skills. If any Halvarian shows their face, they shall quickly find it full of arrows."

The attack plan required the army to reorganize its order of march, a difficult thing to do in the narrow confines of the mountain passes, yet it was soon completed with grit and determination, not to mention plenty of Dwarven cursing.

Elven archers spread out along either side of the gorge, their arrows ready to loose on a moment's notice. Shalariel, accompanied by a pair of Forest Wardens, moved up to stand before the bridge of spikes. The entire area fell silent as she raised her hands on high. Strange sounds emanated from her mouth, words of power that bent arcane forces to her will.

The air surrounding her buzzed as her magic built, and then a cracking noise issued from the bridge, followed by a strange groaning as a chunk of rock split off from the spikes and plummeted to the gorge below.

A pair of Halvarian archers appeared atop the tower, their bowstrings pulled back, but before they loosed their missiles, an arrow took one in the throat while his compatriot was hit in the eye.

Shalariel ignored them, concentrating on controlling the magic flowing through her. Another chunk of rock slewed off, and then a colossal rumble erupted as half the bridge disintegrated, the avalanche of stone hitting the bottom of the ravine in a thunderous crash.

She lowered her hands and fell quiet, watching the last of the Halvarian bridge collapse, the timbers mixing in amongst the rubble below. A cheer went up from the Dwarves while the Elves remained silent.

Lord Arandil approached the Grey Wardens, the elite Elven cavalry now waiting at the front of the column. He began casting, his hands moving very little while his voice boomed out, echoing off the mountainside as words of power flowed forth.

The riders' armour seemed to glow slightly, and Gelion rubbed his eyes to ensure he wasn't imagining things. Shalariel now moved closer to the cliff face, casting yet again. This time, however, her voice sounded calmer, as if she caressed the magic rather than forced it out.

Roots sprang out of the ground, crawling over the edge of the cliff face, then reappeared, flattening themselves into planks of wood as they migrated towards the other side of the gorge. At first, they grew slowly, but as the spell progressed, their growth accelerated. Soon, they were halfway across the span, with a railing growing up on either side to prevent people from falling.

Gelion had no idea how much power was required for this feat of magic, but it was clearly draining Shalariel, for she'd grown pale. He moved closer, peering over the gorge, and was surprised to see massive roots already digging into the other side, with shoots heading upward to support the planks that would carry their warriors across.

The Elf ceased her casting, and the spell continued for a heartbeat, with the roots that clutched at the far side of the ravine sinking even deeper.

Lord Arandil barked out a command, and the Grey Wardens trotted forward, mail glittering in the sunlight, their swords hanging at their waists, while each held a bow, an arrow nocked, ready to let loose.

Gelion stepped back to give them room to pass, watching them traverse the bridge, four abreast. Arrows flew from the tower, some even finding their target, but the Elves' speed was such that they were on the other side before any serious damage was done. Once the two hundred horses rode across, the Elven foot followed, shields and swords at the ready.

The sound of fighting drifted to Gelion's ears. By his reckoning, several hundred Halvarians had retreated from the attack on Stonecastle, and there was a strong possibility that reinforcements had arrived from their homeland, yet those numbers didn't even slow the Elves as they pushed past the tower and continued onward, disappearing from sight.

"Bring our people forward," said Khazad, "and we'll deal with those in the tower."

"Aren't the Elves going to take it?"

"We agreed that would be our responsibility. After all, you can't expect a woodland Elf to assault a tower made of stone."

Gelion wanted to remind him that was precisely what Shalariel had done but thought better of arguing with the vard. "Yes, Majesty." He gave the order, and the doughty warriors of Stonecastle advanced, the arbalesters leading, with the axe-wielding warriors of the Undermountain following. Last came the Vard Guard, though he much preferred the term Hearth Guard. Problem was, the name had already been used, up in Ironcliff, and Khazad wasn't the sort of vard who wanted to be accused of stealing someone else's thunder.

Gelion stood there, watching them pass, then realized his place was up front. He hurried to get ahead of them, only to find Murdan leading. "What in the name of Gundar are you doing here?"

"You made me captain when you were promoted," replied the arbalester.

"Did I? I don't remember doing that."

"Too late to change your mind now!"

Gelion grinned. "I'm just pulling your beard. There's no one else I'd have leading my old company." Hearing a grumbling behind him, he turned and spotted the engineer, Golmar Hengesplitter, huffing and puffing his way towards them. Over his shoulder sat a yoke with a pole attached, a leather bag slung on each end of it. "Do you need help carrying those?"

The old Dwarf growled. "Touch these, and you're likely to blow yourselves to bits. Now, out of the way, and let me at the base of that tower."

Murdan ordered his men to the opposite side of the road, where they loaded their arbalests and kept bolts trained on the tower lest any Halvarians attempt to loose arrows from it.

Gelion joined them, watching Golmar with great interest. "I'm eager to see what that fire powder of his is capable of. I understand it's relatively new?"

"It is," replied Murdan. "They say the only other person who knew the recipe was one of his apprentices. Unfortunately, he was killed when he accidentally set alight a small sample."

"How small?"

"I'm told no more than the size of an Elf's purse."

"Is that large?"

The arbalester chuckled. "Do I look like someone who spends a lot of time around the woodland folk?"

They fell silent as Golmar removed the yoke from his shoulders and dug through a sling bag, producing what looked like a taper, which he jammed the end of into a bag. He pulled forth another and moved to the second bag, where he repeated the process.

"What in Gundar's name is he doing?" whispered Gelion. "I thought those things were supposed to ignite. Can't he just strike his flint and be done with it?"

"Watch and learn, my friend. I think you'll find it most entertaining."

"You've seen it before?"

"Aye," replied Murdan. "He demonstrated this fire powder of his after the siege was lifted." He paused for a breath. "Oh, that's right, you were off in Wincaster getting healed, weren't you? Sorry. I should have realized."

Golmar drew out a flint and steel, striking them together near the end of the first taper. Once it caught, the engineer bent it slightly, using the tip to light the second. That done, he rose and ran full speed towards the watching arbalesters.

"Cover your ears," he shouted, then crouched, doing precisely what he'd suggested.

The tapers burned down quickly, and then a jet of sparks flew forth from the bag on the left, with the same soon happening on the right. Before Gelion could say anything, a tremendous explosion rent the air, followed by a blast of wind that threatened to knock him from his feet. An intense wave of heat came next, leaving him wondering if he'd been sent to the Underworld.

The explosion drilled into the tower, slicing off a chunk of rock to expose the wooden frame beneath. Mere moments later, the second bag exploded, sending a massive sheet of flame skyward.

With his ears ringing from the power of the explosions, Gelion tried to make sense of the horrendous damage that such small bags of powder had wreaked. As the smoke cleared, the sound of cracking stone issued forth.

"Back!" yelled Golmar. "Get away from that thing before we're all crushed!"

Murdan followed this with his own command. "Run!"

Now weakened on one side, the tower tilted, and then the entire thing toppled, large chunks of stone being dislodged from the wooden frame. As it struck the road, it sent up a massive plume of debris.

Gelion held his breath while others choked. When the dust settled, little more than rubble was left of the tower.

"Amazing!" said Murdan. "You brought that down in one fell swoop."

"Technically, it was two," replied Golmar. "And it would've failed had it not been for the terrible construction."

"But it was a stone tower?"

"That tower was made of wood. Their Earth Mages got lazy and placed a thin layer of stone over it to protect it from flaming arrows. Had they built a proper stone tower, my powder would've failed."

"How much more of that stuff have you got?" asked Gelion.

"Very little, and its ingredients are rare."

"How rare?"

"That powder cost more than what building a new tower would." He clapped his hands to remove the dust that had settled on them. "Now, let's get this debris cleared out, shall we? We've got a lot of work to do."

"Work?" said Murdan. "What are you talking about?"

"We're going to build a new tower on this side of the bridge." Golmar paused, shaking his head. "No. Not a tower, an entire gatehouse. Never again will outsiders try to force their way across Kharzun's Folly."

"And how long will that take?"

"Months, but I have workers coming to take care of that. We just need to keep the road clear for our supplies."

"You are injured," said Lord Arandil.

Blood trickled from the corner of Shalariel's mouth. She produced a handkerchief and dabbed it away. "The spell was most taxing."

"You must conserve your strength. This campaign will be long, and we cannot afford for you to be incapacitated."

Shalariel furrowed her brow. "Do I detect a note of concern about my well-being?"

He returned her gaze. "We have been together for more than a thousand years. In all that time, have I ever expressed my emotions in front of outsiders?"

"I do not believe so."

"Then I think it time I begin."

She stared back, a look of shock on her face. "Are you ill?"

"No," he replied, "but my time amongst Humans has, I think, altered my view of the world."

"So you would go against millennia of tradition to reveal your emotions to outsiders?"

"Only in this," he replied.

From somewhere behind them came the sound of a lute, accompanied by the tender voice of the bard, Delsaran:

"The king of the Darkwood, Arandil,
did pledge his love out loud,
To Lady Shal' of Thorolandrin,
In front of Dwarven crowd."

Delsaran paused. "Hmmm. It needs some work. Should I shorten Thorolandrin as well, do you think?"

"That's enough out of you," said Lord Arandil. "I suggest, in future, you confine your efforts to songs of battle."

EIGHT

Command

SPRING 968 MC

Lord Alain Heinrich, the Duke of Erlingen, rubbed his hands together as he paced. "I face a difficult decision," he said. "With General Fitzwilliam no longer with us, whom do I appoint as commander of my army?"

His barons stared at each other as if sizing up the competition. Alongside them stood the officers commanding the Temple Knights of Saint Agnes and Mathew.

"This is no easy choice," replied Temple Captain Vitaly. "Lady Beverly led us to victory over the Halvarians, which is to be applauded, but only one person here has anywhere near the experience of the Mercerian's background."

The duke nodded. "You speak of Temple Commander Marlena?"

"I do, Your Grace. She's fought the Halvarians several times and thus is familiar with their tactics."

Augustus Strappe, the Baron of Salzing, cleared his throat. "I might remind everyone the good Temple Commander has yet to command an entire battle. She was also on the losing side of her first two encounters of this campaign."

"Who would you put forward as an alternative?" asked the Mathewite.

"Myself. I was a Knight of the Sceptre long before I became baron. That alone shows my devotion to the Crown."

"It is not your devotion that is in question," said Lord Hagan Stein, Baron of Mulsingen. "It is your experience or lack thereof."

"I've fought my share of duels."

"Doubtless, you have, but that hardly gives you the skills necessary to command an army." Stein turned to the duke. "Your Grace, we cannot afford to gamble on an inexperienced general when the entire realm is under threat of invasion."

"Invasion?" said Strappe. "We defeated one of their vaunted legions."

"True, but as General Fitzwilliam already implied, the Halvarians learn quickly. The next time they come, they won't make the mistake of splitting their army."

"He speaks the truth," replied the duke. "And let there be no mistake, gentlemen; our next encounter will be here, on Erlingen soil."

"Could we not advance into Angvil again?" asked Strappe. "That would keep them from crossing into our lands."

"No. As Lord Hagan pointed out, the enemy won't fall for the same trick a second time. We can hold the bridge at Zurkirk for the moment, but I fear it's only a matter of time before they find another way across."

"The river will protect us."

"Not necessarily," offered Temple Commander Marlena. "We thought the river a secure border back in Arnsfeld until the empire used Water Mages to lower the water."

"Then why are they not crossing as we speak?" asked Strappe.

"We must assume they're waiting for reinforcements. We dealt them a heavy blow at the Battle of the Pines. It will take time for them to make up those losses."

"An interesting observation," said the duke. "Where would these extra troops come from?"

"From the other legions occupying the conquered kingdoms, which grants us a reprieve to recover. After all, we might've won the battle, but we still took losses."

"If I placed you in command, what would be your strategy?"

"I would reorganize the army. Your current structure is inefficient, with each baron commanding their own men. We need to present a solid line of battle, not individual clusters of warriors."

"I'm intrigued," said Lord Alain. "Tell me more."

"With our present numbers, I'd group the army into three divisions. Two consisting of the footmen, archers, and a small number of horse. The remainder of the cavalry, including the Temple Knights, would be massed in a reserve division, along with the remaining foot and bow."

"How large would these divisions be?"

"By my estimates, nine hundred men, with the reserve being slightly smaller."

"Nonsense," said Strappe. "Why have footmen in reserve? Wouldn't it be better to split them amongst the other two divisions?"

"Placing them in reserve allows them to replace casualties as needed."

"Good luck with that. I can't see any baron agreeing to give up command of the men they've paid for."

"I disagree," said Stein. "If this is the best chance of saving the realm, then we must all make sacrifices." Many of the other barons in the room nodded. Likely they didn't fancy the idea of going into battle and were content to let others ride into danger.

"Who would command these divisions?" asked the duke.

"I'd take personal command of the reserve," replied the Temple Commander, "the better to deploy them as needed."

"And the other two divisions?"

"With your permission, I would assign the Temple Captains to command them."

"Not my barons?"

"With all due respect," replied Marlena, "Temple Captains are trained in tactics and strategy. Can you say the same for your nobles?"

"You make a compelling argument. Wherever did you come up with such an idea?"

"The enemy. Their organization makes them more flexible in terms of strategy. Each legion is a complete army, with a balance of horse, foot, and bow, divided into four cohorts. Admittedly, our divisions would be slightly larger than their cohorts, however we lack the numbers of a full legion."

"How long would it take for this reorganization?"

"That depends on the cooperation of your nobles. On paper, it's a simple matter of informing everyone about the new command structure, but I imagine it would take at least a week for them to acclimatize."

"I'm confused," said Strappe. "First, you say it's a simple matter, then you claim the men need time. Which is it?"

"Changing a commander is easy," replied Marlena, "but each division must camp as a separate entity. In some cases, that means a single baron's companies may find themselves split up into different divisions."

The duke nodded. "I applaud you, Commander. You've given this much thought. I shall consider the matter at some length before I make my final decision. I wonder if you might give further consideration as to which companies will go into each division?"

"Of course, Your Grace." She bowed.

"You are all dismissed. We shall reconvene first thing in the morning."

"Am I doing the right thing?" asked Marlena.

"Most assuredly," replied Johanna. "You have more experience fighting the empire than anyone else here."

"Perhaps, but Lord Augustus made an excellent point; they've defeated me twice already."

"Wasn't it Saint Agnes herself who said you learn more from your mistakes than from your successes?"

"Yes, it was. Thank you for reminding me."

"You have this in you, Commander. We Temple Knights all know it."

"It's not the order I need to convince."

"No," replied Johanna, "it's not. It's yourself. Put aside your doubts. Go in there tomorrow and be confident, knowing you're doing the right thing."

"How do I know if I am?"

"The only way to do the wrong thing is to do nothing."

"More words from Saint Agnes?"

"No, Saint Ragnar."

Marlena stared back. "Not thinking of joining them, are you?"

"Saints, no," replied Johanna. "I was only curious about their role in the Church."

"And what did you discover?"

"Aside from the usual hunting down Necromancers, nothing. In any case, it matters little. As far as I can determine, they don't allow women entry."

"I think you'd be surprised," said Marlena.

"What does that mean?"

"Simply that the order has more at their disposal than just Temple Knights. Sister Charlaine once told me that when she was in Ilea, she met a Life Mage who worked for the Ragnarites. It doesn't take a stretch of the imagination to speculate they would employ other gifted individuals."

"Fascinating."

"There's more," added Marlena. "Aside from hunting down Death Mages, they're employed as scouts for the Holy Army, possibly even spies."

"You mean they were," replied Johanna. "They broke with the Church, much as we did."

"Yes, they did. The Temple General was very clear on that."

"I thought we weren't supposed to talk about her in public?"

"In case you haven't noticed," said Marlena, "we're camped amongst our own knights. If we can't trust them to keep the secret, then we've no hope at all."

. . .

The duke had switched his headquarters to one of Zurkirk's inns, but as his barons filed in, he began to wonder if perhaps a larger venue would've been more appropriate. The temple officers were last to arrive, remaining near the door due to the packed nature of the room.

Lord Alain cleared his throat, garnering everyone's attention. "I have given this much thought," he began, "and I decided to award command to Temple Commander Marlena." This brought an immediate response from his barons. Most nodded, but Lords Augustus Strappe and Marten Drachmann, Baron of Hutfeld, voiced their dissent.

"What about the commanders?" Lord Hagan's question interrupted their grumbling.

"I will allow the Temple Commander to appoint whomever she sees fit. If those individuals are Temple Captains, then so be it."

Everyone tried to speak at once, but the duke wasn't having it. He raised his hands to quiet the room. "This is not a matter of status or of picking favourites; it is about choosing those who, in her opinion, are the most qualified to bring us victory. Now, having said my piece, I shall ask the Temple Commander to come forward and take her rightful place."

Marlena moved through the crowd. Most allowed her easy passage, but Strappe forced her to push her way past him. Finally, she stood before the duke. "Thank you, Your Grace, for giving me your support. I shall do my best to prove myself worthy."

She turned, facing the rest of the room. "Yesterday, you heard how I intend to reorganize the army. I'm certain you have questions, particularly concerning how we move forward in the face of Halvarian aggression, but before I get to that, I'd like to clear the air concerning my ideas. As barons, you are an essential part of the ruling class. My intention is not to usurp your influence; it is to protect you, for Erlingen needs its nobility to help rebuild after this invasion. Fear not. You shall all have a chance to speak your minds, but let there be no mistake. When it comes to military matters, my decisions are final. Now, I would invite questions."

Lord Hagan's voice broke through the crowd. "I think the question on everyone's mind is where we fit into this. I understand your intention is to ensure our survival, if possible, but should we wish it, are we able to assist in some manner?"

"Most assuredly," replied Marlena. "I invite anyone who wishes to participate in the coming campaign to do so, be that in an advisory capacity or as soldiers standing shoulder to shoulder with their own men, but ultimately, all companies are expected to follow the commands of those in charge. If a baron contradicts those orders, then that noble will be removed from their position. Do I make myself clear?" The vast majority of the barons nodded, while one or two remained apprehensive. Or was it fear? It suddenly occurred to her that, despite the bluster, most of the nobles of Erlingen feared what was to come.

"I have complete trust in the Temple Commander," said the duke. "And I expect you to abide by her commands." He nodded at Marlena. "Perhaps you could explain the strategy you intend to employ?"

"Most certainly. The Battle of the Pines gave us some breathing room, but eventually, the enemy will replace its losses and cross the border. I've seen first-hand what they're capable of, and I assure you, they won't sit back and wait for long. When they do return, it will be in greater numbers, and I doubt they'll make the mistake of splitting their forces a second time. To that end, we must prepare to face two full legions."

"How do we prevent them from overriding the entire duchy?" asked Hagan.

"Simply put—we don't. We have limited manpower and can't be everywhere at once. The harsh reality is we will be forced back until we find a defensive position where we can gain some tactical advantage."

She paused, waiting for questions, but when none were forthcoming, she continued. "I must warn you; the empire is not above using trickery to weaken us. Back in Angvil, the duchess's army took in what were reportedly survivors from the Armies of Gotfeld and Rudor. At the time, they thought these extra men would make it easier to hold back the Halvarians. In truth, they were loyal to the empire and turned on us at a critical time."

"Pardon my asking," said Lord Marten, "but are you suggesting the Angvil survivors can't be trusted?"

"I am saying precisely that," replied Marlena. "We'll still employ them but will relegate them to less-critical duties, such as guarding our towns and villages. As for the overall strategy, I intend to borrow a tactic from my former Temple Commander. We shall withdraw southeast, towards Torburg, leaving small groups behind in the hills north of the road, as well as the woods to the south. Their task will be to tie down as many Halvarian troops as possible by means of hit-and-run raids on their supply lines, forcing them to divert some of their men to secure the area, thus weakening their main army."

She paused. "If all goes according to plan, we should make our stand on the outskirts of your capital, which, I'm told, has favourable terrain."

"Why not make a stand here, at Zurkirk?" asked Drachmann.

"That would be fine were I certain of the enemy's strategy, but if they cross in the south, at Grozen, we risk being cut off and attacked from the rear. To that end, we shall be leaving a small garrison here while we withdraw the bulk of the army to Anshlag, where we will undergo our reorganization. Numbers alone preclude us from taking the offensive, so we are forced to adopt a defensive stance, reacting to the enemy's movements. I know it's not ideal, but once they cross into our territory, we'll get a much better idea of what they intend."

"Will we burn our villages to prevent them from supplying the enemy?"

"No," replied Marlena. "The common folk have already suffered enough. We don't need to add to their woes by burning them out of their homes."

"You've all heard the commander," said Lord Alain. "Now go explain this to your men so we can ensure an efficient change of command."

Marlena stared down at the map of Torburg and its surrounding areas, trying to decide where best to eventually make her stand. Johanna, her aide, entered, hesitating before speaking, a sign something was bothering her. "There's someone to see you, Commander."

"What is it you're not telling me?"

"He's a Temple Captain," she replied. "A Cunar."

"What does he want?"

"He says he's come to help, but in light of recent events, I doubt we can trust him."

"Send him in," said Marlena, "and gather six knights, just in case."

"You think we'll have to arrest him?"

"It's certainly a possibility."

Johanna nodded, then exited, leaving Marlena to assess the situation. The Cunars were no allies of her order. Why, then, would they come offering help? Was it a ruse to gain insight into her plans? Ordinarily, she would take the word of a fellow Temple Knight without hesitation, but recent events had proven the Cunars untrustworthy.

The door opened to a familiar face.

"Temple Captain Waleed," said Marlena. "You're the last person I expected to see here."

The Kurathian bowed. "May the Saints be with you. It has been many years since we fought beside each other in the Five Sisters. I'd enquire if you've prospered, but with the prospect of an invasion looming, that would seem a poor topic."

"We missed you in Reinwick. What happened?"

"Shortly after we fought off the Halvarians, I was ordered to Ostrova. We had no commandery there, but I was assured we were considering building one. Only after I arrived did I realize I was sent there as punishment."

"For what? You distinguished yourself in battle."

"True, but that was in cooperation with your order, along with the Mathewites. In light of more recent events, I now doubt my superiors' motives. Thankfully, I had some contacts at the Antonine and obtained a transfer to Lubenstahl, where I've been for the last two years."

"Are you familiar with the politics of the Antonine?"

"If you're referring to the official disbanding of your order, then yes. Over the last two years, I've acquired Temple Knights who feel the order has become… I'm not sure what I'd call it."

"Corrupted?"

"That term will suffice. When we heard the empire launched its campaign, I gathered those loyal to me and rode west, our intention being to offer what assistance we can."

"You'll pardon me for my skepticism, but this wouldn't be the first time the empire has tried to trick us."

"I assure you the knights under my command are earnest in their desire to bring about the end of the empire."

"How many have you?"

"Two companies," replied Waleed. "Many who are veterans of our shared campaign in Reinwick, which is the reason they disagreed with the disbanding of your order, although from the looks of it, it has done little to lessen your own numbers."

"And do they still wear the grey of your order?"

"They do, but only as a matter of practicality. Present us with other colours if you wish, as we no longer serve the Cunar Grand Master."

NINE

Abandoned

SPRING 968 MC

Exalor cursed, slamming his fist down on the table beside him. He'd intended to return to Varena to secure his position, but events in the north now demanded his attention. Facing the prospect that his entire campaign had faltered, he tried to control himself before addressing Idraxa. "Tell me again how the siege is going, and this time, the truth."

She swallowed, fighting to remain calm. "We failed to breach the front door to the Undermountain, but we may have discovered another way in."

"Go on."

"Our Earth Mages believe we can batter away at the mountain, collapsing tunnels close to the outside."

"How long do they expect this bombardment will take?"

"We've already made progress. A small hole appeared this morning, so I gave the order to concentrate on that one location."

"You say a small hole?" said Exalor. "How small?"

"Large enough for a man to crawl through, but it's easily defensible. My intention is to widen it until our warriors can charge in three abreast."

The High Strategos mulled over this new information. If this turned out to be a way into the mountain, then the end of Ironcliff would soon be at hand. "How long before you can begin the full assault?"

"Two days, perhaps three."

"You've done well, Idraxa. Keep up the good work."

"Will you be remaining to oversee the assault?" she asked.

"No. My attention is required in the capital. However, I've arranged for replacement warriors to fill your ranks, and they will arrive by the end of the week, in time for the march into Norland. I've also taken the liberty of choosing primarily footmen, as they'll take the greatest casualties once you get into that mountain."

"Understood, Your Grace. I shan't let you down."

"Good, because once I'm done in Varena, I shall be recommending you to the position of High Strategos."

"But… that is your position."

"At the moment, yes, but once I seize the Throne, I need someone reliable to look after the legions. I trust you have no objection to assuming that duty?"

Idraxa bowed. "I would be honoured, Your Grace."

Exalor let out a deep breath. "I know this campaign has come with its share of surprises, but you've adapted to them with grace and dignity. I wish the same could be said for my other marshals."

"I assume the other attacks failed?"

"The attack on Stonecastle was repulsed, and the Third Legion has retreated. I left orders to destroy all bridges, but I fear the marshal is rising to the level of his incompetence."

"And the naval assault?"

"The Fourth has been unable to make any headway. It's not all bad news, for the fleet is still there, cutting off trade, forcing the Mercerians to maintain a presence in the area, but I fear the swamp will soon bring sickness to the legion."

"Is there no hope at all?"

"I cannot act while my future in the empire is so precarious. I must return and cleanse Varena of my enemies, then remove that figurehead of an emperor once and for all."

"You'll need men if you intend to hold the capital."

"Fear not," said Exalor. "I've compiled a long list of enemies deserving of retribution and a longer list of allies. My justice will be swift and merciless."

"Are you suggesting we should abandon our attack on Ironcliff?"

"Not at all. We need a victory, Idraxa, to prove we are still a force to be reckoned with."

"I shall not fail you."

"See that you don't. Now, I must be on my way."

She bowed, then left him. As a Shozarin, Exalor trusted her, but would that be true of his other allies? As head of his line, he'd assumed he could count on his fellow Enchanters, but was he gambling his life on that loyalty? He shook it off, then closed his eyes, concentrating on casting a spell.

· · ·

Wingate fretted. He'd received word Exalor was returning to Varena, but he was now overdue. He then sensed the familiar buzzing in the air, and his master's voice echoed in the room. "I shall be returning shortly. See that my guards are in place."

"Yes, Your Grace."

Wingate felt the connection break. Exalor's fartalk spell was a strange sensation, almost as if he were talking with a ghost, yet it had proved extremely useful over the years.

Wingate called for the guards, leading them below, where the enchanted circle waited, deep in the bowels of the Shozarin estate. Needing to bring guards was not normal, but these were dangerous times, and Lord Exalor wasn't taking any chances, even here in the heart of his power base.

They arrived as the circle activated, the runes glowing, their light reflecting off the white marble walls. After a flash, Exalor appeared in the centre.

"Welcome, Your Grace," said Wingate.

The High Strategos didn't waste any time on formalities. "I used my magic to send you back here to determine what's happened. What have you to tell me?"

"It's not good, I'm afraid. We received news that an assassin killed the Governor of Herani three days ago, and there's been an attack on that of Zefara as well. It appears someone is attempting to cleanse the line."

"Who is behind these attacks?"

"That remains to be seen, Your Grace, but rumours are the Sartellians are attempting some sort of power grab."

"That makes sense, considering they arranged for one of their own to take command of the campaign in the Petty Kingdoms."

"What shall we do about it?"

"Do?" replied Exalor. "What else can we do but retaliate? Doing otherwise would show signs of weakness."

"Where would you like to start, Your Grace? With Edora Sartellian in the Petty Kingdoms?"

"No. Much as it pains me to admit it, her loss might endanger the great dream. We need someone here, in Varena, with a large enough presence that their death will make waves."

"Enelle, perhaps? She is, after all, the High Purifier?"

"No, too obvious. We must aim higher." Exalor snapped his fingers. "Agalix Sartellian."

"The head of the family?" said Wingate. "Are you certain that's wise, Your Grace? You could incite a line war."

"The time has come to cleanse this city of their corrupt influence."

"What about the Stormwinds? They work very closely with the Sartellians amongst the Petty Kingdoms."

"True, but the destruction of the Volstrum put an end to their influence, leaving them nothing more than a regional power. If they continue their decline at their current rate, they'll be virtually unknown in five years."

"Agalix will be heavily guarded," warned Wingate.

"Which only makes it more of a challenge." Exalor rubbed his hands together. "I've been waiting for this opportunity for years."

"Will this be a matter of stealth or an outright assault?"

"Stealth, at least to begin with."

"I'm not certain I understand."

"There will be others," replied Exalor, "but Agalix will be the first to feel my wrath. Send our best agents. I want him dead by nightfall."

"Yes, Your Grace."

Agalix lifted the poker, using it to stir the embers. The fire was dying despite his best efforts. His magic had sustained it, but even magical flames needed a source of fuel to burn, and he wasn't about to waste any more of his inner magic.

He got to his feet and placed another log atop the fire. A wave of his hand was all that was needed for it to burst into flames, and then he returned to his seat, relishing the heat.

A distant crash interrupted his thoughts. Likely a servant dropping a plate. Agalix cared little for such things, instead turning his attention to the news he'd received from Edora. Her campaign against the Petty Kingdoms had suffered a setback, but she was confident her new plan of attack would put them back on the path to victory.

The Mercerian, General Fitzwilliam, had thwarted her original strategy, but he was confident Edora wouldn't be fooled a second time. The door behind him creaked as it opened.

"Not now," said Agalix. "I'm thinking."

Despite his words, the footsteps drew closer, and he turned in irritation, expecting one of his servants. Instead, a man dressed in black approached with a sword held out before him.

"Ah," said the mage. "You've come to kill me."

"Nothing personal," the assassin responded.

Agalix chuckled. "I can think of nothing more personal than murder. Tell me, if you would be so kind, is my death to be quick or lingering?"

"It makes no matter either way, so long as you're dead."

"Might I finish my wine?"

"Most certainly."

Agalix lifted the cup and turned slightly, offering it up as a salute. The assassin stood no more than three paces away, the tip of his sword temporarily lowered. And why wouldn't it be? Agalix was an old man, far too ancient to present anything in the way of opposition.

He felt the power building within him. Part of him wanted to burn the fellow to ashes, but that required a much more overt display of magic, one that would undoubtedly give time for the sword to pierce his heart. He contented himself with warming his wine. The metal cup glowed slightly as he poured his magic into it. He made a show of struggling to get to his feet as the wine started bubbling within the cup.

Agalix suddenly hurled the boiling hot contents at his would-be murderer, splashing the villain in the face, his pain-filled screams filling the room. The old mage prepared to follow up his attack by causing the unfortunate soul to erupt into flames, but a crossbow quarrel took him in the chest. He stared down at it, not quite comprehending what had transpired, then fell to his knees as he tasted blood.

The second assassin loomed over the Fire Mage, drawing a knife to finish off his target, but it proved unnecessary. Agalix Sartellian breathed once more and then crumpled to the floor, lifeless.

Bryn Vilani watched from an alleyway as her people moved into position. The Marshal of the South, Castimar Stormwind, was marching to the capital along with his three legions, but the power structure here required thinning. Her target, Enelle Sartellian, was wandering down the street, stopping at different stalls as her guards stood back, looking on, providing the perfect opportunity for Bryn's people to strike. They'd already arranged for the deaths of two Sartellians and three Shozarins, but to her mind, she needed at least one more to push the two families into open warfare.

When her eyes met those of her associates, she gave them a nod. A wagon rolled out into the street, its driver struggling to control the horses. Commoners rushed to get out of the way, and as it drew closer to Enelle, it swerved, not into her, but towards her guards. They jumped back to avoid being trampled, effectively separating them from their mistress.

Bryn's people gathered around Enelle Sartellian, their clothing suggesting they were nothing more than commoners; indeed, two had even manned a stall. They converged on the mage so quickly she had no idea what was happening.

Bryn watched as the throng of people backed up, revealing a blood-splattered Enelle. The mage collapsed without a sound, and those who'd surrounded her now melted into the gathering crowd.

By the time her guards realized she was under attack, it was too late. Enelle Sartellian, the High Purifier of the Halvarian Empire, was dead.

Kelson Shozarin wandered through the streets of Varena. He'd noticed he was being followed three blocks ago but decided against taking immediate action. He continued along, acting as though he were unaware of the danger.

He stopped at the open window of a bakery, luxuriating in the smell, giving himself the time he needed to decide on his next move. There was no telling who'd sent his pursuers, but he held no doubt they were there to put an end to him.

He continued, ducking down an alleyway as he passed the corner of the building. Ordinarily, it would've been a simple matter for those following to discover his whereabouts, for the alley only led one street over. What they would doubtlessly forget, however, was the power of his magic.

Kelson called on his inner magic, letting the spell build as his features altered, his height diminishing even as his girth increased. He quickly removed his cloak, turning it inside out before he threw his hat to the side and pulled the cloak's hood close to hide his features. He stepped into the street, making a show of looking behind him as if someone had bumped into him.

Three men rushed past, eager to pursue their victim, unaware they'd just passed him. Kelson counted to five before letting loose with the blend spell, which allowed him to walk along and be ignored by those around him as if his very presence wasn't out of the ordinary.

He watched the alleyway from across the street, eager to learn more about the trio. They emerged a short while later, arguing with each other. Kelson followed as they went on their way, hopefully to report to their superior.

An aged sign announcing to the world that the business was known as the Oaken Cudgel hung over the door they stopped at. It appeared to be in good repair despite being in a poorer neighbourhood, with the noise emanating from within indicating the popularity of the place.

Kelson's blend spell wouldn't last much longer, and he didn't want to expend any additional energy in case he needed to fight his attackers, so he settled on finding a nearby alleyway that gave him a good view of the front door.

The Cudgel got even busier as it filled up with dinnertime patrons. He waited, watching with the patience of the dead, but none who came or went were of any consequence.

As night fell, he began to wonder if he wasn't wasting his time or if he'd missed another entrance to the place. Then a familiar face stepped out into the moonlight: Kestia Stormwind.

Kelson was immediately on the alert, for her presence was unlikely to be a coincidence considering the usual patrons of the Oaken Cudgel. As a member of the Inner Council, the true governing body of the Halvarian Empire, she was one of the elite, yet here she was, visiting the same place as the trio who'd just tried to kill him. He stopped himself. Were they truly out to murder him, or was he being paranoid? Admittedly, it was difficult not to be when Shozarins were being murdered left, right, and centre.

It suddenly occurred to him there had to be more to the spate of recent killings than a line war. No, this was much more dangerous: a realignment of the ruling families. The Sartellians, Shozarins, and Stormwinds had always been political rivals, but until recently, they'd held to a truce of sorts designed to allow the Empire of Halvaria to thrive. Something had changed to alter that balance, and only the fall of the Volstrum came to mind. Its destruction at the hands of the Therengians had taken everyone by surprise. That a renegade student of the Stormwinds was responsible for this tragic situation developing in the first place, put the blame entirely on the shoulders of the matriarch, Marakhova Stormwind.

The problem with this line of thinking was that the loss of their academy would've weakened the Stormwinds, not emboldened them. Why, then, would they make plans to murder him, a Shozarin?

Kelson shook his head. It would do no good to speculate. He needed actual proof, not idle conjecture, and to decide on his next course of action now, not wait until it was too late. With only Shozarins and Sartellians being targeted, was this a move to seize power by the Stormwinds or a way to reduce their influence so that all three families were once again equal?

He was also forced to consider the possibility that another faction was involved. Despite these families holding the reins of control for over five hundred years, there were other mages in the empire more than capable of seizing power should the opportunity present itself. Perhaps this wasn't the work of a family so much as the clever scheming of a gifted individual!

TEN

Ironcliff

A cylinder of light leaped up to the ceiling, temporarily blinding the Dwarven guards stationed there. Used to such displays, they looked aside, waiting for the light to dissipate to reveal their visitors.

"I don't know that I'll ever get used to that," said Herdwin. "It's very disorienting."

Albreda frowned. "Would you rather have walked all the way to Ironcliff?"

"It's convenient, I'll give you that, but I always feel as though a part of me got left behind."

"No. You're all here," said Kasri. "Trust me. I'd know if anything was missing."

The guards snapped to attention, their gold armour reflecting the torchlight.

"It's good to be back," she continued. "Captain Durgan, good to see you again."

"And you, Commander," replied the guard. "Shall I have the guards escort you to the vard?"

"If you would be so kind."

He called on two of his warriors, who, in turn, opened the doors leading out of the casting circle, and then he led the way himself.

"How have you fared in my absence?" asked Kasri.

"We lost the outer city, but that was expected. Everyone was brought beneath the mountain well in advance, although we took some casualties in the first assault."

"And the current situation?"

"We are sealed up inside the Undermountain, my lady. I'm told the High Ranger of Merceria has a plan, but I believe it best if the vard explains it to you."

"This place is different from Mirstone," noted Albreda, "yet I notice touches here and there that suggest a common ancestry."

"That's hardly surprising," noted Herdwin. "After all, Dwarves will be Dwarves."

"As far as I know, Ironcliff is the only Dwarven stronghold to clothe their warriors in plate armour."

"Only our elite companies," added Kasri.

"And those would be?" asked the Druid.

"The Hearth Guard and the vard's personal warriors. The rest are equipped with simple mail."

"Simple, she calls it," quipped Herdwin. "There's a lot of work that goes into making a mail shirt, and it's a very repetitive process."

"I didn't mean to suggest it wasn't," replied Kasri. "Dwarven mail is far superior to what most Humans use. It's a wonder they don't use it themselves."

"They can't. They don't have the forges for it."

"None at all?"

"Well," said Herdwin, "except for maybe Aldwin's back in Bodden that he used to smelt skymetal. Of course, I had to send him detailed instructions to do so."

"Don't tell the Guild Master of the Smiths Guild," said Kasri. "He'd likely tear out his beard."

"Do they not share their knowledge here in Ironcliff?"

"No. Quite the reverse. Those secrets are reserved for the most senior members of the guild, which is one of the main reasons so few of our warriors wear plate armour."

Herdwin laughed.

"You find something funny?" asked Kasri.

"My pardon. I was wondering what this guild master of yours would look like beardless."

"I was merely speculating."

"That I understand," replied Herdwin, "but what he doesn't realize is I've learned how to make plate armour, and I'm under no restrictions as to who I teach."

"Who taught you?" asked Albreda.

"I taught myself. Kasri allowed me to examine her armour, and I worked out how to reproduce it, even added a flourish or two of my own. My objective was to make armour for the Queen's Guard Cavalry. Aldwin was supposed to help me, but he went and got lost in the east… Well, I suppose that wasn't the only problem. Truth be told, all those Halvarians put a damper on the whole endeavour. Still, I'll get back to it, eventually."

"You are a remarkable individual."

"Thank you."

"We're here," announced Captain Durgan. Two guards adorned in silver plate armour flanked the door before them. At their approach, one opened the door, admitting the group into the great hall of Ironcliff.

Vard Thalgrun sat on his throne while Garnik Hardhand, the Guild Master of the Warriors Guild, argued with Selia Ironfist, the head of the mining guild.

"Your warriors can't be in there while the enemy is still battering the walls," Selia was saying. "Those walls are unstable."

"Isn't that the entire point?" replied Garnik. "I need my people in those chambers before the Halvarians enter; else, how are we to surprise them?"

Thalgrun, idly playing with a thread on his tunic, noted the arrival of his daughter. "Kasri!" his voice boomed out, cutting off the argument. "I was wondering when you might deign to put in an appearance."

Kasri made her way towards the throne and bowed, an action Herdwin and Albreda repeated.

"My vard," she said. "As promised, I've returned to help liberate Ironcliff."

He rose and stepped down from his throne to embrace her before holding her at arm's length, taking a good look at her. "Unharmed, I see." His eyes flicked to Herdwin. "And who is this magnificent Dwarf?"

"We've met before," replied Herdwin.

Thalgrun winked. "Of course. I could hardly forget you. You must excuse an old Dwarf's teasing. It's meant only as a sign of affection." He leaned in closer, lowering his voice. "Don't mind the guild masters; their arguing is nothing new."

"What is our situation?" asked Kasri.

"No worse than expected. The High Ranger came up with a plan to lure in the enemy, but it'll take some time to put everything in place."

"And that plan is?"

"We're weakening some of the upper chambers, those closest to the mountainside, to let their siege engines break through, and then we'll wait for them to send in their warriors."

"Where doubtless you'll have all manner of traps prepared."

"Precisely."

"And where is the High Ranger now?" asked Albreda.

"Overseeing the galleries," replied Thalgrun. "Meaning the tunnels I mentioned."

"Might I offer my own contribution to the cause?"

"By all means. We'd be fools not to listen to the Lady of the Whitewood. What is it you're suggesting?"

"That I use my magic to lure a deep one into those very same galleries."

The vard visibly paled. "Are you certain that's wise? Once unleashed, those creatures are virtually unstoppable."

"Do you doubt my magic?"

"No, of course not, but if anything happens to you, we'd be trapped in a forge with no quenching in sight."

"I assure you, I have no intention of dying in the near future."

"The Hearth Guard will watch the deep one," offered Kasri. "If something should happen to Albreda, we'll take care of it."

"I can agree to that, but Albreda will have to guide it through the halls of Ironcliff."

"We shall prepare a route for her. Of course, we can't do anything until she actually finds one."

"I can help," offered Selia. "We've identified a nest of them down in the lower depths."

"A nest?" said Herdwin.

"Well, a collection. We haven't an actual term, so I thought I'd use one the Druid might be familiar with."

"The Druid?" replied Albreda. "I do have a name, you know."

"I am the Guild Master of the Mining Guild. I can use whatever term I wish!"

"Now, now," said Thalgrun. "Let's not say anything that might cause an argument. We're all on the same side here."

Herdwin turned on Selia. "Albreda is the most powerful mage in all of Merceria!"

"And I lead the most influential guild," replied Selia. "You should watch your tongue, especially considering your current guildless standing."

"You are talking to the future bondmate of your next vard," said Kasri, raising her voice. "I suggest you hold your tongue!"

"While all this is quite fascinating," interjected Albreda, "I think it's time we looked at this nest, don't you? Perhaps the guild master might see fit to have someone show us to it?"

Selia made an exaggerated bow, then turned, snapping her fingers at one of her underlings.

The fellow rushed forward, bowing deeply. "If you'll come with me, I'll show you the way."

They left the room, following their guide.

"What was that all about?" said Herdwin.

"Whatever do you mean?" replied Kasri.

"All that bickering?"

"That's just the guilds trying to show dominance. It's not unusual for the guild masters to exert their influence over guests, particularly when they'll be staying for a while."

"So she's trying to put me in my place?"

"That's about the size of it, yes."

"A dangerous game when dealing with Albreda."

The Druid chuckled. "I'm more than familiar with Dwarven customs, and Mistress Selia's response was much milder than expected."

"That's Master Selia," replied Kasri. "As in the master of the guild."

"I stand corrected."

"How far to this nest?" asked Herdwin.

"Quite some distance," replied their guide. "It's down in the deepest depths of the mountain."

"How far down?" asked Kasri.

"Just below the twenty-seventh deep."

She halted, causing the entire party to do likewise, save for their guide, who continued for a few paces before realizing he was no longer being followed.

"Something wrong?" asked Herdwin.

"Breathing below the twenty-fifth deep is difficult, if not impossible."

Their guide grinned. "Don't worry. We have a solution."

"That being?"

"Enchanted helmets that let us breathe. A variation of an air bubble."

"That's an Air Magic spell," said Albreda. "Wherever did you find someone to cast it?"

"I couldn't say. We've had them for some time."

"How long a time?" asked Kasri.

The fellow shrugged. "A few centuries, at least."

"And you didn't see fit to inform the vard of this?"

"Why would we? It's guild business, and it's not as if he ever goes down to those levels."

"I suppose that makes sense. Lead on, my good Dwarf."

It took a considerable amount of time to reach the lower depths of Ironcliff, giving everyone a new appreciation for just how big the Dwarven stronghold was. At the twentieth level, they were led to a long room with benches on either side and a door at the far end, opposite the entrance.

"If you'll wait here, I'll see to your helmets."

"Before you go," said Herdwin, "could you introduce yourself?"

The fellow bowed deeply, his beard touching the floor. "My apologies. My name is Rurik Deepdelver, senior mining supervisor."

"Is that high up in the guild?" asked Albreda.

"It is right below the deputy guild master."

"Then we are honoured by your presence."

"Out of curiosity," said Herdwin, "how long have you held that position?"

"I've only been the senior mining supervisor for thirty-two years, so I'm considered relatively new to it. Now, you'll pardon me while I retrieve the helmets." He disappeared through the far door.

Herdwin shook his head. "It's Stonecastle all over again. The guilds have a stranglehold there."

"As they do here," replied Kasri. "We'll make changes once I'm vard."

"We?" said Herdwin. "I'm a nobody here."

"That's not true. You won't have an official title, but you'll wield immense influence. Just you wait and see."

Rurik reappeared, carrying, by the chinstraps, what looked to be four full helms. "I know these might seem a little odd, and you'll find your vision somewhat restricted once you don them, but I assure you, they work." He passed them out, holding the last in reserve for himself.

"How do we activate them?" asked Kasri.

"You don't. They just work."

She donned the helm, its strap falling around her neck. "Is this strap entirely necessary?"

"Oh, yes," replied Rurik. "Without it, if you fell and lost the helmet, you'd pass out almost immediately."

"This is remarkable," said Herdwin. "Though I must ask what that horrible smell is?"

"The results of centuries worth of miner's sweat."

"I'm sorry I asked."

Rurik waited until everyone donned their helmet. "Follow me, and I'll take you to the lift."

"Ah, now that's something I'm familiar with. We have one guarding the western approaches to Stonecastle."

They followed their host, turning to descend a long flight of steps leading to a square room carved out of stone, holding a metal cage with benches on either side.

"Best to take a seat," said Rurik. "The ride can be a little bumpy, and we don't want anyone falling over."

Everyone sat, including their guide, and then he rang a bell that hung inside the door.

"One bell signifies we want to descend," he explained. "Two means we wish to return to this level."

"And if we run into trouble?" asked Kasri.

"Then we ring the bell until help comes, but that hasn't happened in over five hundred years."

"The lift is that old?"

"This particular one is only about two hundred, but its predecessor was around for close to three hundred."

"Why was it replaced?"

"It was wooden and worked fine for centuries, but the deeps were getting… well, deeper, and the old lift was never made to go down that far. This new one is metal and treated with a preserve spell to prevent rusting."

"Remarkable," said Herdwin. "I should very much like to see how it works."

"And I'd be glad to show you," replied Rurik, "but I fear now is not the time. Perhaps when the war is over?"

"You have a deal, my friend."

They felt a bump before they swung slightly.

"They've removed the stops," said Rurik. "Now we'll start to move."

Sure enough, the lift began its descent. It was a strange sensation, although admittedly, they'd all experienced something similar on the way to Stonecastle.

"How far down does this thing go?" asked Albreda.

"Down to the twenty-fifth deep."

"Is that far?"

"The levels are numbered based on the entrance hall. Above, you have what's commonly referred to as the heights, while below, you have levels, of which we have twenty, then there's the deeps, beginning with the first deep."

"Are you suggesting we are going forty-five levels below the entrance?"

"More or less. Not all the floors are level, and some have higher ceilings, but yes, I believe that's what the engineers would say. Now, this level we're headed to leads out onto a ledge overlooking an immense cavern. There's a railing to stop you from falling, but I'm afraid it's Dwarf-sized, not Human, so you'll have to be extra careful, Albreda."

"I shall bear that in mind," she replied.

"It's not that I don't trust your magic," said Herdwin, "but how in the name of Gundar are you going to convince one of those deep ones to enter this lift?"

"Are you familiar with the habits of bears?"

"I've heard of them, but I'm not overly familiar with their habits. Why?"

"They go into a deep sleep in the wintertime, and I can recreate that state using a spell called hibernate."

"Why would you want to do that?"

"There are several reasons. For example, if the pack were starving, I could place them in a state of hibernation to conserve food. The spell also enables them to heal wounds at a faster rate, although they are effectively unconscious the entire time. My intention is to cast the spell on one of the deep ones, and then the miners can drag it up to the higher levels."

"That sounds dangerous."

"Not as dangerous as mining," offered Rurik. "Though, it'll likely take at least ten of my Dwarves to haul one up here."

The lift came to a halt, swinging slightly.

"Mind your step," he said, then exited.

The immense chamber before them stretched off into darkness, with three magically glowing spheres attached to poles illuminating the imme-diate area. A long, wooden railing ran beside where the lift stood, while a drop into nothingness lay on the other side.

"Where are the deep ones?" asked Kasri.

"Listen, and you'll hear them," replied Rurik.

Off in the distance came a shuffling noise, as if someone was dragging their boots as they walked.

"That's them, though there's no telling how many are down there."

"Let's find out, shall we?" said Albreda, weaving her hands before her, calling upon her arcane powers. The air buzzed, and then her eyes, barely visible through the helmet's eye slit, glowed with an inner light. When she finished casting, she stepped to the railing and gazed down.

"What was that?" asked Kasri.

"I gave myself night vision," replied Albreda. "It doesn't work in total darkness, but thanks to these glowing orbs, I can see the bottom."

"And do you see any deep ones?"

"Several. They are clustered around a large crystal."

"We've found several of those in the lower depths," said Rurik. "We believe they might be some sort of amethyst."

"It's not amethyst," she snapped. "It's how they reproduce."

"How in the name of Gundar would you know that?"

"I had a vision back in Wincaster, which is what gave me this idea in the first place."

"Your vision being?"

"One of those deep ones emerging from just such a crystal. I cannot speak to how it came to be, merely that those crystals are how they reproduce."

"Then we must take care not to damage any."

"A wise precaution," said Herdwin. He looked all around the lit area. "This is quite the chamber, but if Albreda's going to put one of those things to sleep, we'll need to get up close and personal with it. That being the case, how do we get down there?"

ELEVEN

Reinwick

SPRING 968 MC

Beverly entered the city of Korvoran on foot, leading Lightning rather than riding him so she was the same height as the Ashwalkers. Aubrey and Cyric followed her example, but Owen remained in the saddle, claiming it gave him a better view.

The Orcs, including Krazuhk, had remained quiet for the majority of the trip, keeping to themselves, but once they were in the city, they suddenly became more talkative.

"*Korvoran is the capital,*" said Marag, "*containing the residence of His Grace, Lord Fernando, the Duke of Reinwick.*"

"*And your people live here?*" asked Krazuhk. "*How did that come to be?*"

"*It is a recent development. Just over a year ago, a Human named Athgar visited our people, convincing us to help the duke fight off his enemies. In recognition of our help, the duke granted us the Thornwood to call our own.*"

"*The Thornwood?*"

"*Yes. A forest on the border between Reinwick and Andover.*"

"*Did you say Athgar?*" asked Aubrey, using the Orcish tongue.

"*I did. Do you know him?*"

"*Not precisely, but I know of him. I have communicated with Shaluhk, Shaman of the Red Hand, and his name came up on quite a few occasions.*"

"*He has done much for our kind. In the east, Orcs and Humans live side by side, and while the same is not true here, our lives have improved significantly.*"

"*So much so that you now serve the duke's interests?*"

"*War is of concern to all of us, and there is no love lost between our people and the Halvarians. We do not know the particulars, but any tribes in the areas that succumb to the empire fall silent.*"

They navigated through the narrow streets of the city, and then, as they passed a warehouse, the bay most unexpectedly came into view, with hundreds of masts rising into the air like some kind of forest, reminding Beverly of her time in Riversend.

Cyric pointed. "Those over there are the Temple Ships. You can tell by their flag; it's white with three red waves, the reverse colours of their surcoats."

"Why reversed?" asked Beverly.

"If I understand correctly, it's to avoid being mistaken for pirates. Apparently, they favour the colour red; historically, it was a sign of rebellion amongst mercenaries."

She grinned. "That's exactly why the new Merceria flag has red in it."

"Interesting," said Cyric. "I should very much like to see those ships up close."

"Perhaps later. Delivering our letter to His Grace is our first priority."

"Yes, of course. I must apologize, but the fabled Temple Fleet is something I never dreamed I'd see in person. They have quite a storied history. Even though they were only formed thirteen years ago, they've defeated the empire in two sea battles, not to mention bringing piracy in the north to a virtual standstill. They say sea trade has grown significantly as a result. Does Merceria operate a fleet?"

"No, but until recently, we had no access to the sea."

"I thought you had a southern coast?"

"We do," replied Beverly, "but it's a gigantic swamp, which is not the sort of coastline that promotes trade."

"Yet you just said you recently acquired access to the sea."

"The Trolls founded a town on the coast and cleared out the mouth of the river, allowing trade."

"Trolls?" said Cyric. "I've heard of them; everyone has, but only in children's stories."

"They're large, at least a head or two taller than a Human, with hard skin, like stone, but they've proven to be loyal allies."

"However did you find them?"

"We fought them on the battlefield. They were led astray by invaders after being pushed out of their traditional homeland. They've always preferred living in the swamp, so our southern coast was ideal for them."

Cyric nodded. "Fascinating. I should very much like to see them one day."

Beverly chuckled. "You're starting to gather a list of things you'd like to see: first, the Temple Fleet and now the Trolls. As to the latter, we could arrange something once this war is over, although I daresay it'd be a long trip to get there."

"I'm a patient man."

"This way," said Marag, turning up a side street. "The duke's estate is up the road."

"Your command of the common tongue is surprisingly good," noted Aubrey. "Is that a recent development?"

"It is. Once the Ashwalkers were given permission to claim the Thornwood, we thought it best to send someone to the duke's court to represent our interests."

"And so you were chosen?"

"I volunteered, along with two others, allowing us to send messages back and forth without abandoning Korvoran completely."

"I would have thought you'd use shamans."

Marag looked at her in surprise. "You know of spirit talk?"

"I do," replied Aubrey. "Kraloch of the Black Arrows taught me the spell."

"He must hold you in high regard. That is a spell we would not willingly share with outsiders."

"I took an oath to keep it secret, and I stand by that decision."

"You are a strange people," said Marag. "So unlike the Humans of the Petty Kingdoms. Where are your people from?"

"Merceria lies west of the Halvarian Empire. We're descended from mercenaries."

"You have those of Therengian descent amongst your number." She nodded at Aldwin. "Do they suffer under your rule as they did here?"

"No," replied Aubrey. "Until we came here, we didn't even realize they existed. In our home, we don't judge others by the colour of their eyes."

"And is the same true of Orcs?"

"I wish I could say it was, but some still fear what they don't understand."

Marag nodded. "That is to be expected. Even amongst the Ashwalkers, not all trust you Humans."

"Yet your tribe helped the High Thane of Therengia."

The Orc grinned. "We did, but we do not consider that realm part of the Petty Kingdoms. I find it interesting those lands farthest east and west of us value our presence while here we are still viewed with suspicion."

"It takes time for meaningful change, but thankfully, the Continent seems to be heading in the right direction."

· · ·

A circular road in front of the duke's estate allowed carriages to enter and exit at will. The shape of the building reminded Beverly of the Royal Palace in Wincaster, although much smaller.

A pair of guards stood out front, and as their party neared, a trio of grooms came forth to take their horses. The two guards only acknowledged their existence with a slight nod towards Marag.

Beverly held out Lightning's reins to a stable hand who hesitated at the sheer size of the warhorse. "Don't worry," she said. "He won't bite."

"Are you certain?"

"I was talking to my horse."

"My apologies, madam."

"That's General," corrected Aubrey.

The groom bowed deeply, then led Lightning away, trying to stay as far from the horse as the reins permitted.

A woman appeared in the doorway, offering a bow. "His Grace sent me to offer you greetings in his name."

"And you are?" said Beverly.

"Enid, one of the duke's servants. I've been asked to bring you to him."

"How did he know we were coming?"

"A runner was sent from the gates."

"But you don't even know who we are?"

"True, but you are in the company of Ashwalker Marag, whose return His Grace has been eagerly awaiting."

"After you," said Beverly, indicating the Orc should go first.

They filed into the building, Enid leading them through a maze of hallways and corridors to a large room reminiscent of the great hall in Wincaster. Unlike that place, however, this was decorated with all manner of paintings and sculptures and packed with people ranging from guards to senior officers and their wives. It appeared to be a celebration, although, to Beverly, the conversation was muted. Had they received word that Halvaria was on the warpath?

Marag led them directly towards a particular trio of people. The tallest, a well-attired man in his mid-forties, stood beside an older fellow with a meticulously manicured long beard. The last of them, a woman wearing the trappings of a Temple Knight of Saint Agnes, had gold waves on her tabard instead of the standard white.

The tall fellow turned at their approach. "Ah, Marag. You honour us with your presence. Was your trip successful?"

"It was, Your Grace," replied the Orc. "However, I fear the news I bring is not what you were hoping for."

His gaze wandered to the rest of the group. "And who have you brought to me?"

"This is General Beverly Fitzwilliam, Baroness of Bodden, and Lord Aldwin Fitzwilliam. With them are Lady Aubrey Brandon, Brother Cyric, Sir Owen, a knight of Erlingen, and Krazuhk, a master of air." She turned to the group. "May I present, His Grace, Lord Fernando Brondecker, Duke of Reinwick."

Beverly bowed. "We are honoured to meet you, Your Grace."

"What brings you to Reinwick, General?"

"I bear a message from His Majesty, King Dagmar of Andover." She pulled the scroll case from her belt, holding it out.

The duke took it but refrained from opening it, instead questioning the Ashwalker. "You mentioned you had news?"

"Temple Knights of Saint Cunar attempted to prevent these people from passing. I fear they may have intercepted our messengers to Andover."

He turned to face the bearded fellow. "What do you make of that, Marius?"

"Considering all that has befallen the Church recently, I can't say I'm surprised."

"Marius used to be the Admiral of the Holy Fleet." The duke paused. "Where are my manners? I haven't introduced Admiral Danica, who commands the Temple Fleet."

To Beverly, the woman appeared far younger than she'd expected, and she was about to say as much when Brother Cyric stepped forward, offering his hand.

"Pleased to meet you."

"Pardon me," said the admiral, "but did she say your name was Cyric?"

"Indeed."

"I believe we have a mutual acquaintance. Temple Captain Giselle?"

The Mathewite smiled. "Yes. I've known her for years. Might I ask how you made her acquaintance?"

"It was my great honour to serve under her in Ilea."

"With Temple Commander Charlaine, no doubt."

"Indeed," replied Danica, "though it's Temple General now."

"Hold on a moment," said Aldwin. "Wasn't she the one who disappeared along with five hundred Temple Knights?"

"Yes."

"Where is she?"

"She is safe," replied Danica, "and will surface when the time is right. That's all I'll say on the matter at present."

"The admiral is full of mystery," added the duke, "but we must respect her accomplishments." He looked down at the scroll case as if suddenly realizing its import. "If you will excuse me, I need to read this." He backed away from the group.

"Cunars," said Danica, shaking her head. "No offence, Marius, but they've proven nothing but trouble these last few years."

"Which is precisely why I left them."

"And your advice to the Temple Fleet has been exemplary. We're lucky to have you."

"I assume you know each other?" said Beverly.

"We met many years ago," replied Danica, "at the Battle of Alantra, and we share a passion for ships. I was only a Temple Knight at that time, not that there's anything wrong with that. I'm curious about you, though. It's not often we see a general in our travels, especially a woman. In whose army do you serve?"

"Merceria. Are you familiar with it?"

"I can't say I am. Where does it lie?"

"Far to the west, beyond Halvaria."

"You're a long way from home."

"We were stranded here by magic," said Beverly. "My cousin could tell you more as she's the expert in such things."

"Lady Aubrey is a Life Mage," explained Cyric. "A skill she put to great use in Erlingen."

"Were you trained by Elves?" asked Danica.

"No," replied Aubrey. "Why? Are your Elves known to use such magic?"

"An old friend of mine was taught Life Magic by an Elf named Gwalinor."

"Does she serve in the Temple Fleet?"

"No. She's with the Five Hundred. Perhaps you'll meet her someday."

"I would like that."

A woman wandered over to them. "Excuse me for interrupting," she said, "but I couldn't help but overhear you talking about magic. It's an area in which I possess some expertise."

"And you are?" asked Aubrey.

"Galina Marwen."

"Galina was instrumental in toppling the Stormwinds," explained Danica, "and has only just returned to us."

"Toppling?" said Cyric. "I'm afraid you'll have to explain that one to me."

"I was originally Galina Stormwind, a member of that... Well, I hesitate to use the term family. In any case, I have the honour of being good friends with Natalia Stormwind, the Warmaster of Therengia."

"We're familiar with her name," said Aubrey. "I've communicated several times with Shaluhk, Shaman of the Red Hand, although admittedly, not since we were stranded here amongst the Petty Kingdoms."

"Natalia led the assault that destroyed the Volstrum and broke the family's power. Even more remarkable was the manner in which she did it."

"Don't hold us in suspense," said Beverly.

"We moved a large army into Ruzhina unopposed, by means of her magic."

"We've used magic to transport people back in Merceria, but our mages can only take a few at a time. How could she possibly move an entire army?"

"It's a spell called frozen arch, which can be used to connect two locations, providing one is a power node."

"Power node," said Aubrey. "That's where the ley lines cross."

"I'm surprised you're familiar with them," replied Galina. "Most mages assume they only run north-south."

"An east-west one was what brought us here."

The duke returned, his face a shade paler than when he'd left. Despite this, he managed to smile, although it appeared forced. "Lady Galina, how nice of you to drop by. I trust all is well?"

"As well as can be expected under the present circumstances. There is, after all, a war threatening to engulf the entire Continent."

His Grace ignored the remark, instead turning to Beverly. "I read His Majesty's letter, and you may rest assured the Army of Reinwick will march to his aid."

"That bodes well for Andover," she replied, "but what of Erlingen?"

"I cannot answer that until I speak with Dagmar."

"Those legions are a threat to everyone," said Beverly. "Can you not see that?"

"Our agreement is for our mutual protection. It says nothing of carrying on a war outside of our borders."

"But Reinwick has an alliance with them, doesn't it?"

"It does, along with an agreement with Therengia, but that's unlikely to bear fruit when they're more than a thousand miles away."

"I wouldn't be so quick to dismiss them," offered Galina. "In addition to being a powerful mage, their warmaster is an exceptional strategist. Her presence alone would be worth more than a thousand men. You should know, Your Grace, she was with you at the Battle of Ebenhof."

"I agree completely with your assessment, but there is still the matter of distance. Even if we sent a ship this very day, it would be weeks before it reached her."

"That's not entirely true, Your Grace. I can get word to her much sooner."

"Still, Therengia would have to mobilize their entire army, not to mention get it here. Even the Temple Fleet doesn't have the numbers to transport so many warriors. I fear the war would be over well before they could set foot in Korvoran."

"The first step," said Galina, "is for me to contact the warmaster. Once that's done, we can discuss how best to employ them. It might well prove more useful to transport them directly to the battlefield."

"What in the name of the Saints are you talking about? You're not suggesting they march clear through the Petty Kingdoms?"

"You must learn to think in new ways, Your Grace. You witnessed powerful magic at Ebenhof. Now you must allow yourself to fully embrace it. Not as a caster, but as the leader of Reinwick's army."

"The Army of Merceria uses magic all the time," added Beverly. "So much so that mages have become an integral part of our forces, which allowed us to defeat enemies considered unbeatable only a few decades ago."

The duke shook his head. "And you truly believe the warmaster can transport an entire army here in a timely manner?"

"I'm told they did precisely that in Ruzhina, Your Grace, to great success."

"What do you think of this claim?" the duke asked Admiral Danica.

"Word is the Stormwinds are scattered, Your Grace, forced out of Ruzhina by a great calamity. Galina's explanation seems to fit the facts as we know them."

"Yes, but do you trust her?"

"I have no reason not to."

Fernando nodded. "Then we should contact Natalia Stormwind and see what her thoughts are on the matter."

"I shall do so at once, Your Grace." Galina bowed, leaving in a hurry.

"What do we truly know about the Therengians?" asked Sir Owen. "Can they be trusted?"

"I'd stake my life on it," said Aubrey.

TWELVE

Scheming

SPRING 968 MC

Castimar Stormwind, Marshal of the South, paused on a hill overlooking his forces. Three full legions stood ready to march, men hand-picked for their loyalty and devotion, who would give their lives, if necessary, in pursuit of his aims.

He turned his head, meeting the gaze of Morven Rassi, his second-in-command. Ordinarily, the commander-general of each legion would report directly to the marshal, but with so much at stake, and so many pieces in motion, he'd taken the unusual step of appointing his own senior officer to oversee the others. Morven was a commander-general until a run-in with the High Strategos led to his removal from the position. Castimar then snapped him up, appointing him to the ancient rank of marshal-general, determined to put his talents to good use.

It had paid off magnificently. Now, more than seven thousand men were prepared to undertake this campaign of conquest. Varena would fall, and with it, the ancient line of emperors dating back to the foundation of Halvaria.

The marshal urged his horse into a trot, heading towards his waiting army, then noted his other advisors and altered course to intercept them.

Cadmus Aldmeyer held the honour of being the oldest of the group. His high, nasally voice could be annoying at times, yet there was no denying his dedication to the cause. Castimar had first met the Air Mage more than twenty years ago, during the pacification of Calabria. Having recently been conquered, the people there rose up against the empire. It didn't go well for them, but Castimar had the good fortune of being introduced to one of the greatest Air Mages in all of Halvaria. Cadmus had only two objectives in life: the accumulation of influence and wealth, both of which Castimar showered upon the fellow.

His other advisor, Egreth Blackthorne, was a little more complex. Her voice, harsh with age, was grating and low, but thankfully, she didn't speak much. She had a wealth of knowledge, particularly regarding the magic of the earth, but her reason for joining his cause was more altruistic. Rather than seeking fame or fortune, she wanted Halvaria opened up to those she felt more deserving of ruling, though what those particular qualities were was open for debate.

"Your Grace," said Cadmus, "is it not the perfect day to begin the campaign? The clouds have parted, revealing a glorious sun to inspire the men on their march."

"Indeed," replied Castimar. "Have you given much thought to my suggestion?"

"I have. Fear not. I shall summon a bird of prey and keep an eye on the road ahead. If anyone reveals any signs of resistance, we'll know of it soon enough."

"It's not signs of resistance I'm worried about; it's riders taking word of our approach to the capital. We must have total and complete surprise for this enterprise to work."

"It shall be as you wish, Your Grace. I believe the marshal-general already dispatched scouts to ensure no one learns of our approach."

"Excellent news, though I daresay I expected nothing less. Morven has always had a good head on his shoulders."

"Yet the current regime removed him from his command," offered Egreth. "A gross error in judgement, in my opinion."

"Mine as well," added Castimar, "and you may rest assured, Exalor will pay for the slight with his life."

"That might prove difficult, Your Grace. After all, he commands the Western legions. Once word of your success reaches him, he may hide behind his own army."

"If he chooses to do that, it is of little consequence to me."

"You would think differently if he marched on the capital."

"I would welcome it," replied Castimar, "for it gives me the opportunity to defeat him on the field of battle."

"He is a dangerous man and a seasoned leader."

"As am I. His appointment to High Strategos was nothing more than an act of political expediency. Oh, he's a battle mage, I'll give him that, but he's no more qualified for the position than dozens of others. And as for his army…" Castimar shrugged. "Reports indicate they've been whittled down, thanks to the efforts of our enemies."

"I'm not complaining," said Cadmus, "but how do you intend to handle those the empire is currently at war with?"

"I've given that a great deal of thought. The Dwarves lack the numbers to invade our lands, so we're safe in leaving them be, at least while I consolidate my power. Merceria has proven themselves to be wily adversaries, but they haven't the resources for a prolonged war. I should think an offer of a truce would be met with a favourable response."

"And the Petty Kingdoms?"

"That is a little more complicated, as it relies entirely on Edora Sartellian. If she defeats the major powers of the Petty Kingdoms, then we welcome her as a Hero of the Empire."

"Assuming she's willing to bend the knee," added Egreth.

"Naturally," replied Castimar.

"And if she faces defeat?" said Cadmus.

"I think that the less likely outcome, but stranger things have happened. We must also consider what nature that defeat might take. If she returns to our territory with even a portion of her army intact, there is still hope to negotiate a truce."

"The empire doesn't negotiate."

"It certainly hasn't in the past, but once I'm on the Throne, I can do as I please." He noted the look of disgust on Egreth's face. "You don't agree?"

"If the Petty Kingdoms defeat Edora's legions, they won't settle on a truce. They'll march across the border and invade our lands."

"They haven't the numbers to occupy the entire empire."

"True, but each province they conquer is another blow to our sovereignty that incites other provinces to rebel."

"I think you overestimate their chances," said Castimar, "but if that should come to pass, we can cede a couple of the northern provinces and let them have their win."

"What about the great dream?"

"The great dream was never intended to come to fruition. It was only an ideal for people to strive for, something to give focus and divert their attention from other matters."

"That being the case," said Egreth, "what would replace it?"

"A desire for eventual revenge. It won't take long for those provinces to realize how good they had it under our rule. In a few years, they'll petition to rejoin the empire."

"We could hope."

"Hope has nothing to do with it," said Castimar. "The triad of power that has ruled the empire for centuries has caused us to stagnate. I intend to sweep away the cobwebs, returning us to the supreme power we were always intended to be."

"Good," said Cadmus. "It's about time. It feels like we've been flailing around in the dark ever since Arnsfeld."

"It wasn't only Arnsfeld," said Egreth. "It started with the loss of our fleet at Alantra, which left our enemies in control of the Shimmering Sea."

"It matters not," replied Castimar. "We do very little sea trade, and the Church is no longer a threat to us since their falling out with the Temple Knights, so we're unlikely to see another seaborne invasion."

"Still, strength is power, especially now, when you're considering negotiating a peace."

"You make an excellent point. I shall keep that in mind, going forward."

Egreth smiled, a rare occasion for the Earth Mage, but it revealed just how invested she was in the Marshal of the South's plan.

"You must excuse me," said Castimar. "I must ride over to our glorious marshal-general and give him the go-ahead to begin the march." Castimar rode directly for the head of his army.

Morven Rassi spotted his approach and raised his sword in salute. "Your Grace," Rassi called out. "The men are set to march on your command."

"Glad to hear it." The Marshal of the South slowed, coming to a halt beside the leader of his army. "A fine showing. They appear ready to take on all of Eiddenwerthe."

"They would willingly give their lives for you, Your Grace, should that become necessary."

"I am humbled, but let us hope that shan't be required." Castimar paused, looking over his men. "You may begin the advance."

The marshal-general turned and barked out a command. The First Legion moved forward as one, keeping their formation. Morven led them for the first few paces before he turned aside, letting their own commander-general take the lead.

"They look eager," said Castimar.

"Thank you, Your Grace. They're excited to finally be doing their part."

"It's a long march to Varena."

"That won't dampen their spirits: quite the opposite, in fact. I'd wager that the closer we get to the capital, the more enthusiastic they'll be to do their duty to their new emperor."

Castimar nodded. "It's been a long time coming, my friend."

"Ten years," replied Morven. "Ten years of swamps, jungles, and savage greenskins, but it'll all be worth it once you're on the Gilded Throne."

"Yes, and then we can eliminate the requirement for all marshals to be battle mages. You've proven yourself over the years, Morven, and you shall be my new High Strategos."

"You honour me, Your Grace... or should I say, Your Eminence?"

Castimar chuckled. "In all likelihood, I'll make do with Majesty, but let's stick with Your Grace for the time being, shall we?"

"Yes, Your Grace."

Bryn Valani swirled the wine in her chalice, her mind occupied by other matters. Running a large criminal organization was always time-consuming, but today had been particularly difficult. A war had erupted between the Shozarins and Sartellians, and although it was of her making, it had taken all she had to place the blame on others.

A knock at her door interrupted her thoughts. "Who is it?"

"Vola," came the reply.

"Come in." Bryn waited as the fair-haired bureaucrat entered. "You have news?"

"I do. I received word that the Marshal of the South has commenced his march towards Varena."

Bryn smiled. "It's about time. I was beginning to think it would never happen."

"Are your people in place?"

"They have been for weeks." Bryn paused, mulling over the news. "Where are my manners? Have a seat. We'll have a drink to celebrate." She rose and grabbed a bottle from behind her, topping up her own chalice and filling another for her visitor.

"Thank you," said Vola, then she sat, taking time to smooth out the front of her dress. She was an odd sight here, a woman clad in austere clothing in amongst a den of thieves and ne'er-do-wells, but Bryn liked her. Perhaps it was respect for her devious mind or the way she charmed information out of the most stalwart of individuals. Under other circumstances, they might've been enemies, but their introduction, arranged at the behest of the Marshal of the South, resulted in a bond of trust seldom seen in Bryn's line of work.

"You look busy," said Vola. "I hope I'm not interrupting anything important?"

"This?" replied Bryn, waving her hand over the papers littering her desk. "This is nothing noteworthy. I'm far more interested in your news. When did you hear from the marshal?"

Vola smiled, which had a calming effect on Bryn's worn nerves. "I came straight here once I heard."

"Any details you'd care to share?"

"He started off early this morning with three full legions, as expected. We are to keep an ear out for any rumours concerning his approach and take measures to ensure he maintains the element of surprise."

"I expected as much."

"My people at the palace are ready to intercept letters should that prove necessary, but they aren't so numerous that they could seize the place."

"Do we know where the Royal Guards stand in terms of their allegiance?"

"Unfortunately, no. The emperor's personal guards will protect him, but the rest of the palace guard will likely be less inclined to interfere."

"I'm surprised to hear that," said Bryn.

"You shouldn't be. To become a palace guard, an individual must be nominated by their superior and then approved by at least two council members from different lines, which will likely result in split loyalties."

"Ah, yes. Family politics. Seems to be everywhere these days." Bryn chuckled.

"You find that entertaining?"

"My pardon. You obviously haven't heard the news. The Shozarins and Sartellians have begun a purge—at least, that's what they believe."

"Let me guess, you're the one who's pulling the strings?"

"It helped that we received news of the Volstrum's destruction. With the Stormwinds seemingly weakened, it was only a matter of time before the other two lines were at each other's throats."

"Clever," said Vola. "Have you done enough to entice them to continue the murder spree on their own?"

"I believe so, though it will take some time to know for certain. With a bit of luck, you may soon find them battling in the halls of the palace itself."

"Finally, something to look forward to. Will this bloodbath reach all the way to the throne?"

"That wasn't my original objective, but so much the better if it does. It would be less work for Castimar when he gets here."

"What's our next step?"

"You keep your ears open for any new developments. Once the army gets closer, we'll be taking a more active role in things."

"Can you be more specific?" asked Vola. "I shouldn't like to find myself facing a bloodthirsty bunch of palace guards."

"Don't worry. I'll keep you safe."

"How?"

"I've hand-picked twenty men to help secure the palace, but they're experts at hit-and-run tactics, not fighting like trained warriors, so I don't want to commit them until the last moment. Have you a safe place to take refuge should it prove necessary?"

"I do."

"Glad to hear it." Bryn was about to change the subject but noted Vola shifted nervously in her seat. "I sense you're not completely comfortable with this arrangement. What can I do to help?"

"Would it be possible to send a few now rather than later? It might raise too many questions if they arrive right as everything begins to fall apart."

"I'll see to it this very day. Should I send them to your office as if they were seeking employment?"

"That would suffice nicely. Thank you."

"Out of curiosity, what do you do at the palace?"

"Officially, I'm responsible for the Imperial Bureaucracy, which means I'm the person who hires all the servants and ensures they're qualified for their positions."

"Does that include all the other parts of government?"

"An astute observation. I hire scribes and such, but the higher offices of state are supposedly appointed by the governing council. Although, in truth, they are usually familial assignments or rewards for service to one line or another."

"Do I detect a note of revulsion?"

"Indeed," said Vola. "Running this empire would be a lot more efficient if we could do away with such blatant favouritism. If I had my way, we'd hire the most qualified person for the position."

"Is that why you're supporting Castimar?"

"Yes. What of yourself?"

"There are no family members in my organization."

Vola chuckled. "No. I meant, why are you supporting him?"

"I have numerous business arrangements that would do much better without the interference of the Purifiers."

"And Castimar agreed to end their influence?"

"He did," said Bryn. "And it's about time; they're nothing more than a corrupt group of bastards. They'll say anyone is lying if given enough coins."

"Wouldn't that work to your advantage?"

"Aye, it would if their prices didn't keep increasing. I don't mind a bribe here or there, but it's beginning to seriously dig into my profits."

"You should go to the top and cut out the middleman."

"That would be Enelle Sartellian. I'm told she's not the sort of person who'd be willing to take coins from someone like me."

"No," said Vola. "I suppose that's true, but that's not really a problem anymore, is it? Considering that she's dead."

Bryn's sly smile revealed her involvement. "A nice coincidence that. Still, those in charge are always ready to nominate a successor."

"Perhaps they'll pick someone a little more willing to look the other way?"

"Anything is possible, but I won't count my blessings just yet, as it'll probably end up being another Sartellian. They seem to have a lock on that particular office."

"It's unfortunate," said Vola, "but practically every government position is like that. The only positions of power that aren't claimed by a single line are the three marshals, although the death of the Marshal of the North did put a Shozarin in place when it should rightfully be a Sartellian. The good news is, it typically takes months to choose a new high officer, so there's every likelihood Castimar will be on the Throne long before that becomes an issue."

THIRTEEN

Holdcross

SUMMER 968 MC

The Orc shaman, Rulahk, bowed his head, severing the connection to Kraloch. "It has begun," he announced in the common tongue.

"They're early," said Lord Calder. "Waverly has yet to arrive. We can't march on Ironcliff with what we presently have!"

"Slow down," replied Heward. "You're reading too much into this." He regarded the Orc. "Can you be more specific?"

"Yes," said Rulahk. "The Dwarves of Ironcliff have weakened one of their walls, hoping to draw in the Halvarians, and the tactic seems to have worked. They report the enemy is preparing to do exactly that."

"What in the name of Saxnor does that mean?" said Calder. "Are they beginning the assault or not?"

"For the Halvarians to get inside the Dwarven fortress, they must first climb up the side of the mountain. They are presently gathering rope and organizing their men to attempt the ascent. Kraloch said their attack will likely commence once they are satisfied that the route up to the breach is passable."

"When was Waverly due?"

"He'll be here soon," replied Heward, "though we have no idea of how many men he'll be bringing."

"Hopefully, he'll bring some horse," said Calder. "We're weak in that area."

"I'd prefer footmen, as they'll bear the brunt of the fighting."

"Nonsense. Cavalry will be the decisive factor, and the enemy has loads of it."

"With all due respect, Lord Calder, the only cavalry used by Norland is light, and we already have an abundance of that. What we need are knights, but those only exist in Merceria, and as far as I know, they're all employed down by Trollden."

"Then we shall have to pray Queen Bronwyn sends us what we need." Calder gave Heward a side-eye. "You were pretty chummy with her when you were at court, weren't you?"

"Chummy?"

"Do I have to spell it out for you, man?" He cleared his throat. "Is there, perhaps, a budding romance between the two of you?"

"Not on my part, I assure you."

"But you're not married, are you?"

"I am not."

"Have you another woman in your life?"

"Not at present, no, but I have been rather busy of late, what with the war and everything."

"But you're the Baron of Redridge."

"Your point being?"

"You need an heir."

"I do," agreed Heward, "and I'll have plenty of time to deal with that once this war is over."

Calder wasn't finished with his interrogation. "You can't look at it that way. For Saxnor's sake, what if something happened to you? People die in war."

"If I am to die, then so be it. My title won't follow me to the Afterlife."

"You Mercerians are always so…"

"Pragmatic?"

"I was going to say stubborn," replied Calder, "but I suppose it amounts to the same thing." The earl changed targets, looking over at the Orc shaman. "What of your people, Rulahk?"

"We have no titles or lands to inherit."

"Do you mean to tell me the vaunted Queen of Merceria hasn't seen fit to grant you a reward for your service?"

"Recognition is all we seek, and we do not own the land."

"What sort of rubbish is this? Everyone owns land. How can you have a kingdom without land?"

"The land surrounding Ravensview is ours to nourish, not control."

"But you must plant crops?"

"Orcs are hunter-gatherers," said Heward. "They don't farm."

Calder knitted his brows. "Are you telling me they feed their entire population by hunting?"

"Yes. Why do you find that so difficult to accept?"

"It isn't natural."

"It is for Orcs," said Rulahk. "To us, the ways of Humans are most confusing."

"How?"

"We hunt to survive, taking measures to ensure we do not deplete the area of game. You Humans hunt for the pleasure of the kill, a most disturbing characteristic by Orc standards."

"Not all do so," offered Heward. "There are some who hunt to feed their families."

Rulahk offered a bow. "And these individuals, we understand. Lord Heward, does your queen organize royal hunts as her father did?"

"No. She has too much respect for Albreda."

"Albreda?" said Calder. "The Witch of the Whitewood? Why does a Mercerian queen care what that woman thinks?"

"She is not a witch," replied the Orc. "She is a powerful Druid, at one with nature. Some say she is the Meghara reborn."

"What in Saxnor's name is a Meghara?"

"A powerful wielder of magic who comes to our people in times of great need," explained Rulahk.

"What utter nonsense."

"Is it?" replied Heward. "You haven't seen her magic at work."

"But she's not an Orc. How can she possibly be this Meghara person?"

"Nowhere in our history," said Rulahk, "does it say she must be an Orc."

"But you don't have a history, do you? I thought your people couldn't read?"

"Our history is an oral one, passed down by the spirits of our Ancestors."

"Spirits?" said Calder. "Are you trying to tell me your people actually speak to the dead? I find that difficult to believe."

"It is true. Shamans like me use magic to communicate with those whose spirits linger."

"What do you mean by 'linger'?"

"When an Orc dies, they go to the Afterlife, much as Humans do, but occasionally, their connection to the land of the living is so strong that their spirit remains, and these spirits are the ones our magic can contact."

"So you talk to ghosts?"

"I believe that would be the explanation easiest for you to comprehend."

Heward chuckled. "Not that this isn't interesting, but I have other matters to attend to, so please excuse me." He was about to leave them but then paused. "Have either of you seen Master Kharzug?"

Rulahk pointed towards the Singing Crow. The inn wasn't much to look at, but as one of the tallest buildings in Holdcross, its flat roof made an excellent place to observe the area. Sure enough, up on the roof were two Orcs staring off to the south.

Heward headed straight to the building and entered, ignoring those inside. He climbed the stairs, emerging onto the roof to see the master of earth, Kharzug, talking with his chieftain, Ghodrug. At the sound of his approach, they both turned.

"*Sorry to interrupt,*" said Heward, using the language of the Orcs.

"*There is no need to apologize,*" replied Ghodrug. "*What can we do for you, Commander?*"

"*I was hoping Kharzug might use his magic to look for any signs of our reinforcements.*"

The master of earth swept his arm towards the south. "*See for yourself.*"

Heward moved up to the edge of the rooftop to get a better view. All he could see in the distance was a blur on the horizon. "*Are you certain that's them?*"

"*Indeed,*" replied the shaman. "*I have had eyes following them for most of the morning.*"

"*A deer?*"

"*No, a fox. They have superior eyesight.*"

"*Any idea as to numbers?*"

Kharzuk chuckled, his voice a low baritone. "*Animals do not count as we do. To him, he's found a mass of Humans to be avoided, nothing more. I can tell you, however, that amongst their numbers are a few horses, for they range out in front.*"

"*And these are Norlanders and not Halvarians?*"

"*For them to be Halvarians, the empire would have had to find some way to slip past us unobserved unless you are suggesting they sent an entire army across those mountains?*"

"*That is highly unlikely,*" replied Heward.

Ghodrug stepped closer until she stood beside him, staring south. "*I sense their arrival means we will soon be on the march again.*"

"*Yes, although I'd like to give them a day of rest before we move eastward.*"

"*Are we to attack those who are besieging Ironcliff?*"

"*That's the plan, yes,*" replied Heward. "*I've been informed Ironcliff has a little surprise arranged for the Halvarians, one which will keep them busy while we make our approach. The idea is to time our attack to coincide with a major push from Ironcliff.*"

"*I did not think the Dwarves had the numbers to do so?*"

"*Apparently, the marshal had new recruits training down in Hawksburg, and they're now on their way to the Dwarven fortress, courtesy of the magic circle there.*"

"Have we any idea of the numbers involved?"

"No," said Heward, *"but if I know the marshal, he'll have ensured they're well-trained."*

Lord Waverly's command marched into Holdcross, four hundred strong. Half were footmen, with one hundred archers and the same number of horsemen, although admittedly, they were light cavalry, as had been suspected.

Heward watched them march past, then spotted Lord Waverly and waved him over. The Earl of Marston's exhaustion had him slouching in the saddle, leaving him looking considerably shorter than his usual height, which was even taller than Heward. His dour expression was likely the result of an extended time in the saddle, but he acknowledged the request and rode over.

"Lord Heward," said the earl. "Her Majesty, Queen Bronwyn, sends her sincerest regards. I'm pleased to announce I bring you four hundred warriors to bolster your defences."

"Thank you, my lord. We greatly appreciate the men, but I'm afraid they won't be here for long. I intend to march to Ironcliff the day after tomorrow."

For the briefest of moments, Waverly's jaw dropped open, but he snapped it shut and quickly regained his composure. "Are you certain, Commander? I was led to believe we came to Holdcross to prevent the Halvarians from entering Norland territory?"

"You were," replied Heward, "but recent events have changed our situation considerably. Rather than defending here, we'll be taking the offensive."

"In only two days?"

"I thought it best to give your warriors tomorrow to recover."

"That is much appreciated."

"How was the march?"

"Difficult. The men weren't used to such exertions, but they've done quite well, all things considered. I daresay they've trimmed up remarkably in the last two weeks. We set a slow pace at first, but then we averaged almost twenty miles a day. I'm led to believe that's a considerable accomplishment?"

"It is," replied Heward. "A typical march would cover only about fifteen, so you've done well."

"I should see to my command."

"I have people standing by to show them where to set up camp. I'd like you to meet the other commanders while they're busy with that."

"Yes, of course. Where are my manners?" Waverly climbed out of the saddle, though perhaps dropped would've been a more apt description. The poor fellow was no longer a young man, and the trip had worn him down. "Lead on," he insisted.

Heward brought him inside the inn, which had become their headquarters. "You know Lord Calder, but I don't believe you've met Lord Lanaka."

Waverly regarded the Earl of Tewsbury. "He's a Kurathian."

"So glad you noticed," replied Lanaka.

"And this," continued Heward, ignoring the exchange, "is Ghodrug, Chieftain of the Black Ravens."

"Greetings," replied the Orc. "I trust my presence will not be too unsettling for you?"

Waverly straightened his back. "Not at all. I welcome the chance to work alongside our allies."

"I wonder," said Calder. "What finally convinced the other earls to send help?"

Waverly cleared his throat. "Let's just say the queen has impressive powers of persuasion."

"They must've been impressive indeed to scrape together four hundred souls. When I left, they could barely manage fifty!"

"Let us not dwell on how we got here," said Heward. "Instead, we should concentrate on how we move forward. Your men, Lord Waverly, brings our total to thirteen hundred, a sizable army by any measure."

"Perhaps," noted Calder, "but that still pales in comparison to a Halvarian legion."

"What is the strength of a legion?" asked Waverly.

"What we know so far," said Heward, "is that they number twenty-four hundred at full strength."

"And how do we know this?"

"Lady Aubrey used her connection with Kraloch to relay the events happening in the Petty Kingdoms. They've had a lot of experience fighting the empire over there, though admittedly, it's usually on the losing side."

"How many warriors does Ironcliff possess?"

"At last count, only six hundred, which includes four companies of Mercerians. Mind you, we just learned the marshal intends to send more now that our recruits are trained."

"How many more?" asked Waverly.

"At this point, I can only hazard a guess, but I believe the bulk of it will be footmen."

"What makes you say that?"

"He's sending them to Ironcliff; it's not as if cavalry would be useful in a Dwarven mine."

"But there would be bowmen, surely?"

"There may well be some archers amongst them, but training them is much more time-consuming."

"Why would you think that?" asked Calder.

"Archery requires a certain level of expertise, particularly when it comes to estimating the effect of wind or distance. In my experience, anyone can be taught to fight with a sword or spear, but it takes an exceptional individual to master archery unless they've grown up with it."

"Will that be enough to liberate Ironcliff?"

"The marshal wouldn't undertake such an attack if he didn't feel we had a good chance of success. He's not the type to throw lives away needlessly."

"But isn't that the lot of the common soldier?" said Waverly.

"It is no small thing to lose men, my lord, and Gerald Matheson is most cautious with the lives of his men. It's what makes him so effective."

"Are you telling me this entire campaign rests on the shoulders of a man who's become too timid to command properly?"

Heward found his temper rising. He closed his eyes and took a deep breath. "I said he was cautious, not timid."

"His men adore him," added Calder. "I hate to say it of a Mercerian, but I envy the love his warriors have for him."

"When have you been around the Mercerians?" asked Waverly.

Calder nodded towards Lanaka. "Did you forget our cavalry?"

"Half of those are Kurathians."

"Those Kurathians are, in fact, Mercerians now," said Lanaka. "But for the uninformed, I also have the honour of commanding the Wincaster Light Horse, trained by Lady Beverly herself."

"Your pardon," said Waverly. "I withdraw my statement. Now, Lord Heward, how is this campaign of ours to proceed?"

"Lord Lanaka will use his light horse to screen our advance, giving us warning once the enemy comes into sight. Now remember, we're marching into the Gap, a wide corridor bounded on two sides by mountains, but that gap can be up to thirty miles wide at various points, so there's still a chance they could flank us. To that end, we shall march in a relatively tight formation, ready to form up for battle on a moment's notice. To minimize the risk, we'll travel parallel to the northern edge of the Gap, keeping our left flank right up against the mountains. If we have to turn and fight, that will prevent anyone from getting behind us."

"And if the enemy cavalry makes their presence known?"

"We'll be marching in two columns. The more southern one will consist of our footmen, while the northern one will be our archers. If the enemy threatens, everyone will turn to the south, allowing the archers to form a line behind our foot."

"That's all well and good," said Waverly, "but how do we eliminate the element of surprise? If their horsemen appear unexpectedly, they could do serious damage before the men have a chance to form into their line of battle."

"You need not worry on that account," said Ghodrug, displaying her mastery of the common tongue. "Our master of earth will have eyes and ears out, watching for any signs of the enemy. We will know of them long before any of our warriors are threatened."

"I wish I had your confidence."

"It is not confidence I rely on; it is magic."

"May I make a recommendation?" asked Lanaka.

"Of course," replied Heward.

"The Orc cavalry is not trained to operate as scouts. Therefore, I suggest they be kept in the middle of our columns as a fast reserve, able to fill in any holes in the line should we be caught unawares. That would, I believe, soothe Lord Waverly's fear."

Waverly puffed up his chest, looking like he was about to explode, then took a deep breath, slowly releasing it, forcibly calming himself. "Do not mistake caution for fear."

"My apologies, my lord," the Kurathian replied with a wink. "My mastery of the common tongue is still less than perfect."

"What about the issue of command?" said Calder. "Are we all to command our own men?"

"For now," said Heward, "but once we liberate Ironcliff, that will change. The marshal's intention is to balance out the brigades prior to marching into Halvaria."

"Balance them, how?"

"He intends to organize the army into two similar-sized brigades, each with foot, horse, and bow, but I can't speak to numbers until we know how many Mercerians the marshal sends to Ironcliff. My gut tells me he would keep the Norland companies in one brigade and the Mercerians in a second, but that might leave one or the other short on cavalry."

"Are you suggesting we send some of our horses to help the Mercerians?"

"Yes, although it might be the opposite, with some of their cavalry coming over to us."

"Fascinating," said Waverly, "but back to the attack on Ironcliff. How will we know when it's the right time to advance?"

"Our attacks will be coordinated through our shamans," replied Ghodrug. "Rulahk on our part, Kraloch on the marshal's."

"The marshal's?" said Calder. "Are you saying the Marshal of Merceria will be there in person?"

Heward grinned. "I can pretty much guarantee it. This is a complex operation requiring close cooperation between two separate commands. I don't imagine he'd be willing to leave that in someone else's hands."

"So he'll command the second brigade himself?"

"No. That will likely fall on the High Ranger's shoulders."

"Wouldn't we be better off if he commanded it himself?"

"I understand your trepidation, but I assure you, the other brigade is in good hands. The marshal has spent years reorganizing the Army of Merceria, populating the senior ranks with those who know their business."

"Let's hope you're right," said Waverly, "or we'll all be marching into a massacre."

FOURTEEN

Grand Strategy

SUMMER 968 MC

Aubrey felt the familiar buzzing in the air before the ghostly figure of Kraloch materialized before her.

"Greetings," said the Orc. "How are things progressing in the Petty Kingdoms?"

"We've arrived in Reinwick," she replied, "but have yet to learn when the army will march."

"Will they help Erlingen in their fight against the empire?"

"That's difficult to tell. At the moment, the duke says he must speak with King Dagmar first. Their alliance calls for aid in mutual defence but says nothing about going on the offensive, particularly into another Petty Kingdom. How are things there?"

"They are proceeding well. The marshal has a plan to liberate Ironcliff, but it requires time to get all the pieces into place."

"And Trollden?"

"They have pushed the invaders into the swamp, but they are tying down a significant number of our warriors. There is also the matter of their fleet, whose presence offshore remains a danger. Despite that, the marshal has devised an overall strategy to defeat the empire, but it requires the cooperation of the armies of the Petty Kingdoms. Do you think you can arrange their assistance?"

"That's difficult to say. I shall certainly do my best to encourage them, but right now, they're more concerned with defeating the legions marching through their territory than helping us with an invasion of Halvaria."

"That is disappointing. How are the others?"

"They're doing well. While we were spending time at the duke's court, we ran into someone named Galina Marwen. She claims to know Natalia Stormwind."

"I know that name," replied Kraloch. "Galina was once a Stormwind herself."

"Yes, she mentioned that. She contacted Natalia on our behalf. She seems to be under the impression the Army of Therengia might be transported to our location using magic, although I'm at a loss to understand how. Our recall spell can only take a few at a time."

"Have you given any more consideration to finding a ship to bring you home?"

"We've discussed it," said Aubrey, "but we've had our hands full dealing with this war. Why do you ask?"

"For the marshal's strategy to succeed, it requires someone he trusts to interpret his commands."

"Don't look at me. I'm a Life Mage, not a commander." She hesitated. "Oh, you mean Beverly."

"I do, but that means remaining in the Petty Kingdoms for a little longer."

"And Gerald's confident this plan of his would work?"

"It relies on many parts coming together, but yes. And thanks to the queen, we have a working map of Halvaria, but I am afraid there is no way to get it to you." Kraloch paused. "Or perhaps there is."

"Would you care to explain that?"

"I have no way of transporting the map to you, but a shaman could spirit travel to our location and examine it."

"Any shaman?"

"No. It would take great power to do so. Shaluhk would be capable of such a thing, but she is far to the east."

"True, but if the Therengians have a method of transporting themselves to the middle of the Petty Kingdoms, might she come with them?"

"I shall discuss the matter with her when I contact her. In the meantime, you must share the general's request with Beverly. It is not an easy thing to ask someone to remain away from home for so long."

Aubrey nodded. "We all want to get home, but if remaining here helps bring about the empire's downfall, then this is where we'll stay."

"It is not your choice alone," replied Kraloch. "All three of you must be in agreement."

"I understand. I shall bring the matter to their attention as soon as we're done here."

"Where are Beverly and Aldwin?"

"They're discussing military matters with the duke. Beverly is of the opinion we should march with all haste, but His Grace, the duke, feels we should wait until they've heard from Natalia Stormwind. Apparently, he's worked with her before and highly values her opinion."

"I assume you do not agree with this delay?"

"I'm no military expert," replied Aubrey, "but every day we delay is another day Erlingen risks the return of the Halvarians."

"Then we must hope that Lady Beverly's attempts to hasten the march bear fruit."

"I must object, Your Grace. If we rush to battle, it will only lead to disaster." Lord Kurlan Stratmeyer, the Baron of Blunden, sat back in his seat. "I understand the pressure this puts on Erlingen," he continued, "but it's worth the delay if we can get the aid of a battle mage."

Duke Fernando nodded his head. "You speak with great wisdom, my friend, but how long do we wait? Every day increases the peril to our lands, and you can be assured that if Erlingen falls, we're next on the chopping block."

"If I may," said Aldwin. "I have a suggestion."

All eyes turned to him in surprise, for he'd been silent for most of the discussion. In fact, the Lords of Reinwick had discounted him as a mere observer, but now he looked down at the map with an intense stare.

"By all means," said the duke. "Speak your mind."

"I'm not familiar with the idea of a battle mage, but it seems to me there is no other option, at least for the start of your campaign. From what I understand, you are legally bound to march to Andover's aid. Any discussion about what you do after that is, at this stage, mere speculation. It thus makes the most sense to get to the Andover capital of Zienholtz as quickly as possible."

The duke turned to Beverly. "What would you have us do, General?"

"This is not my army to command, Your Grace."

"True, but you have experience in these matters. Do you agree with your husband's assessment?"

"I do."

"And do you mean to accompany us?"

"With your permission, yes. My kingdom is under attack, Your Grace. I will do all I can to deal our common enemy a defeat."

The duke nodded. "We are lucky to have your experience. Speaking of which, I'm eager to hear the admiral's thoughts on the matter."

Everyone looked at Admiral Danica.

She cleared her throat. "I'm an expert at naval matters, not the marching of armies."

"Yet you are a Temple Commander. I'm led to believe your order teaches strategy as part of the promotion process?"

"That is correct, though I must confess recent events have made that difficult."

"I'm afraid you'll have to explain that."

She nervously cast her gaze around the room. "As most of you are aware, there has been a… Well, let's call it a disagreement between my order and the Antonine."

"We are well aware of that," offered Lord Kurlan, "but the duke gave the Temple Knights of Saint Agnes safe harbour here in Reinwick."

"And I'm truly thankful for that," replied Danica. "What I'm trying to explain is that my training as a Temple Commander is incomplete due to those events. Were you to ask my opinion about naval matters, I'd answer without delay, but I hesitate to offer advice on something with which I'm unfamiliar. In any case, I think General Fitzwilliam far more qualified to speak on such matters."

"Then perhaps Brother Cyric might offer his expertise?"

"I am only a Temple Knight, my lord, but it seems to me the admiral has made a fine argument. Might I enquire why you find it so difficult to accept Lady Beverly's advice?"

"She is an outsider," replied Lord Kurlan. "How do we even know we can trust her?"

"King Dagmar thought well enough of her to trust her with his message, not to mention the Duke of Erlingen giving her command over his entire army. If that's not enough for you, then I shall add my own observations. I was present at the Battle of the Pines, my lord, a battle that brought our first victory since this continental war began."

"Yet Erlingen was forced to retreat across the border!"

"That was done to preserve their army."

"I've heard enough," said Duke Fernando. "We shall begin the march to Zienholtz first thing in the morning. I suggest everyone get some sleep. It's going to be a busy day tomorrow."

They all stood and started to file out, and as Beverly was about to exit the room, Admiral Danica called out, "General? I wonder if I might have a word?"

"Certainly."

"Brother Cyric tells me there's a Halvarian fleet off your coast."

"Yes. They landed one of their legions. Our marshal blunted their invasion, but their very presence pins part of our army in place."

"And have you the ships to defeat them?"

"No. Nor, from what I've been told, does our ally, Weldwyn. Why?"

"The Temple Fleet could be of some assistance."

"You'd have to sail through uncharted waters just to get there."

"It wouldn't be the first time. My ships have mapped the entire northern coast of Halvaria these last few years. I doubt I'd have any trouble finding volunteers for a longer voyage."

"The fleet off our coast was immense," replied Beverly.

"Yet I suspect very few are warships."

"Why would you say that?"

"I'm very familiar with the empire's warships. They're designed to stick close to shore, not spend months at sea. There's also the matter of your own ships or lack thereof. The Halvarians don't begin a campaign unless they're knowledgeable about their opponents."

"So you're suggesting they didn't send warships because there's no one to fight?"

"That's the gist of it, yes. Oh, there'll be a few, if only to keep the provincials in line, but I'm confident the bulk would be trading ships, likely cogs, designed to carry troops. It would take a significant number to ferry an entire legion."

Beverly stared back, trying to decide if this was an earnest offer of help or merely a flight of fantasy.

"I know that look," said Danica, "and I can't say I blame you, but the Temple Fleet has a history of fighting a numerically superior enemy. We also have something they don't."

"Which is?"

"Our new ships are far superior to those of the empire. I'm not proposing we send the entire Temple Fleet, as we still need to maintain control of the Great Northern Sea, but I think we could provide enough to see off that invasion fleet. My question to you is, would your people be able to replenish my ships once they arrive in your waters? They'd be fine from the standpoint of the crew, but a trip of that length would deplete their stores."

"There's a couple of ports in Weldwyn that would suit your needs, and I'm certain the king would be willing to lend what assistance he can. If you give me the particulars, I'll have Aubrey pass them on."

"She's in contact with your people?"

Beverly smiled. "Yes. That's just one of the advantages of knowing the magic of the Orcs."

"I wish my fleet had that capability. It would make things so much easier."

"I imagine it would. The ability of the Orc shamans to communicate over great distances has proven vital to the Mercerian Army. Has your order any contacts amongst them?"

"I have yet to see an Orc who likes travelling by sea. In that regard, we Humans seem to be unique, aside from the Sea Elves, that is."

"Sea Elves?"

"Yes," said Danica. "My understanding is they left the Continent rather than go to war with the Orcs. Not that I claim to have any great knowledge of them, but they do have ships."

"And are their ships like those of Humans?"

"They have hulls and masts, if that's what you're asking, but I have to admit to only seeing one down in Ilea, and it's nothing like my current fleet."

"How so?"

"They use magic to fuse the planks together, making for a solid deck and hull, and I'm not entirely certain that's an advantage."

"Why?"

"In the rough northern seas, we experience twisting of the hull, and without planking, the hull would likely rupture. At least that's the prevailing thought."

"Interesting," said Beverly, "but I think for now, I'll concentrate on the land side of things. I meant what I said about your idea. Give me a list of what your fleet would need, and I'll ensure it gets forwarded to the appropriate people."

"I shall do that. Thank you."

"It's me who should be thanking you. After all, you're offering to free up our southern shore."

That evening, Aldwin and Beverly sat before a roaring fire. They were at the duke's estate, guests of His Grace, and were finally enjoying some time together in private.

"This is nice," said Beverly, her hand grasping her husband's. "It seems like forever since we've had time to relax."

He chuckled. "It won't last long. Tomorrow, we'll both be up at the crack of dawn."

The door behind them creaked open.

"Come in, Aubrey," said Beverly.

"How did you know it was me?"

"By process of elimination. Who else would enter without knocking first?"

"Shall I come back later? I don't want to disturb you."

"You're here now. Have a seat."

Aubrey sat across from them. "It's much cooler here than I would've expected."

"Likely the result of the sea," said Aldwin. "They say it brings a cold wind from the north."

"You look troubled," noted Beverly.

"I am," replied the mage. "I talked to Kraloch."

"And?"

"Gerald has a master strategy to defeat Halvaria."

"What is it you're not telling us?"

Aubrey cleared her throat. "For his plan to work, he needs a way of coordinating with the Petty Kingdoms."

"I can guess what that means. He wants me to oversee things on this end."

"He does, but he understands if we choose to return home instead."

"And how do you propose we do that?"

"We could hire a ship," replied Aubrey.

"There's no point in returning home if it's only to see Merceria conquered." She looked at Aldwin. "What do you think?"

"I'm fine with staying here as long as you're with me."

"I guess you have your answer, Cousin,"

"I thought as much," said Aubrey.

"What can you tell me about this grand strategy?"

"Not much at this point. Gerald hasn't divulged any details yet. It also relies on us convincing the Petty Kingdoms to agree to cooperate with us."

"Then that is where we shall begin."

Aldwin knitted his brows. "How do we do that when we don't even know the details of the plan?"

"By having faith," replied Beverly. "Gerald has yet to steer us wrong."

"Not entirely true. He did get captured by Kythelia's army, remember?"

"I remember, but his successes far outweigh his failures."

"I agree," said Aubrey. "So how do we go about doing this? We have to convince the Duke of Reinwick to join us, not to mention the King of Andover."

"And the Duke of Erlingen," added Aldwin. "Although, admittedly, you've already given his army a victory, so I suppose that's not insurmountable."

"We'll start by offering them the tactical advantage."

"How?"

"We get Aubrey to convince the Ashwalkers to lend us their shamans."

"How hard do you reckon that will be?"

"Not very," said Aubrey. "Since we arrived here, Krazuhk has been learning more about them. I'm hoping that familiarity will help us convince them it's in their best interest to assist."

"I think they will," said Aldwin. "It's to their own advantage. By the way, whatever happened to Sir Owen? I haven't seen him since we arrived."

"I have," said Beverly. "He was invited to visit the chapter house of the Knights of the Golden Chalice. I suspect the knights of the Petty Kingdoms consider themselves brothers-in-arms despite being from different realms."

"And Brother Cyric?"

"He's staying at the Temple of Saint Mathew, although I've heard he's spending quite a bit of time looking over the Temple Fleet in port. That reminds me. That admiral of theirs thinks she could sail a fleet all the way to Merceria."

"Is that something worth considering?" asked Aubrey. "By my estimate, we'd be talking about more than a thousand miles."

"Oh, she's aware of the distance. She wants me to arrange for safe ports in Weldwyn."

"And by that, you mean you want me to see to it."

"Naturally," said Beverly. "It's not as if I can use magic."

Aubrey chuckled. "I'll see what I can do. Have we any particulars?"

"Not yet, but I've been assured I'll soon have that information."

"She does realize we're marching tomorrow morning?"

"Naturally. She was at the briefing and appears to be very organized. I suspect we'll have the information in hand at first light."

"In that case, we'd better get some sleep. It's getting late." Aubrey paused, looking at her companions. "That means you two as well. Don't spend all night canoodling!"

"Hey, now," replied Beverly. "We're married, remember? We're allowed to canoodle!"

FIFTEEN

Death Comes Calling

SUMMER 968 MC

The guard captain stood to attention as he entered the High Strategos's office, his eyes darting around in his head as if looking for an escape route.

"Out with it," snapped Exalor.

"Agalix is dead, Your Grace."

"Yes, I know. Word of his demise travelled quickly."

"There is more, Your Grace."

Exalor raised an eyebrow. "More? What more could there possibly be? The man is dead."

"As is our agent."

"What are you trying to say?"

"The man we sent to kill Agalix was also murdered, Your Grace."

"By whom?"

The captain drew in a breath of air. "We've yet to determine that. The body of our man was found at the murder scene, which I'm afraid implicates us."

Exalor chuckled. "It's hardly a secret now, is it? If the Sartellians can't figure out we're the ones killing them off, then what hope have they of surviving?"

"That's just it, Your Grace. Our man didn't kill Agalix."

"I thought you said he was at the murder scene?"

"He was, but a crossbow bolt killed Agalix; our man preferred a blade."

"How did you discover this?"

"I read the official report of his death, Your Grace. I have contacts amongst the Imperial Judiciary."

"This is most unexpected."

"Could it be another Shozarin taking matters into their own hands?"

"Admittedly, anything is possible," said Exalor, "but I find that difficult to believe."

"That is not everything, Your Grace."

"Go on."

"We have reports that Enelle Sartellian was murdered in broad daylight on the streets of Varena."

"I never authorized that!"

"I'm well aware, Your Grace."

Exalor's gaze wandered the room while his mind went elsewhere. Had another Shozarin taken matters into their own hands, or was a different faction at play here? Certainly, the death of Enelle worked to his advantage, but did it signify he'd lost his grip on his own line?

"Have you any orders, Your Grace?"

"Double the guard, and ensure our people keep an eye out for any further developments."

"You fear retribution?"

"It'd be foolish not to think the Sartellians would seek reprisals against us. I doubt it would result in fighting in the street, but then again, I wouldn't have expected someone to murder Enelle in broad daylight. This smacks of a third party trying to manipulate this feud out into the open."

"The Stormwinds, perhaps?"

"That's certainly a possibility, but we must remember there are other groups within the empire who'd enjoy seeing the families toppled from their positions of power."

"Is there anything else, Your Grace?"

"No. You may leave me." The captain bowed before quietly departing.

Exalor was uncertain which was more likely: that the Stormwinds, weakened by the Volstrum's loss, were trying to incite violence between the other families, or an outsider was attempting to seize power? The loss of two powerful Sartellians would bring a swift response, but who would benefit most from that?

He was aware that some officers within the army wished to be free of the tight control the three families held over them, but they were more suited to military action, not murdering people in broad daylight. Could it be a criminal organization? In her role as the High Purifier, Enelle Sartellian had undoubtedly brought a slew of criminals to face justice. Perhaps this was a revenge killing?

Exalor immediately dismissed the idea. Had it only been Enelle, he might've believed it, but the death of Agalix didn't fit that scenario.

His thoughts turned to the Shozarins. Exalor considered himself the true power behind his line, but there always were others seeking to replace him. Was this the manoeuvering of a potential rival? In all probability, any reprisals for the deaths would target him, leaving a power vacuum, so who benefits most from his own death? Only one name stood out from the rest.

"Kelson," he said under his breath, though he was loathe to admit it. He raised his voice. "Wingate! Get in here! I need you."

After a short wait, the door opened to his out-of-breath aide. "You called, Your Grace?"

"Yes. We have work to do. Someone has been interfering in my personal vendetta, and I intend to find out who."

"Where would you like to start?"

"Excellent question. I am of two minds on this: either a third party has taken an interest in our affairs, or someone within my own line has taken it upon themselves to interfere."

"You think someone is trying to seize control of the Shozarins, Your Grace?"

"Our family history seems to indicate that the most likely cause. Wouldn't you agree?"

"There has certainly been strife in the past, Your Grace, but I have a hard time believing someone would dare try to usurp your position."

"Be that as it may, I must still consider the possibility. To that end, I want you to send word to Kelson that I wish to see him."

"Will you travel to his location, Your Grace, or summon him here?"

"Here. It sends a message that I'm not to be trifled with."

"Am I to summon anyone else, Your Grace? We have many Shozarins in positions of influence who might benefit from your…removal."

"Good point. Gather their names and add them to my kill list.

"Yes, Your Grace."

"And Wingate?" said Exalor. "No word of this to anyone. You understand?"

His aide offered a bow. "Completely, Your Grace." With that, he was gone, leaving his master to contemplate recent events yet again.

Exalor found it difficult to believe Kelson might've betrayed him, especially when he'd healed him after the attack on his person. He was suddenly struck by a thought. What if Kelson arranged the assassination attempt to get closer to him? After all, the perpetrator was never caught, which suggested either a very astute assassin or a cover-up at the highest levels. Who better to hide the individual than the High Sentinel himself?

. . .

"He wants to see you in person, m'lord." Captain Heliot stood at the door, his hand, as always, resting on the hilt of his sword.

"Where?" replied Kelson.

"At his estate."

"Was there any indication of his mood?"

"The messenger said immediately, m'lord, which suggests he's in a foul temper. Shall I call more guards?"

"To do what? Meet the High Strategos with an army of warriors? I doubt that would be well received."

"You should be protected, Lord. These are dangerous times."

"So they are. I'll take four guards, along with yourself. Would that make you happy?"

"Indeed, m'lord. I shall make the arrangements."

Kelson turned back to his guest. Praxar Shozarin, by all rights, should be overseeing the Third Legion's evacuation from the mountains surrounding Stonecastle, but recent events had put that entire operation in jeopardy.

"Exalor's nervous," said Praxar, "and so he should be. He's made a right mess of this campaign."

"You are entitled to your own opinion," replied Kelson, "but this campaign was never about subjugating Merceria. No, it was always meant as a means for him to amass an army to take the Gilded Throne."

"Then why attack in three places when he should've massed all the legions together?"

"Yet he very nearly succeeded. If not for the stubbornness of those pesky Dwarves, our legions would be marching on the Mercerian capital as we speak."

Praxar cleared his throat. "With all due respect, Kelson, it is precisely what he should've expected. We learned long ago how difficult it is to pry those people out from under their mountains."

"I might remind you that you were charged with overseeing the attack on Stonecastle."

"That was the legion commander's fault, not mine. Had he carried out the assault according to the plan, none of this would've come to pass. Now, we're faced with an army of Elves marching into our territory."

"Can you stop them?"

"Most certainly. They lack the numbers to do anything other than make a nuisance of themselves."

"Then why are you here," asked Kelson, "rather than in the west commanding what remains of the Third Legion?"

"You worry too much. My magic will have me back where I'm needed long before dark. My question still stands: what are you going to do about this situation we find ourselves in?"

"To which one do you refer? The losses to our legions or this purge that Exalor's begun?"

"Both, not to mention the troubling rumours coming from the east."

Kelson sighed. "You refer to the news that Reinwick is marching south?"

"I do. If Edora doesn't act soon, she'll be too late."

"Let me worry about the campaign in the Petty Kingdoms. You need to take care of those annoying Elves. Have we any idea of the forces at their disposal?"

"It is a small army," replied Praxar, "predominantly comprised of foot, with a smattering of archers and horse."

"I noticed you didn't mention the Dwarves."

The Marshal of the Empire shrugged. "They are of no tactical advantage, and their short legs will slow the advance."

"Still, you mustn't underestimate their contribution. You yourself mentioned how difficult it is to dig Dwarves out from under their mountains."

"True," replied Praxar, "but we have the advantage of terrain in this instance. There won't be rocks for them to crawl under in our lands, only wide-open fields, the perfect place for our cavalry to do their business."

"I assume that means you have a strategy?"

"I do. I shall draw their army towards one of our cities, then cut them off from their supply lines. Trust me, they won't last long."

"And which city would that be?"

"There are several that will suffice. I need only wait and see which direction they march once they clear the mountain passes."

"Wait and see? You must have some idea of what they're up to?"

"Oh, I do," replied Praxar. "Common sense dictates they'd march north to attempt to close off the eastern end of the gap, thus cutting off the Seventh Legion. The problem is they're Elves."

"And?"

"The empire has never faced them in battle, so their tactics are unknown to us."

"But you have a breakdown of their army. You told me so yourself."

"We do, and were they Human, I'd have no doubt as to their intentions, but we're dealing with an unknown race here. Who knows how they think?"

"I admire your caution," replied Kelson, "but we can't let them march all over our territory; the results would be catastrophic."

"It's not that bad."

"Perhaps not from a military standpoint, but think of the political ramifications! The vast bulk of the empire is comprised of conquered territories. Allow them to believe we're weak, and we'd have uprisings throughout the land, particularly in the north, where the realms under our rule are relatively new acquisitions."

"Then I shall do all in my power to crush them as quickly as possible."

"Good," said Kelson. "That's precisely what I hoped you'd say. Now, you must excuse me. I have to go and meet with His Grace, the High Strategos before he has a fit and decides to purge our own line."

"You really think he'd go that far?"

"He has an unbridled thirst for power. He'd do anything he thinks he needs to achieve his objective."

"He's here, Your Grace," said Wingate.

"Good. Show him in." Exalor forced himself to relax, easing back into the armchair. He'd elected to meet Kelson in a drawing room rather than an office, an attempt on his part to put his rival at ease. Drinks were laid out, with a fireplace warming the room despite the heat of the day, all to give the impression nothing was amiss. He closed his eyes, taking the opportunity to calm himself. The more he thought about Kelson, the more he became convinced the fellow had betrayed him, but then would he have healed him? Would he ever know the entire truth of the matter? Somehow, he doubted it, but he must make the best of a bad situation. Perhaps he might convince Kelson it was worthwhile supporting his claim to the Throne.

"He is here, Your Grace."

"Thank you, Wingate. That will be all."

His aide bowed reverentially before backing from the room, leaving his master and Kelson Shozarin alone.

"You called for me?" said his guest.

Exalor tried to hide his annoyance, but a twitch at the corner of his eye revealed his irritation. "Have you heard about the death of Agalix Sartellian?"

"Yes, Your Grace. It's the talk of the city."

"And are you also aware Enelle Sartellian was murdered?"

"Indeed, although some claim it was a robbery attempt in her case."

"What are your thoughts on the matter?"

"I've a hard time believing that," replied Kelson. "Enelle would've had personal guards with her, so I can't conceive of any circumstances where mere thugs could've gotten to her. Was that your work, by chance?"

"I was about to ask you the very same question."

"I assure you I had nothing to do with it."

"What makes you think I did?"

"Logic," replied Kelson. "Enelle represents a rival faction. What better way to put them in their place than to remove one of their top people? However, the fact that you thought I was responsible seems to indicate you had nothing to do with it. That being the case, my next question is, who do you think is behind the attack?"

"Still you."

"Were I the one who killed her, it would've been done indoors to lessen the chance of witnesses. An outdoor attack is a bold move, which indicates whoever was behind it doesn't fear reprisals."

"I can't argue with your logic," said Exalor, "but it now begs the question of who is responsible."

"Perhaps this was simply a matter of revenge. It's not as if she didn't have enemies."

"True, but there's something else you're unaware of that indicates otherwise."

"Interesting."

"I sent a man to kill Agalix, but he was murdered alongside his target."

"Are you suggesting someone else was there?"

"I am."

"You know," said Kelson, "the most logical suspect is one of the Stormwinds."

"I thought of that, but I've had people watching their senior members for a while now."

"Might I ask why?"

"The loss of the Volstrum dealt them a heavy blow," replied Exalor. "I feared they might try to weaken the other lines to balance out that loss."

"But their losses were in Ruzhina, not here in the empire."

"True, but it was still a terrible blow to their power base, which will have long-reaching effects."

"I highly doubt that," said Kelson. "They'll build another academy to replace the Volstrum, likely one in a much safer location; it's only a matter of time."

"I don't think you fully grasp the ramifications. Ruzhina was considered the safest place on the Continent, yet it still fell, and from an enemy who came out of nowhere! Had you suggested such a thing possible even ten years ago, you would've been laughed out of the council chambers."

"Are you implying our own academy in Wyburn is at risk?"

"The events leading to the Volstrum's downfall were the result of terrible mistakes on the part of the ruling Stormwinds. We Shozarins pride ourselves on running an efficient and well-managed institution, but like any training academy, we've had our share of failures."

"Could that be the answer?" asked Kelson. "Could a failed student be taking revenge?"

"Against the Sartellians? I think that unlikely."

"Ah, but what if they're trying to start a war between the Shozarins and Sartellians?"

"It certainly bears further consideration, although I do wonder how such an individual would have the resources to murder Enelle Sartellian so openly."

"There is another option," replied Kelson. "It could be a power play from within the Sartellian line."

"Have your sentinels heard any rumours suggesting this?"

"Admittedly, no, although that doesn't necessarily mean I'm wrong. Sentinels can only overhear what is talked about in the open, and our three families are notoriously tight-lipped about private matters."

"That doesn't help us in the least."

"On the contrary," replied Kelson. "We have identified several possible suspects, which tells us where to begin looking deeper. I'll have my people investigate the current status of those individuals who've been dismissed from our academy."

"Good. And I, in turn, will try to learn more about the changing power dynamic of the Stormwinds."

"And the Sartellians?"

Exalor barked out a laugh. "We're at war with them. We can't exactly knock on their doors and ask them if anyone is trying to seize power."

"True, but we can send people into the streets to find out what rumours are circulating."

"That would help." Exalor looked down at his hands. "I think I might owe you an apology?"

"For what?"

"For doubting your loyalty. I should've known better."

"We live in dangerous times, Your Grace. I cannot fault you for exploring all possibilities."

SIXTEEN

Breach

SUMMER 968 MC

Bastien Lambert, Commander-General of the Seventh Legion, lowered his spyglass. "We've almost finished widening the breach in the side of the mountain, but I still dislike this idea of yours."

"Have you a better one?" replied Idraxa.

"The main gate is my preferred method of entry."

"You've so far failed to bring down that door of theirs. Are we to wait until the snow returns?"

"I understand how frustrating this is," replied Lambert, "but to enter that breach, my men must scale a steep slope, not to mention needing to fight once they reach it. An exhausted man is ill-prepared to face the fury of a Dwarven axe."

"I think you overestimate the resolve of the mountain folk. Once your men are inside those tunnels, that mine of theirs will soon fall."

"How can you be so certain? At Dun-Galdrim, they laid all manner of traps."

"I've studied the siege of that Dwarven mine extensively. Their traps were all laid along the expected route of attack, whereas here, we have a chance to assault them where they least expect it. No doubt they'll have some tricks up their sleeves, but it will pale in comparison to what they have waiting behind the front doors to the mountain."

"I still don't like this."

"I'll be sure to make a note of that," said Idraxa, "but I'm overruling your objection. I am the Marshal of the North and in command of this siege."

"The acting marshal," cautioned Lambert. "Get this wrong, and your career is over."

"As will be yours if you don't do as I've ordered. Now, what's it to be, Commander-General? Will you attack as ordered, or will you force me to replace you?"

Lambert stiffened. "I have never refused an order."

"Good. Then your men will begin the ascent as darkness falls, and attack as soon as they reach the breach."

Lambert nodded. "It shall be as you command, Marshal."

"You are dismissed."

Small bits of stone and dust tumbled to the floor as the mountain shuddered.

"That was close," said Herdwin. "Will this ceiling hold?"

"Absolutely," replied Kasri, "but it won't be long before the enemy sends its warriors in."

"How do you know that?"

"Our people report the outside breach is about as large as it can get."

"Does the enemy know that?"

"I suspect they do," she replied. "They brought Earth mages to Stonecastle, and they're bound to bring the same expertise here."

"If I were you, I'd send my arbalesters up to rain bolts down on them as they climb."

"I doubt that would prove effective."

"What makes you say that?"

"Two things, actually," said Kasri. "One, they'd have to cram into the breach, making them an easy target for the empire's siege engines, and two, their warriors will be climbing in the dark, making them difficult targets."

"How do you know all this?"

"It's what I'd do if I were in their boots."

"Thank Gundar you're on our side."

She smiled. "I'll take that as a compliment."

"We should head below. If their assault is coming soon, we need Albreda to manoeuvre the deep one into place."

"You go. I'm needed here to prepare the defences."

"I thought everything was already set?"

"Almost," replied Kasri, "but I must determine the best spot to deploy the Hearth Guard."

"I'll let Albreda know the time has come to do her part." He paused a moment. "Be careful, Kasri. I couldn't stand the idea of losing you."

"My armour will protect me. You're the one who'll be in the greater danger, what with that deep one being nearby. I will, however, take your advice and be careful, providing you do the same."

"I will. I promise."

Albreda stood at the railing, looking into a great pit of darkness. Down there, deep ones roamed, creatures of the depths seemingly made of rock and stone. Some called them elementals: magical creatures of the subterranean world, but she knew they were living, breathing creatures, just as those above the surface of Eiddenwerthe.

She heard the lift well before she saw it, a clunking that reverberated off the walls. Turning, she watched the iron box descend, coming to rest level with the ledge on which she stood.

The door opened, and out stepped a Dwarf, his face hidden by the helm he wore, but his distinctive armour was enough to identify him.

"Ah, Herdwin. I wondered when you might deign to put in an appearance."

"I've come from Kasri," he replied. "She tells me the assault will commence at dawn."

Albreda nodded, adjusting her own helmet slightly. "Plenty of time to convince one of our friends down there to lend us a hand. It's time we descended."

Herdwin moved closer, staring into the darkness. "And how do you propose we do that?"

"We shall start with a little illumination." Albreda closed her eyes, uttering the words of arcane power. The air began its familiar buzzing, and then, at her feet, vines crawled forth, reaching over the edge of the precipice to disappear into the darkness. As the vines descended, small flowers sprang forth, glowing with a pale light that illuminated the area.

She ceased her incantation, moving closer to the railing to look below. The vast cavern was now exposed to her view, lit up by the glowing blossoms. Off to her right, where the vines hit the bottom of the cavern, she could make out a shadowy figure lumbering towards the wall.

"It appears one has taken an interest in my plants," she said.

Herdwin moved up beside her. "That's all well and good, but how do we get him to come up here?"

"What makes you think it's a him?"

"Nothing, I suppose, but I have to call it something. Why? Do you think it's a female?"

"I rather suspect it's neither and both."

Herdwin cocked his head. "I'm afraid you'll have to explain that one to me."

"I've given this a lot of thought, and have come to the conclusion that they reproduce much like a plant; though, rather than seeds, they create crystals. In time, these crystals shatter, allowing a deep one to emerge, much as a butterfly emerges from a cocoon."

"A what, now?"

"Never mind," said Albreda. "It's not important, merely an observation."

"You still haven't explained how we're going to get that thing up here, seeing as we can't get it into the lift."

"I shall go down there and use my magic."

"Really?" said Herdwin. "You know a spell that can lift a deep one?"

"Of course not, but Ironcliff has a magic circle. I'm surprised you didn't remember that, considering that's how I brought you here."

"Ah, I see now. You're going to use that circle to amplify your magic."

"No," replied Albreda. "I'm going to use a spell of recall to take that deep one to the magic circle. From there, we'll escort it to the area where we expect the most trouble."

"What can I do to help?"

"You need to go back to Kasri and ask for a handful of her Hearth Guards to accompany you to the circle to provide an escort."

"Are you saying you'll go down there and face that thing all on your own?"

"How else am I to convince it to accompany me?"

"And how do you aim to do that?"

Albreda shook her head. "Did you forget I'm a Druid? I can use my magic to talk to it. I'm certain it's a perfectly reasonable creature."

"And if it doesn't want to go?"

"Then I shall abandon the attempt and find another way to repel the empire's attack. Now, are you going to stand there arguing with me all night, or are you going to help?"

"My apologies. I shall speak to Kasri at once." He turned and rushed back to the lift.

Albreda cast her gaze once more over the side of the cliff. It was a steep climb, one that would prove most difficult, even with the help of the vines. She had to admit she was getting old, and though her magic was still strong, her physical strength wasn't what it used to be.

It suddenly struck her that there was no reason why she couldn't use the spell of recall to take her directly to the bottom. The normal use of the spell required the caster to target a location containing a magic circle, but Albreda was never one to follow the rules. Yes, it would prove difficult, perhaps even impossible, but it wouldn't cost too much of her magical strength to give it a try.

She closed her eyes and began weaving her hands around in the air. Some scholars believed such an act helped to concentrate on the magic, but to her mind, it was how she gathered the magic permeating the world of Eiddenwerthe.

As the power built within her, stray strands of her hair stood on end. She snapped her eyes open, concentrating on a point on the cavern's stone floor. The energy around her increased until it felt as though she couldn't contain it any longer, and then she pointed, channelling all her magic at her target.

A cylinder of light surrounded her, temporarily blinding her as the familiar tug of magic signified the activation of her recall. The disorientation accompanying the spell overwhelmed her, and then, as the magic dissipated, she stood in mid-air with nothing beneath her feet. She fell to the ground, the impact driving the breath from her lungs, and crumpled to the floor of the cavern. Her spell had worked, but she'd materialized higher than expected, leading to a waist-high fall.

Once her eyes adjusted to the dim light given off by the blossoms, she sat up, surveying her surroundings. The deep one she'd spotted from above was off to her left, about a dozen paces away. Her arrival had apparently drawn its attention, for it lumbered towards her.

She concentrated on summoning more of her magic, intending to use a spell that normally enabled her to speak with mammals, although she wasn't sure if it would work on a creature such as this.

By the time she finished her spell, the creature had advanced and now towered overhead, its emotionless crystalline eyes staring down at her. Panic rose with her, and she fought to get it under control. She concentrated on the deep one, and the familiar surge of power wafted through her, and then she spoke one word, "Stop!"

It froze in place, although she had no idea if that was a result of her spell or its own decision.

"I mean you no harm," she added, thinking quickly. It occurred to her that her helmet muffled her words, and she considered removing it. The air was thin down here, and she certainly didn't want to suffocate, but it made this exchange much more difficult. Reason finally took hold, and she raised her voice to be understood better. "Friend," she shouted.

The deep one opened its mouth, little more than a small slit along its stony face. "Friend?" it replied, its deep voice resonating throughout the chamber.

"So, you can speak. I was beginning to wonder. Now, what shall we talk about? I imagine living down here is a unique experience. How do I go about asking you for your help?"

Kasri crouched behind the barricade. Before her stood one of the upper halls, a long, tall room with a balcony above that ran the length of it. A group of Halvarians had gathered at the far end, using the doorway to protect themselves from the arbalester bolts raining down from above. It was only a matter of time before they rushed to overwhelm her position, but to her mind, it couldn't come fast enough.

She stood, pointed Stormhammer at the enemy, and discharged a bolt of lightning that lit the room as it soared to hit a Halvarian warrior at the other end. The man went stiff, then fell from view, a victim of her weapon's magic.

A deep growl erupted from the far end as men streamed through the doorway, their weapons drawn, seeking Dwarven blood.

"Hold," called out Kasri. If she advanced into the room, it would only give the enemy the advantage. Dwarves have short legs, best suited to defensive positions, and as the warriors of the empire rushed forward, she knew exactly how to utilize the Hearth Guard. "Fall back. Hide of the Drake!"

Her warriors stepped back three paces, forming a line, their overlapping shields locking into place. Those in the second rank leaned forward, the bottoms of their shields resting on the tops of those in the front. Between them came spears, presenting a wall of spiked steel to meet the enemy.

Everyone braced for impact as the Humans made contact, and although the initial charge pushed the Dwarven line back a few paces, the determined warriors of Ironcliff stood strong. Swords and axes clanged against shields, yet the Dwarves held their position.

The arbalesters poured bolts into the enemy warriors, thinning their numbers. In the second rank, Kasri felt a great weight upon her shield and realized, with a start, that an enemy warrior had leaped onto the top of their formation. "Third rank, stand by to repel!"

A man in mail dropped down behind her, and attacked, his axe glancing off the plate armour protecting her back. He was bracing for a second swing when a poleaxe sliced through his side. He lurched forward, collapsing against her, coughing up blood as he died.

When the men of Halvaria realized the tactic had succeeded, more warriors jumped onto the tops of the shields, their weight making it difficult for the Dwarves to maintain their formation. The Hide of the Drake worked well to provide protection from arrows and bolts, but against a foe that outnumbered them up close, its weakness soon became apparent.

"General melee!" shouted Kasri. She stepped back, allowing the second rank to put some distance between themselves and those in front. The Halvarian warriors atop their formation lost their footing, tumbling to the ground, and the Hearth Guard in the second and third rows made short work of them. Those Dwarves in the front, however, began to suffer, for the Human's numerical superiority had given the advantage to the enemy.

She loosed another blast of lightning from Stormhammer, striking a helmet, and then it jumped to another, taking him in the shoulder. Both fell, though likely only stunned.

Additional men poured through the far door, adding their battle cries to the noise reverberating off the stone walls. Disaster was coming. Kasri knew it. By all rights, she should retreat, but her Dwarven stubbornness prevented her from admitting defeat. She planted her feet and swung her hammer around with all the speed she could muster.

The Hearth Guard's front rank disintegrated, and then a great swarm of Halvarians descended on Kasri. Adrenaline surged through her. She was Kasri Ironheart, Dragon Rider, and designated successor to the Throne of Ironcliff. She would not submit! A song of battle came to her, and she embraced it. Time stood still as her hammer swung, loosing lightning and bludgeoning foes with wild abandon. This was the way to die: as a hero worthy of the legends of old!

Albreda opened the door to a scene of carnage, bodies strewn about the room, blood soaking the walls. Dozens of the Hearth Guard lay unmoving, each surrounded by two or three slain Halvarians, yet the fighting continued with a mass of men and Dwarves embroiled in what looked more like a barroom brawl than a battle in the heart of a mountain.

Albreda turned to the deep one, but words proved unnecessary, for the creature lurched into the room, moving at a slow but steady pace. Upon seeing it, a Halvarian warrior rushed forward, swinging his axe, but it only glanced off the elemental's arm, and then the great creature smashed out with a fist, puncturing the fellow's breastplate and crushing his heart. Unmoved by the experience, the deep one continued its advance, swatting away the empire's finest as if they were nothing more than insects.

Herdwin squeezed past the Druid, rushing towards Kasri, his axe striking out with great precision as he went. He dug the head of his weapon into a shin, but his opponent took the Dwarf's weapon with him as he fell. Herdwin drew a long knife from his belt and continued on.

Albreda called forth her magic, sending a tiny spark of light sailing across the room to land near the far door, where it sank into the stone. The floor cracked open, and vines rose from the ground to block the doorway, cutting off any chance of escape. More bolts sang out from above, and then everything went quiet, save for the moans of the injured and dying.

"Are you all right?" said Herdwin, looking at Kasri's blood-soaked armour.

"I'm fine," she replied. "It's only a scratch."

"It doesn't look like it."

"Nonsense. Most of that blood is from the ones I killed." She took a step forward, but her leg buckled, and she fell to her knees.

Herdwin steadied her. "You can't go on like this. You need healing."

Kasri nodded. "Take the Hearth Guard and clear the next chamber. They know what to do."

"Me? I'm just a smith!"

"You're a Mercerian commander, Herdwin, and a Hero of Stonecastle! I hereby give you command of the Hearth Guard until such time as I can resume my duties. Do you understand?"

"Aye. I do." He cast about, trying to piece together their current situation.

Albreda was already moving towards the far door, following in the wake of the deep one. She paused, turning to regard the carnage, her eyes meeting those of Herdwin. "Well?" she said. "What are you waiting for? We have an enemy to vanquish!"

SEVENTEEN

Plotting

SUMMER 968 MC

Beverly bolted awake from a deep sleep, suddenly on the alert. She poked Aldwin, who slept beside her. "Did you hear that?"

He rubbed his eyes. "Hear what?"

"There's somebody out there."

"It's probably just a servant."

Unconvinced, she jumped out of bed and raced towards her weapons and armour, which stood on a rack in the corner of the room. Knowing enough to trust his wife, Aldwin threw off the covers and sat on the edge of the bed, trying to take a moment to wake up, but the door burst open, illuminating the doorway as a trio of individuals rushed in, blades in hand.

Beverly grabbed Nature's Fury and moved up to swing at the nearest foe, striking his left arm but unexpectedly glancing off a metal vambrace hidden beneath the fellow's cloak. He immediately turned to face her, slashing out with a blade that glowed with a sinister green substance. She backed up, realizing that without her armour, even a glancing blow could prove fatal.

The second one rushed towards the bed and leaped onto it, swinging out with his sword. Aldwin barely ducked in time, the blade slicing through the air where his head had just been. He grabbed the closest thing to him—a cup—and hurled it towards his attacker, hitting the fellow in the face, which bought him enough time to get to his feet.

Beverly smashed Nature's Fury into the floor, sending vines creeping out towards her foe, where they wrapped themselves around his legs, pinning him in place before they started crushing him. She followed up with a swift blow that sent her hammer into the man's skull, felling him instantly.

The third assailant had remained by the door after entering, waiting for an opportunity to strike. He lifted a hand crossbow and let fly with a bolt that sailed across the room and grazed Beverly's right arm, drawing blood but doing no real damage. She charged him, using the hilt of Nature's Fury to smash his face. He fell back against the door frame, and she followed with a swing at his leg. Bone crunched under the impact, and he dropped to the floor, blood spouting everywhere.

Aldwin leaned back as his attacker struck again, slicing across the front of his chest. It was a shallow cut, doing only surface damage, but he felt the sting of it. He tried backing up again, only to find himself against the wall. With no way to escape the next blow, he readied his fists and lunged at his assailant, striking out even as the fellow raised his sword.

Years working the forge had made the smith strong, so much so that when his fists struck home, the attacker's neck snapped back. Aldwin followed with a desperate rain of blows, pulverizing his foe's face and bloodying his knuckles. His assailant tumbled backwards, falling onto the bed and lying still.

Aldwin heard movement to his left and twisted around, expecting trouble, but it was only Beverly.

"Are you all right?" she asked.

"I'm fine," he replied. "You?"

She nodded, then moved closer, embracing him. "For a moment there, I thought I'd lost you."

Footsteps approached, and then a pair of warriors adorned in the duke's livery appeared in the doorway.

"We heard fighting," said the shorter one.

Beverly released her husband, turning to face the newcomers. "They burst in here, intent on murder, but we seem to have gotten the better of them."

The guard turned to his companion. "Fetch more men and sound the alarm. There is evil afoot this night." He stepped into the room and knelt down, examining the man near the door. "This one's dead."

"We were fighting for our lives!" replied Beverly.

"It is meant only as a comment, my lady, not a condemnation."

"Sorry. I'm a little on edge."

"That's to be expected under the circumstances."

More footsteps, and then Aubrey appeared, a dressing gown clutched around her. "Are you all right, Cousin?"

"These men attacked us," replied Beverly. She looked at her arm, then pointed at the discarded dagger. "Be careful. That weapon has something on it, likely poison, though the wound from the crossbow bolt appears normal enough." She suddenly remembered the cut on Aldwin's chest and turned to regard him.

"It was only a graze," he said, then his eyes rolled up into his head, and he collapsed to the floor.

Aldwin opened his eyes to see Aubrey standing over him.

"Can you hear me?" she asked.

"I'm fine," he said, then a pain lanced through his skull. "On second thought, maybe not. My brain feels as though it's too big for my head."

"That's to be expected; you've been poisoned. I've used my magic to neutralize it, but your body still believes it's fighting it off."

"How long will my head feel like this?"

"I expect you'll be fully recovered before dinner, providing you drink lots of water. You gave us quite the scare there."

"Where's Beverly?"

"Taking a quick break. She's been up all night with you."

"All night?" said Aldwin. "What time is it?"

"Mid-morning. I'll go fetch her. She'll want to know how you're doing."

"No. If I know Beverly, she'll be busy trying to track down those responsible. Let her know I'm fine, then let me sleep. We can talk once my head returns to normal."

Aubrey nodded. "Oh, just to let you know, Sir Owen is outside the door, and Krazuhk arranged for some Ashwalkers to guard the hallway."

"Any idea yet who was responsible?"

"No, but we're still looking into it. Now get some rest." She pulled up the blankets, tucking him in, then rose, giving her patient one more glance before exiting the room.

Beverly waited outside. "Any news?"

"He's finally awake," replied Aubrey, "and his head is sore. Don't worry, that will wear off in time, but he needs to rest. He's lucky I was nearby; that poison was fast-acting."

"So you know what it was?"

"The most likely candidate is a high concentration of malroot. Back home, we used to employ it to ease the suffering of those who were dying."

"Used to?"

"We have no need of it now that we have Life Mages willing to use their magic for the benefit of all."

"How common is it here in Reinwick?"

"I can't answer that," replied Aubrey, "though perhaps an Ashwalker shaman might be able to tell us more."

"Then I shall go at once and seek one out." Beverly turned, ready to leave.

"Let me, Cousin. You're far too busy dealing with the Halvarian invasion. We don't know if malroot has the same name here in the Petty Kingdoms, so my knowledge will be required to discuss the matter."

"I can't argue with your logic," replied Beverly, "but if you get even a hint of who's responsible for this attack, let me know at once."

"I will. I promise, but you should be cautious. Whoever was behind this had access to the duke's estate."

"I shall find Krazuhk and keep her at my side at all times. Will that suffice?"

"I'm not your enemy, Cousin. I'm only trying to keep you safe."

Beverly took a deep breath. "Sorry. I didn't mean to take it out on you. I know you have our best interests at heart. Will you forgive me?"

"Of course." Aubrey smiled. "Now, we both have things to take care of, and hanging around this hallway accomplishes nothing."

Brother Cyric stared down at the three bodies laid out on the floor. They'd been stripped of their armour to help identify them, but so far, Captain Marwen had nothing to offer on that score.

"Their musculature indicates someone who has spent a lifetime fighting," noted the Temple Knight, "as would the proliferation of scars."

"I would agree," said Marwen, "although I daresay that gets us no closer to identifying them."

"May I see their weapons?"

"Yes, of course." Marwen moved to stand beside a chest. "They're in there, but don't worry, they've been thoroughly cleansed of poison. Lady Aubrey indicated it was something called malroot."

"Yes. I've heard of that."

The captain looked up in surprise. "You have?"

"Indeed. In my role as a special investigator for the order, I've come across all sorts of concoctions."

"Is murder so common in the Temple Knights?"

"Not at all. The cases I dealt with involved worshippers of Saint Mathew, not Temple Knights. You might say murder is my particular specialty." He paused briefly. "Oh dear, that didn't come out the way I intended. What I meant to infer was I've had quite a bit of experience investigating such things."

"And what can you tell me about malroot?"

"It's rare in these parts. I expect someone went to great expense to acquire it."

"That's disheartening," said the captain. "That indicates someone wealthy was behind this. Any ideas as to whom?"

"I doubt this was the work of anyone native to Reinwick."

"What makes you say that?"

"The bodies, for one. These were fighting men, most likely knights."

"Could they be from the duke's order, the Knights of the Golden Chalice?"

"I presume they spend a lot of time at the duke's court?"

"They do."

"Then I highly doubt these individuals were members; otherwise, someone would've identified them already." He crouched beside the chest, pulling forth a sword. "Was this the one who injured Master Aldwin?"

"I believe so, yes."

"A fine weapon." Cyric stood, the sword in hand. "We need some tools."

"For what?" asked Marwen.

"If we remove the handle from this sword, we shall likely see the maker's mark."

"I thought those were found on the blade."

"They are, but this sword is shorter than most, and there's no visible mark above the hilt, which leads me to assume it's farther down."

Captain Marwen produced a knife. "Here. You can cut away the leather wrapping with this."

Cyric got to work unravelling the binding and then removing the wooden grip that lay beneath it. "Ah, here it is." He held the weapon up to the window, the better to examine it. "I know this mark or rather a portion of it." He held it out towards the captain. "The smiths of the Antonine all include the Holy Cipher as part of their mark. Now, I can't tell you which smith made this, but this mark here"—he pointed with his other hand—"is the simplified 'A' that signifies it was forged within the walls of the Antonine."

"Do you realize what you're suggesting?"

"Yes. These three individuals are likely Temple Knights."

"From which order?"

"To my mind, there can be no doubt they are Cunars."

"Why would you say that?"

"You've likely heard rumours concerning the Church of late. What you don't know is the role the Temple Knights of Saint Cunar played in those events. When the Primus ordered the orders to amalgamate, the Cunars enforced that policy, often at sword-point."

"Are you suggesting they turned on their fellow knights?"

"I'm not suggesting anything," said Cyric. "I'm revealing the truth of what happened."

"But how would they know Lady Beverly was here?"

"They accosted us on the way here. Without the assistance of the Ashwalkers, they would've slain us then and there."

"I could understand if they'd attacked you, a Mathewite, but we're talking about an individual who came to us from the west. What possible motive would they have for attacking the general?"

"I don't think you understand the full ramifications of this. They no longer serve the Church."

"Then who do they serve?"

"Isn't it obvious?" Cyric waited for the captain to put the pieces together.

Marwen sucked in a sharp breath. "Are you implying they're now in league with the empire?"

"So far as I know, the Church doesn't have a presence in Merceria. Can you think of any other reason a group of Temple Knights might choose to attack Lady Beverly?"

"Admittedly, no. We should bring this to the attention of His Grace, the duke."

"On that, I concur."

"Are you absolutely certain?" Duke Fernando paced back and forth, his agitation readily apparent to all those he'd gathered.

Brother Cyric nodded. "I'm afraid there is little room for doubt, Your Grace. We must now count the Temple Knights of Saint Cunar as potential adversaries."

"That is only a minor irritation. They have no presence in Reinwick."

"The same cannot be said of those lands which we will march through in our quest to defeat the empire."

The duke turned to Beverly. "You've been remarkably quiet thus far, my lady. I would've thought you'd be eager to see those responsible for the attack on your husband brought to justice."

"Oh, I am," she replied, "but a wise woman reminded me there are other matters equally deserving of our attention. Those who attacked us are dead, their masters likely beyond our reach for the present. If we let this consume us, it will be to the detriment of the coming campaign."

"A keen observation," noted Cyric. "I wonder if that might've been their intent all along?"

"Truly?" said the duke. "Are you of the mind that they weren't out to murder the general?"

"I think their mission was to sow as much chaos as possible, Your Grace. Certainly, the death of Lady Beverly would have dealt a great blow to our cause, but even a failed attempt diverts attention away from greater issues." He nodded towards the general. "No offence, my lady, but tragic as this attack has been, the lives of many more people hang in the balance."

"I agree," replied Beverly. "Which is why I'd like to propose something rather radical, Your Grace."

Fernando put his hand to his chin. "Do go on. I'm most intrigued to see what you deem radical."

"In Merceria, we use Orc shamans to communicate over long distances, which is how my cousin, Lady Aubrey, has been able to keep up with events back home."

"And?"

"I propose that you employ the Ashwalkers in a similar capacity. The presence of their shamans would allow you to coordinate efforts much more effectively than using couriers to carry your orders."

"How many of these shamans would we need?"

"Ideally, one for each of your brigades. Sorry, that's the Mercerian term. I believe you call them divisions. Given the present circumstances, I'm certain they'd be willing to assist in repelling the empire."

"Our current army is organized into four divisions, although two of those are much smaller, intended to form our reserve. It seems to me the ability to communicate over large distances would be better employed to coordinate matters with our allies from Andover rather than within our own army."

"Are there any Orc tribes residing in Andover's territory?"

"Not that I'm aware of, which means we'd have to lend King Dagmar one of ours. That, in turn, raises another issue, for as far as I know, no one in the court of Zienholtz speaks their language."

Captain Marwen cleared his throat. "I've been learning their language ever since the war with Andover, Your Grace. If you'd permit it, I'd accompany whichever shaman they send south, assuming they agree."

The duke raised his eyebrows. "I must say this comes as a bit of a surprise."

"As you know, Your Grace, my wife has friends in Therengia, and they, as a realm, embrace the Orcs as full members of their society. With the arrival of the Ashwalkers to our lands, I thought it only proper that someone learn more of their ways, including their language."

"Your foresightedness is most appreciated, Captain, but if I send you to King Dagmar, you will need a proper escort lest those cursed Cunars try to interfere again." He addressed Beverly once more. "You must tell me more of how the Army of Merceria employs these shamans, General, for I haven't the faintest idea how this would be organized."

"I shall be delighted, Your Grace."

Admiral Danica walked through the door.

"You're a little late," noted the duke.

"My apologies," she replied. "I was combing through the charts of the Temple Fleet."

"Might I ask to what end?"

"I'm told a fleet of Halvarian ships is threatening the southern coast of Merceria. I was seeking what information I could find concerning the northern shoreline of the Continent."

"And what did you discover?"

"Between our own expeditions and captured Halvarian charts, we have a good understanding of the empire's northern waters. The area to the west, though, remains largely a mystery."

"I sense there's more," said Duke Fernando.

"There is, indeed, Your Grace. For the past few years, we've been rewarding merchants who provide us with any scraps of information concerning Halvarian waters. Late last year, Captain Zivka of the Temple Ship *Illustrious* encountered a merchant who claimed he'd once been blown off course, ending up far to the west."

"As far as Merceria?" asked Beverly.

"Do they have a northern coast?"

"No, only a southern one."

"Might I ask what lies to your north?"

"The realm of Norland, which has mountains forming its northern border."

"That's quite interesting," said Danica. "You see, this same merchant talked of passing by two separate mountain ranges, both of which ended at the sea. Could this be the mountain range you speak of?"

"Quite possibly, though I've seen little of them, save for those near Iron-cliff. Was the coast difficult to sail?"

"He spoke of smooth sailing once he got past the mountain ranges, but the waters between the two were rough."

"But that would make it dangerous sailing, would it not?" asked the duke.

"For normal ship captains, yes, but the Temple Fleet typically sails far out to sea, avoiding treacherous shorelines."

"Without the shoreline to guide you, how would you navigate?"

"They'd use the mountains," said Beverly. "I imagine you could see them for miles."

"They'd still be navigating an unknown coast," insisted Duke Fernando.

"We would," replied Danica, "but we have smaller craft to lead the way, ships far more nimble than the rest of the fleet. They'd range ahead, keeping an eye out for danger."

"That is madness! You'd risk losing control of the Great Northern Sea."

"Not so," said Cyric. "I know without a doubt that the seas are navigable."

"How?"

"An old acquaintance of mine, a fellow named Captain Runell, sailed to Weldwyn some years ago."

"Runell?" said Beverly. "Would that be Harnen Runell of the *Swift*?"

"Yes. How do you know of him?"

"His ship was anchored in Loranguard while we were there eight years ago. I didn't meet him in person, but Dame Hayley spoke fondly of him."

"And who, might I ask, is Dame Hayley?"

"The High Ranger and the Baroness of Queenston."

"How extraordinary that we should both be familiar with the good Captain Runell."

"Amusing," said the duke, "but it still doesn't get to the heart of the matter. The admiral risks control of the seas in what is, quite frankly, a dangerous and ill-conceived desire to explore unknown waters."

"You are entitled to your own opinion," replied the admiral, "but ultimately, it's my choice to take such an undertaking. It is called the Temple Fleet, not the Navy of Reinwick."

Duke Fernando bowed his head. "You are correct. I only hope you're not making a terrible mistake, for it could have dire consequences for all of us."

EIGHTEEN

Crossroads

SUMMER 968 MC

The wind stirred the leaves, distracting Wingate as he was staring out the window, imagining himself frolicking beneath the tree's boughs, a comely young woman at his side. He'd dreamed of that life for many years but, somehow, never found the time to pursue it. Instead, he'd spent his days in service to the empire, first in the imperial bureaucracy and then to the High Strategos himself.

Those thoughts had him searching for his reflection in the window. His best years had passed him by, and now all he saw was grey-tinged hair adorning the countenance of an old man, no longer the fellow who'd draw a lady's favour.

It had not been for nothing, for he'd accumulated almost enough savings to see him live the rest of his life in comfort, if not as one of the empire's elite. Then, his thoughts turned bitter. Exalor was not the type of man to reward those beneath him; instead, he would exhaust them, drawing their last breath from their lungs in his service if it forwarded his ambitions. The man was a martinet, insisting on everything being done his way, which had propelled him to heights unimaginable to others and perhaps even to the Throne of Halvaria if he had his way, yet it had made enemies of his rivals.

Wingate smiled. He'd made use of those individuals, selling information in exchange for coins, which had allowed him to double his savings in the last year alone, but it was still not enough to give him the life he desired.

Now, his master was on a murder rampage, ordering the death of his most vocal critics. He'd created a list of individuals for his agents to elimi-nate, a list to which Wingate had added a couple of names, eager to remove those who could reveal his treachery. It was a gamble, and if his master got wind of it, it would be the end of his career, even his life. On the other side of the coin was the fact that somebody else was out there eliminating people, so an extra death or two was easily explained away.

He'd briefly considered coming clean with Exalor, blaming his treachery on some imaginary blackmail, but quickly dismissed the idea. These were perilous times, and any sign of deceit, no matter how small, could potentially send him to the grave. Better, he thought, to make the most of the situation and demand payment upfront lest his contacts be eliminated before they had an opportunity to pay.

A bell tolled outside, reminding him the world continued on with its daily life whether he was a part of it or not. With a start, he realized he'd been dwelling on his own fate for so long that he'd forgotten he was supposed to meet with Kelson Shozarin, a meeting he was most definitely not going to report to the High Strategos. He turned from the window and gathered up his notes, pleased he'd be receiving yet more coins this day.

Kelson Shozarin sat beneath the statue of Erkinwald, the first Emperor of Halvaria, situated in the middle of Victory Park, a space dedicated to the great battle successes the empire had accumulated over the centuries. The place held the advantage of being centrally located within the city while still offering a modicum of privacy thanks to the heavily wooded grounds.

Wingate was late, which was uncharacteristic of someone who prided himself on his punctuality, leading Kelson to wonder if the fellow had suffered a change of heart regarding their arrangement. Not that he faulted him. Exalor had quite a temper on occasion, and those who betrayed him were often swept aside or "cast to the wolves" as the High Strategos was fond of saying. Still, it was enough to raise suspicions on Kelson's part.

He finally spotted the aide approaching along the walkway, glancing left and right to ensure he wasn't being followed.

"It's about time you showed up," said Kelson. "Something wrong?"

"Not in the least, although some unexpected business delayed me at the last moment."

"Something I should know?"

"Nothing that need concern you. I have, however, a list of names you'd be most interested in." He reached into his belt pouch and retrieved a folded piece of paper, brandishing it as if it were loathsome to the touch.

"Might I ask the reason for this list?" asked Kelson.

"Now that there's open warfare between the families, the High Strategos has added additional names to his termination list. All these people have, in some way, earned the wrath of His Grace."

"I hope I was convincing enough in our meeting earlier to ensure I haven't been added to this list."

"You weren't," replied Wingate, "though if Exalor learns of this meeting, you might soon find yourself joining it. We both would, if truth be known."

"You may rest assured there is no danger of me telling him of our meetings," said Kelson, "and on each and every occasion, I've taken steps to ensure that others are unaware of these discussions."

Wingate nodded. "I never doubted you'd be careful."

"May I examine this list?"

"Most assuredly," replied the aide. "That's the very reason I'm here today. I knew as soon as he told me it was something you'd be interested in."

Kelson took the note, unfolding it slowly. Wingate waited for him to read it before continuing, "You'll note that several Shozarins are on there."

"I find that surprising, although I suppose I shouldn't. Exalor was always wary of rising stars within the line."

"Agreed. He sees them as potential rivals to his power rather than allies. To this day, I still don't understand how he came to trust you so much."

"I took great pains to present myself as an ally rather than a rival," replied Kelson. "It was difficult at times, especially when our High Strategos was in one of his moods, but that's to be expected."

"Do you think he's right to suspect the people on that list of working against him?"

Kelson looked once more at the names, his gaze lingering on one or two. "Perhaps, in some cases, but there are few here that don't deserve to suffer his wrath. You say all these people are to be eliminated?"

"Yes, my lord."

The High Sentinel refolded the paper and handed it back. "An interesting collection of individuals. Tell me, how many names did you add?"

"None, my lord."

"I command the empire's sentinels. Do you think I can't tell a lie when I hear it?"

Wingate stared down at the note in his hands. "I have no idea what you're talking about."

"Tell me the truth. None of those people are of particular import to me one way or the other. If you want to add names, I have no objection, providing I know the ones on Exalor's true list."

"I added two. Grafford and Edora Sartellian."

"I can well understand the addition of Edora, considering she commands the assault on the Petty Kingdoms, but Grafford? The man's so low in seniority he barely rates as a Sartellian at all. The last I heard, he was participating in the assault on the mountain passes. Considering the Third Legion is now in retreat, there's a good chance he's already dead."

"Perhaps," said Wingate, "but I'm nothing if not thorough."

"Might I ask why he's of any consequence? Is this a feud, or has he wronged you in some way?"

"I'd rather not say."

"You may keep your secret if you wish. I shall breathe no word of it."

"Thank you, my lord."

"It is I who must thank you," said Kelson. "I have a feeling the information you've provided today will prove most useful."

"I thought you said the names on that list were of no particular import?"

"And they aren't… yet, but I have hopes they soon will be."

"I don't understand?"

"That's because, as able as you are at administration, you don't know people, whereas I do. Many on that list would pay handsomely to know Exalor is looking to eliminate them, and I intend to capitalize on that fear."

"For coins?"

Kelson forced a smile. "My dear fellow, there is so much more to life than coins."

"Such as?"

"Power and influence, for one, or rather two. Like it or not, our empire doesn't exist in a void. Power is there for the taking. Exalor is a prime example of that, and without influence, his rule would be destined to fail."

"Are you suggesting you want the Gilded Throne for yourself?"

"No. I much prefer to rule from behind the throne than atop. There's far less danger to my life if I'm operating from the shadows."

"And you believe you can control Exalor?"

"You tell me," said Kelson. "You know him far better than I ever could."

~

The column halted, waiting as Lord Arandil Greycloak surveyed the area. The path before them led down into a fertile land peppered by farms, with a large city visible in the distance. "What do we know of the region?" he asked.

Delsaran, nominally a bard, had been put in charge of gathering information from prisoners. He now fumbled through his notes, finally selecting a parchment with a crude map sketched upon it. "That, my lord, is the city of Edgefield. It is, I believe, a regional capital, which means it is the only city of any consequence in the immediate vicinity."

"Remind me how this empire of theirs is organized."

"Halvaria is, it seems, divided into three parts called prefectures. Within each of these are three provinces, although I am led to understand they are large by our standards."

"How large?"

"If our sources are to be believed, a single province would be capable of holding both Merceria and Weldwyn, with land to spare."

"Are we to believe such a vast area could be governed by a single entity?"

"Not at all," replied Delsaran. "Each province is then divided into smaller regions, under the direction of a governor of sorts." The bard hesitated. "I am still trying to clarify the details, my lord, so I apologize for my ignorance about what these individuals are called."

"You have done remarkably well, all things considered. You say Edgefield is a regional capital. I assume that means it has a garrison?"

"Indeed, though not a legion. It appears legions are the offensive arm of the empire, while their cities are defended by what we consider a more traditional garrison."

Lord Arandil nodded his head absently, his eyes glued to the distant city. "Have we any idea of the size of this garrison?"

"Not an exact count, but from what I gleaned from interrogating the prisoners, I think it safe to assume it will be substantial. The empire appears to be a military institution, with most of its territory acquired through conquest. The presence of a strong army in the region would be needed to keep opposition to a minimum."

"So they oppress their own people?"

"I assume most go about their business with little interference from the government, my lord, but there are bound to be some who oppose being ruled by outsiders."

"You appear to be assuming a lot, Delsaran," said the Elven lord. "We are about to enter enemy territory, and I need to know as much about the enemy as possible."

"Shall I fetch Andurak, my lord? He may know more."

Lord Arandil considered the bard's suggestion. The Orc shaman had accompanied his army to allow communication with the Mercerian Marshal, Lord Matheson. Even though he found the Orcs irritating, he had to admit that the presence of one who could communicate across great distances had certain advantages.

"My lord?" prompted Delsaran.

Startled from his thoughts, the Lord of the Darkwood turned to his bard. "We are the first alliance army to march into Halvarian territory. I doubt he has much to add. I am interested, however, in knowing your thoughts on how to proceed."

"My thoughts? I am but a simple bard, my lord."

"I admire your modesty, Delsaran, but this is a time for boldness, not timidity. Were you the enemy, how would you garrison that city?"

"Considering their history, I would see to it the garrison was comprised of people taken from another region, which would ensure there was no regional loyalty amongst the troops should the locals rise up."

"That makes sense," replied Lord Arandil. "I suspect the enemy would too. Now, how many people would you say inhabit Edgefield?"

"I cannot say, my lord."

"You can see the city as well as I. How does it compare with those of Merceria?"

"I do not know. Aside from Stonecastle, I have never travelled outside the Darkwood. You campaigned with the Mercerians, did you not?"

"I did."

"And your conclusion, my lord?"

"Edgefield is considerably smaller than Wincaster, though I suspect it might rival the lesser cities, such as Tewsbury or Hawksburg."

"And how large are the garrisons there?"

"They are much smaller than what you suggested," replied Lord Arandil, "but then again, the Kingdom of Merceria isn't a conquered land ruled by an oppressive emperor."

"Then let me change your perspective," said Delsaran. "Were you in command of the empire, how many warriors would you station within its perimeter?"

"Hah! I see what you did there, my friend—a very shrewd move." Arandil pondered the bard's question. "I would not be surprised to discover a garrison of eight hundred or more; though, from this distance, I observe little in terms of defensive structures. The city has no walls, and from our viewpoint, there is no castle or keep. Under such conditions, their garrison would be better employed taking to a field of battle rather than hiding behind meagre defences."

"If word has reached them about their legion's defeat, they will be trying to raise more men."

"A good point. Let us put the garrison a little higher, then, shall we? Say, a thousand men?"

"That does not bode well for us, my lord. With numbers like that, we only have a small numerical advantage."

"We've got enough to defeat them."

"True, but victory over Edgefield requires us to leave a garrison there, thus weakening the rest of our army."

"You surprise me once again," said Arandil. "You are becoming a master strategist."

"I thank you for the compliment, my lord. Given these estimates, are we to march directly for Edgefield?"

"I do not command this army in isolation. I must confer with Vard Khazad and learn his wishes before proceeding any farther."

"Shall I fetch him?"

"Fetch him? He is the Vard of Stonecastle, not a common servant to be sent for. Invite him, on my behalf, to meet with me at his earliest convenience and suggest it might be beneficial for his commander to be present so that we may have the benefit of the fellow's thoughts."

"Yes, my lord."

The sun was starting to sink below the mountains as they gathered. Lord Arandil was joined by Lady Shalariel and several Elf captains, while the Dwarven Vard, Khazad, brought Commander Gelion along with his engineer, Golmar Hengesplitter.

"Over there"—the Elven lord pointed to the southeast of their present location—"is the city of Edgefield, our first objective in the empire's homeland."

Khazad looked east, squinting. "If you say so. All I see down there is a road leading off into nothing."

"My apologies," added Lord Arandil. "I sometimes forget that those of your race are not gifted with long-sight."

"No offence taken," replied the Dwarf. "I don't need to see it to know it's there. I trust your eyes. I suppose the reason you asked for this meeting is that you want to capture it?"

"It would provide us with a secure location from which we can extend our campaign into Halvaria."

"I might remind you this expedition is meant to draw the enemy away from Ironcliff, not conquer the empire. We destroyed the legion that came for Stonecastle and scattered them to the four winds, but we haven't the numbers to consider an extended campaign."

"True, but capturing that city forces Halvaria to take our threat seriously."

Khazad lifted his eye patch and rubbed the socket. "Aye. I can't very well argue with logic like that. How do you propose we proceed?"

"My intention is to lure their army out onto ground of our choosing."

"That suits me fine. We Dwarves are much better at fighting defensively, though I advise we proceed cautiously. There's a considerable amount of ground between us and that city, and I'd hate for someone to show up on our flank."

"Then I shall send riders out on either side," said Shalariel, "to watch for signs of enemy movement, as well as tasking them with collecting as much information about the region as possible. I want to confirm their numbers before we face them on the field of battle."

"It's their horses that worry me," said Khazad. "We Dwarves aren't exactly swift on our feet, and if there's one thing we learned from that legion of theirs, it's that they like their cavalry."

"Your concerns are noted," said Lord Arandil. "I assure you, we shall do all in our power to keep your forces intact." He shifted his gaze. "Have you anything to add, Commander Gelion?"

"How many roads lead from that one down there to Edgefield?" asked the Dwarf.

"Only the one, though others branch off as it goes along."

"Then I propose we send the Army of Stonecastle straight down that road, with your Elves on either side. You're much more mobile than us and can react faster to any threat that presents itself. As for our deployment, I'd alternate our foot with our arbalesters, allowing us to improvise a quick redeployment should that prove necessary. Have we any idea how long it will be before we are in contact with the enemy?"

"That largely depends on how they respond," replied Shalariel. "At our present pace, it could be a week or more before we see any serious challenge to our presence."

"Then we are in agreement," said Lord Arandil. "We shall commence the second phase of our campaign first thing tomorrow."

NINETEEN

Southport

SUMMER 968 MC

The ship rocked gently at anchor but it was still enough to make Brogar clutch the handrail. "This is madness," he said. "We Dwarves belong on land, not sailing around on flimsy pieces of wood."

"We shall be ashore soon enough." Althea pointed towards the docks. "Once we're all on solid ground, we'll follow the coast eastward, then turn north and cross into Merceria at Colbridge."

"What did you say the name of this city was?"

"Southport. Why?"

"Much as I hate to ask, why aren't we sailing straight on to Bramwitch? That's farther east, isn't it?"

"It is, but it's more of a fishing town."

"Why does that matter?"

"They pull their boats up onto the shore each night." She noticed his look of confusion. "It means they don't have a proper dock, and it would take forever to unload everyone by ship's boat."

"It's just as well," replied Brogar. "I'd much rather march for days on end than spend another moment aboard this thing." To emphasize his point, he slapped the railing.

Glisnak appeared beside them, standing on the tips of his toes to peer over the railing. "Big enclave," he said.

"We started at Loranguard," replied Althea, "and that's much larger. And for the record, it's called a city, not an enclave."

"Ah, yes. Big pile of Humans. How many live there?" He pointed towards the city.

"A few thousand, although I can't be absolutely certain."

"Thousand? Glisnak not understand the word." He possessed a ring that allowed him to speak the common tongue of Humans, but there were still concepts beyond his comprehension.

"You remember Drakewell," replied Althea. "Now, imagine a whole bunch of Drakewells clustered together, and you wouldn't be too far off the mark."

"Drakewell is already much larger than Stonewall. How many Drakewells make up Southport?"

"At least six groups of six sixes." She smiled, for she'd learned about the Goblins' preference to think in terms of the number six. It had the desired effect, although she could swear she saw a vein ready to pop on the Goblin's bare head as he worked out the numbers. It wasn't his fault: Goblins weren't unintelligent, merely uneducated in the ways of Human civilization, but her experiences of the last few months taught her they were quick to learn.

Glisnak shook his head. "I must tell Grazuk. She will be most interested." He turned, ready to rush below, but lingered for a moment. "Will the Humans of Southport fear Quickpaw?"

"Yes," replied Brogar before Althea could answer. "But we Dwarves will debark first and reassure the townsfolk that you are allies." He looked at his mistress. "I assume you have no objection? She is a mountain wolf after all."

"None whatsoever," replied the princess.

"Good. I'll head below decks and inform the Dragon Company that we'll be heading ashore."

Glisnak watched the Dwarf disappear through a hatch. "Brogar not like being on water."

"Do you?" asked Althea. "This must be very strange for you, being so far from home, especially travelling across a large body of water."

The Goblin shrugged. "It is far too exciting for me to worry about such things."

A loud bang sang out. They both jumped, then looked towards the ship's bow, where the crew had just dropped a boarding ramp to facilitate access to the wharf.

"I must go," added Glisnak. "My people will be eager to see this." With that, he was off, disappearing below with such speed that it defied all logic. The Goblins were a dexterous people, their small stature proving an immense advantage aboard the cramped confines of a ship.

Althea moved to the other side of the deck, staring out into the bay. The remainder of the fleet, small as it was, stood at anchor, awaiting their turn to unload their cargo of warriors. Darkness would have descended by the time all was said and done, meaning the march couldn't begin until tomorrow morning. She hoped they wouldn't be too late, for they hadn't received any news about the invasion of Merceria for some time.

A voice beckoned her from the dock. "Highness?"

She returned to the port side and noticed a well-dressed courtier waving to get her attention. "You wanted me?" she called back.

"I bear greetings from Lord Beric Canning, Earl of Southport. He invites you to dine with him this evening."

"I should be happy to, providing I can bring my advisors?"

Her request caught the man off guard, but he recovered quickly. "I shall inform His Lordship of your decision, Highness. Might I enquire as to numbers?"

Althea considered whom to bring. She had to take Brogar—he was her bodyguard, but who else? Her husband, Lochlan, was aboard the *Tempest*, waiting to unload his warriors, but surely he would be finished before dinner was served. "Three," she said at last, then corrected herself. "No, make that five."

She smiled, wondering how the earl would react to two Goblins at his table. It suddenly struck her that she had no idea how Glisnak might react to sitting at a dining room table to eat, let alone his pit-sister, Virdu.

There was, however, the satisfaction of knowing it was Lord Beric's problem, not hers, for the earl had objected to her marriage to Lochlan. Rumour had it, he'd supported the idea of marrying her off to Lord Elgin, enabling Elgin to claim the Throne instead of her brother Alric. Perhaps Beric was attempting to make amends for the insult, but Althea wasn't in a forgiving mood, particularly today, as she prepared to march to war.

Lord Beric's manor house matched the opulence of the Royal Palace in Summersgate; at least it did before the dragon had destroyed it. The invaders had captured Southport during the war but had seen fit to leave this manor house intact instead of plundering its contents, a situation most beneficial for the Cannings.

Althea arrived on foot, as did her companions. Glisnak chattered excitedly with Virdu in their native Garspeak, a language that consisted of rushed words spoken in a relatively high tone, at least compared to Humans.

"Impressive," said Brogar, "though I don't much fancy those columns. They don't look strong enough to support the roof."

"They're decorative," replied Althea. "It's a common enough sight in Summersgate. I'm surprised you haven't seen their like before."

"Oh, I have; I just don't particularly like them. To my mind, there's no sense in having a column if it doesn't perform some useful function."

"I've seen Mirstone myself, Brogar. Not all the columns there were built out of necessity."

"I'll give you that, but you must admit, we Dwarves build decorative columns on a much grander scale."

"On that, we can agree. Now, shall we go see what His Lordship has to offer in the way of food, or do you wish to remain out here, critiquing the architecture all night long?"

The Dwarf grinned, rubbing his hands together. "Let's go and eat, shall we?"

Two guards bedecked in the green-and-yellow livery of the Earl of Southport stood at the door. One snapped to attention and held his sword out in salute while his companion opened the door and stepped aside.

Althea nodded before she proceeded, the rest of her party trailing along behind her. The same fellow who'd approached her at the dock met them.

"Is Lord Lochlan here yet?" she asked.

"Not yet," the man replied, "but we received word he'd be arriving soon. I believe he had to arrange supplies on behalf of your army?"

"I told you," said Brogar. "You've taught him to look after all the details."

"He's always been a scholar at heart," she replied. "His attention to detail is what makes him stand out from all the others."

"Others?" said Glisnak. "What others?"

"It's an expression," replied Brogar. "It's meant to imply he's exceptional."

"Just like Glisnak. Glisnak very different from other Goblins."

The Dwarf chuckled. "Yes, you are."

Virdu uttered something, but no one, save her pit-brother, understood.

"What did she say?" asked Brogar.

"She said Virdu is special, just like Glisnak."

"She understood what we said?"

"Yes. Her mastery of the common tongue is improving, though she does better listening than talking."

The earl's man cleared his throat. "If you'll follow me, Highness, I shall escort you to the dining room."

"Thank you," said Althea. "You may proceed."

He guided them along a long hallway that led to the very back of the manor, where a pair of double doors stood, one set on each side of the wall. "This way," he said, opening the ones on the left that led into a large room holding an immense table.

Lord Beric sat at the far end but rose as the door opened. "Ah, Highness. So good of you to accept my invitation." He kept smiling as he took in

Brogar, but at the sight of the Goblins, his eyes twitched in irritation. "I'm afraid you have the advantage of me," he said, recovering quickly. "Would you be so kind to introduce your companions?"

"Of course," she replied. "This is Brogar Hammerhand, one of my advisors." She swept her arm to indicate the Goblins. "And this is Glisnak, Chieftain of the Stonewall Enclave and Virdu, the Shaman of Stonewall."

"Bender," corrected Virdu.

"I'm sorry?" said the earl.

"My apologies," said Althea. "Virdu is indeed a bender rather than a shaman."

"Which is?"

"One skilled in bending bones back into shape."

"Isn't that the same thing as a shaman?"

"Unlike shamans, benders utilize poison on occasion. They also don't talk to their Ancestors like the Orcs do."

Lord Beric stared back, not exactly sure how to respond. Finally, he swept his hands towards the chairs. "Please, sit. I shall have the servants bring us some food."

They took seats, the two Goblins watching with interest as other servants pulled chairs out for them.

"I trust your journey was uneventful, Highness?"

"We are marching to war, my lord. I doubt anything proves eventful when compared to that."

"I must admit to some surprise. I wasn't aware the Clans employed the smaller green folk."

"They are our allies, not warriors for hire."

"The difference being?"

"They came of their own free will at no cost to us, volunteering their services to aid in freeing Merceria from the invasion of their land."

"And what do they expect in return—plunder?"

"We came to help Al-tea," replied Glisnak. "Is that not common between allies?"

"Allies?" the earl scoffed. "Allies bring armies, not collections of pint-sized raiders."

Althea stood, her legs shoving the chair away from her. "You insult the Clans, my lord, not to mention the character of our allies. I would consider carefully your next words, or you might find yourself in displeasure at the court of my brother, King Alric."

"My apologies, Highness. I did not intend to demean the nature of these Goblin friends of yours. I merely call into question the quality of their contribution. They are less than half the height of a Human warrior. Do you seriously expect them to pose a threat to the Halvarians?"

"Glisnak and his companions assisted us in the killing of a dragon. I can think of nothing more dangerous to illustrate how much of a threat they can be when the occasion demands it. Can you?"

"No. I suppose not."

"Tell me, Your Earldom," said Brogar. "Are you in the habit of insulting the Royals of Weldwyn, or is this a special occasion?"

"That's 'my lord' or 'Your Grace' to you, Dwarf. Know your place."

"Brogar's place is at my side," said Althea, "and as for your own hospitality, I can only assume it comes with an ulterior motive. I think it's time we left." She waited as her party stood, then strode from the room, the rest marching behind her in solidarity.

They'd stormed out the front door and were already halfway down the path when Lochlan appeared, surprise overtaking him at meeting her here. "Am I too late?" he asked.

"No," said Althea. "You're just in time." She marched right past him, grabbing his hand to pull him along.

"Where are we going?"

"Some place where we'll be welcomed with open arms."

Glisnak watched the Army of the West, as he liked to call it, march past, his own modest group of Goblins standing to one side. Clan warriors led the column, while behind them came the men of Weldwyn, a smaller group hastily raised by their king.

"*There are so many of them,*" noted Virdu in Garspeak. "*In contrast, we are few, like the flies that swarm the carcass of a dead animal.*"

"*Perhaps,*" he replied, "*but flies multiply fast. Left to their own devices, they would quickly grow to enormous numbers.*"

"*Is that your plan for Stonewall? You want to reduce our losses of runts, but is that for the betterment of all or to make us more of a threat?*"

"*I have no desire to expand beyond the walls of our mine.*"

"*Yet here we are, marching to fight the war of others.*"

Glisnak nodded. "*That we are, but we do this to show we have value. Our part in this campaign may be small, but it demonstrates we will do all we can to help our friends in their time of need.*"

"*Friends? We know no one from Merceria.*"

"*True, but they are friends to Al-tea, and it is important to her, making it important to us.*"

Virdu mulled it over. "*This is not typically our way, Glisnak. Most enclaves grow more aggressive when their numbers swell, leading to conflict with others.*"

"*Or themselves. Perhaps this is a better way. By directing our natural tendencies towards outsiders, we avoid such violence.*"

"*You are a strange one, pit-brother. Never before have I seen one of our race who thinks so much about the welfare of our people.*"

"*You make it sound like something bad.*"

"*Not bad,*" she corrected, "*just different. Your rule over Stonewall has allowed our numbers to flourish, but we have yet to see the long-term effects of that. I hope we will prosper, but you must not be surprised if the inborn violence of our people overwhelms us in time.*"

"*It won't,*" he replied.

"*How can you be so certain?*"

"*I have given this a great deal of consideration. I believe the violence of our people is the result of idleness. When an enclave grows, there are more hunters than are needed to support the enclave. Resentment builds as those out seeking food work, while those who remain behind turn their efforts to prove their worth in other ways.*"

"*Yes,*" added Virdu, "*by trying to display their dominance over others. It is an age-old tale, but what makes you believe you can stop it?*"

"*I will keep them busy,*" he replied. "*Unlike other enclaves, Stonewall trades with the Humans, which requires more diggers in addition to all the other roles taken on by our people.*"

"*Is that why you want to train more tinkers?*"

"*It makes sense, doesn't it? We mine iron, but the value of our trade would increase greatly if we made objects of iron instead of selling off the ore.*"

"*Where in the name of the mountain did you get that idea?*"

"*From the Humans. Look around you, pit-sister, and you will see all manner of things—things they call 'finished goods.'*"

"*Like the armour of our grunts?*"

"*Yes! Flint has already learned much from the Dwarves. One day, he will master making metal armour, and that will fetch a high price.*"

"*To what end? What are coins to a Goblin?*"

"*Remember Snarlak?*"

"*Of course. He was a brutal chieftain who very nearly killed you. He ruled because he had the toughest Goblins helping him.*"

"*Yes, and everyone else was envious because he had the best weapons, the best food, the best everything.*"

"*What is it you're getting at?*"

"*More coins means more of the things everyone craves, enough to fill everyone's belly and keep them from feeling the pangs of hunger. A well-fed Goblin will be interested in other matters: better weapons, armour, that sort of thing."*

Virdu's wide smile revealed her pointed teeth. *"Which you are already doing by having Flint make better stuff for everyone. You are clever, Glisnak. A lesser Goblin would have kept the wealth to themself; by sharing it, you are buying the loyalty of all."*

"My intent is not to use coins to purchase support. Doing such opens the enclave to the influence of others with coins. Remember the Red Wizard?"

"I could hardly forget. He was a blight on our people and nearly led us into a war. His death was a turning point in all our lives. But if not to buy loyalty, why covet coins?"

"To make our people's lives better. From what I have learned of Humans, when they are happy, they are prosperous, but war is the result when anger rules."

"Like what we are now marching towards?" Virdu chuckled. *"We may not be fighting the Red Wizard's war, but we are still seeking battle, although it's at least far from our home."*

"You do not approve?"

"You are my chieftain and my pit-brother. I shall follow you to the end of my days, but I'll let your head worry about these things instead of mine."

Grazuk rode over on Quickpaw, halting to offer a slight nod of her head. *"The end of the army is approaching, Glisnak. How would you like us to proceed: lobbers first or the grunts?"*

"I think the wolf riders should lead, don't you? They're the most important."

Grazuk visibly straightened, her grin spreading across her face. *"It shall be as you command."* She turned and rejoined the rest of their small horde, ordering them into place.

"She is good, that one," said Virdu. *"As is Tarzil. Rare is the chieftain who can leave others in charge and expect to return without a challenge."*

"They have come to believe as I have," he replied.

"As 'we' have," she corrected. *"Remember, in this, you are not alone."*

TWENTY

The Temple Fleet

SUMMER 968 MC

"**M**ost curious," noted Cyric. "I always assumed that Halvarian warships were the grandest on the seas, but your new ships put them to shame."

"Ours are three masters, like the empire's," replied Danica, "and they might be a little longer, but the biggest difference is the hull. Ours are slightly narrower, making them much more seaworthy."

"I'm surprised to hear you say that. I was under the impression Halvaria's warships have dominated the seas for decades."

"And they did, but only in their primary role of supporting their legions. The empire designs its ships to hug the coast, not sail in the treacherous waters of the Great Northern Sea, which we learned after we captured some of their ships at the Battle of Temple Bay. We initially tried to copy their design, but their shortcomings soon came back to haunt us. As a result, we designed a new boat from the keel up, giving us the *Redoubtable* here, along with her sister ships."

"From what you've shown me so far, I'm quite impressed. Have you always been so knowledgeable concerning ships?"

"I was born in a fishing village," replied the admiral, "but aside from small boats, I had minimal sea experience. You might say it was joining the order that excited my passion, though it took some time."

"And we are the better for it." Cyric glanced towards the stern, where Aubrey leaned over the railing, peering at the sea. "Careful, my lady. That's a long drop."

She straightened and came towards them. "Might I ask a question?"

"Of course," replied the admiral.

"How many ships have you in your Temple Fleet?"

"Seventeen are currently afloat."

"Meaning you have more under construction?"

"We do," said Danica, "but they are meant only as replacements for older vessels." She moved to the railing, pointing. "That ship over there is the first of the fleet, the *Valiant*. She was originally designed as a fast merchant, but she's getting a bit long in the tooth."

"She has a strange sail compared to the others."

"Yes, her triangular one allows us to sail closer to the wind."

"Closer?" said Aubrey. "I'm afraid I'm not familiar with sailing terminology."

"It means she can sail almost directly into the wind, a task that's difficult for most other vessels. *Valiant* and her sister ship, the *Valour*, are both equipped with similar sails, while the third sister, the *Vigilant*, is of a more traditional arrangement."

"Do all your ships begin with a 'V'?"

"We've taken to naming them based on their design. The Valiant class is our smallest, while the *Fearless* and *Illustrious* are captured Halvarian vessels. This ship is our own design, as I was just explaining to Brother Cyric."

"Were you serious about intending to sail all the way to Merceria's shores?"

"We Temple Sisters tend not to joke about such things. Why? Do you doubt our resolve?"

"Your resolve? No. I'm more worried about numbers. I'm told the fleet off our coast is immense."

"It wouldn't be the first time we were outnumbered. Are you familiar with the Battle of Lidenbach?"

"No, but I'm open to learning more."

"As am I," added Cyric. "That was back in oh-three, was it not?"

"It was," replied the admiral. "We'd been expecting the empire to take some sort of naval action in support of their invasion of Arnsfeld. Their fleet left their home port and sailed with a large complement of warriors, aiming to land them behind the Army of Arnsfeld and cut them off from the capital."

She scanned the nearby ships, then pointed. "That ship there, the *Furious*, was my flagship. Our forces then numbered nine vessels, although one was the *Sprite*, a tiny ship we used to carry messages."

"And against you?" asked Cyric.

"Fifteen warships, along with four immense cogs they used to transport the bulk of their warriors. Several of their warships were large three-masted vessels, though the majority had two."

"It must've been quite the battle."

"It was," replied Danica, "and could've ended in disaster had it not been for the quick thinking of our crews. As it was, we ended up losing the *Invincible*, but that pales in comparison to what we achieved. Four enemy warships were lost to fire, while we captured seven, which doesn't include the cogs, which all ran aground and were destroyed."

"So some warships escaped?"

"They did, but once the battle was over, we tracked them down, and just last year, we caught the final one, the *Majestic*, sheltering in a secluded bay in Halvarian waters. It now rests at the bottom of the sea, or rather, its charred remains do."

"Fascinating."

"But is it enough?" asked Aubrey. "The fleet off our coast is enormous."

"I would need more information, naturally, but I suspect the bulk of those vessels are cogs used to transport their warriors. Was it an entire legion that landed?"

"It was."

"A legion numbers twenty-four hundred men at full strength, requiring a significant number of transports, which represent little in the way of a threat to the Temple Fleet, but their warships are another matter. Is there any way for you to learn more about them?"

"My magic allows me to communicate over great distances, and my understanding is that Albreda viewed the fleet from above, so she may be able to provide the answers you seek."

"Even so," said Cyric, "they're likely to have dozens of warships to guard a legion. You can't possibly send your entire fleet; you'd need to keep some here to stop the pirates from taking over once again."

Admiral Danica smiled. "There's more than one way to even the odds." She ushered them along the deck to the foremast, where a tarp covered a large object. "Ever seen one of these?" she said, pulling off the tarp.

"It looks like a Dwarven arbalest," said Aubrey. "The Dwarves in our area use them, though this appears much larger."

"That's because it is. This particular deck-mounted arbalest was designed and constructed by a good friend of the order, along with several highly specialized bolts."

"Meaning?"

"We can use it to grapple an enemy vessel, damage its sails, or…" She reached down into a box mounted at the weapons base and retrieved an odd-looking bolt with what looked like a bulb of clay instead of the usual metal head. "This particular bolt head shatters upon impact, spewing a sticky substance that burns on contact with air. Do you remember the *Majestic* I mentioned earlier? We used a bolt like this to set it alight."

"How many of these do you have access to?" asked Cyric.

"They're difficult to produce, but every warship of the fleet is equipped with three or four. For safety's sake, we only keep one up here in the locker, with the rest stored below in special containers to prevent accidents."

"Remarkable."

"We also have another advantage," continued the admiral. "The fighting complement of all our ships consists of Temple Knights equipped with plate armour, which makes a difference when compared to Halvarian naval troops."

"These are multipliers," said Cyric. "By that, I mean it allows each ship to be as effective as two or three. Taking that into account, you could conceivably attack with only a third of their strength in warships, providing you have that many to spare."

"As I mentioned to General Fitzwilliam," said Danica, "I'm more than comfortable navigating unknown waters, but my ships would need to replenish both food and water before engaging the enemy."

"Not after?" asked Aubrey.

"I must consider the possibility of a loss, in which case, we'd have no time to take on supplies. I shouldn't like testing the odds of trying to sail back here with empty stomachs and parched mouths."

"The nearest friendly port to the invasion sight would be Southport."

"Are you familiar with it?"

"I am," replied Aubrey. "During the campaign to retake Weldwyn, I was there when it was liberated. It could easily accommodate all these ships." She swept her arm to encompass those vessels nearby.

"Excellent. Let me know what you learn about the empire's fleet the next time you contact home. If I'm not up at the duke's estate, I'll be here, aboard the *Redoubtable*."

"I'm due to contact Kraloch this very evening."

"Then I look forward to our next conversation."

"There were hundreds of ships," said Kraloch, "but Albreda's report indicates the vast majority were small, likely there to expedite ferrying the warriors ashore."

"And the rest of the fleet?" Aubrey found herself holding her breath in anticipation. If the number was too large, it would doom the idea of a naval expedition to free the coast. She forced herself to relax.

"Seventeen larger ships, likely traders the empire called upon to transport men with horses."

"And warships?"

"That is difficult to say. From a bird's point of view, there is little difference between a warship and one carrying cargo. Albreda only identified the transports because they had no sign of warriors remaining aboard their decks."

"Did any utilize catapults or other visible engines of war?"

"Yes, at least twenty, although they vary considerably in size. She also couldn't identify the purpose of some vessels due to a lack of anything noteworthy on the deck, and she only had so much time left on her spell. Albreda is a powerful mage, but even she has limits to her magic."

"Thank you," said Aubrey. "You've been most informative."

"There is more," offered the Orc. "She has travelled to Ironcliff with Herdwin and Kasri, and the marshal believes the siege will soon be lifted thanks to her help."

"Have you any details?"

"None at present, but I will let you know when I learn more."

"Have we any news from Lord Arandil?"

"We have," replied Kraloch. "Andurak reports the Dwarves and Elves entered the empire's lands and are marching towards a city called Edgefield." He took a breath. "There is also the matter of the marshal's strategy against the empire."

"I understand. You want to know what we've decided," said Aubrey. "We voted unanimously to remain here in the Petty Kingdoms and see this thing through to the end."

"The marshal will be pleased. How did the Duke of Reinwick respond?"

"We haven't gotten to that yet," replied Aubrey. "They're concerned with the legions to the south right now, not taking the fight to the lands of the enemy."

"Will the Northern Alliance march to Erlingen's aid?"

"That largely depends on King Dagmar of Andover, but it's looking more likely, thanks to recent events."

"Why? What has happened?"

"Someone tried to murder Beverly in her sleep. The attackers were slain, but Brother Cyric is of the opinion they were Temple Knights of Saint Cunar."

Kraloch's ghostly image nodded. "That would fit with what I have heard about their order. Therengia has had nothing but trouble from them in the past. Speaking of Therengia, has there been any word from Galina about a response?"

"From what I understand, Natalia cannot make that decision herself. She has to take the information to the ruling council, which requires all the thanes of Therengia to travel to one location. We just have to be patient."

"I must stress how important this is. Therengia has an experienced army, not to mention multiple shamans, which will allow instant communication, much like we do here in Merceria. Such tactics would give our new allies a great advantage."

"I'm well aware," replied Aubrey, "and Beverly's stressing that to the duke, but there's only so much we can do without upsetting people. As to their army, she's brought up the idea of the Ashwalkers lending the aid of their shamans, but from what I've seen, the Orcs don't have many."

"This is sad news," said Kraloch. "I was hoping they would be able to play a larger role."

"If it's any consolation, their hunters make a sizable contribution to the alliance's army."

"Have we any idea of numbers?"

"Three hundred is my understanding, and if they're anything like your own tribe, I expect half would be archers. The good news is they have masters of fire, so we have something to counter the possibility of enemy mages."

"An interesting development, but our experience against the empire indicates they rarely employ their spellcasters in battle: rather, they use them in a support role like crossing Kharzun's Folly."

"Then the addition of masters of fire on our side gives us an advantage."

"I shall inform the marshal of all we discussed."

"And I shall meet with the admiral to relay the information about the Halvarian fleet and see if she's still interested in sailing to Merceria. I look forward to our next conversation."

"As do I."

Aubrey broke the connection, the Orc shaman's image fading away.

"*Did you learn anything new?*" asked Krazuhk.

"*You startled me,*" the Life Mage replied, effortlessly switching to Orcish. "*I wasn't even aware you were here.*"

"*You were deep in the throes of your spell when I arrived. I did not want to interrupt. I bring news from the Ashwalkers.*"

"*You asked them about the malroot?*"

"*I did. It is scarce in these parts, but the tribe used to live farther south, on the northwest border of Andover, where it is more plentiful. However, it is a notoriously difficult plant to identify, often being mistaken for greenweed.*"

"*Meaning it would take considerable expertise to identify it.*"

"That would be my assumption as well. It also means those attackers had some knowledge of its preparation, for it loses its potency quickly."

"How quickly?"

"A day, perhaps two. In its weakened state, it causes drowsiness instead of death. Could it have been their aim to abduct Lady Beverly rather than kill her?"

"I doubt it," replied Aubrey. *"It's one thing to sneak into the duke's estate, quite another to carry an unconscious body away without raising any suspicion. There's also the matter of Aldwin. I doubt three assailants could have carried both Beverly and Aldwin at the same time."*

"We should be thankful they failed," said Krazuhk. *"Her loss would have dealt the Petty Kingdoms a heavy blow."*

"Tell that to the duke. I don't believe he's entirely convinced of her value."

"Perhaps, but I suspect that will soon change. I have talked at great length with Rugal, Chieftain of the Ashwalkers, and he believes, as do I, that Beverly is the key to the success of this campaign."

"How? Her command of the Army of Erlingen was a temporary measure, and it's unlikely the duke or the king will grant her a similar position over their forces."

"True," replied Krazuhk. *"But you must take a broader view of things. If our efforts here bear fruit, we will see the Northern Alliance and Erlingen working together, perhaps even Therengia. I doubt any of those armies would support handing over command of their warriors to another realm. Beverly, on the other hand, is an outsider with no troops of her own."*

"I see your logic," said Aubrey, *"and she certainly has the experience and the expertise. I'm just not certain we can convince all the others of that fact."*

"Then we shall take it one step at a time. Did I hear you mention the Temple Fleet?"

"You did. I now have an assessment of the number of Halvarian ships sitting off the coast of Merceria, but I'm afraid it's not good news. They appear to possess a significant numerical advantage compared to what those Temple Knights can muster."

"You must trust in the admiral's expertise in the matter, much as we would trust in yours when treating a patient. Tell her what you know and let her make her own decision."

"Wise words. Anything else you'd care to share?"

"Yes, there is. There are forces working here which we have little to no understanding of, forces that saw fit to deliver your group to where and when you were needed most."

"Are you suggesting the Gods sent us here?"

"Gods, Saints, Ancestors: it matters little to whom we attribute this good fortune. What does matter is how you seize this opportunity to bring about a victory over the empire."

"And by 'you' you mean 'we'. You're a part of this too."

"I suppose I am," said Krazuhk. "It is strange to think that not so long ago, I was but a master of air in training. Now, here I am, many ten-days from home, assisting in the greatest war to ever engulf Eiddenwerthe—at least in recent history."

"You're talking about the Great War between the Elves and Orcs. What do you know of it?"

"Not much. As you are aware, we Orcs do not maintain a written history. Ours is passed down through the Ancestors and word of mouth. We know only that our people were driven from their cities, forced to live a life of wandering hunters and that our numbers dwindled as a result, but we tend not to dwell in the past. If you wanted to learn more, you would need to talk to the Elves, for their lifespans mean that they could have experienced it in person."

"And if we should encounter Elves here in the Petty Kingdoms?"

"I do not understand the question."

"This Halvarian invasion spares no one. It's quite probable that the Elves will eventually come into conflict with the empire. My question to you is how you feel about that, considering what they did to your people."

"That would largely depend on the Elves. To my people, that is but a distant event, but the Elves are said to have longer memories. Having said that, it would be in both our interests to defeat the empire. You have Elves back in Merceria, do you not?"

"We do," replied Aubrey. "But Lord Arandil is an exception. He brought his people into seclusion rather than take part in the destruction of your people."

"And do your Elves and Orcs get along?"

"For the most part, yes, although they have differences of opinion every now and again. We try to keep them separate on the battlefield to avoid such conflicts."

"Then let us hope the same can be done here."

TWENTY-ONE

Countermarch

SUMMER 968 MC

Edora Sartellian had stripped the frontier of its occupation force to ensure she possessed the numbers necessary to march into Erlingen, a campaign that, until now, she'd been loathe to continue. The news from the east, however, had changed the situation dramatically.

She waited until all three of her commander-generals were present. Hamath Nordin had died in battle, leaving the Fifth Legion, now battered and bruised, under the command of the former captain-general of the First Cohort, Joachim Battista. His reputation as a fierce warrior had been proven true in the legion's most recent battle, in which, despite the loss, he'd still distinguished himself. Unfortunately, the losses incurred there reduced his legion to less than half its full strength, presenting problems for the coming march into Erlingen.

Vorinus Moreau, Commander of the Ninth Legion, had the most victories under his belt in this campaign and was eager to add to the list. The last was Umberto Rakert, commanding the Eighth Legion. His men had been pacifying the recently conquered Kingdom of Gotfeld, but Edora had seen fit to pass that duty over to the Eleventh. Now, they were within a three-day march of the Fifth and Ninth Legions, giving her army a much-needed boost in numbers.

There was no love lost between these men, for each craved influence and notoriety, which only came with a victory where you didn't have to share it with others.

Edora cleared her throat, causing them all to pay attention. "We have good news," she began. "Our allies are finally on the move and ready to play their part."

"Allies?" said Rakert. "I was under the impression we were alone in this?"

"That was by design," replied Edora. "I thought it best to limit knowledge of my full plan until I could put it in motion."

Moreau's wrinkled nose and pursed lips belied his frustration at being kept in the dark. "And who might these so-called 'allies' be? Are you certain we can trust them?"

"They are a highly disciplined and battle-hardened order of knights who we've swayed to our side."

"And has this order a name?"

"Indeed." She paused, knowing her answer would shock them. "The Temple Knights of Saint Cunar."

Battista spat out his wine. "The Cunars? Are you mad? They're sworn to oppose us!"

"Not anymore, they're not. Years ago, our people infiltrated their order, and ever since, they've been working their way to the very top. Once there, they broke the backs of the other fighting orders and are now dedicated to helping us conquer the remaining Petty Kingdoms."

"But the other orders weren't disbanded," said Rakert. "We've fought against Agnesites three times during this campaign and Mathewites at least once."

"They are no more than a few scattered companies, hastily assembled in an attempt to slow our advance."

"Pardon me for asking," added Moreau, "but how are these newfound allies of ours to help us?"

"I received word this morning that the Army of the Antonine, as we like to call it, is marching through the Petty Kingdoms even as we speak. They've already brushed aside the meagre army Ulrichen had assembled and are ready to threaten Erlingen directly."

"What about the armies of Ardosa and Galoran?"

"They, too, have been crushed by the might of the Church."

"Have we any idea of their numbers?"

"As of this moment," replied Edora, "they are fielding twelve hundred men, the bulk of which are Temple Knights."

"I would've thought they'd all be Temple Knights," said Rakert.

"Not so. The army recruited from the conquered regions as it advanced north. There are now footmen and archers flocking to the 'Holy War' against what they've been told are heretics in Erlingen."

"Have we a timetable for their arrival?"

"We do," said Edora. "They will cross the border within the week and advance on Torburg, the duke's capital. To take full advantage of this development, we will shortly be crossing the border ourselves."

"Shortly?" said Moreau. "I would've thought speed of the essence. Are we not to combine our legions with this Holy Army to wipe out Erlingen?"

"No. The plan is to wait until the duke's army withdraws back to Torburg to face this new threat. Once we have confirmation they are in retreat, we cross but keep our distance. We will eventually engage, but not until they're committed to a battle with the Temple Knights."

"Crushing them between us? A brilliant strategy, but what if the Northern Alliance comes to their rescue?"

"Then we shall save ourselves a lot of work. We have two and a half legions at our disposal, gentlemen, with half a legion of Cunars on top of that. That is more than enough to deal with the numbers they can field, assuming they even make it here in time to be of any assistance."

"True," added Rakert, "and our legions are used to working together, whereas the so-called Northern Alliance—Reinwick and Andover—were fighting each other only two years ago."

They were all smiles, save for Battista.

"What troubles you?" asked Edora.

"General Fitzwilliam. She's already pulled one victory out from under her cloak. How do we know she hasn't something else under her helmet?"

"She caught your predecessor by surprise," said Moreau. "One of the things the empire's legions are good at is learning from past mistakes."

"That's easy for you to say," said Battista. "You weren't there. Her presence alone is worth a thousand men, possibly more."

"I couldn't agree more," replied Edora, "which is why we've taken steps to remove her from the picture."

"What steps?"

She smiled. "The court of Reinwick is easily infiltrated. By now, she's resting comfortably in a coffin somewhere."

"I admire your confidence, but I'll believe she's dead when I see the body for myself."

"It's not practical to bring her body here, but perhaps I can arrange for the man responsible to come here in person. Would that soothe your ill humour?"

"It would."

"Good. Now, I suggest you all get a good night's sleep, gentlemen. Beginning tomorrow, you must prepare your legions to cross the river into Erlingen."

Joachim Battista stared across the water. His legion was charged with crossing the river and seizing the village of Grozen, which, as far as they knew, held no garrison. To put it bluntly, this task was a deliberate insult—the Fifth's punishment for being defeated by the Army of Erlingen. It had not been his fault, for he'd been under the orders of his predecessor at the time, but the defeat still stung. Battista had not sought promotion. He'd been happy commanding a single cohort, but now it appeared fate had revealed a new destiny for him, one that would bring him fame and ever-lasting glory to the empire.

He looked to his left, where the remains of the Fifth Legion waited to cross. The three Water Mages who'd accompanied the legion were supposed to do something with the water to allow his men to cross, but the seasoned veteran harboured doubts. They'd assured him that such a tactic worked to perfection in Arnsfeld seven years ago, yet that campaign failed spectacularly. True, the water crossing had succeeded, as the riverbed there had proven quite passable, yet he suspected they would encounter nothing but silt and mud here, which was sure to cause delays.

He turned to his aide, a sergeant named Marfor, a veteran of more than a dozen campaigns. "You may inform the mages they are to begin."

"Yes, sir." Marfor marched off, heading straight for them.

Battista considered himself a patient man, but he found the mages an annoyance. If he had his way, he'd have used boats to cross instead of relying on magic, but word had come from the marshal to proceed in this manner, so he'd reluctantly agreed.

He watched Marfor interact with the mages; though, from this distance, he couldn't hear what was being said. The sergeant then left them, heading directly for his superior. He'd noticed a certain attitude to these mages, for they were Stormwinds, a powerful family who didn't take well to orders. Even now, with the eyes of the empire on them, they remained in place rather than proceeding to the water's edge.

Sergeant Marfor came to attention before his new commander-general. "They've been informed, sir, but they don't appear to be in any hurry to carry out your orders."

"That is to be expected," replied Battista. "They are mages, after all, not warriors."

"Are you implying they won't follow orders?"

"Oh, they will… eventually, or they'll be forced to endure the displeasure of Edora Sartellian. Unfortunately, since she's not here, we'll have to put up with their petulant behaviour, at least until we're on Erlingen soil."

"It's not too late to build rafts, sir."

"We have close to twelve hundred men to cross, Sergeant. I think you underestimate the time required for such an endeavour."

Marfor fell silent and, like his commander, watched the three mages with intense interest. The trio finally moved to the riverbank and began waving their hands around in the air, presumably to conjure forth whatever magical power lay within them. One bent down, touching the surface of the water. Battista was unsure what was happening at first, but then he noticed the water solidifying as it turned to ice. The other two mages joined in, placing their hands on the frozen water, the ice thickening as it spread out into the main channel of the river.

Battista watched, fascinated, as the ice crept across to the far bank. "It seems our friends, the Stormwinds, aren't going to lower the water after all."

"Will the ice bear the weight of our cavalry, sir?"

"It had better, or I'll see to it personally that those mages take the blame. Just to be on the safe side, though, we'll send our foot across first."

"Permission to go with the lead elements, sir?"

"Eager to make a name for yourself, are you?"

"I've fought the length and breadth of the empire, sir. It would be nice to be in front for the final campaign."

"I admire your spirit, Marfor. Get yourself over there and take the first company across, and if their captain gives you any trouble, tell him it was my decision."

The sergeant grinned before he marched off, his back stiffened with resolve. Battista watched as Marfor took command of the first company, and then they were marching across the ice, weapons at the ready, though there was no sign of any opposition.

Men like the sergeant had built the empire, fighting everything from wild hillmen to the Orcs of the Southern Continent. The Petty Kingdoms had fallen in a steady progression, Halvaria absorbing more than a third of the entire Continent, and now, as Marfor indicated, the great dream was finally in full swing.

His men had suffered extensively in the recent battle against Erlingen, particularly his provincial troops. Most of his imperial footmen were still intact, but his cavalry had taken a beating, leaving him with few riders to perform the duties of scouting and reconnaissance, not that it mattered much here, in the middle of nowhere. Besides, the enemy was expected to withdraw to their capital, clogging the only road and relegating his command to little more than a reserve. He briefly considered taking matters into his own hands and marching south towards Salzing, but Edora Sartellian was not the sort of marshal who'd reward the disobeying of orders.

· · ·

Miles to the north, the Ninth Legion marched across a bridge, the village of Zurkirk unknowingly waiting for them. The marshal's orders had been precise; capture Zurkirk but do not advance any farther. He understood the risks, for if the threat appeared too great, the Army of Erlingen might turn around and march back, offering battle before Edora's plan could be put into place.

Moreau expected little trouble, for he'd witnessed the enemy army abandon the village, marching out of Zurkirk in a hurry, a veritable horde of refugees following in their wake, and he didn't mind that in the least. Refugees would place a strain on the duke's supplies, something that would work to the empire's advantage.

He urged his horse forward, falling in behind the lead company. Moreau had elected to send his footmen across first, their only task being to secure the end of the bridge, thus allowing his horsemen to cross unopposed. As he reached the far side, he pulled off the road, turning to watch as his imperial cavalry rode past, heading directly towards the streets of Zurkirk.

The sun shone brightly with little in the way of clouds, the perfect weather for an occupation. With his cavalry past, more footmen paraded across the bridge, spreading out on either side, soon filling up the flat ground beside the riverbank.

The sound of fighting drifted to his ears, and it took him a moment to realize where it came from. He turned towards the village, but the buildings there blocked his view. Moreau elected to wait, confident his horsemen would make short work of any opposition. The sounds of fighting trailed off, and then a lone horseman appeared, riding directly towards him.

The sergeant took his time getting there but finally came to a halt before the commander-general. "We were ambushed, Your Grace, but have secured Zurkirk."

"Ambushed? By whom?"

"A group of Temple Knights. They drove us back, then disengaged and fled to the southeast, along the road to Torburg."

"Temple Knights? I didn't think the warrior women of the Continent had it in them."

"It wasn't the Agnesites, Lord; these were garbed in brown and covered in mail."

"Mathewites? I'm surprised they could field enough men to engage us. Any idea of numbers?"

"Perhaps twenty, my lord."

Moreau felt his temperature rising. "Are you telling me less than two dozen archaic knights held off an entire company of our horse?"

"They utilized the element of surprise, taking us in the flank. We recovered quickly, but by then, they'd already begun to withdraw."

"Withdraw? You told me they fled. Which is it, man? Did they withdraw in good order or flee in a panic?"

The cavalryman mumbled something.

"What was that?"

The sergeant raised his head, meeting Moreau's gaze. "They withdrew in good order, Your Grace." He waited while his commander-general absorbed this new tidbit. "Shall we pursue?"

"No. Our orders were clear. We are not to do anything that might draw the Army of Erlingen towards us."

"So we just let them go?"

"Tell your captain to take his company to the other side of the village. He is to watch the road like a hawk. If he sees any signs of the enemy, he is to send a rider at once. Do you understand?"

"Yes, Your Grace."

"Good. Now, be off with you before I choose to hold you personally responsible for this debacle."

The rider departed in great haste, leaving Moreau to ponder this new development. He'd expected some sort of token resistance, but not at the hands of disciplined Temple Knights. Though he hated to admit it, the Church's fighting orders were superior to his own cavalry, presumably due to their fanatical devotion to their Saints, not to mention their rigid and inflexible discipline. It would be interesting to pit the brown-clad Mathewites against the empire's newest allies, the Cunars, although there was very little doubt in his mind who'd prove the superior warriors.

His thoughts turned to the coming campaign. In a few days, they'd march on, and then he would bear witness to the most triumphant victory in the history of the empire, that of the destruction of Erlingen's army. After that, they'd turn north and crush the so-called Northern Alliance, ending all opposition. With the war over, the entire Continent would fall before their feet, and pride swelled in Moreau's chest, knowing he would be the instrument of this great victory.

Edora would take all the credit, but there was always a chance she might fall in battle. After all, a marshal couldn't sit back and watch such a momentous battle from a distance, not when the end of the great dream was so close at hand.

Moreau contemplated what it might entail to encourage such a fate. Could he arrange for the marshal to fall victim to a stray arrow? She didn't wear armour, so such an accident was not beyond the realm of possibility. He imagined her falling to her death, an arrow in her eye, he himself bearing witness before he picked up the pieces of her shattered dream and led them all to victory. It would be glorious!

A rider came across the bridge, halting before him and disturbing his reverie. "The Eighth Legion is ready to cross, Your Grace. They wait only for us to clear the way."

Moreau hid his annoyance at the interruption, adopting a diplomatic smile. "You may inform His Grace, Commander-General Rackert, that we shall do so at once."

TWENTY-TWO

Breaking the Siege

SUMMER 968 MC

Lanaka ordered the advance, and the cavalry surged forward, descending upon the Halvarian legion as the sun rose behind them, illuminating them like some sort of chosen force. He'd ridden them all night, looping around to fall upon the enemy from the east, using the blinding light of the rising sun to mask their allegiance.

At the sight of them, the Halvarians gave no warning, and why should they? Only reinforcements would be coming from that direction.

Heward watched from a distance, his presence hidden by the mountain range. His own forces had been pushed up against the side of the mountains, but now, with the enemy distracted, they marched out into the open, taking up a line of battle.

This had all been carefully orchestrated, with the warriors within the Undermountain of Ironcliff even now preparing to launch their own attack against the besiegers. He was unaware of the specifics, but the marshal led this offensive himself, and Heward didn't want to disappoint him.

The men of Norland finished forming their line with the foot in front and archers to the rear. The Orcs formed on his south, their mighty warbows ready to deal with any attempt on the part of the Halvarians to flank them.

Rulahk, the master of earth, stood beside Heward, his eyes closed as he watched the battle unfold through the sight of a wolf. "It has worked," the Orc announced. "Commander Lanaka is tearing through their encampment and wreaking great damage."

Heward nodded to the man beside him, who stood ready with a horn. "Signal the advance," he ordered.

A single note disturbed the silence of the morning, echoing off the walls of the Gap. As one, the Army of Norland, as it had come to be called, advanced slowly, maintaining their formation.

He feared they were severely outmatched, for their army numbered only thirteen hundred, whereas a legion had, in theory, almost twice that, but the Dwarves had lured many of them into a trap, evening up the numbers. At least that's what he'd been told, but it was still unnerving marching forward to confront what appeared to be a numerically superior enemy.

Ghodrug, the Chieftain of the Black Ravens, walked beside him, calm as ever. As if sensing Heward's thoughts, she turned to him, speaking in her native tongue. *"All is proceeding according to plan. By nightfall, we shall have them on the run."*

"I wish I had your confidence," replied Heward, responding in the language of the Orcs.

"The Grey Wolf will bring us victory. The Ancestors have declared it so."

"The Grey Wolf?"

"Our name for the Marshal of Merceria. Fitting for one so skilled in the hunt."

"It's to battle we march, not a hunt."

"Is it not the same thing?" replied the Orc. *"We seek to kill to protect our way of life rather than for food, but the result is the same, save for the number of individuals involved."*

"I concede the point," said Heward. *"Now, let us concentrate on the task at hand. We will soon be awash in the blood of our enemies."*

Kasri Ironheart held Stormhammer with an iron grip. They'd pushed back against the Halvarians who'd dared to enter the mountain during the night; now, it was time to complete the trap.

Before her, Agramath stood waiting. On her signal, he would open the concealed door, allowing her command, the Hearth Guard, to flood in behind the empire's assault troops. Albreda was with Herdwin, pinning the enemy warriors in place while this second phase was put into play. Kasri nodded to the master of rock and stone, who then pressed his hand against a hidden rune. A portion of the wall popped out a finger's breadth, the latch securing it now released.

"I always thought this was a bad design," he grumbled as he struggled to get a grip on the edge of the door. "A handle would've been nice."

"Aye," she replied, "but then it would hardly be a concealed door, would it?"

"No, I suppose it wouldn't, but that doesn't make it any easier to open."

"Stand aside, Master Agramath. My people can handle it from here." She nodded at Captain Durgan, who moved up to take the mage's place. Rather than using his fingers, he jammed the end of his shortened poleaxe into the small space, prying the door open.

"Lead on, Captain," added Kasri.

Durgan stepped through, weapon at the ready. Behind him followed two more of the Hearth Guard, in their distinctive golden armour, stepping to either side once they were through. "It's safe," announced their captain.

They stood still as the heir to the Throne passed through the doorway. Kasri had spent decades amongst these halls, but this tunnel was unfamiliar. "You'd best get up here, Master Agramath. We need your guidance." She waited as the elderly mage entered the corridor.

He looked both ways, then pointed to his right. "That leads to the breach in the upper chamber. If you went down there and turned left, you'd see sunlight streaming in from outside." He pointed in the opposite direction. "That leads to the upper halls where the bulk of the fighting has taken place. Either direction would be useful in cutting off the enemy's retreat. Why, you could even remain here near the concealed door and build some fresh barricades."

"No. I'd rather take the fight to the enemy."

"Why not do both?" asked Durgan. "The hallways here are constricting enough. The entire Hearth Guard can't possibly be used. Allow me half, and we'll seek out the breach and fortify it, preventing any reinforcements from reaching the invaders while you take them from behind."

"I like your way of thinking," replied Kasri. "That's precisely what we'll do."

"Where would you like me?" asked Agramath.

"With the captain. Your Earth Magic would be better for closing up that entrance."

"Or," offered Durgan, "we could use it to launch another attack on the Halvarians."

"Wouldn't that be dangerous?" asked the mage. "After all, you'd only have half a company."

"Aye, but you forget all those Mercerians waiting with our Dwarves to attack from the front gate, not to mention that army of theirs coming from the west. Under those circumstances, I doubt they'd have many men to spare to face us. Add in that deep one of Albreda's, and there's not much that can stand in our way."

"Then I'd best get moving," said Kasri.

~

Gerald rubbed his forehead, worry creasing his brow. He'd arrived in Ironcliff along with a significant number of warriors, but the process had exhausted the magical strength of most of the kingdom's mages. Only Kraloch was spared, for his ability to communicate with Heward's command was vital to the plan.

The marshal turned around, observing all those who'd gathered. King Thalgrun had brought the bulk of his warriors to the great hall, where they prepared to march out the front gate, assisted by more than six hundred newly trained warriors, half of whom were Orcs, skilled in close-order battle and Mercerian tactics.

Hayley stood nearby, her rangers ready to do their part, but the initial push would be up to Thalgrun. The Vard of Ironcliff had insisted on leading the counterattack in person. His pride was so fierce that it had taken a great deal of convincing to even let his allies assist, but in the end, he'd given in to reason.

Revi Bloom watched from the sidelines, his magical energy temporarily exhausted from moving troops. Beside him stood Kharzug, the master of earth, looking just as worn out.

Gerald heard Kraloch's voice and turned to see him standing alone. He waited patiently until the Orc finished, then watched as he drew closer.

"Heward is advancing," said the shaman. "We cannot communicate with Commander Lanaka, but I am told the cavalry is in amongst the rear of the Halvarian encampment."

"Send a runner to Kasri to let her know, and while you're at it, pass word on to Albreda that the final assault has commenced."

"Yes, Marshal."

Vard Thalgrun beckoned to Gerald. "How much more of this waiting?" asked the Dwarf, adjusting his crown slightly to make it more comfortable.

"Lanaka is effectively cutting off their supply lines, so they'll be eager to see him off, allowing Heward to strike from the west. I don't presume to dictate when you should attack, Majesty, but were I in charge of this offensive, I would wait until Heward's forces engage the enemy before leaving the gate. With the losses they've experienced inside your mountain, they'll have few warriors left to oppose you."

Thalgrun laughed. "You do not presume to dictate but then turn around and tell me to wait? That's very diplomatic of you, Marshal. Your friendship with Queen Anna has obviously rubbed off on you. Not bad for an old grey wolf, I'd say."

"Grey wolf?"

"That's what the Orcs have taken to calling you. I heard Kraloch mention it while he was using his magic."

"I wasn't aware you spoke their language."

"I'm old," replied Thalgrun, "older than you by far. What else was I to do with all those years if not learn new things? I needed something to keep my mind sharp." He glanced at the Mercerians lined up behind his own warriors. "I must admit, I never thought I'd see the day so many non-Dwarves would be packed into this hall. It's a pity it must be under such circumstances." He paused as he contemplated something. "I'd like to ask a favour," he said at last.

"Favour?"

"Yes. Now, before you object, let me finish what I have to say. I'm not the youngest Dwarf these days, and there's every chance I might not live to see the sunset."

"We all take that chance going into battle," soothed Gerald.

"Aye, and I've accepted that, but if that should prove true, tell Kasri I've made arrangements, and Agramath has the details."

"Arrangements for what?"

"For her ascension as vard."

"I would've thought that all done. My understanding is she's been your designated successor for decades."

"She has, but some recent developments have occurred that I haven't had the time to inform her about, what with this siege and everything. Don't worry. She's still my successor. It's those cursed guilds; they can be problematic at times, so I've taken steps to curb their more argumentative tendencies."

"Dare I ask how you accomplished that?"

"You may," Thalgrun replied, "but that doesn't mean I'm going to tell you." He lowered his voice. "And quite frankly, I'm surprised it even worked, but there you have it." He returned to his normal volume. "Now, let's get this army of mine closer to the gates, shall we? I'd hate to waste any time once they're open."

Heward kept his men at a steady pace, advancing towards the legion besieging Ironcliff. Thanks to Lord Waverly, he now commanded more than he'd ever before, yet even so, it would be a difficult victory. He had no idea how many Halvarians had been lost trying to take the mountain or if any reinforcements had arrived, swelling the Seventh Legion's numbers. This entire plan was a gamble, and if the Army of Ironcliff couldn't break through to come to their aid, it might well be the death of him.

The Halvarians before him had formed into a line, their numbers roughly equivalent to his own. Were he commanding Mercerians, he would have no concerns with those odds, but the Norlanders were another matter. Any army will break, given enough casualties, but these men had fallen apart at the first sign of trouble in their clashes with Merceria. Would it be the same here today? He'd stiffened their resolve with the Orcs of the Black Ravens, but there was only so much he could do. He must now put his trust in Saxnor that victory would be his.

He glanced at Rulahk and grinned. *"You may inform your Grey Wolf we are about to engage."*

The Orc shaman halted and closed his eyes, calling on his magic to contact Kraloch. A small group of his tribe mates hung back with him as the rest advanced with the army.

A distant trumpet sounded from somewhere behind the Halvarian line, followed by three high notes, a signal from Lanaka that all was proceeding to plan.

"Steady!" he shouted in the loudest voice he could muster. "Keep the pace even." Sergeants took up his call, and the ranks straightened, making his entire command appear as if they were on parade.

A few stray arrows came their way but fell short. It did serve, however, to give his own archers a better idea of the range. The Orc hunters were first to test this, loosing arrows from their warbows in small groups, peppering the enemy. They did no damage, but Heward noticed some Halvarian defenders wavering in their resolve. He hoped the line might even break before contact, but then the empire's officers moved up, steadying their men.

More Orc arrows flew forth, taking down two Halvarians, and then the enemy line retaliated, striking shields. Though some swearing came from the Norlanders, no one fell.

As the advance continued, the volleys increased in frequency. The first Norland casualty was an archer, and his comrades sent a hail of arrows towards the enemy, though it proved largely ineffective.

The Halvarians directly opposite Heward wore mail, identifying them as imperial troops rather than provincials. He couldn't decide if that was good or bad, but it definitely meant this fight would be a tough one.

Lanaka sliced down, cutting into the Halvarian's lightly armoured shoulder. The cavalryman tried to pull his horse back from the assault, but the Kurathian took another swing, his sword striking his foe's helmet, sliding off to slice into the already damaged shoulder. The enemy's arm went limp, and he yanked on the reins with the other arm, trying to escape, but the cavalry commander wasn't in the mood for it. A final strike, a stab this time, finished the fellow off, and then Lanaka steered his mount through the crowd.

He'd begun the attack at dawn, riding into the enemy camp with the sun behind them as planned, taking the legion completely by surprise. He and his men were soon in amongst the siege camp, setting fire to tents and carving their way through the portion of the camp set aside for the mighty siege engines.

The enemy commander-general had reacted quickly, dispatching cavalry to counter the threat, and now there was a running melee surging through their camp like a panicked snake. Chaos reigned, with the Kurathians angling off in random directions, until the resistance finally organized themselves, slowing Lanaka's progress, but he knew they'd done their part by tying up much of the Halvarian horse.

~

Thalgrun met the gaze of Malrun Bronzefist, the Master of Revels, and nodded. He, in turn, gave the command, and the great gears controlling the front gate of Ironcliff sprang to life, soundlessly turning.

First, the immense iron bar holding the doors to the Undermountain shut retracted into the walls on the right. With these hidden away, a horn sounded, and the grand double doors began to swing in, daylight flooding the entryway.

They were only half-open when Vard Thalgrun ordered the advance. Four hundred Dwarven warriors moved as one, their weapons in hand, their glorious vard leading the way.

The Halvarians, having sent the majority of their warriors up the side of the mountain, had left little to fend off a counterattack. A smattering of arrows fell in amongst Thalgrun's guard, rattling their plate armour, but the fearsome Dwarves ignored them.

The sun beat down upon Thalgrun's face for the first time in weeks as he led his warriors through the ruined outer city of Ironcliff. He approached the shattered gates, while behind him, the Mercerians advanced even as he gazed down into the Halvarian camp.

Clusters of horsemen fought as they rode hither and yon amongst the campfires, while to the west, two long lines of warriors butted up against each other, fighting for supremacy. He risked a quick glance up to where they'd engineered the breach of the mountainside. Gold-plated warriors streamed down the side of the mountain, heading on a parallel course to his own.

This glorious day would cement his legacy as one of the greatest vards to ever sit upon the Throne of Ironcliff!

Gerald waited until the Dwarves passed through the doors from the Undermountain before he nodded to Hayley. The Queen's Rangers were the first Mercerian troops to exit, breaking off on either side with bows, ready to chase down any enemy warriors lying in wait.

Next, came the footmen, moving at a slower pace than usual to avoid colliding with the Dwarves. There was no finesse to this tactic, merely marching through the outer city, then straight down the grand stairs directly into the enemy's camp. Ordinarily, this would've been suicidal, but with Heward pushing in from the west and Lanaka's cavalry already keeping the enemy horsemen busy, there was little to oppose them.

A curse off to his right drew his attention. Halvarian crossbowmen, hidden amongst the rubble, were loosing off bolts at the Dwarves in an effort to break their formation. Gerald thought the tactic was futile, for the mountain folk's plate armour was thick and resistant to such things, but as he was about to dismiss the threat, a hue and cry went up in front of him.

He ordered two of his companies to assist the rangers in clearing out any Halvarians hidden in the debris, then rushed forward, heedless of the danger.

The Dwarven advance had halted, the vard's personal guards forming a circle. At the marshal's approach, they closed ranks, but then their captain waved him through.

Thalgrun lay on his back, an arrow protruding from the side of his head, penetrating just below the line of his crown, which he'd insisted on wearing. His death would've been easily prevented had he only donned his helmet, but such was not his way.

A great sorrow built up in Gerald, and he cursed aloud. He turned to the Dwarves, ready to take command, but the Dwarven captains had already decided on their reaction. The enemy had slain their vard, and now they would pay the price! The vard's personal guards moved him aside, and then the Dwarven warriors continued the advance, a low rumble coming from their throats. Gerald stepped aside, trying to understand the sound.

"It's a death chant," said one of the vard's bodyguards. "The enemy has killed our vard—Gundar help any that stand in our way."

TWENTY-THREE

Bad News

SUMMER 968 MC

Beverly moved off the road, allowing the Army of Reinwick to continue without interruption. Twenty-two hundred men, mostly on foot, marched south, supported by three hundred Ashwalkers, although the Orcs preferred to march on either side of the column.

Aubrey soon found her, coming to a halt just as the duke's knights rode past, Sir Owen amongst them. "I must say," she began, "I'm a little disappointed. I hoped we'd hear from the Therengians before we marched, but it looks like we're out of luck on that score."

"It can't be helped," replied her cousin. "There's no use in delaying the march if we're too late to help Erlingen."

"Do you think we'll get there in time?"

"That largely depends on what's happening down there."

"Well," said Aubrey, "I have some good news on that, at least. A messenger returned this morning informing the duke that the King of Andover will be ready to march as soon as we arrive. It appears everything is now in motion." She hesitated. "Did we hear anything else about the Temple Fleet?"

"Not yet, but then again, a lot is happening right now. Brother Cyric remained in Korvoran, and he'll send word letting us know when the admiral decides."

"I have to admit, it feels good to finally be doing something useful. I don't know about you, but all that time at court wears me down."

Beverly chuckled. "You never seemed to mind the court in Wincaster."

"That's different; that's home. Besides which, Queen Anna doesn't dither. When it's time to make a decision, she acts, not like this bunch." She jerked her thumb to indicate the marching army.

"That's not a fair comparison. The politics here are much more complicated than back home."

"Oh, I don't know," said Aubrey. "They both involve wars, traditional enemies, and, oh yes, a massive foreign army threatening friendly territory."

"I stand corrected. Then again, Merceria only has two neighbours, but from what I understand, it's not unusual for a Petty Kingdom to have five or six. I can't imagine how difficult that would be to deal with."

"All I'm saying is it wouldn't hurt if the Duke of Reinwick was a little more…"

"Decisive?"

"Yes, precisely."

"He loathes war," said Beverly, "and I can't blame him. We're from a warrior culture, but there's no such tradition here. It will be interesting to see how this Northern Alliance performs compared to our own army."

"You led Erlingen to victory. What's your opinion of them?"

"We won because we were able to take the enemy by surprise. I doubt we'll be that lucky a second time."

"But they did win the battle."

"They did," replied Beverly, "but I think they would've suffered in a more traditional engagement. Erlingen's warriors have heart, but their overall lack of experience is their weakness, and the same for Reinwick's men."

"How do you overcome that?"

"Additional training, but the only true way to stiffen their resolve is for them to win a few battles. Unfortunately, we're not in a position to make that happen. It's far more likely this campaign will end in one massive battle. I only hope the men of the Northern Alliance are up to the challenge." Beverly twisted in the saddle, peering back along the line of march. "You haven't seen Aldwin, have you?"

"He's on the other side of the column with the Ashwalkers, along with Krazuhk." Aubrey hesitated, unsure how to broach a difficult subject.

"It's not like you to hold back, Cousin. Out with it."

"The duke's court is not to his liking."

"Yes, he mentioned they acted differently when I wasn't around."

"They do," replied Aubrey, "but I don't think it has to do with him being a smith; it's his grey eyes."

Beverly shook her head. "I don't understand why they're so focused on eye colour."

"Those grey eyes mark him as a Therengian, and the Petty Kingdoms' nobility all fear the once great kingdom re-emerging and enslaving them all."

"I've got news for them; it's already been reborn, although admittedly far from these lands."

"Yes, and on paper, at least, it's allied with Reinwick."

"Yet they still haven't come to Reinwick's aid in the face of Halvarian aggression."

"I think it's a bit more complicated than that," replied Aubrey. "Imagine how much preparation would be involved in supporting an army operating so far from home. Speaking of which, have you seen the back of this column?"

"No. Why?"

"Their idea of supply wagons pales in comparison to what we're used to."

"I should've thought of that," admitted Beverly. "I've been so involved trying to work out the empire's strategy, I didn't think to consider something as basic as feeding the army. I need to have a word with His Grace, the duke. Thank you, Aubrey."

"For what?"

"For reminding me of what's important."

Temple Commander Marlena stared at the hastily written note that had arrived from Torburg. She looked up at the messenger. "Are you absolutely certain of this?"

"Yes, Commander. The duke's seneschal gave me this message."

"Bad news?" asked Lord Hagan.

"It appears we face a new threat. An army has crossed the border and reportedly seized Galmund."

"Galmund? That's clear across the other side of the realm. Who's responsible?"

"It doesn't say, other than they came from the south and appear to be mostly cavalry. What country borders Galmund?"

"Ulrichen," replied the baron, "but they're a poor kingdom, mostly wilderness, with no real army to speak of."

"I've a sinking feeling I know precisely where this army came from."

"Where?"

"The Antonine. Unless I miss my guess, those horsemen are Temple Knights."

"That's good news, isn't it?"

"Good news?" replied Marlena. "Hardly that. They're not here to help us, my lord; they're here to destroy us."

"Why would you say that?"

The Temple Commander took a steadying breath. "They officially disbanded the Temple Knights of Saint Agnes, then tried to arrest those in the Antonine."

"The Five Hundred?" said Lord Hagan. "I thought that a myth?"

"I assure you it's not, and ever since then, the Cunars have been hunting us down."

"But you prospered in Arnsfeld."

"As we did in Erlingen, but not every ruler in the Petty Kingdoms will willingly disobey the Church of the Saints. It's likely the Primus has declared a crusade in the name of eradicating our order, which will swell his ranks with volunteers, allowing him to augment his precious Temple Knights with footmen and archers. This"—she stared down at the note—"is the result."

"What do we do?"

"There's only one thing we can do: we march back to Torburg."

"But the empire is on our doorstep!"

"I'm well aware of our predicament," said Marlena, "but we have no choice. If we remain here, guarding the frontier, this new threat will advance into our rear, and then we'll be caught between a hammer and an anvil."

"The timing is suspect, is it not?"

"Most definitely, but something tells me this is no coincidence. We've known for some time that the Antonine was corrupted by the Halvarians. I just never believed it'd come to this."

"You knew and yet said nothing?"

"I had little choice," she replied. "If I'd informed you of the true schism within the Church, your duke might've sided with the Antonine, and then where would we be? Under the thumb of the empire, that's where." She crumpled the note. "Have we a map of Erlingen?"

"Yes, of course." Lord Hagan moved to a table and then dug through several papers to extract a large scroll. He unrolled it, using cups to secure the corners. "Here you go."

Marlena moved closer, her mind absorbing all she saw. "How accurate is this?"

"Very. After our last invasion, His Grace, the duke, insisted on sending out men to survey his realm. I doubt, though, that he thought we'd need it so soon."

"Torburg is roughly halfway between us and Galmund, with only one road between the two. Their most logical strategy would be to force us into a showdown outside the capital, where the Halvarian legions can march and attack us from the rear." She traced the road with her finger. "Have we received any word from Lady Beverly?"

"Not as yet, Commander."

"Send a messenger to Andover. Tell the king we're continuing our withdrawal to Torburg and urgently need their assistance."

"Even if they marched today, they wouldn't have enough time to reach us."

"Then we must take all measures to delay Halvaria's legions."

"But what about the Holy Army?"

"They won't attack until the empire is in position. To do otherwise could end in disaster for them."

"What makes you say that?" asked Lord Hagan.

"Simple numbers. The Cunar army couldn't chase down five hundred sister knights. I doubt they have the numbers to face more than two thousand men in battle."

"You're taking an incredible risk."

"I am?" replied Marlena. "The enemy is dictating our moves, not me. If I stand to face Halvaria, the Holy Army will sack Torburg, then squeeze us between the two armies. If I march past Torburg to the Holy Army, then the legions adopt the same tactic. By choosing to retreat to the capital, we at least have the freedom of choice."

"But you said it yourself—we have no choice!"

"Our choice is to stall for time, time that allows our allies to come to our aid."

"But we don't know if they'll even condescend to send help! As far as we know, they'll remain behind their borders and wait it out."

"You must look at the grander scheme. If Andover and Reinwick want their kingdoms to survive, they have little choice but to fight the empire, and it's far better for them with our numbers on their side than without."

"Which places a great deal of faith in our potential allies; I only hope it's warranted." He paused, raising his eyebrows. "What of the other Cunars? The ones who claim to have joined our cause?"

"I have no reason to doubt the loyalty of Temple Captain Waleed."

"But he's a Cunar!"

"Who has forsworn his allegiance to the Antonine and pledged to our cause."

"How do we know it's not a ruse meant to lure us in with a false pledge of loyalty? They could turn on us at a moment's notice, jeopardizing everything!"

"Do you doubt my ability to lead this army?"

"No, of course not," he replied. "His Grace appointed you himself. I would never doubt his wisdom."

"Then you, too, must have faith that I will do all within my power to ensure we survive. Now, I suggest you gather your nerve; attacking my strategy does little to aid us in these dark times."

"I'm sorry. I shall leave you to it, then." He remained composed as he left, although upon reaching the door, his pace increased.

Sister Johanna stepped into the room, barely avoiding a collision. She watched the baron disappear, then turned to face her commander. "I heard raised voices. Is there a problem?"

"This campaign is nothing but problems, but yes, there's been a new development. Come over here, and I'll tell you all about it."

Temple Captain Waleed looked over his knights before he turned to regard the Temple Commander. "Well? What do you think?"

The ex-Cunars had donned new surcoats, the traditional grey of their old order replaced by ones of an entirely different colour.

"White?" said Marlena. "You're apt to be mistaken for Augustines."

"Not so," he replied. "If you recall, the Augustines were disbanded, and their brethren ordered to join the Cunars. White also represents purity, and we're trying to demonstrate that we've chosen a more righteous path than our old order."

"There's no symbol adorning your new surcoats."

"We have yet to earn one. I will not adopt a sigil for our order until others see fit to bestow one upon us."

"Those others being? Remember, you're not serving the Antonine anymore."

"There's every chance that by the end of this conflict, my knights will all be dead, thus rendering the question moot." Waleed kept his eyes locked on Marlena. "We will prove ourselves to you, Commander. I swear it."

"Your former brothers are marching towards Torburg as we speak."

"Yes, and it appears our army is marching to face them in battle, but the Halvarians may soon be coming this way. Might I offer a solution to both our problems?"

"Are you offering to stay and fight the empire?"

"Yes, though I swear we would not be throwing our lives away. Rather, we will employ hit-and-run tactics aimed at slowing down their advance, thus buying you time to deal with this new development."

"Interesting," said Marlena, "but some of the duke's nobles don't trust you, especially after hearing about the Holy Army's approach. What would you say to them?"

"I swear to you, by all the Saints, we will do whatever it takes to defeat this invasion, even give our lives if necessary."

"I believe you, but others are not as trusting."

Waleed nodded. "Perhaps I can assuage their lack of faith. I command two companies of Temple Knights, give me two more companies of Erlingen cavalry, and they can bear witness to our dedication to the cause."

"We are expecting a battle ourselves; I can't afford their loss."

"Then find a handful of volunteers. Surely there must be some barons who'd be willing to observe us in action?"

"I make no promises," replied Marlena, "but I'll see what I can do."

"Thank you. I appreciate your faith in us."

"Faith is something that has been much on my mind of late."

"As it should be. You are a Temple Knight, and faith is the founding virtue of our respective orders." He quieted for a moment. "Or at least it was. I was shocked when I heard about the commands sent out from the Antonine. The Saints taught us tolerance, not hate; were they to see what the Church has become, they would surely turn in their graves."

"The teachings of the Saints live on, but we must be vigilant; otherwise, they, too, will become corrupted just as the Primus was."

"I don't suppose there's any chance of him coming to his senses?"

"No," replied Marlena. "The Primus is an agent of the Halvarian Empire. I'm afraid he always has been."

"How do you know this?"

"I was informed by the Temple General."

Waleed brightened. "Ah, yes. The mythical Charlaine deShandria."

"Mythical? You've met her yourself. She's as Human as the rest of us."

"Sorry. I meant no disrespect, merely that the stories of her accomplishments have grown to great heights since her disappearance from the Antonine. Anyone who could make five hundred Temple Knights vanish is going to attract a considerable amount of attention. Dare I ask what she's been up to since her flight from the Antonine?"

"Survive these next few weeks, and you may find out, but it won't be from me. I've taken an oath to keep such things to myself."

"Yet you're still in communication with her."

"I was before the empire crossed into the Petty Kingdoms, but I've heard nothing since. That's not surprising, considering the circumstances, but I have no way of getting word to her of our current situation."

"So… no army of sister knights coming to our rescue?"

"That about sums it up, yes."

"Then we shall have to hold on to what little faith we have left."

The torrential rainstorm threatened to wash the road away, and in any other kingdom, it would have, too, but the past kings of Andover had the foresight to ensure proper drainage for the major thoroughfares of the kingdom, allowing the men to continue unhindered. Lord Fernando pushed them at a brutal pace, a necessary evil if they wanted to arrive in time to help Erlingen, but the speed of the march took its toll.

Beverly rode through the camp, navigating her way with a lantern held aloft by a rain-soaked footman dispatched by the duke to find her. Aldwin struggled along behind, his horse showing signs of fatigue, unlike Lightning.

They finally arrived at the duke's tent. "Right this way," said their guide.

Beverly dismounted, waiting as Aldwin did likewise. Once they'd passed their reins off to a guard, they entered to see a familiar face in discussion with the duke.

"Ah, there you are," said His Grace. "You remember Galina Marwen?"

"I do," replied Beverly. "I assume your presence here brings good tidings?"

"It does," said Galina. "I have news from Natalia Stormwind. They are willing to lend their assistance."

"If I may be so bold to ask, what form would that assistance take?"

"The Army of Therengia will march to our aid, but she has one stipulation before it does."

"That being?"

"She wants to meet you, General... in person."

TWENTY-FOUR

The Gilded Throne

SUMMER 968 MC

The sun was at its zenith, its rays caressing the fields of barley and grain. Castimar Stormwind stared out from his vantage point, fondly looking over the familiar countryside. "It's been so long since I trod these fields."

Morven grumbled. "The fields are for peasants, Your Grace. Beyond lies the real treasure." He pointed towards the distant city of Varena. "There it waits, the Gilded Throne."

It was like any other city of the empire from this distance, a grey smudge amongst a sea of green, like some horrible blight.

"Patience, my friend," soothed Castimar. "We will be within its walls soon enough."

"Provided Vilani does her part."

"I'm confident she will, but you must be ready to take advantage of the opportunity."

"I assure you my men are more than ready to take the gate, but if she fails to open it, the assault will fail."

"We've gone over this before. Each of us has our part to play, but we must trust each other to see this through to completion. Now, gather your commander-generals. I wish to address them."

"Yes, Your Grace." Morven nodded, then left to gather his men.

The marshal noted Egreth Blackthorne, the Earth Mage, walking by and waved her over.

"You wanted me, Your Grace?"

"I called you over because I need your expert opinion."

"How may I help?"

"We shall be assaulting the gates of Varena this evening."

"And you want to know if my magic is capable of breaching the city walls?"

"Yes. Back at the Volstrum, I learned about Earth Magic."

"But not, it seems, precisely how such magic can best be applied."

"I am well aware of my shortcomings in that regard," replied Castimar, "but the magic of the earth is not common amongst the Petty Kingdoms. I also realize that theory and actual experience are often different from each other."

Egreth smiled. "It's refreshing that one of your importance is willing to acknowledge that I know more about the matter than you do."

"That is all well and good, but can you get us through those walls or not?"

"I was under the impression one of the gates was to be open from the inside."

"It is, but I want a contingency plan in case something goes wrong."

"Shaping stone is a time-consuming process requiring physical contact. Once the spell is cast, the stone becomes soft to the caster, who then manipulates it like soft clay. As to your question of whether I can get you through the wall, the answer is yes, but I must warn you, if the wall is thick, it could take all night. That's assuming you wanted a hole big enough for your army to move through."

"Have you any other spells that may be of use?"

"Several, in fact. I could produce vines that would allow some of your men to climb the walls, although that might prove a difficult feat in armour. Or, I could try transmuting stone to dirt, which might, in theory, collapse part of the wall, allowing entry."

"Are you implying it might fail?"

"There is a limit to how much stone I can transmute, and the walls of Varena are thick."

"Could you not use that spell on the hinges? They are set in the stone."

"I hadn't considered that, but now that you mention it, it might work. The only problem with that approach is the area in question would need to be within sight for me to target it, which is a little difficult, considering we are outside the city rather than in it."

"So you're telling me I should look elsewhere?"

"I would think Cadmus better suited to such things since he's an Air Mage. He could change several of your men into a gaseous cloud, allowing them to easily enter the city, or, even better, he could create a portal to put your men atop the wall."

"How many men?"

"You'd have to ask him that. I've heard of the spell, but I've no idea of the specifics. Shall I fetch him for you?"

"If you would be so kind."

She left in a hurry, eager to make a favourable impression. Egreth was by far his oldest supporter, in terms of time and age, but she was also dedicated to ending the monopoly of power held by the three families, and Castimar was more than happy to oblige.

Cadmus drew closer, his high, nasally voice breaking through the marshal's ruminations. "You wanted to know about my magic, Your Grace?"

"I want to know if you can use it to put people atop Varena's wall or, better yet, its gatehouse."

"Of course, though I must warn you, once there, they'd need to be prepared to fight. The city gate would have a strong garrison, and I can only send so many people through at one time."

"How does this spell of yours work?"

"I'm surprised you don't know," said the Air Mage. "I would've thought a battle mage would be educated in the use of the air gate spell."

"I'm familiar with the concept, but I need to know the details to determine its suitability here."

"Ah. It's a lengthy ritual. First, I open a portal here, or gate, as we like to call it, and then I open another at the proposed destination. Once the link is established, it's only a matter of walking through."

"How many men could pass through?"

"It's not a case of how many, so much as how fast. I can keep an air gate open for a length of time, or I can create a larger portal that allows more men to step through at once. In either case, it consumes an amount of energy relative to the size and duration of the spell."

"How close would you need to be to target the gatehouse?"

"Within sight. For a wall, that would mean a height advantage; otherwise, I can't anchor the other end."

"That doesn't help," said Castimar.

"On the contrary. I've seen several nearby hills that might suffice. Why, I could even use another spell to see the area in question up close."

"Could you allow a group of ten men to go through this portal at once?"

"That would involve a considerable draw on my power, but providing I didn't have to maintain it for long, yes."

"Excellent. Here's what I want you to do..."

Bryn Vilani peered around the corner of the building and spotted one of the gate guards patrolling back and forth. Doubtless, there were more within the gate tower, but she had to start somewhere. She waited, seeking to learn if he had a pattern. With a bit of luck, he might grow bored or turn at regular intervals, making it that much easier to approach unseen.

Instead, the man kept to an irregular pattern, leaving her to think rushing him was her only option. It would alert the other guards, but she was running out of time. If she didn't act soon, the entire operation would be in jeopardy. She glanced back in the direction of the palace, where her people were already fighting to secure the building. The plan hinged on them seizing it and holding it until Castimar's army came to their aid, but if this gate didn't fall, all that would be for naught.

She raised her hand, ready to signal the advance, and then something told her to wait. The guard stopped his pacing, now moving with purpose towards the base of the gatehouse. She tried to figure out what he was doing, and then it dawned on her—he had to relieve a full bladder.

Her arm swept down, and her rogues went into action, rushing across the intervening space at a fast yet quiet pace. The guard, intent on his business, never saw the knife—one quick slash, and it was all over, the fellow falling to the ground into an ever-expanding pool of blood.

Bryn followed, tightly gripping her dagger as she scanned the area. At this point, the biggest threat was the archers, for they could rain arrows down with impunity. She searched for them along the top of the wall and found something completely unexpected—warriors exiting from a glowing circle.

At first, she couldn't comprehend what had happened, but as these new men cut down those manning the top of the gatehouse, she realized the Marshal of the South had sent them.

She slowed, taking a more casual approach to the endeavour. With the threat of archers neutralized, all her people had to do was take the fight inside the cramped confines of the gatehouse, which was their element.

The sound of fighting came from inside the building, but she wasn't worried. Quicker than she'd expected, one of her men poked his head out a window, catching her attention.

"All good," he called out. "We'll have the gate open in a trice."

The clank of chains echoed through the early morning air. Four of her men rushed out to lift the heavy crossbar securing the city's doors, and then they were pulling them open.

Bryn held her breath, for all this effort would be wasted if Castimar's men weren't ready to take advantage of their work. She needn't have worried, for no sooner were the doors thrown wide, horsemen thundered past her, heading straight up the city streets towards the Imperial Palace, while other warriors, footmen this time, set a more sedate pace.

. . .

After all the men had entered the city, Castimar Stormwind appeared, surrounded by his personal guard.

"Ah, there you are," he said, looking at Bryn. "I must commend you on your work here today. Your people have done an outstanding job."

She bristled. "Is that why you chose to send warriors to the top of the gatehouse?"

Apparently, nothing could wipe the smile off the fellow's face, for he waved his hand as if swatting a fly. "Merely an extra hand to help see you through this difficult task."

What he really meant, she thought, was that he didn't trust her. She began to think maybe she should've revealed his treachery to the emperor and claimed the reward, but then realized she was in too deep, and doing that would've exposed her own role in the plot. Instead, she pasted a matching smile on her face. "It is much appreciated. One can never have too much assistance."

She'd thought he might acknowledge her remark, but he ignored her, concentrating on trying to catch a glimpse of the palace. He leaned left and right, but the nearby buildings obscured his view, turning his smile into a frown.

His marshal-general approached from within the city, his horse lathered. He'd ridden through with the first horsemen and had obviously met some opposition, for blood was spattered on both his clothes and the blade of his drawn sword, which he used to point in the general direction of the palace. "This way, Your Grace. We've cleared the road for you."

They rode off together, leaving Bryn to wonder why she'd bothered to join this cabal in the first place.

"There it is," said Morven, nodding at the palace. "You'll soon be seated on the Gilded Throne, the first Stormwind to take his rightful place as the Emperor of Halvaria. This is a most auspicious occasion."

"So it is," agreed Castimar, "but we mustn't get ahead of ourselves. The palace is not yet ours, nor the crown, for that matter."

"Ah, but it's now only a question of time, Your Grace. What will be your first official act as emperor?"

"I must consider a great many things, chief amongst them ensuring my head remains attached. To that end, I shall order the arrest of my rivals."

"A wise move that will send the message that your rule is not to be trifled with."

"Precisely my intent. Once that's out of the way, we'll begin a systematic review of the empire's governors. I can't afford for the Sartellians or Shozarins to continue wielding any form of influence."

"Many in your legions would be pleased to serve you in this, Your Grace. Say the word, and I'll have them dispatched across the land to arrest those you deem unworthy."

"One thing at a time, I think. Varena must be secured before we spread our wings any further. I assume you have begun making arrests?"

"Yes, Your Grace. Our men are descending on the houses of Shozarins and Sartellians even as we speak. It won't be long before they've all been dealt with."

"I do hope you sent enough men; these are mages of considerable power."

"I've ensured sufficient numbers and given strict instructions to use force before any resistance is in evidence, thus minimizing the risk to our men."

"Excellent. Have we any updates on the palace?"

"We've secured the grounds, thus preventing any escape, but I'm afraid the building itself is still being contested. It's a rat's nest of corridors, making it difficult to judge our progress."

"Have you an estimate of how long it will take to complete its scouring?"

"Two days, by my reckoning. We want to ensure it's absolutely safe for you before you enter, Your Grace. We can't risk the enemy getting within striking distance after all you've accomplished. I should also point out that we've seized every magic circle within the palace and have warriors standing by to eliminate any who might seek unauthorized use of them."

"More good news. It seems you are full of cheer today."

"I aim to please, Your Grace, although there is something which requires some clarification."

"It's not like you to hesitate," noted Castimar. "Speak your mind, Morven."

"I refer to Emperor Nevarus."

"What of him?"

"Is he to be eliminated?"

"I can hardly become the ruler of Halvaria while he lives."

"That is not what I meant, Your Grace. Clearly, he must die, but what manner is that death to take? Are we to ensure he dies as we seize the palace, or do you prefer a public execution?"

"I hadn't considered that. What are your thoughts on the matter?"

"A public execution illustrates you are to be taken seriously but may incite opposition towards your rule. However, if he died during the palace assault, there's the chance he might become a martyr around which a rebellion could eventually materialize."

"So you're saying we lose either way? Surely you're not going to recommend a lengthy incarceration?"

"No, Your Grace, but there is another, less straightforward way to deal with his death."

"I'm listening."

Morven took a deep breath. "What if he dies during the assault, but we don't announce it until several weeks later? That gives us time to spin a yarn about how cowardly he was and paint him as a villain rather than someone who'd inspire loyalty."

"I like that. Do it your way."

"And Karoulus, his heir? Killing somebody so young might be seen as too barbaric by the masses."

"Execute him now, but to the commoners, he must appear to have disappeared in the chaos and confusion."

"Those in opposition to your rule will go to great lengths to locate him, Your Grace."

"All the better, for they'll waste their time looking for a corpse. Anything else on which you require clarification?"

"The emperor's staff?"

"They must also die to protect our secrets. We can't have someone blabbing that we killed the God-Emperor, not when we're pretending he's in custody. Think of how it would make us look. I want my reign to begin on a positive note."

"I'm not certain that's possible," replied Morven. "You're seizing the Throne through force of arms, a violent undertaking by any measure."

"True, but once I'm crowned, I shall offer amnesty to any who opposed us, providing they lay down their arms and swear an oath to their new emperor."

"I fear that would be a mistake, Your Grace."

"Not so," said Castimar. "By then, we'll have eliminated anyone of any import, crushing any opposition. People will want to get back to some semblance of a normal way of life. By embracing the more important members of society, I will be ensuring my legacy."

"Embrace? I thought the idea was to replace everyone?"

"Not everyone. I know many people who'd willingly follow my orders even if I wasn't the emperor. Remember, my friend, it takes a military man to place a crown upon one's head, but it takes a diplomat to keep it there."

"Wiser words were never spoken."

TWENTY-FIVE

Reinforcements

SUMMER 968 MC

Glisnak proudly stood on the barge with his fellow Goblins as it was towed across the river to Colbridge. Althea waited for him on the far side, along with the rest of her army, ready to march south and meet up with the Mercerians.

"*This is most unusual,*" said Virdu, in Garspeak, "*and worrisome.*"

"*How so?*" he replied.

"*Were they to abandon us, we would be lost forever unless you know the way home?*"

"*I do not, but fear not; Al-tea will not abandon us.*"

"*How can you be so certain? Were she a Goblin, she could easily take advantage of the situation and have us eliminated.*"

"*The Clans need our iron,*" replied Glisnak, "*and their people don't like going into mines.*"

"*What if the Dwarves decided to return? Stonewall was originally theirs.*"

"*True, but they abandoned it. A spear, once discarded, belongs to whoever picks it up. A mine is no different.*"

Virdu pondered this, then smiled wide enough to reveal her pointed teeth. "*I still don't understand how you became so wise. When we first crawled from the pit, you could barely stand.*"

"*I was tired from pulling you out, pit-sister. Or did you forget?*"

"*I forget nothing.*" She looked around, noting the presence of the Weldwyn warriors wearing mail, something the Goblins were too physically weak to bear, yet she knew Glisnak wanted armour like this for the hunters in his enclave. Her thoughts drifted to their tinker, Flint. He was a quick study, having learned to make metal helmets from the Dragon Company's smith, but he could only produce so much.

"*You are thinking,*" said Glisnak, grinning.

"*That's your influence.*"

"*What is it that consumes your thoughts?*"

She pointed at the mailed warriors. "*I was wondering if there was some way to equip our grunts like that.*"

"*I have already given it a great deal of thought.*"

"*And your conclusion?*"

"*We are a people of small stature, and though we could never hope to wear such armour, there is no reason why our tinkers could not make something suitable to our size.*"

"*But what about the weight?*"

"*Look closely,*" said Glisnak. "*I see nothing to indicate the rings could not be made smaller and thinner. They wouldn't give us as much protection, but they would be far superior to the simple leather we currently wear.*"

"*Once again, you have out-thought me.*"

"*But you understand, now that I explained myself?*"

"*I do.*"

"*I was like you when I first encountered the Humans, struggling to comprehend strange and different customs. I'm confident that, in time, you'll learn to think as I do.*"

"*I look forward to it.*"

The ferry bumped into the dock, and Grazuk, already atop Quickpaw, was the first ashore, quickly followed by the other wolf riders. Glisnak nodded towards the Weldwyn captain, Darvin Fairhand, indicating he and his warriors should debark before the rest of the Goblins.

"No," said the Human, sweeping his arm towards the dock. "After you."

Glisnak stepped onto the dock with Virdu right behind him, then moved aside so the rest of the Goblin horde could disembark. Brogar broke away from Althea and approached.

"Master Glisnak," said the Dwarf. "There's to be a meeting of leaders once we rendezvous with the Mercerians. The princess wants you to stay close."

"I'm happy to do so," replied Glisnak. "When will we meet them?"

"They're camped south of Colbridge, outside the swamp. I hope they'll have space for the sudden influx of so many reinforcements."

"Influx?"

"Sorry. I keep forgetting you're unfamiliar with many of our terms. It simply means a whole lot of people arriving at the same time."

"Humans have such strange words."

"Its origin is actually Dwarven, not that it matters."

"Until we meet these others," said Glisnak, "where would you like my Goblins?"

"I think it's best if you continue marching in the rear for now. Once we reach the swamp, I imagine Tog will wish to make more use of your people."

"Who is Tog?"

"He's the brigade commander."

"Strange name for a Human."

"That's because he's not," replied Brogar. "He's a Troll." He grinned. "Another new experience for you."

"I look forward to it."

Two days passed before they rendezvoused with the Mercerians in a tent erected in an open field. Glisnak pushed aside the canvas door and almost bumped into an immense, grey-skinned giant. At first, he was inclined to flee, but then reason took hold, for this must surely be a Troll.

"Greetings," boomed a deep voice. "I am Tog. You must be the Goblin Chieftain, Glisnak."

"I'm surprised you know my name. Our horde is so small compared to everyone else."

"All are important here. Now come, the rest are waiting." Tog positioned himself at the end of a table. "Here is a chair for you to stand on so you may look over the maps."

Glisnak climbed up to see papers strewn about the surface. Al-tea had introduced him to the concept of maps while they sailed to Southport, so he wasn't completely lost.

A Human man clad in armour that looked like it was made of solid steel nodded at the princess. "Your arrival brings our total to over fifteen hundred, Highness, including some much-needed archers."

"Thank you for that, Lord Preston," said Tog. "Now, my strategy is to divide our army into three smaller commands. Preston will lead the Mercerian contingent while Lord Tulfar commands the Dwarves of Mirstone. The third contingent will be under the command of Her Highness, Princess Althea."

"What about us?" asked Glisnak.

"If you have no objection, I'd like your Goblins to accompany the Dwarves. Your wolf riders are faster than them and able to move quickly to either flank should they need to."

"The Dragon Company goes with the princess," announced their captain, Haldrim. Those in the room fell silent, surprised at the Dwarf's open defiance.

"I have no objection," replied Tog. "As for the two hundred men from Weldwyn, in the absence of their king, they shall be placed under the command of Princess Althea. I trust that will not be a problem?"

"Not at all," replied Lochlan. "We travelled with them all the way from Loranguard, so we've become accustomed to their presence."

Lord Tulfar cleared his throat. "Might I enquire where His Majesty is?"

"Back in Summersgate," replied Althea. "He's overseeing the training of a new Weldwyn army."

"I would've thought he'd have done that by now. It's been a while since the war."

"If they hadn't lost thousands of men when King Leofric marched into Norland, recruiting might be more successful. And with the threat of the Clans neutralized, we had no impetus to reform a large standing army."

"Have we any idea when this rebuilding might be finished?"

"No," replied Althea, "although I'd expect it's some way off. In the meantime, we must be thankful for the two hundred men my brother sent us."

Osbourne Megantis, the Weldwyn Fire Mage, stepped up to the map and pointed. "I've scanned the area using a phoenix. The enemy legion is encamped in the swamp north of the shoreline."

"Would the village not be more suitable?" asked Lochlan.

"It would've been," replied Preston, "had Tog and his people not set fire to it when they retreated."

"That will put their backs to the sea should we attack."

"You mean when we attack," said Tog. "From what Arcanus Osbourne tells me, the men of the empire are suffering greatly."

"Suffering how?"

The Troll's grin was somewhat menacing. "The swamp is not the natural habitat of Humans, and their thin skin does not protect them much from disease and sickness."

"Doesn't that present a problem for us as well?" asked Lochlan.

"Do not worry. Your exposure will be brief, and if any fall ill, we have Kurghal to look after them."

"What's a Kurghal?" asked Glisnak.

"I am." An Orc stepped forward. "I am a Shaman of the Black Arrows and sister to Urgon, its chieftain."

"Ah, I see. Does that mean you climbed out of the pit together?"

"They are brother and sister," added Althea, "much the same as King Alric is my brother." She noted his look of confusion. "They share the same mother?"

The Goblin shook his head. "My pardon. I still have trouble understanding the ways of others. My apologies if I offended you, Kurghal. How long have you been a bender?"

The Orc knitted her brows. "Bender?"

"Their word for shaman," offered Althea.

"Then, yes, I am a bender. Have you a bender amongst your people?"

"Yes, my pit-sister, Virdu. Why do you ask?"

"If she is capable of using Life Magic, we might be able to teach her to use spirit talk. Does she understand the common tongue?"

"A little. I've been teaching it to her."

"Wait," said Preston. "How is it you're willing to teach a Goblin you just met and not our Life Mages?"

Kurghal shook her head. "Humans have a history of letting magic corrupt them. This is not an issue with Goblins."

"But your people taught it to Aubrey."

"She has proven herself and is an Orc friend."

"Let us not fall into arguments," said Tog. "Having another gifted with this ability would make it far easier to coordinate our attack."

"We haven't the time for that," insisted Lord Preston. "We need to drive those Halvarians from our shores. The marshal needs all the men he can get for the invasion of Halvaria."

"If she were able to speak your language," said Glisnak, "how long would it take for her to learn this spell?"

"That depends on her magical ability," replied Kurghal. "Were she an Orc shaman, I could have her proficient before nightfall."

"Then make time to do so. I will see to her ability to understand the common tongue."

"It would be easier if she spoke our language."

"It matters little which language you need; the result will be the same."

The Orc looked at Glisnak with raised eyebrows.

"You must take him at his word," said Althea. "I guarantee he speaks the truth."

"Once we are done here," added Glisnak, "I shall speak with Virdu."

The conversation devolved into a discussion about the upcoming strategy, a topic with far too many terms Glisnak was unfamiliar with.

Althea motioned to him, and they stepped outside for some fresh air. "I assume you're going to give your ring to Virdu?"

He nodded. "She can be of great help if she learns this spell of Kurghal's. It will also be useful when we return to Stonewall so we can talk with you over great distances. And it gives our horde something important to do in the coming battle."

"And what would that be?"

"Keeping Virdu safe."

"I shall mention that to Tog," replied Althea. "If she proves capable of casting that spell, it may change his strategy."

"Yes. Now, I must go and find my pit-sister and explain what we need her to do."

"Are you certain about this?" Virdu looked down at the ring on her finger. *"Without this, you will be unable to talk to the Humans."*

"I will take it back once the battle is over," replied Glisnak. *"This is a great opportunity for you. You will learn a spell no other Goblin in the Sunset Peaks has access to. Think how that could change our lives!"*

She stared at her finger some more, holding up her hand to let the sun reflect off the ring. *"How does it work? Do I have to do something to speak another language?"*

"No. The magic it contains lets you speak any language known to those around you. You have merely to be in someone's presence when they speak. I know it sounds strange, but the language will come to you naturally."

"And if I wish to speak Garspeak instead?"

"Then you simply do so. Your head will sort things out when the time comes. I should warn you, though; your mastery of the language will only be at a basic level."

"Basic being?"

"Similar to what a runt knows, or someone who just learned the language."

Virdu nodded. *"So it will be difficult to discuss complicated matters?"*

"Precisely."

"I understand. Even so, it would be nice if we could get more of these."

"Perhaps one day we shall. Someone with magic had to create that ring, so it only stands to reason they could do so again."

Grazuk appeared, leading the Orc shaman. *"You have company,"* she called out in Garspeak.

"Greetings," said Kurghal in the tongue of the Orcs. *"I am Kurghal, Shaman of the Black Arrows."*

"And I am Virdu, Bender of Stonewall Enclave," Virdu answered in Orcish, and her eyebrows went up. *"I am speaking your language!"*

"So you are," replied the Orc. *"A most impressive achievement."*

"My pit-brother told me I am to learn a new spell. How do we begin?"

"It might be best if you tell me which spells you already know."

. . .

They set out early in the morning, with the Human cavalry, few as they were, leading the way, followed by Tog's Trolls. The rest of the Human footmen came next, interspersed with their archers, then the Goblin horde, their lobbers leading, with Virdu and Glisnak following. The grunts brought up the rear while the wolf riders screened their flanks. Behind them all marched Tulfar's Dwarves and the Dragon Company, along with Princess Althea.

Glisnak surveyed his horde. He had two sixes of grunts and an equal number of lobbers at hand. The wolf riders, under Grazuk, also numbered twelve, of which Grazuk was one, leaving himself and Virdu as the odd ones out. He was beginning to wonder if he shouldn't have brought four more to fill out his group to an even number of sixes. He tried to dismiss the feeling as mere superstition, but deep down, he worried he'd made a mistake.

He observed the men of the Clans marching in front of them. They, like their Mercerian counterparts, were organized into groups of fifty, a number so vast as to be almost unimaginable to an enclave dweller. If he attempted to muster that many Goblins, there'd be none left to hunt. The thought of it swirled around in his head, and he saw a different future, one in which his people grew to fill the old Dwarf mine. He'd learned from Brogar that Mirstone fielded hundreds of warriors, yet that wasn't even half the population of his home. Could Stonewall grow to such immense numbers?

Glisnak imagined a horde of green, marching to war with metal armour and helmets to match. Grunts typically used spears, but he had a hard time believing those crude weapons would suit such a sight. Most Humans he'd seen favoured swords, although the Clansman preferred axes. Neither was particularly well-suited to hunting, but an army was a different matter. Would this horde of his eventually adopt either weapon?

He soon came to his senses. Stonewall might raise an army, but who would he use it against? The Clans were friendly, though Al-tea had once told him the Clansmen had frequently fought amongst themselves in the past. Would his horde be the protector of their lands?

There was always the possibility the other enclaves of the Sunset Peaks might take exception to his success. After all, he'd lured away many of their Goblins to join him in the old Dwarf mine.

"*You are thinking again,*" said Virdu. "*I can tell. You keep glancing at the Humans and their metal armour.*"

"*And what do you think consumes my thoughts?*"

"*You seek to conquer the other enclaves.*"

"Would that be so bad? Any chieftain who possessed the strength would do no less."

"And that would make you no better than them. You founded Stonewall to give us another life, one filled with hope rather than dread. We look after our sick and injured, ensuring no one takes what does not belong to them. Would you now throw that all away by becoming another Snarlak?"

Glisnak considered her words. Snarlak had terrorized Crag, quite literally had his enforcers beat him within a fingers-breadth of his life and then toss him over a cliff to die in agony.

"You're right," he finally said. *"Were we to go to war with the other enclaves, too many lives would be lost. I want our people to prosper, not dwindle through battle losses."*

Virdu nodded. *"Your wisdom serves you well. Make the enclave strong and drape your hunters in the metal armour you so covet, but remember, they are there to keep Stonewall safe, not force our way upon others."*

"There has always been trouble between enclaves. How long before one of them comes, trying to take what is ours?"

"The Red Wizard's death drained much of the fight from them. In time, they will recover, but by then, this war will be over, and our horde will have returned armed with the one thing no other enclave possesses."

"And what is that?"

"Experience."

"True," said Glisnak, *"but you're forgetting something of even greater value that they lack."*

"That being?"

"Friendship."

TWENTY-SIX

Warmaster

SUMMER 968 MC

Galina Marwen stood in the middle of the camp while those watching stood silent. It was a strange sight, for the sun had just risen, and a low fog was still burning off, its blanket of mist obscuring the ground and making it appear as though they were standing on clouds. The words of power emerged from the mage as she traced intricate patterns in the air.

"Fascinating," said Aubrey, keeping her voice low so as not to disturb the Water Mage. "It's so different from the spell of recall."

"She's only just begun," replied Beverly. "I'm surprised you could tell."

"The preamble is different."

"Preamble?"

"Yes. The first words of power link the mage to the element in question —in this case, water."

"But aren't there four elements? Besides which, you're a Life Mage."

"We actually have two preambles, one for the physical realm and one for the world of spirits."

"You've certainly made understanding magic your life's work."

Aubrey smiled. "I'm nothing if not thorough." She was about to say more, but Galina's casting began to bear fruit. "Look," she said, nodding in the direction of the Water Mage.

Two pillars of ice were forming, the air around them growing frosty as they rose beyond the height of a tall man, reaching towards each other to create an arch. Then came a snap, and suddenly, the view through the arch changed to that of a distant field with large standing stones off in the distance.

"That looks similar to the one that brought us here," said Beverly.

"She must be using it as an anchor point, like our magic circles back home."

Two figures approached the arch from the other side: one, a pale woman with black hair, the other, an Orc.

"Shaluhk!" said Aubrey.

The two travellers stepped through, and then the Orc grinned. "Lady Aubrey, it is so nice to finally see you in person."

Galina turned to Lord Fernando. "Your Grace, you remember Lady Natalia Stormwind?"

He bowed. "It is good to see you again, Warmaster."

"And you, although I wish it were under better circumstances. Let me introduce you to Shaluhk, Shaman of the Red Hand."

"We are honoured by your presence."

"As am I," replied the Orc. "And this must be Beverly Fitzwilliam. It is particularly fortuitous that we meet this day."

Beverly was taken aback. "You know of me?"

"Indeed. Kraloch has told me all about your accomplishments." She suddenly switched to Orcish. "*I understand you are fluent in my native tongue?*"

"*I am.*"

"*Good. The warmaster will talk with the duke in private first. You will be placed in command of the alliance's army by the time she is done.*"

"*I will?*"

"*You should not be surprised. Nat-Alia herself would command, but the Petty Kingdoms would never allow a Warmaster of Therengia control over their armies, and we Therengians will not willingly serve a kingdom that once subjugated our people. You are an outsider with no loyalties to either of us. Thus, you are well-suited to present a neutral view of things. In addition, this campaign requires someone of exceptional skill, and your experience makes you the perfect person to lead us to victory.*"

"*I don't know what to say,*" replied Beverly. "*Except that I am humbled.*"

"*That is a good sign. It illustrates that your head has not swelled with victory. I am told that often happens with successful Human generals.*"

Beverly chuckled. "*You needn't worry about that. Aubrey wouldn't put up with that nonsense, nor would my husband.*"

"*Good. Now, say nothing of this to the others, save for perhaps your cousin Aubrey and your bondmate.*"

"*I understand.*"

A sound like the shattering of glass interrupted their conversation, and they both turned to see chunks of ice where the arch had so recently stood.

"I must go," said Shaluhk, reverting to the common tongue. "Nat-Alia will want me at her side. We shall talk again once we are done with the duke." She left them, running to catch up to the warmaster, who was already heading towards the duke's pavilion.

"I always thought you should command," said Aubrey. "Although, it's nice to know someone else feels the same way."

The expected conversation with Shaluhk never occurred, for the duke summoned all his commanders and barons to his command tent. Beverly squeezed in beside Aubrey, although Aldwin elected to remain outside, confident his wife would fill him in on all the important details.

His Grace, the duke, was already speaking when they arrived: "… and so I've gathered you all here to discuss strategy."

"If I may be so bold," said Captain Marwen, "would this discussion not be better served when we rendezvous with King Dagmar?"

Natalia stepped forward. "There's an old saying I learned in my training as a battle mage that says it's better to ask for forgiveness than for permission. This campaign requires decisiveness and quick thinking, neither of which are facilitated by consensus."

"My apologies, my lady, but wouldn't that decision be up to His Grace, the duke?"

"She makes a good point," replied Fernando. "I understand the Northern Alliance is between our two realms, but we find ourselves having to cooperate not only with Erlingen but with Therengia as well. In the interests of victory, we must choose someone to lead whom all of us can agree on."

"That person being?"

"General Beverly Fitzwilliam, providing she agrees."

The mention of her name set the room alight with objections, but Lord Kurlan Stratmeyer, the Baron of Blunden, first put voice to them. "Are you certain, Your Grace? We know little of this woman other than what she's told us. How do we ensure the empire hasn't sent her to lead us to disaster?"

Natalia Stormwind straightened, her calm demeanour somehow dominating the room. "I have it on the finest authority she is who she claims to be. I might also remind you that she has already bested the Empire of Halvaria once, and I'm confident she can do so again." She leaned forward, resting her hands on the map table. "Unless you'd prefer me to command?"

The baron drew in a sharp breath. "I withdraw my objection, Your Grace."

"Lady Beverly, I'm told your marshal has devised a campaign strategy to defeat the empire once and for all. Would you care to elaborate?"

"Certainly, Warmaster." Beverly stepped forward to join Natalia. She glanced down at the map, which purported to represent the Petty Kingdoms, but aside from Reinwick and Andover, it lacked many details. "We cannot even consider invading the empire's homeland until we deal with the more immediate problem we're facing, that of the recent Halvarian incursion."

She glanced around the room, searching for dissension, but they were all hanging on her every word. "We defeated one of their legions by using their own strategy against them. They divided into two columns in hopes of taking us by surprise, unaware that we were onto their plans."

"That's all well and good," said Captain Marwen, "but how do we do that a second time?"

"That largely depends on our Therengian allies. As for our immediate plans, nothing has changed. We must still rendezvous with the Army of Andover and then march south into Erlingen. What we do once we arrive is contingent on what has occurred in my absence. My suspicions are the enemy will have waited for reinforcements before pushing across the border."

"How many reinforcements?"

"By my reckoning, we destroyed half a legion, but there's bound to be at least two more they can call upon."

"Saints be with us," said the duke. "Are you suggesting we'll be facing three legions?"

"It is a logical assumption," replied Natalia. "The empire learns from its mistakes. To ensure their victory, they'll pull from their army of occupation, which is exactly what we want."

"It is?"

"It means," added Beverly, "the realms they've marched through won't be properly garrisoned. That, in turn, will hurt their supply lines, especially once they begin their retreat."

"Retreat?" said Lord Kurlan. "How can you speak of forcing them to retreat when we haven't even faced them in battle? Three legions mean we'd be facing more than seven thousand men!"

"I might remind you, my lord, that by the duke's reckoning, the Northern Alliance has more than four thousand warriors, and Erlingen, the last I checked, had almost twenty-five hundred, and those numbers don't take into account the Army of Therengia."

"And just how many can we count on from the great eastern empire?"

All heads swivelled to the warmaster. "We are not an empire," replied Natalia, "but to answer your question, we are standing by with over one thousand warriors, amongst which we count a number of spellcasters."

"And the composition of this army of yours?" pressed Lord Kurlan.

"This is neither the time nor the place to speak of such things."

"Then how in the name of the Saints are we to use them if we don't know what you've got?"

"I shall take General Fitzwilliam back to Therengia so she may see the army for herself."

"I don't like this one bit," said Lord Kurlan. "We need numbers to ensure victory, not the weak promises of a non-believer."

"With all due respect," replied Beverly, "this is not a matter of religion or regional politics. We are here because the Empire of Halvaria wants to conquer us all. You must put aside your differences to allow us to find a path to victory."

"I couldn't have said it better myself," said Duke Fernando. "I apologize for my earlier remarks, Warmaster, but these are dangerous times, and many of us feel we are in over our heads."

"I agree," said Captain Marwen. "If I may, perhaps it would help to describe how the command structure will work. Are we to take orders directly from General Fitzwilliam?"

"No," replied Beverly. "Each individual army will still be commanded by its respective leaders, but I shall be in command of overall strategy."

"And how do you intend to coordinate all of this?"

"That's where we come in," said Shaluhk. "Our shamans can communicate over great distances, and Therengia is blessed with an abundance of us."

"Yes," added Natalia. "We also have other mages available, including Earth, Fire, and Water, all of which have been trained to use their magic in battle."

"My pardon," said Lord Kurlan, "but where is your High Thane? Does he not think us important enough to come here in person?"

"He is assembling the Army of Therengia, but I assure you, he will join us once the battle commences. Now, unless there is other business you wish to discuss, I need to take the general east so she can best decide how to utilize our forces."

"You are all dismissed," said Duke Fernando, "except for those the general requires."

"That's you, Cousin," said Beverly, "along with the warmaster and Shaluhk."

The duke ushered everyone else out. "Send word when you're finished, General." With that, he left.

"When will I be able to see this army of yours?" asked Beverly.

"There's no time like the present," replied Natalia.

· · ·

Aldwin stepped through the frozen arch with Beverly, both bearing witness to the set of standing stones, much like those that had brought them to the Petty Kingdoms. They turned to leave the hill the stones were on, only to see the Therengian Army spread over a large field on their left.

"Saxnor's balls," said Aldwin as he noticed the massive beasts assembled with the warriors. They had to be twice the size of a warhorse, with Orcs mounted atop, holding long spears.

"What are those?" he asked, pointing.

"Those are tuskers," replied Shaluhk. "My brother, Laruhk, commands them."

"We also have Temple Knights of Saint Agnes," added Natalia, "though only two companies worth. Unfortunately, that's all the cavalry we have at present. It's mostly thick forest here, which is not the best terrain for raising horses. Now, come. Let's get you closer for a better look, shall we?"

They walked down the hill to inspect the warriors whose mail was similar to what the majority of Mercerians wore. However, unlike those warriors, women comprised nearly half of the Therengians' forces.

"This is the Thane Guard," began Natalia. "We have an even larger contingent back home, what we call the fyrd, but they're only utilized when the kingdom is in danger. These men and women, however, constitute our permanent, professional army."

A smile broke out on the warmaster's face as an individual wandered over. "And this is Athgar, the current High Thane of Therengia."

He stepped closer, then embraced Natalia, planting a kiss on her lips.

"He is also my bondmate," she added.

He released her, then turned to his visitors, staring at Aldwin. "Ah, a fellow Therengian. Can't say I was expecting that. Welcome." He shook their hands. "And you must be Beverly?"

"Majesty."

"Oh, please," he replied. "I think we can dispense with the formalities, don't you? Besides, I'm not a Majesty."

"Then what are you?"

"I suppose if you were to call me anything, it would be lord, but I'd much prefer we keep this informal." He turned to his bondmate. "I thought you said there'd be three?"

Aldwin snapped his head around. "My wife's cousin Aubrey is here somewhere."

"She is examining the standing stones," offered Shaluhk. "Shall I go and fetch her?"

"Don't worry. She can catch up with us later," replied Athgar. "What do you think of our army, Beverly?"

"Impressive. Might I ask how you utilize your archers?"

"They're trained to loose volleys over the heads of our shield wall, but on rare occasions, we put them on the flanks."

"I would've thought that tactic more common."

"And were this any other army, I'd agree, but the Orc tribes typically guard our flanks."

"Ah, yes. The Orc warbow. I'm told we have you to thank for those."

Athgar's eyebrows raised. "You use them in Merceria?"

"We do, though in limited numbers. You appear to have far more at hand, which I suppose shouldn't be surprising, considering how many tribes live in Therengia. Between Kraloch and my cousin Aubrey, I've heard quite a bit about this kingdom of yours."

"We prefer the term 'realm'. I might be the High Thane, but that's not a lifetime appointment. When the time comes, I'll step down, and they'll elect someone new."

"Elect? So you follow the Orc custom?"

"We do. The tribes are an intrinsic part of the realm and have full representation on the Thane's Council, the same as we Humans do, which is one of the reasons it took so long for us to send word that we were coming to the aid of the Petty Kingdoms. We had to bring together everyone to vote. Having said that, we're fully committed to this campaign. As for strategy, I'll leave that up to Natalia. She is, after all, our warmaster."

"Don't be fooled by the title," added the Water Mage. "We do not seek conflict. The title of warmaster is merely indicative of my expertise and training. In the Petty Kingdoms, I'd be a general or marshal, but we prefer to use the Orc term for the position."

"A question, if I may?" said Beverly. "Do you employ commanders in addition to the warmaster, or do you use some other method of command?"

"We have commanders," replied Athgar, "much as you do. I knew Natalia would be bringing you here to see the army, so I've arranged a little get-together."

"It's still morning for them," said Natalia. "The sun rises earlier here than in the Petty Kingdoms, so they've only just had their breakfast."

"That's all right," piped up Aldwin. "I don't know about the rest of us, but I can always find room for something to eat."

Athgar grinned. "A man after my own heart. Follow me, and we'll show you our hospitality."

Beverly leaned back, resting on her elbows. They sat on the ground, partaking of plates of food passed around the fire, Aldwin nibbling on a rib while she and Aubrey had eaten their fill.

"Kargen will join us shortly," said Shaluhk. "He is bringing the last group of hunters with him from Runewald."

"Yes," added Athgar. "The villages of Therengia are spread over a wide area, making it a time-consuming process to gather the army."

"It seems you've been planning to help us for a while," said Beverly.

"Ever since Galina contacted us. Of course, we didn't say anything then since we didn't know if the Petty Kingdoms would welcome our presence. You might say we've been fighting the empire for years."

"I wasn't aware their influence reached this far east?"

"I'm not sure if you know this, but Natalia trained at an academy called the Volstrum, and it turned out the people who ran that institution were in league with the empire."

"Were?"

"Yes. It's gone now, destroyed by Natalia's magic."

"Destroyed?" said Aubrey. "Are you suggesting she razed the entire building? Why, that would take an immense amount of power."

"It did," said Natalia. "So much so that it very nearly killed me in the process and would have without the ley lines." She hesitated. "Mages at the Volstrum were not taught how to harness their power; I worked it out on my own."

"That sounds like Albreda. She's what we call a wild mage. Some claim such knowledge is dangerous, but I think those individuals are uncomfortable with something they don't understand."

"I'd like to meet her. Perhaps, once this war is over, I'll pay her a visit."

"It's a long way to Merceria."

"Nonsense. With the power of the ley lines at your fingertips, there's no limit to what can be achieved. I'm not saying every wielder of magic is capable of harnessing such power, as it requires a certain frame of mind to even contemplate, but there is a small group of mages, such as this Albreda you speak of, who could expand their magic by leaps and bounds." She leaned forward. "And from what Shaluhk tells me, you may very well fit into that category yourself."

TWENTY-SEVEN

Chaos

SUMMER 968 MC

The door burst open as three armoured men entered the hallway. A young woman holding a tray of bottles turned at the interruption and then dropped what she was carrying. The warriors, blood dripping off their swords, rushed towards her, but she proved too fast for them, running down the corridor at a breakneck speed and almost careening into Janek as she went round the corner.

"Watch yourself, girl," he shouted, but she ignored him, dashing past without a word. Heavy footfalls grabbed his attention, and then he spotted the interlopers kicking open doors, searching for something or someone. He gasped, realizing, for the first time in his life, how close to death he was.

Janek backed up against the wall, hoping they hadn't seen him. He couldn't quite comprehend what was happening, but a sense of dread overwhelmed him. The distinctive clash of steel on steel drifted to his ears, meaning fighting had broken out in the Imperial Palace, but who was responsible for this travesty? He resolved to make his way to the emperor's quarters, provided he could do so without further exposure to danger.

Six warriors wearing the emperor's livery rushed past him, turning into the corridor where the serving girl had run from, their spears held at the ready. Janek seized the opportunity, making a bid for safety as he followed them, staying well back as they clashed with the trio who'd been searching the rooms.

He knew he needed to get through the door up on the right, so he pushed himself against the wall, sliding past the melee, then raced for the door, shutting it behind him. Along the far wall, a concealed door led to the servants' hallway. When they'd built the palace, the rulers of Halvaria had wanted their servants out of sight, leading to a complex series of parallel corridors and secret entrances, which would now work to Janek's advantage as he plotted a course to his emperor.

~

"Did you hear that?" Nikki pressed her ear to the door. "Something's going on out there."

Arnim looked up from the book he was reading. "And by something, you mean?"

"I can't be certain, but it sounds like fighting."

At her words, he tossed the book aside, rose from his chair and crossed to her side. "Let me have a listen."

They stood silently for ten heartbeats. Sure enough, the distinctive sounds of melee echoed in the hallway outside.

"This is grave news," said Arnim. "It sounds like someone's trying to take the palace."

"They must be after the emperor. Should we warn him?"

"He's not our ally, Nikki. He's the ruler of the very empire that's invaded our home."

"True, but we're only alive because he took an interest in us. I hate to say it, but our fate is tied to his. If he dies, we'd be of no further interest, and from what I've seen thus far, these Halvarians don't impress me as the type to simply let us go."

"I agree, but we have three problems: One, we have no weapons; two, the door's locked, and we have no key; and three, we have no way of knowing how to reach the emperor's quarters."

"Oh, ye of little faith," she replied. "I shall have this lock picked in no time." She reached under her dress, withdrawing the lock picks concealed beneath.

Arnim looked at her in surprise. "You've had those all along?"

She grinned. "Other than patting me down for weapons, they took very little interest in me. I'd call that a win, wouldn't you? Now, make yourself useful, and see what you can find in the way of weapons."

He glanced around, his gaze coming to rest on the table where they ate their dinner, or more accurately, the two chairs sitting on either side of it. He crossed the room and lifted a chair, then smashed it against the floor. It resisted his first effort, but the second attempt broke off a leg he intended to use as a club.

She took a moment to admire his handiwork. "Nice, though perhaps a little more decorative than I would've liked."

"It's a makeshift club, Nikki, not a real weapon."

She stuck her tongue out the side of her mouth as she worked on the lock, a testament to where her true concentration lay. A loud click caused her to smile in triumph. "I've still got it!"

"I never doubted that for a moment. Let me go first. We may have to fight our way out of here, and I have more weapons training."

"With chair legs?"

Arnim chuckled. "Well, when you put it that way, I suppose not." He backed up, offering her a bow. "Would you care to lead the way, m'lady?"

"Under the circumstances, I'm far more willing to let the battle-hardened warrior go first."

He moved up, opening the door a crack and peering into the corridor. "I don't see anyone." He remained there, looking out. "It seems whatever we heard has quieted down, at least for the moment."

"They've likely moved on to greener pastures."

Arnim closed the door. "If you were going to seize this palace, what would be your primary target?"

"The emperor, naturally."

"Then that must be where they're headed. This place is a maze. Do you remember the way?"

"I used to navigate the slums of Wincaster. This is simple by comparison."

"Simple? Hardly that."

"It makes perfectly good sense when you look at it objectively. The palace is meant to project power and wealth while hiding away those individuals they rely on to keep things running."

"Meaning?"

"There are servants halls everywhere," replied Nikki, "and concealed doors to hide their presence."

"I never noticed."

"Of course not. You're not the type to worry about such things."

"And you are?"

"You forget my past. I used to infiltrate the houses of nobles, posing as a servant, remember? I learned a lot about such things. Trust me, they're all over the place. You just have to know how to look. Now lead on, my dear. The faster we go, the more likely we are to survive this."

"What exactly do you think you witnessed?" Nevarus paced, a clear sign of how upset he was.

"Fighting, Eminence," replied Janek, "between the palace guards and a group of armed intruders."

"Ruffians?"

"No. Warriors, and they seemed to be looking for something. You are in danger, Eminence. We must get you to safety."

"My bodyguards will protect me."

"Perhaps you haven't noticed, but your personal guard appears a little light today."

The emperor was not pleased. "Are you suggesting my own people have turned against me?"

"I'm not suggesting anything of the sort, Eminence, but doesn't it seem odd to you that members of your guard are missing the very day the palace is attacked?"

"They are loyal!"

"Loyalty only goes so far," said Janek. "I don't doubt their devotion to you, but that they're not here when needed is telling."

"What would make them abandon their post?"

"I can think of several things, the most likely being someone has threatened their families."

"These are dark times indeed," replied Nevarus.

"So you'll abandon the palace?"

"Not yet, although I fear I won't be here much longer." He halted and turned to face Janek. "Go and fetch Karoulus and bring him here. I would have my son by my side in my last hours as emperor."

"Your last hours? Surely you don't mean to die here?"

"I do not," replied Nevarus, "but I shall not abandon my son to suffer his fate at the hands of these… these interlopers."

"I'll do what I can to find him, Eminence, but the palace halls are extremely dangerous."

"Then take two guards with you and hurry. Time is of the essence."

Arnim peered around a corner before quickly ducking back and pressing a finger to his lips as he looked at Nikki. They held their breath as a group of warriors ran past, too intent on their destination to even notice them. She waited until they were out of sight before pushing herself away from the wall. "Those weren't palace guards."

"No," he replied. "Nor the emperor's personal bodyguards."

"They don't move like criminals, either, which means they're soldiers."

"Yes. Soldiers who don't want to announce who they're working for. Your thoughts?"

"Likely one of the three ruling families trying to grab all the power for themselves, but it makes little difference which one, at least from our perspective. We must move quickly and find the emperor before it's too late." She glanced left and right. "This way."

As they crept down the hallway, a serving woman approached, pressing herself against the far wall, trying to stay as far away from them as possible.

"How much farther?" asked Arnim.

Nikki halted at the next corner.

"Well?" he pressed.

She turned to give him a smile. "See for yourself."

He moved up, glancing down the corridor to see two of the emperor's guards standing outside a door. "What do we do now? March up and introduce ourselves?"

"I don't believe that will be necessary. Look!" Janek entered through the other end of the hallway, accompanied by a youth and two more of the emperor's guards.

Nikki immediately stepped around the corner. "Janek?"

"Lady Nicole! What are you doing here? It's not safe."

"We came to offer our help."

"Then you'd best come inside while you can." He nodded at the guards, who, in turn, opened the door. They followed him in, wondering who the boy was.

The emperor smiled. "Ah, Karoulus. I'm glad you're safe."

The lad, who couldn't have been more than twelve, stiffened. "No one would dare hurt me, Father."

"I fear that is no longer the case."

Karoulus turned to Nikki and Arnim, a sneer on his face. "And who are these peasants?"

"I'm Lady Nicole Caster," replied Nikki, "and this is my husband, Lord Arnim Caster, Viscount of Haverston."

"Names I am not familiar with."

"We're from Merceria."

The youngster ignored the comment, turning on his father with a raised eyebrow. "Why must I subject myself to the presence of these two?"

"We are under siege," replied Nevarus. "Before long, warriors will be at our doors, demanding our heads."

"They wouldn't dare! We are gods!"

"Even gods can die," said Arnim, "or do you think yourself immortal?"

Nevarus put his hand on his son's shoulder. "We carry the blood of gods, but it can be spilled just the same. My father died, as did his father before him."

"I will not run," said Karoulus, shrugging his father's hand off his shoulder. "To do so only shows weakness."

"We must leave. I implore you to come with us."

"How do you expect to get away without being recognized, Father?"

"We shall take him in disguise," replied Nikki.

"The very idea is revolting. I will remain here to face down the criminals who dare oppose our rule."

"But you will die!" said Nevarus.

"Then I shall do so with my head held high. Go, if you must, Father, but I will not slink from the palace like some sort of vermin."

"Can you see us clear of the palace?" the emperor asked Arnim.

"You're more familiar with this place than us. You tell me."

Nevarus looked to Janek, and the servant swallowed hard, his fear evident. "We could leave through the gardens, Eminence, but not with you dressed in Royal Robes. We must find you something more suitable that will not draw unwanted attention."

"Make him look like a servant," suggested Nikki.

"And if you succeed?" said Karoulus. "What then? Is my father to become a pawn in the politics of the Petty Kingdoms, or is he to be thrown into a dungeon, living out his life in misery?"

"I cannot guarantee his fate, but I know this: if he remains here, he will die."

"How can you possibly know that?"

"Simple logic," replied Arnim. "Whoever is behind this will eliminate him to prevent a possible future return to his rule. By the same argument, your own life would be forfeit."

"I am not intimidated by idle threats. My loyal guardsmen will protect me."

"Protect you?" said Nikki. "They'll be struck down like yourself. Let us take you to our queen."

Karoulus laughed. "Your queen? What utter nonsense! She is more than a thousand miles away, not to mention the other side of an entire mountain range. Even if you were, by some miracle, able to get my father there, what would be the result? Imprisonment? Death? Or would he be placed back atop the Throne so your blessed queen could pull his strings? Your promises do not fool me, Lady Nicole. I will take my chances here, remaining in the palace."

"I am your emperor!" shouted Nevarus. "I order you to come with us."

"I no longer consider you the ruler of Halvaria," his son replied. "You gave up that responsibility when you agreed to flee alongside these heathens."

"We're wasting time here," said Arnim, advancing on Karoulus. "I can knock him out and carry him."

"No!" shouted Nevarus. "You cannot lay hands on a God-Emperor!"

"He's your son," insisted Nikki. "You can't leave him behind. They'll kill him."

Nikki went to speak again, but Armin shook his head. "Leave it," he said. The room fell silent. Arnim waited for the emperor to tell his son to follow, but some small part of Nevarus had died, leaving a broken man wearing a look of abject misery in its stead.

Janek must have seen it as well, for he moved closer. "Eminence, please. We need to leave at once before the enemy is at our very door. Let me fetch you some clothes to hide your identity."

The emperor nodded, then moved to slump down in a chair.

Karoulus stood even straighter but avoided eye contact with his father, turning instead to meet Arnim's gaze. "This is all your fault."

"I had nothing to do with this," replied Arnim.

"Then how do you explain this open defiance?"

"I'm no expert on the politics of Halvaria, but if I had to guess, I'd say someone else covets the Throne."

"Who?"

"You know more about this empire than I."

"My guess," said Nikki, "would be that the three families are fighting over ascendancy. If that's the case, they'll stop at nothing to clear the path to the Throne, including murdering both you and your father."

"Gods have no fathers," replied Karoulus. "We are born of stardust."

"What utter nonsense. You're flesh and blood, same as the rest of us."

"That's precisely the response I would expect from an unbeliever."

Janek returned, carrying a bundle of clothes. "I found these, Eminence. I hope they fit." He fell silent as he took in the defiant High Regent.

"My son will not be accompanying us," said Nevarus. "He has elected to remain here to face down our enemies. I wish it were otherwise, but he has made up his mind. Now he must see it through to its inevitable conclusion." He rose, then moved to stand before his son. "There is much I should've told you, Karoulus, and for that, I am truly sorry, but now that the end is nigh, there is scant time to even say goodbye." He held out his hand to Janek, who handed over the clothes. The emperor took one last look at his son before he returned to his chair and began removing his shoes.

"Your behaviour here will not be forgotten," said the High Regent. "Your name will be forever associated with the act of cowardice."

"I forgive you your insult," replied Nevarus, "for you lack the years to comprehend the fate you've chosen for yourself."

Karoulus opened his mouth to speak, but his father held up a hand to forestall him. "I know what you're going to say, but hear me out. You've been raised in a glass bottle, one whose top has been sealed against the outside world. You may believe yourself invincible, but I assure you such is not the case. I have learned much these last few months and have come to realize this palace, opulent as it is, is no more than a gilded cage."

"But you are the emperor!"

"You believe that because that's what you've been told, but I know it isn't true, at least not anymore."

"What are you babbling on about?"

"I'm certain our predecessors possessed true power, but think back on your lessons. When was the last time an emperor made a decision about governing the empire?" He held up his finger to emphasize the point. "I'll tell you when—more than one hundred years ago! The empire is not what you think it is, Karoulus."

The High Regent placed his hand over his chest. "In here beats the heart of the empire. I will not surrender to those who would usurp my right of birth!"

"Then the time has come for us to part." Nevarus stood, his fine clothing now replaced by the simple garb of a servant. "Come, Janek. It is time we were free of this place."

"And the guards, Eminence?"

He turned to face the men in armour. "You have served me faithfully for years, but I must now ask you for the greatest sacrifice of all."

They both knelt, clutching fists to their chests in a salute. "We shall die in your name, Eminence."

"Thank you, gentlemen. May your journey to the Afterlife be swift and merciful."

Arnim moved to the door, opening it to peer outside. "It's all clear, Eminence."

The God-Emperor of Halvaria moved to the door, halting to take one last look at his son. Karoulus stood with arms crossed, defiant to the end. Nevarus turned, wiping away a tear as he exited the room.

TWENTY-EIGHT

The Grey Wardens

SUMMER 968 MC

The Halvarians marched out of Edgefield, eager to put the invaders in their place. Gelion Brightaxe watched, relieved that they had little in the way of cavalry.

"Not much to look at," mused Vard Khazad, "and we appear to have the advantage of numbers, for once."

"That we do, Majesty, although only if the Elves do their part."

"We have no reason to believe they wouldn't. Stonecastle and the Darkwood have been neighbours for centuries. We even fought beside each other during the Mercerian wars."

"We did," said Gelion, "but that was under the direction of the Marshal of Merceria."

The vard lifted his eye patch and rubbed the socket. "Are you suggesting you don't believe Lord Arandil is up to the task?"

"I have no doubt the Elves will fight, but they've never before faced the full might of the Halvarian Empire. Who knows what tactics these Humans will employ?"

"You worry too much. We have the numbers, and with Lord Arandil's cavalry, we can outmanoeuvre them. You should also remember we're facing a city garrison, not a legion. Those warriors over there appear inexperienced. I certainly wouldn't march out into the open like that were our roles reversed."

"And so we sit and wait," said Gelion, "presenting them with a weak line."

"Weak enough that it convinced them to march out of their city." The vard slapped his commander on the back. "This is it, my friend. The moment we repay them for the affront to our people."

"I wish Herdwin were here."

"As do I. He's our most experienced commander, even though the guild won't acknowledge him, but I suspect that won't be an issue in the future."

Gelion looked at him in surprise. "What makes you say that?"

"Someday, Kasri Ironheart will become Vard of Ironcliff, and we both know she and Herdwin intend to forge."

"And?"

"Don't you see? The guild will view him as a valuable source of influence."

"But our guilds have no presence in Ironcliff."

"True, but that's not through lack of trying." The vard lowered his voice. "I'll deny this if you ever repeat it, but the Guild Master of the Smiths Guild is very interested in exporting goods to Ironcliff."

"Wouldn't their own guild resist such efforts?"

"Most likely, but word is they can't keep up with demand. And it's not only the smiths guild that's rubbing its hands in glee."

"Who else?"

"The warriors guild."

"I'm a member in good standing, and I've heard nothing."

"Of course you've heard nothing. The last thing they want to do is blab it all over the city. This war has revealed the Army of Ironcliff's weakness. Apparently, Vard Thalgrun called on the guild to increase the size of the army, but they lack the trained warriors, which is where our guild comes in."

"Are you suggesting our people would relocate all the way to Ironcliff?"

"Not permanently," said Khazad. "The proposal on the table is that they'd be hired on a temporary basis, filling in till Ironcliff trains up their own people."

Gelion shook his head. "And no doubt the guild would take their percentage of everyone's wages."

"Now you understand. What about you?"

"What about me?"

"Would you consider going to Ironcliff under such circumstances?"

"Of course not. Margel would have my beard! I can't expect her to give up her seniority just to go north with me. How would this even work? We've barely enough warriors to fill out this army, let alone sending some to Ironcliff."

The vard nodded. "My point exactly, but you know how the guilds are—always thinking about how best to fill their coffers."

"Is there nothing you can do to curb their behaviour?"

"Oh, trust me, I've tried many a time. Admittedly, I've managed to restrain their more excessive qualities on a few occasions, but you know how we Dwarves get when we discover a new source of gold!"

"Not all of us," replied Gelion.

"My apologies. I didn't mean to cast aspersions. You're right. There are still noble Dwarves, like yourself, dedicated to serving the greater good. Unfortunately, those like you seldom advance to the higher levels of the guilds."

"I won't deny it. My promotion has been a long time coming."

"You deserved it. Now, let's get back to the matter of beating these Halvarians, shall we? They appear ready to commence their attack."

Kyre Banburn sat on his horse, focusing on his cavalry as it manoeuvred on his left-hand flank.

"'Tis a fine day, Captain-General."

He turned to his aide, who'd interrupted his concentration. "And by that, you mean?"

"This victory shall put your name on the emperor's lips. It is a great opportunity."

"You feel that certain of a victory? I might remind you, Cassius, this is not a legion, only a garrison unlucky enough to be in the path of an invasion, something that, only a year ago, would've been inconceivable."

"Perhaps, but you can't deny it's an opportunity to distinguish yourself." Cassius stared at the enemy line. "Look at how pathetic they are. Do they truly believe so few warriors stand a chance against us?"

"They are Dwarves. We'd be wise not to underestimate them."

"They've marched all this way with such a puny force. Why, we must outnumber them nearly three to one! I say we should let the cavalry loose on them and watch them flee from our lands."

"I may not be one of the empire's marshals, or even a commander-general, but even I know Dwarves don't retreat. They don't surrender, either, meaning this battle, no matter how short, will be a bloodbath on both sides."

"What matters if it serves the needs of the empire?" Cassius grinned. "Imagine the rewards that will come our way once news of our victory reaches the capital?"

"I might remind you we still need to defeat these Dwarves first."

"Yes, m'lord. I assume this will be a frontal assault?"

"Why else would I mass my footmen in such a manner?" Kyre sighed, for it appeared his new aide was devoid of any military knowledge whatsoever. "As we approach them, our archers will release a series of volleys designed to thin their numbers and sow discord."

"And then our lines meet?"

"Yes, but I've added a little flourish. While our footmen keep them pinned down, our cavalry will encircle them to attack from the rear."

"Brilliant, m'lord! It should be over and done with well before dinner. Who would've thought that today would be the day for such a momentous victory?"

Kyre forced a smile. It would do no good to antagonize someone with Cassius's family connections. He was, after all, a Sartellian, although admittedly not a spellcaster.

"Here they come," said Gelion.

"What do you make their numbers to be?" asked the vard.

"At least twice ours, not that I can see them all. But their archers will be next to useless."

"Then let's give them a taste of Dwarven arbalests, shall we? Oh, and sound the horn. We don't want Lord Arandil's people to miss out."

Upon Gelion's command, the Dwarven archers loosed bolts towards the enemy. Several Halvarians went down, a testament to the power of the arbalests, but the remainder of the city's garrison kept marching, ignoring the loss.

Closer and closer they came until their own arrows fell in amongst the warriors of Stonecastle. The lines made contact, and the Humans pressed in, using their superior mass to force the Dwarves back. The clash of arms filled the air, drowning out any thought of talking.

Gelion spied the empire's horsemen on his flank and immediately recognized the threat. They were riding wide, avoiding the fight altogether, and the only reason they'd adopt such a tactic was that they meant to get around behind them!

~

Shalariel peered out from behind a tree, watching as off in the distance, the Halvarian cavalry rushed past, intent on outflanking the Dwarves of Stonecastle. She turned to the Grey Wardens waiting patiently behind her and nodded. They moved from the cover of the woods, taking but a moment to form a line before advancing towards the enemy.

Their swift horses could easily outpace the Halvarians, but more importantly, these were the finest mounted archers in all of Eiddenwerthe, having honed their skills over centuries. Armed with small composite bows capable of picking off targets at range, they approached at a fast gallop, standing in their stirrups, their legs controlling their horses' movements.

Arrows flew, and ten of the empire's riders went down in the first volley. The Halvarians turned to engage the Elves in melee, perhaps thinking them weak in that regard, but nothing could've been further from the truth. The two masses of riders met with an audible clang as swords careened off Elven mail.

Shalariel watched with great interest. The Grey Wardens had not ridden to war in more than two thousand years, yet today, they fought as if they'd been doing so their entire lives. They made short work of the enemy horsemen before advancing towards the footmen threatening their allies.

Lord Arandil came up beside her. "I have given the order to advance," he announced. Moments later, four hundred Elven foot stepped out of the woods, their silver armour gleaming in the noonday sun. Behind them came two hundred archers armed with the mighty Elven bows that had proven so effective in the Weldwyn campaign.

Gelion grunted as a mace smashed against his shield. The blow did no damage, but the impact forced him back a step, then a bolt struck his attacker in the head, and the fellow toppled over.

"By Gundar!" yelled the Dwarf as he pushed forward into the enemy line. If he'd been using his two-handed axe, he would've been able to cleave through the Halvarians at a faster pace, but then he wouldn't have his shield to deflect blows.

He suddenly realized the fighting had subsided, with some of the Humans running away in fright instead of continuing the exchange of blows. "Hold your position!" he called out.

The Dwarves fell back a step to redress their line. Arbalesters let loose with bolts, inflicting horrendous casualties while Gelion tried to fathom why the fight was waning. Then a horn blasted two high notes, which told him all he needed to know—the Elves would take it from here.

Vard Khazad appeared at his side, his armour rife with dents and scratches. He lifted his visor and rubbed his missing eye socket. "That was grand," he said, his beard dripping with sweat, "but I need to catch my breath. I'm getting a little old for this sort of thing."

"We've won," replied Gelion, "thanks to the Elves."

"Aye, well, it is an alliance after all. We've done our part. Now, we must let Lord Arandil do his."

"And once he's done?"

"Then we march into Edgefield."

"Do we sack it as they did our outer city?"

"No," said the vard. "That does not fit in with the marshal's plan."

"Which is?"

"We are to take steps to be seen as liberators, not conquerors."

Gelion shook his head. "What of Dwarven vengeance? Many of our people died."

"Would you have me add more to that list? Occupying Edgefield will serve no purpose if we must continually crush uprisings."

"And what does Lord Arandil think of this strategy?"

"He agrees with it, as do I." Khazad removed his helmet, then retrieved a small cloth from somewhere and mopped his brow. "I know it's a difficult thing to ask, but you must ensure our warriors properly understand the circumstances. A false move on the part of even one of our people could jeopardize everything."

"Fear not, Majesty. My Dwarves will maintain their discipline."

The vard smiled. "You're a good commander, my friend. Were it up to me, I'd make you a general, but the guild would never permit it."

"I've only just made commander, Majesty."

"Aye, that's true, but I consider myself a good judge of character, and you have enough of that to fill a mine cart. I may not be able to promote you, but I can appoint you as master of the outer city, putting you in charge of every Dwarf guarding the outer walls. Of course, you'd have to work with the stonemasons guild to repair all the damage, but I think you'd rise to the challenge."

"Most assuredly, Majesty."

"Now, enough of this Majesty nonsense; we're not in the great hall."

"You are the vard. How else should I address you?"

"We'll borrow the Mercerian tradition, and you can call me sir. I am, after all, your superior in terms of rank."

"Yes, sir."

It was late afternoon by the time they entered Edgefield. The townsfolk watched in fear as Dwarves and Elves marched down the street. For most, this was their first encounter with such folk, resulting in many of them peering out partially opened shutters or doors held slightly ajar, unsure what would happen once they occupied their city.

Delsaran stared at the buildings, unused to such sights. The architecture here was unlike anything he'd seen back in the Elven lands, and while the houses of Stonecastle were similar in size, they were built almost entirely of stone. Here, tall wooden bell towers reached up to the sky while even larger houses, complete with columns and roofs of copper, sprawled out in all directions.

"Remarkable," he said. "I have never seen their like."

"You should visit Wincaster," replied Lord Arandil. "You would find it very similar."

"And the purposes of so many of those tall buildings?"

"They are temples dedicated to worship. Humans gather together to celebrate their religion, rather than doing so in the privacy of their own homes."

"What strange customs," replied the bard. "Am I right in assuming these Humans worship the Gods?"

"Not here in Halvaria, at least not out in the open. According to the Mercerians, they only worship one deity, the God-Emperor."

"Surely you are not suggesting their ruler is an actual god, my lord?"

"I am not suggesting anything of the kind, merely that their religious practices are built around such a belief."

"And which god do they think is ruling them?"

"That is a fascinating question," replied Lord Arandil. "Unfortunately, we have yet to determine the answer." He glanced around, his gaze meeting that of one of the townsfolk peering out of a doorway. Upon realizing this, the fellow slammed the door shut. "They fear us."

"They are right to, considering all they have done to our allies. Will they resist our rule?"

"I doubt it. They have no army left to fight with, and once they realize we mean them no harm, I believe they will return to their regular lives."

"Surely they will object to our presence?" insisted Delsaran.

"Some will, but we are not here to tax them or beat them into submission. With us, they will have more coins to spend on food, and I have yet to hear of a full belly that complains about who rules."

"You appear to have given this much thought, Lord."

"We are at the forefront of the invasion of Halvaria, and though our offensive is limited in scope, it provides us with valuable information."

"Such as?"

"How the common folk of this land will respond to our liberation. It also tells us how long before the emperor reacts to our presence. No ruler can afford to allow a foreign army within their border for any length of time without doing their utmost to remove them, which means, sooner or later, they shall send a legion to fight us. The question is, how long will that take them."

"And in the meantime?"

"We garrison Edgefield and let the population carry on as they have for hundreds of years, minus the empire's interference."

"And if the empire comes in great numbers to repel us?"

Lord Arandil chuckled. "You are full of questions today."

"My apologies, my lord."

"There is no need to apologize; you seek to educate yourself about the campaign, which is to be lauded. Now, as to strategy, our plan is simple. We shall remain in possession of Edgefield for as long as possible, but if the enemy comes in sufficient numbers, we withdraw westward, back towards the mountain passes."

"Even the Dwarves?"

"Vard Khazad has assured me they would. Why? Have you reason to doubt him?"

"They are short-statured, my lord, and as such, are slow to march. I fear they may be quickly overrun by those more swift of foot."

"Then it will be our responsibility to ensure they are well-protected during the withdrawal. I will not abandon our allies."

Delsaran watched a group of Grey Wardens dismount and enter a Halvarian temple. "What are they doing?"

"Searching for maps or anything else that might be of use," replied Lord Arandil. "We have it on good authority that places of worship are used to store things of that nature. We are also searching all buildings belonging to the Crown, or, I suppose I should say, belonging to the emperor, as it seems he owns everything."

"Owning land—that's a very Human custom."

"Do we not claim the Darkwood as our own? And what about the Dwarves? You have seen Stonecastle. Can you claim the mountain folk are any different?"

"I see your point," replied the bard, "but I was referring to the idea of individuals owning a part of nature. Are our lands not held in common for the good of all?"

"Who is to say the same is not true here? Perhaps the idea of the emperor owning everything is merely their way of saying it is held in common. Take the time to learn as much as you can about these people, Delsaran. Such knowledge can only serve the greater good."

"I shall do as you wish, Lord."

TWENTY-NINE

Zienholtz

SUMMER 968 MC

A frozen arch formed yet again, with the familiar snap that opened the portal echoing off the trees.

Natalia admired the spell's effect. "Galina has become quite proficient with her magic; it's a long way to Andover, which would require a great deal of her energy. I shall have to remember to mention it to her."

"I wish we had more time," said Aubrey. "I would've loved to swap spells with you, Shaluhk."

"You still can," replied the Orc. "I shall be marching with the Army of the North."

"As will I," added Natalia. "Assuming General Fitzwilliam has no objection?"

"I'd be glad of the company," replied Beverly. "I'd also welcome the chance to discuss strategy with you. Having now seen your army, I have several ideas on how they might best be utilized."

"Then we shall be certain to make that a priority. Now, I suggest we go through the arch before Galina grows tired of holding it open for us." She took a step, her image rippling slightly as she passed through. Shaluhk motioned for Aubrey to proceed and then followed.

Beverly turned to her husband. "All set?" He reached out, taking her hand, and then they stepped through together. She felt a moment of dizziness, but it passed once they were on the other side. She looked at Aldwin to find him smiling. "What are you grinning at?"

"It makes a nice change to be amongst people with the same eye colour as me. Not that I ever noticed back in Merceria, but you must admit, the Petty Kingdoms haven't been the most welcoming."

"That'll change once we defeat Halvaria."

"I wish I shared your optimism, but from what I've been told, some rulers in these parts fear grey eyes more than the empire."

"Then we'll have to change their minds."

She spotted Lord Fernando walking towards her. The Duke of Reinwick nodded at Natalia as he walked past her but kept heading for Beverly.

"Lady Beverly, did you see the Army of Therengia for yourself?"

"I did, Your Grace."

"And?"

"They will be a valuable addition to the campaign."

"When can we expect them to arrive?"

"My strategy is for them to meet us in Erlingen. Bringing them earlier will only slow us down."

The duke looked less than pleased. He opened his mouth to object but then changed his mind. "Have you an accurate accounting of their numbers?"

"I do."

"And?"

"I shall reveal everything once we arrive in Zienholtz."

"You are marching with my army. I would appreciate knowing how you will employ them?"

"And you will, I assure you," replied Beverly. "But before I can finalize our strategy, I must seek the opinion of King Dagmar. We all must understand what's at stake."

"Are you suggesting I don't?"

"No, Your Grace, but I do wonder why you seem so concerned. Has this something to do with the presence of the warmaster?"

"No. We fought alongside each other two years ago."

"Then why all the questions?"

Lord Fernando took a cleansing breath before answering. "It is one thing to accept advice from a Therengian Warmaster, quite another for their army to be here, in the middle of the Petty Kingdoms."

"You fear treachery?"

"The Cunars have already betrayed us," replied the duke. "How do you know that the empire's influence hasn't spread farther east?"

Natalia, having overheard the discussion, moved closer. "I can assure you, Your Grace, nothing could be further from the truth. I've spent many years fighting the influence of the Stormwinds, which includes, by extension, the Halvarian Empire."

"Please," said Beverly. "This bickering only benefits the empire. We should be concentrating on how we'll defeat the enemy, not dredging up fears from five centuries ago."

"Yes, you're right," said the duke. "My apologies. I should know better than to accuse an ally of treachery."

"I know it's difficult to overcome past prejudices; we faced the same problem back in Merceria."

"With the empire?"

"No. With Weldwyn and Norland, our two neighbours. Weldwyn is now our closest ally, and Norland is much more sympathetic to our cause."

"Are those the only realms adjacent to your own?"

"That largely depends on how you define realms," replied Beverly, "or adjacent, for that matter. The Elven Realm of the Darkwood lies to our east, as does the Dwarven Realm of Stonecastle, although that's more of a city-state."

"And were they once your enemies?"

"The Elves were. In fact, we Mercerians fought a long and bloody war when we first encountered them centuries ago."

"And the Dwarves?"

"They live in the mountains, so we've had minimal contact with them."

"Yet you came to their aid, didn't you?"

"We did," replied Beverly. "They helped us suppress an uprising, so we returned the favour when Halvaria invaded." She hesitated. "I don't suppose there are any Dwarven realms in these parts?"

"No, though there are lots of Dwarves who choose to live in Human cities. In fact, I believe there's a smith back in Korvoran who makes weapons for the Temple Fleet."

"I hate to interrupt," said Natalia, "but you need to prepare the army to march. We still need to meet up with King Dagmar's forces."

The next day, they topped a rise to see the capital of Andover, an army camp spread out before it.

The duke, pleased with this discovery, insisted on riding ahead to greet his ally while Beverly remained with the Army of Reinwick to oversee the preparation of their encampment.

Natalia stared at King Dagmar's army with a frown.

"Is something wrong, Warmaster?" asked Beverly.

"I was expecting more men. When we faced off against them two years ago, they fielded three and a half thousand; we'll be lucky if this army before us has much more than two."

"Is the Army of Reinwick smaller as well?"

"I haven't an exact count, but I'd say it's similar to what they fielded at the Battle of Ebenhof."

"Was that a difficult battle?"

"It was a very close affair, and had we not captured King Dagmar, it might've turned out quite differently."

"Still, they ended up as allies."

"You must give Duke Fernando the credit for that. He could've easily thrown Dagmar into his dungeons or even executed him, but he chose instead to offer the hand of friendship. Were it not for his foresight, there'd be no one to march to Erlingen's aid."

"Thank Saxnor for that."

"I hate to admit it, but this Halvarian invasion has done the one thing that's eluded the Petty Kingdoms for centuries."

"That being?"

"United them. Although, only time will tell if that sense of solidarity continues once the empire is crushed."

"You think it won't?"

"I hope I'm wrong," replied Natalia, "but I suspect they'll fall back into old habits."

"But not Therengia?"

"Despite a reputation as conquerors, we are actually a peaceful people."

"Yet I'm told your borders have expanded."

"They have, but more through happenstance than planning. We harbour no territorial ambitions other than perhaps eventually expanding eastward into the wilderness. Unfortunately, we border the Petty Kingdoms, resulting in the need for a large army."

"You're here to show them how strong you are, aren't you?" said Beverly.

"We want the empire destroyed as much as Reinwick or Andover," replied Natalia, "but I'd be lying if I said that's the only reason for our presence. A strong Therengia sends a message to the rest of the Continent that our people are not to be underestimated. Did you know that Andover once had a death penalty for anyone with grey eyes?"

"Barbaric," said Beverly.

"And Andover is not alone in their hatred for our people. Our presence here, fighting on the side of the Petty Kingdoms, will, I hope, demonstrate to all of Eiddenwerthe that we are the same as them, regardless of eye colour."

"A noble sentiment."

"Have you had a similar problem in your home?"

"Not with eye colour, but there's a lot of objection to the Orcs' presence within our lands. Not by the queen or any of us here in Andover, but you know how politicians can be fickle and willing to seize on any opportunity to advance their own quest for power."

"We had the same problem back in Therengia. Before my bondmate became the High Thane, our people were ruled by a hereditary king."

"What happened to him?"

"He made the mistake of challenging Athgar, and it cost him his life—not that there was much of a chance of it ending any other way. We have since changed our laws to prevent a ruler from abusing their position."

"Our queen faced a similar situation, although in her case, it wasn't settled by a duel—rather, it was a civil war."

"There is nothing civil about war," said Natalia.

"We agree on that. On another matter, what are your thoughts on King Dagmar?"

"What would you like to know?"

"Is he likely to accept me as general?"

"He will have little choice, but I suspect he'll have no objection."

"What makes you say that?"

"Dagmar impresses me as someone who wants to feel important, as if he's changing the world. A victory over the empire will elevate Andover to new heights in the eyes of the other Petty Kingdoms."

"So you're saying he'll help because of his ego?"

"You catch on quickly," replied Natalia.

They all gathered at the palace in Zienholtz, its red stone walls standing in stark contrast to the rest of the city. King Dagmar proved a gracious host, insisting everyone get to know one another before settling down to business.

Finally, after endless amounts of polite but frivolous conversation, the king led them into a dining hall, but instead of plates and cutlery, a series of maps were spread out, depicting Andover, Erlingen, and even Angvil.

"If I may have everyone's attention," said Dagmar. "I believe General Fitzwilliam is ready to reveal our strategy for the coming campaign." He nodded his head towards her. "If you'd be so kind, Lady Beverly?"

"Thank you, Majesty," she replied. "As you know, Reinwick and Andover have gone to great lengths to improve the organization of their respective armies, dividing their forces into divisions to simplify control in battle. We Mercerians have adopted a similar strategy, though we call them brigades, so you must excuse me if I sometimes use that term."

Beverly paused, drawing a cleansing breath. She'd done this sort of thing before. Why was she so nervous now? Was it because she was now dictating to rulers, or was it simply the scope of this campaign that caused her such distress?

"You've got this," whispered Aubrey.

"With the Armies of Reinwick and Andover now combined, we have more than four thousand warriors ready to march to the aid of Erlingen. When I last saw them, they had just over two thousand men under arms, giving us a combined total of six thousand, which does not include the Army of Therengia, which adds another thirteen hundred."

The mention of actual numbers appeared to impress those assembled, so she waited, letting them sink in.

"Unfortunately," continued Beverly, "only one road leads into Erlingen from here, and bringing the Therengians to our location will do nothing for us if the road becomes clogged. I therefore propose to wait until we are within striking distance before having the warmaster's mages use their magic to bring their warriors through. As to the order of march, I shall rely on Duke Fernando's men to lead the way, starting with the cavalry reserve."

"The cavalry?" said Lord Kurlan. "Wouldn't the footmen be more appropriate?"

"The horsemen can travel faster, allowing them to meet up with the Army of Erlingen as soon as possible."

"Wouldn't that leave the rest of us without cavalry support?"

"The empire will be far too busy trying to crush Erlingen, and unless I've misread these maps, they have little choice in the matter. The only road from Angvil leads to the Erlingen capital of Torburg, which is where I expect the duke's army will make its final stand."

"I would've assumed the border would be preferable," said Lord Fernando.

"And if Erlingen were able to stand alone, you'd be right, but all his hopes are pinned on us reaching him. He'll withdraw to Torburg to buy us time to come to his aid."

"And once we reach Torburg?" asked King Dagmar.

"I can't make any decisions on how the battle will be fought till we learn the enemy's dispositions."

"So you're going to take a wait-and-see attitude?"

"I prefer to think of it as improvising, something we Mercerians have made a habit of. I'll need to make myself more aware of the strengths and weaknesses of our army, so I'll be riding back and forth during the march south to see to that."

"Coordinating a march of thousands of men will be difficult."

"It will," replied Beverly, "but we have a secret weapon." She turned to her cousin. "Aubrey, if you'd be so kind?"

"My pleasure," replied her cousin. "Thanks to our allies, we possess the ability to communicate over great distances. Each division will have an Orc shaman assigned to them to relay commands in a fast and efficient manner."

"But none of us know the Orc language," said King Dagmar.

"Some of the shamans speak common, and those who don't will have a Therengian to translate."

"And to whom will these shamans report?"

"To me, and I, in turn, will report to the general. I should also point out that we'll have a number of elemental mages we can utilize, giving us yet another advantage."

"But the Halvarians have those, too, don't they?"

"They do, but they tend to be used sparingly, most often staying close to their generals. Whereas we'll place ours in amongst our warriors, where they can be more effective."

"I know this is a lot to absorb," added Beverly, "and you don't have much time to get used to these ideas, but I promise you, they will be of great benefit."

"If I may make a suggestion?" said King Dagmar.

"By all means."

"Might Andover's cavalry reserve accompany Duke Fernando's? My men might not be as heavily armoured, but they'd still be of benefit to Erlingen."

"An excellent idea," said Beverly. "I shall amend my orders to that effect. Any other questions or suggestions?" She waited, but no one spoke up. "I must stress to all of you the importance of using the shamans to keep in touch. Should you encounter anything in the way of enemy troops, no matter how insignificant you deem them to be, you must pass it on to me. At this point, I'd like everyone to report to their respective armies. We shall march at first light."

"Where do you want Shaluhk and I for the march?" asked Natalia.

"You can join my group, but I'd like your shamans to be available tonight if possible. We'll need to make introductions."

"I shall see to it at once."

The room began to empty, and then Aldwin appeared at Beverly's side. "You were magnificent. Gerald would be proud."

"You're only saying that because you're my husband."

"No. I say it because it's true. You were the very model of calm decisiveness. If I didn't know better, I'd swear you'd done this dozens of times."

"It didn't feel like it to me."

"Why? You've been a general for some time."

"I have, and I've even led the Army of Merceria, but this... this feels different."

"Different, how?" asked Aldwin.

"More monumental. Does that make sense?"

"In a manner of speaking, it is. After all, it's not only one Petty Kingdom that needs a victory—it's all of them."

"That doesn't make it any easier."

"You must do what the marshal does and trust in those under your command."

"I wish I could," said Beverly, "but I know all the Mercerian commanders on a first-name basis. I can't say the same here."

"There's still time, and if I know you, you'll have that rectified before we reach Torburg."

They crossed the border two days later, entering the village of Lieswel, to find out that a messenger from the Duke of Erlingen was waiting. He was immediately brought to Beverly, who was busy watering Lightning.

He dropped to one knee and held out a scroll case. "Message for you, General." Aldwin took the scroll, removed its contents, and passed them to his wife who read it over.

"Bad news?" he asked.

"It appears a new threat has emerged."

"Where?"

"A Holy Army has seized Galmund and is marching on the capital."

"Galmund? That's southeast of Torburg, if I recall."

"I'm surprised you remember. I didn't think you paid attention to such things."

He chuckled. "I'm a smith. I pay attention to every little detail. I just like to maintain an air of mystery. Any indication of how large this Holy Army might be?"

"It doesn't say."

"Your pardon, General," said the messenger, "but Temple Commander Marlena suspects there may be as many as one thousand." He noted their stares. "The duke chose her to replace you as the leader of his army."

"A good choice. Might you know how she came to this estimate?"

"She revealed that the Holy Army had set upon her own order some years ago, and it was unable to stop the Five Hundred. Fearing that the Temple General might see fit to interfere, they'd likely try to field superior numbers to prevent a similar outcome."

"Have you rested?"

"I have, General. I was just getting ready to ride into Andover when the Army of the North arrived. Shall I return to Torburg with a reply?"

"Yes. Tell the Temple Commander we will march with all haste, and she is to do all she can to delay the advance of the Halvarian legions."

"Yes, General." He rose, gave a bow, then rushed back to his horse.

"It appears things are moving quickly," said Aldwin.

"Indeed."

He smiled. "You sound just like your father."

"I shall take that as a very high compliment."

"As you should. Shall I fetch Krazuhk? Her Air Magic may be of great use for us as we march."

"An excellent idea. I knew I kept you around for something other than your sparkling conversation."

THIRTY

Torburg

SUMMER 968 MC

"This is it," said Edora. "The moment we've all been waiting for. The Holy Army will hit the duke's army from one side while we strike from the other. It's only a matter of days now."

"I'm not so certain of that," said Moreau. "We've encountered stiff resistance ever since we left Anshlag. I fear it won't get any easier as we approach their capital."

"Those raids are little more than a nuisance."

"Oh, they're much more than that, Your Grace. They strike as we're about to march, forcing our men to take up defensive positions, and then they withdraw, repeating the process numerous times a day."

"Then hunt them down," replied Edora. "You have the horsemen to do it."

"It's not quite that simple. They are armoured."

"There are eight hundred horsemen at your disposal—use them!"

"Yes, Your Grace."

"We're so close I can taste victory," she said. "Centuries of conquest in the name of the empire, and it all comes down to this—one final battle that will crush all resistance."

"Have we any new information regarding our allies?"

"They halted two days shy of Torburg and are awaiting my orders."

"Which will be?"

"To advance to battle, but I shan't give that order until we're ready to finish the encirclement, and I can't do that unless your legion clears the road."

"I shall send every horseman I have," replied Moreau.

"On second thought, move your men back up the road. The Eighth Legion will take your place."

"I must object, Your Grace. The Ninth has not fought clear across the Petty Kingdoms only to be relegated to the rear."

"I'm not punishing you; rather, I'm rewarding you. Let Rakert's legion wear itself down, then you can strike the final blow against the Army of Erlingen."

Moreau offered a deep bow. "You honour us, Your Grace."

Temple Commander Romanus stood there, pleased with all he'd accomplished. The efforts of his master, Talivardas, had finally borne fruit, and now, years after they'd infiltrated the Church, he was about to strike the final blow. The Holy Army would trap the Army of Erlingen between themselves and the empire's legions, annihilating the Petty Kingdom's resistance once and for all.

Rostyslav, his aide, appeared at his side. "The men are restless, Commander."

"And by the men, you mean the volunteers?"

"Yes."

It amused Romanus no end that he'd used the Church's influence to entice people into their service. If they discovered the army's true purpose, they'd abandon the march, but the Holy Fathers had excelled at preaching that Erlingen was full of heretics and in need of cleansing. It had served them well, with more than four hundred warriors joining their so-called Holy Crusade. Not that he relied on them, for the bulk of his army was comprised of Temple Knights of Saint Cunar, warriors whose reputation alone put fear into the hearts of men.

"Might I ask a question, Commander?"

"Certainly."

"Once the battle commences, will we be able to utilize our magic out in the open?"

Romanus cast his gaze about, worried someone might have overheard, but it appeared his aide had been careful. "No," he finally replied. "Doing so would risk these Temple Knights learning of our true nature. Presently, they all believe we are on a righteous path, marching to punish unbelievers. Were we to employ spells, they would soon see through our ruse, which would lead to catastrophic results."

"Even if it puts our lives in danger?"

"I'm afraid so. I know this makes things difficult, but we are about to complete the Great Dream. Surely you can pretend to be a Temple Knight for another week?"

"I shall do my best, Commander."

"Good. Now, have our scouts reported anything of interest?"

"No. We have eyes on Torburg, but their army has yet to arrive. Are you certain we wouldn't be better off to capture the city while we can?"

"While that might sound like a good idea, it requires us to garrison it, leaving us shorthanded once battle commences. Better to leave that responsibility to the enemy. We are tasked with tying up the Army of Erlingen while our Halvarian allies manoeuvre in behind them. If we move too soon, we'd be facing superior numbers, and then where would we be?"

"We are half a legion strong, Commander. Surely that's enough to defeat the Duke of Erlingen's forces?"

"I appreciate your eagerness," said Romanus, "but the Five Hundred are still out there somewhere."

"If they were still a threat, why haven't they marched?"

"I might remind you they played havoc with our plans for Hadenfeld."

"Yes, but we've heard little of them since. I put it to you that they've disbanded. It takes coins to house and feed five hundred Temple Knights; without the Church's financial support, how would they continue to exist?"

"You raise a good point, but their Temple General has proven herself to be a master of surprises. If a way existed for her to support her people without the Church, she'd have found it."

"We chased them out of the Antonine," said Rostyslav. "Do you really expect them to show up here in Erlingen?"

"Your version of events and mine differ."

"How?"

"We did not drive the Agnesites from the Antonine; in fact, we were trying to do just the opposite, but their Temple General outwitted us."

"I was led to believe we sent a Holy Army after them."

"Oh, we did, but it met with failure."

"I don't understand," said Rostyslav. "I was told we'd decisively defeated them."

"That was a lie, meant to cower those who still opposed us in the Antonine. The truth of the matter is that they escaped into the eastern reaches of Hadenfeld."

"Hadenfeld? But we sent the Holy Army to subjugate them, didn't we?"

"Yes. Two years ago, but it failed."

"Failed? We forced their king to accept the Church. I'd count that as a victory."

"You misunderstand the purpose of that campaign. The Primus painted it as a victory, but I assure you, it was nothing of the sort. We marched in there with the intent to force them to accept a garrison of our knights, thereby neutralizing any military threat that Hadenfeld might have deployed against the empire."

"But wasn't that achieved?"

"No," replied Romanus. "Unfortunately, King Ludwig proved a more capable commander than we expected."

"So the entire campaign was all for nothing?"

"Not nothing. The king agreed to let the Church continue performing services but refused to allow our order to garrison troops there. A particularly galling result, considering he gave refuge to Mathewites."

"Were you there?"

"No. I was travelling the Petty Kingdoms trying to convince the rulers not to give sanctuary to the disbanded orders. Not that my efforts yielded much in terms of success. It did, however, give me access to the Temple General of our own order, which is how I learned what happened in Hadenfeld."

"What a disgrace."

"I would agree, but I wasn't there to see things first-hand. I did, however, discover they relieved the Temple Commander who led the invasion of his command. Those brother knights who survived were also sworn to secrecy." Romanus grinned. "That's one advantage of having such a strict order. We don't have to worry about word getting out."

"But surely Hadenfeld could tell of our defeat?"

"True, but we've seen no evidence they've done so. My guess is the king wants to avoid being the target of another crusade."

"Is Hadenfeld hiding the Five Hundred?"

"I couldn't say. Official reports from the campaign were considered too sensitive to be placed in the Church's archives."

"But our Temple General would've known, wouldn't he?"

"Perhaps, but if that's the case, he chose not to share the information."

"I doubt it matters much," said Rostyslav. "Any threat from Hadenfeld would have to march clear across Zowenbruch. And if they did defeat our crusade, they would've taken casualties."

"Even a reduced army could prove troublesome to our plans," said Romanus, "which is why we must remain vigilant."

"I'll be sure to post extra sentries, Commander."

"Good. Now, let's carry out some drills, shall we? Our new recruits look like they need seasoning."

. . .

Temple Captain Waleed watched the Halvarians advance, their cavalry in the lead, but rather than the typically lighter provincial warriors, these were their imperial horsemen, and much like the knightly orders of the Petty Kingdoms, they wore plate armour.

The empire's horsemen trotted cautiously down the road—and why wouldn't they? Waleed's command had been harassing the enemy advance for days, yet the Halvarians refused to send men to clear out the woods to their south—the very woods that concealed his white-clad Temple Knights.

His plan was simple: wait until the leading edge of the column passed, then charge the footmen following. He turned, surveying his Temple Knights. Most were second sons from wealthy families, trained from childhood to be knights. More than half had served in battle, either before joining the order or after, and he was confident they'd do their duty this day.

He returned to watching the roadway, where the cavalry had passed, and footmen now clogged the road. The Halvarian legions had a reputation as a highly disciplined army, perhaps even rivalling the Temple Knights, but Waleed saw none of that here. These men were worn out and ill-equipped, leading him to surmise they were provincials, not imperials.

He flipped down his visor, then drew his sword, raising it into the air. All around him, his knights repeated the gesture, signalling their readiness to begin the charge.

It started slowly at first, with the Temple Knights emerging from the woods in ones and twos. They halted in the open, forming up into their ranks while Waleed assumed his position on the right side of the line, then gave the command to advance.

First came the trot, the riders keeping to a tight formation. In theory, they should've been stirrup to stirrup, but such a close formation was notoriously difficult to maintain, so for this campaign of hit-and-run tactics, they'd adopted the habit of leaving a foot or so between stirrups.

The Halvarians, perhaps mistaking them for their own cavalry, at first ignored the presence of the knights, but as they advanced in a fighting formation, the footmen scrambled to present a defence.

Waleed ordered the charge, the command repeating down the line. They increased their pace, first to a canter, then to a gallop. The earth shook with the pounding of their hooves, and then they struck the column, pushing aside footmen or crushing them beneath their horses.

He was soon in the midst of a chaotic melee, slicing down with measured strokes, conserving his strength while using clean, well-practiced swings. To him, it wasn't a battle; it was a series of individual encounters chained together, one after the other. Halvarians fell by the dozens, their counterattacks useless against the Temple Knights' plate armour.

Waleed heard a sword scrape across his thigh, then struck out with a blow from on high that tore into his foe's helmet, splitting it. Blood gushed, reddening his blade, but he ignored it, pulling back to swing at another target.

Three more warriors fell beneath his weapon, and then he broke through the mass of men, forcing him to bring his horse around, ready to carve once more into the column, but the provincials had broken, many dropping their weapons and running in fear. They'd destroyed at least one company, perhaps more, but then Waleed realized he'd miscalculated, for a large force of armoured cavalry was coming up the road from the enemy's rear.

He sheathed his sword, replacing it with the mace tucked in his belt, ready to meet this new challenge, but it would all be for naught if his men weren't prepared to do the same. He flipped up his visor, shouting, "To me, to me!"

The Temple Knights heard his call, and before long, they'd formed up on either side of him, ready to meet this new threat. Wounded footmen lay on the ground, many screaming out for mercy while others bled to death. Waleed ignored them, concentrating on the approaching cavalry, who were still some two hundred paces away. He gave the command, and for the second time today, his knights advanced in two ranks, keeping their line steady. Closer and closer, they rode until he gave the signal to charge.

It was as if a peal of thunder had been released from the sky. The line shot forward, the horses lathering under the continued strain of the charge. For a moment, it felt as if time stood still, and then they were in amongst the enemy, reaching out with mace, axe, and hammer, smashing at the plate armour of their adversaries.

Waleed had the presence of mind to flip his visor down just before a mace struck his helm, twisting his head painfully, but years of practice allowed him to take the blow and counter with a swing of his own, denting a vambrace.

All around him, his Temple Knights continued the fight, trading blows in an endless series of strikes and counterstrikes, a relentless assault that could only be performed by muscles accustomed to such exertions. With his visor down, Waleed could see little, save for his immediate foes, but the clangs of battle told him what he needed to know. The enemy was weakening, the training of the Temple Knights proving superior.

Something struck his side, and his armour buckled. The taste of blood flooded the back of his throat, but he managed to strike back, smashing the head of his mace into an elbow joint. His opponent fell back, cursing and swearing while all around, the sound of metal on metal was deafening.

Waleed slowed, allowing his knights to push past him while he tried to recover. He took a deep breath and almost doubled over in pain.

A familiar voice called out, "Commander, are you injured?"

He flipped open his visor to see Brother Nicolas. "A blow to the side," he replied through gasps. "I think it cracked a rib or two. How goes the battle?"

"We broke their cavalry charge, Commander, but I fear more horsemen are on the way."

"Then we shall withdraw and allow them to deal with their wounded. Did we suffer any losses?"

"No dead, sir, although we have some wounded."

"Organize a rearguard to keep an eye out for pursuit."

"Yes, sir."

Waleed forced himself to sit up straight, an act he soon regretted as pain lanced through him. He turned his horse around and began riding back towards Lord Wulfram, the Baron of Regnitz, who'd been watching from the safety of the woods. He prayed his men had done enough this time to prove their loyalty and that he'd survive to witness their acceptance.

"This is unacceptable!" shouted a furious Edora. Once again, the enemy had struck, this time with devastating effects, despite her warning to strengthen their cavalry screen.

Umberto Rackert, the commander-general of the Eighth Legion, knew better than to speak, waiting instead for her to finish venting her anger.

"By all rights, I should have you dismissed," she was saying, "but I have no time to train a replacement. Well? What have you to say for yourself?"

"I offer no defence, Your Grace."

She took a deep breath, letting it out slowly. Once done, she again looked at Battista, though her anger had abated. "Who attacked you?"

"Knights, Your Grace, although we know not which order."

"Prior to invading the Petty Kingdoms, you were given explicit instructions to familiarize yourselves with the orders of chivalry we might run up against. Are you now claiming you failed in your duty?"

"No, Your Grace, but these individuals wore no symbol that identified their order nor carried a banner. They also fought with great passion and discipline."

"They wore surcoats, surely?"

"They did, but they were white, with no adornment. Could they be Temple Knights of Saint Augustine?"

"Of course not. That order wasn't trained to fight in battles, and the Church disbanded them, with all their knights taken into service as Cunars."

"Then I am at a loss as to who they might be, but they won't surprise us a second time. However, our advance will be slowed even further while we clear them from the woods."

"How many were there this time?"

"It's difficult to give an exact number, given the circumstances, but I can't imagine there were more than, say… one hundred?"

"You don't sound very confident of your answer."

"The engagement was chaotic, and we've yet to speak to all the survivors. In time, we'll learn more about them, but for now, we've forced them to withdraw."

"Promising," said Edora, "but not the news I'd hoped to hear today. Return to your legion and ensure your men are ready to continue the march. If we hope to finish off the Army of Erlingen, we must be swift."

THIRTY-ONE

Trollden

Glisnak crouched in the boat, watching as they travelled downstream in the dark, the mushrooms they'd brought from Stonewall allowing him to see as clear as day. He glanced over at Virdu, who sat in the bow of another boat, some of the wolf riders and their wolves crammed in the small vessel along with men from Weldwyn. The comical sight made him smile as he thought about the more serious task they undertook, that of travelling to the mouth of the river and then moving down the coast, cutting off the Halvarians' access to their ships.

Grazuk, sitting behind him, reached out, touching his elbow. *"How much farther?"* she whispered in their native Garspeak.

"Not far now. I can hear the sea."

"Any sign of their ships?"

"No, but they're likely farther down the coast, which is good for us, as it means we can get ashore without fear of them interfering." He glanced back to see her rubbing the top of Quickpaw's head.

"Why us?" she asked. *"Surely they have others better able to do this?"*

"Perhaps," replied Glisnak, *"but none can move with the speed of you wolf riders, and we need that to cut off their retreat."*

"There are only twelve of us riders."

"True, but our lobbers and grunts are here to help, and don't forget the men of Weldwyn."

They both looked at Captain Fairhand in the other boat. He and his men had travelled with the Goblins since Loranguard and were quick to volunteer for this task. Glisnak was happy to have support but worried about their lack of experience, not that the Goblins could necessarily claim more, but the Mercerian army had been teeming with those who'd spent a lifetime as warriors.

Warriors—Goblins had no term for someone who fought for a living. Back in the enclaves, hunters were referred to by how they hunted. Thus, they had grunts who pushed spears, lobbers who threw arrows, and wolf riders who… well, that was obvious, at least to Glisnak.

Humans, on the other hand, referred to their warriors as footmen, archers, and cavalry, the latter mounted on immense horses, at least by Goblin standards. He'd always thought a Mountain Wolf large, but they paled in comparison to the great warhorses the Guard Cavalry of Merceria employed.

However, what the wolf riders lacked in size they more than made up with their speed, and not only that, a wolf could be stealthy when required or inspire fear with their howling and growling.

He'd only brought two sixes worth of riders from Stonewall, but he'd told Grazuk to space them out before they made their presence known. He hoped that wolf howls coming from the shoreline would be enough to dissuade any Halvarians from attempting to flee in that direction.

He smiled, remembering Al-tea's plan. Once his group cut off the coast, the rest of the army would approach from the north, blocking the Halvarians in. They'd have nowhere to flee, for the river flowed along the west, and to the east was only more swamp and the massive creatures called three-horns.

Glisnak had never seen a three-horn, but looked forward to laying eyes on one. He was told they were even bigger than the Mercerian Chargers, but it wasn't their size he found fascinating; it was their horns.

He tried to imagine riding into battle atop such a beast, its head swinging left and right, tossing aside the enemy like pebbles of sand.

Grazuk nudged him from his reverie. *"We're almost there."*

Glisnak stood and pointed towards a sandbank. He waited as quiet whispers carried the message to the man at the tiller. The craft turned to the left, while the river current carried them downstream, leading to it feeling like they floated sideways.

The boat ground to a halt as it struck the sand, but the stern remained in deeper water, twisting around until it, too, was stuck fast.

Quickpaw jumped from the boat first, Grazuk wading along behind her. Glisnak followed, landing in chest-high water, another strange sensation, for back in the Sunset Peaks, no Goblin would dream of immersing themselves this deep in water.

The other wolf riders followed suit, then the grunts. He heard the second boat scrape across the sand, and then the lobbers joined those in the water, along with Captain Fairhand's men.

"Over here," Gliznak called out, using the common tongue, happy he no longer needed to rely on the ring's magic to communicate, for he'd unknowingly picked up the language during his time travelling with the Army of the West.

Quickpaw stepped from the water and commenced shaking herself, drenching those nearby, as did the other wolves, leaving a noticeably wet patch on the ground.

Glisnak stepped ashore, seeking out Grazuk. "*You know what to do,*" he said, switching once more to Garspeak.

She grinned back. "*This is far more interesting than hunting.*"

"*Don't get too used to it; we'll be returning to Stonewall once we're done here.*"

She nodded, then barked out an order to her fellow wolf riders, and they all rushed off into the distance.

Captain Fairhand came up beside him. "My men are ready to march. Are you going to be all right down here alone?"

Glisnak had only two sixes of grunts and an equal number of lobbers, but the addition of Virdu would be a great help. He imagined hordes of Halvarians approaching from the north, dragging themselves out from the swamp only to come across his defiant band of Goblins. Brogar had regaled him with the rich history of the Dwarves and how it was an important part of their culture. Would this moment be remembered by future generations of his own people?

"Glisnak?" prompted the captain, rousing him from his daydream.

"Yes. We're ready. You may march out and do your part."

The men of Weldwyn comprised the largest section of the expedition, forming the centre of a line stretching along the coast from the river to a point east of the Halvarian encampment. There were two parts to this excursion: cut off the Halvarian's retreat while preventing the fleet from landing more warriors.

He watched the captain's men advance along the coast, leaving his own small command with the boats. Glisnak suddenly felt alone, as if his tiny group was in the middle of a hunt surrounded by danger. He shuddered at the thought, but then shook it off, concentrating instead on how to deploy his people. He spotted a large piece of driftwood and ordered his grunts to retrieve it to be used to form a makeshift barricade, behind which his grunts would stand, their spears ready to stab out at anyone who tried to cross the obstacle.

Behind them, he had the lobbers create a raised area by hauling sand, wood, and anything else they could manage and piling it up. Standing atop this would give them a height advantage that allowed them to lob arrows over the heads of his grunts.

He wandered out in front once they had everything in place, pretending he was the enemy. To his mind, it was a solid defence, although it only covered a small area. This was a sobering thought, and he began to worry. Where he'd once imagined the enemy breaking against his line, he now saw them swarming them, flooding to the sea and leaving nothing but Goblin blood in their wake.

Grazuk set about arranging the wolf riders, instructing the first to halt, then continued on, stopping the second within sight of the first. Once deployed, their spread-out line would give them eyes and ears over a far greater distance than if they were all bunched up together.

They were to commence howling once the moon reached its height, but she had no idea how long that would take. She rode back along her line, taking up position to the west, allowing her to help should the men of Weldwyn come under attack.

She heard them before she saw them approaching, their armour making it almost impossible for Captain Fairhand's men to move quietly. Words were exchanged, although she understood little. She was getting used to the common tongue of Humans but was certainly no expert. The noise quieted, and then the long wait commenced.

Tog surveyed his army. The Dwarves constituted the centre of his advance, with the Clansmen marching on the west, while his Trolls, more able to navigate the tricky terrain of the swamp, came from the east. He realized it wasn't the most advantageous terrain to mount an attack but consoled himself with the knowledge that the enemy was in the same situation. He glanced up at the moon, noticing it almost directly overhead.

"Sound the advance," he commanded.

A horn blared out, with others taking up the call, the signal repeating down both sides of his line. Tulfar's Dwarves advanced at a steady pace, with the left and right wings matching their speed.

The uneven ground beneath their feet was soggy or soaked, with only the occasional dry spots jutting out of the water to offer surer footing. The army was forced to split their ranks when they came across areas where the water was too deep, making the line undulate like some ancient serpent slithering across a field. They continued through the swamp until, far off in the distance, the baying of wolves erupted, signalling all was in place.

Upon reaching the enemy camp, Tog was surprised to see they were unprepared for battle. Instead, individuals walked around on a dry spot while hundreds lay on the ground, many writhing about in a fevered state.

"They are sick," noted Kurghal. "The swamp has done the job for us."

"Perhaps," replied Tog, "but by my reckoning, there should be double that or more." He scanned the area, his gaze coming to rest on Osbourne Megantis. He waved the Fire Mage over. "I need you to summon your phoenix."

"By all means, Commander. I assume you wish to discover the whereabouts of the rest of the legion?"

"I do."

Osbourne settled his mind, digging deep into the flame burning within him. He imagined a bird of fire slashing through the air, sparks trailing and then felt the release as the energy coursed through him. He looked up at the phoenix overhead, closing his eyes and establishing a connection to guide the conjured creature over the enemy.

He flew his view south, where he spotted a large mass of Halvarian warriors heading for the coast. There must've been two or three hundred, and unlike their sick comrades, they looked full of fight.

"Commander?" he said, still watching the scene from above.

Tog rumbled a reply, "Yes?"

"There's a large force, perhaps three hundred, heading straight for Captain Fairhand's position."

"I shall relay that information," came Kurghal's voice.

~

Virdu stared at the ghostly image of the Orc. It was a strange feeling to communicate with someone who wasn't close, but she heard Kurghal clearly.

"Trouble," said the Orc in the common tongue. "Many Humans are headed for the middle of your line."

"I shall inform Glisnak," she replied, the magic of Glisnak's ring allowing her to understand all she heard. Once the spectre of the Orc dissipated, she turned to her pit-brother, reverting to Garspeak. *The enemy is heading for Captain Fairhand.*

"I thought that might happen." He dug into the sling bag Al-tea had given him and withdrew a horn, blowing a single note that echoed off the trees, followed by two more in rapid succession, indicating position two was in

trouble. He waited before repeating the signal, with only silence in response. Then off in the distance came a howl telling him the message had been heard.

"*It's done,*" he said. "*We can do nothing now but wait.*"

"*Should we not go to his aid?*" asked Virdu.

"*No. To do so would leave this area unguarded. We must let Grazuk take care of it.*"

~

Quickpaw heard the horn first, her ears pricking up, and then she howled in response. A moment later, the other wolves repeated the call with howls of their own. Grazuk waited as her wolf riders rushed to her side. She did a quick count, ensuring everyone was present, then led them westward towards the Weldwyn position.

She saw them fighting, the mushrooms still allowing her to see in the dark. Grazuk tightened her legs around Quickpaw's chest and lowered her spear, prepared for the charge. She yearned to scream out a challenge, but doing so would reveal they were coming. Instead, she led her wolf riders on in silence, each ready to tear into the unsuspecting enemy.

A group of Halvarians had engaged Captain Fairhand's men, and he was in danger of being overwhelmed. Grazuk picked a target at the back of the assailants, then settled into a crouch, her short spear held firmly in her grasp. The small weapon was designed to strike as Quickpaw's jaws snapped at the target, and they timed the attack to perfection.

The spear sank in, ripping through the Halvarian's chain armour, and the fellow screamed out in agony as the teeth of her Mountain Wolf went for his throat. It was all over in a moment, and then they continued past, the spear remaining in the Halvarian's body.

Grazuk unslung her axe while Quickpaw wheeled about, ready to charge once more. A few Halvarians had turned to deal with her as the rest of the wolf riders struck. From her point of view, the enemy suddenly fell face down, the blood-soaked teeth of the other wolves bearing witness to the ferocity of the attack.

She scanned the area, trying to get her bearings. Ten men had gone down in the initial charge, but plenty of Halvarians still fought the men of Weldwyn.

She urged on Quickpaw, directing the Mountain Wolf with her legs. Her axe took down a warrior from behind, cleaving into his neck even as Quickpaw tore into the fellow's leg. Someone to her left thrust out a spear, the tip digging into her wooden shield and passing through, narrowly missing her arm. She dropped it, then swung her weapon overhead to smash against her attacker's forearm. It didn't penetrate the armour, but she felt the bone beneath and was convinced the blow had broken it.

She was surrounded by a cacophony of growls, snarls, and the ripping of flesh as the great Mountain Wolves tore into their victims. The Goblin riders struck out when they could, but under such circumstances, they were forced to concentrate on not falling from their mounts.

Grazuk spotted Captain Fairhand, who'd managed to form a rough circle, the banner of Weldwyn at its centre, but his warriors were suffering terrible casualties. All around them lay the dead and wounded from both sides, making it difficult to move, let alone fight. It reminded her of the Sunset Peaks, and she imagined the bodies as a rockfall, just the type of terrain her people were used to.

She held her axe aloft and let loose a high-pitched scream that pierced the din of battle. Within moments, her small command answered the call, withdrawing from their individual melees and coming towards her.

For the wolf riders, there was no forming of line or wedge; such things were alien to them. Instead, they rushed forward much as a wolf pack would, tearing after their prey.

They leaped over bodies, their lips folded back, exposing the teeth of both rider and wolf. Without exception, they headed straight for Captain Fairhand and his beleaguered men.

Quickpaw barrelled into one Halvarian, using her pony-sized bulk to push him aside even as her teeth sank into another. Grazuk struck out with her axe, the head of her weapon sinking into the wood of his shield. As she pulled it free, the fellow hit back with his sword, the blade scraping along her chest, cutting into her Dwarven leather but narrowly missing her flesh. Quickpaw turned her head and bit down into the man's arm, shaking her head from side to side, her massive teeth tearing into his limb.

Blood splattered Grazuk, and she took a moment to wipe it from her eyes. Before her, Captain Fairhand was down with an enemy warrior standing over him, sword raised. She leaped from her wolf, her axe slamming against the Halvarian's back even as the force of her body knocked the fellow from his feet, sending him tumbling forward onto the captain. Grazuk, being more dexterous, landed on her feet, moving to stand over the prone bodies, and then she struck the Halvarian's back, hitting the man dead centre, and though it failed to break through the chainmail, the bone beneath wasn't as lucky. The Halvarian twitched, his arms and legs flailing for the briefest of moments, and then he went completely still.

She attempted to drag the body from atop Captain Fairhand but didn't have the strength. Quickpaw, sensing what she was attempting, grabbed a boot and dragged the Halvarian from atop the Weldwyn captain.

He sat up, battered and bruised, blood covering his armour, and said something; though, in the midst of such a loud fight, Grazuk didn't understand a word of it.

The fighting around them died down, the remaining Halvarians fleeing north. It appeared to be all over, but then she spied a long line of troops coming towards them. Just as she was about to order her riders to flee, she realized it was Lord Tulfar's Dwarves who approached. The battle was over, and they'd won a great victory.

THIRTY-TWO

Fighting for Position

The Army of Erlingen had finally reached Torburg, marching onto the tournament fields south of the city. They'd marched day and night until exhaustion overtook them, yet everyone knew more was to come. The enemy would soon be upon them, forcing them to make a final stand against the invaders.

Marlena watched as the last of her command moved into the camp. Morale had hit an all-time low as they retreated, forcing many to consider whether it wasn't better to abandon this campaign to survive. She'd found their lack of faith disturbing, but she could do little about it. The duke's men had captured a few deserters, making an example of them by hanging them by the road, but it did nothing to endear him to his men and only made matters worse in her mind.

She longed to be free of the burden of command but couldn't bring herself to resign. She'd accepted the responsibility in good faith and couldn't abandon these people to the clutches of the empire without a fight.

Marlena shook off her despair, trying to concentrate on the positives. The retreat, hard as it had been, was over, and the Holy Army had yet to make an appearance. With a bit of luck, the Army of Erlingen might be able to rest and regain its strength.

Sister Johanna rode over, her expression anything but encouraging.

"I bear news," announced the knight. "The army from the Antonine is massing to the southeast."

"As we expected. I don't suppose we have a better idea of their numbers?"

"I'm afraid not, Commander, but reports place them at the fork in the road that leads to Mulsingen. They halted there and made camp, at least they had two days ago."

"Send my compliments to Temple Captain Petra and ask her to deploy her cavalry along the approaches to Torburg."

"And if they encounter the enemy?"

"Then they are to warn us as soon as possible. Oh, and once she's seen to that, have her report to me, along with Temple Captain Vitaly. We must make plans."

"Should I include His Grace, the duke?"

"That would probably be for the best."

"Anyone else?"

"Not unless Temple Captain Waleed has returned."

"I shall make enquiries, Commander." Johanna turned around and trotted off, her horse as exhausted as the knight.

It was late in the afternoon by the time Marlena was able to meet in her command tent with her division commanders. Lord Alain, the Duke of Erlingen, was also in attendance, although he had little to offer in terms of advice, looking to the Temple Commander for answers when questions arose.

Sister Johanna arrived, charging in and interrupting the proceedings. "Help is coming," she said, the words rushing out.

"What help?" asked the duke.

"The Northern Alliance will be here come morning. A messenger has arrived from the north. Shall I bring them in?"

"By all means," replied Marlena.

The tent flap opened, and an Orc stepped in. "Greetings," she said. "I am Shaluhk, Shaman of the Red Hand. I am here to assist in coordinating efforts with General Fitzwilliam."

"It's about time," said the duke. "I was beginning to lose all hope. How many men has the Northern Alliance brought?"

"It is not only the Alliance. The Army of Therengia has consented to assist, but only if you agree to place your army under the command of General Fitzwilliam."

"I am more than willing to step aside," offered Marlena, "but the enemy is near, and we haven't much time. What is the general's plan?"

"She will tell you herself." Shaluhk turned to Sister Johanna. "I rode here in the company of Galina Marwen. Would you be so kind as to invite her in?"

The Temple Knight offered a slight bow. "With the commander's permission." She looked at Marlena.

"Of course. Bring her in at once."

The woman who entered wore no armour, but something about her carried an air of… power. "Greetings," she said.

"What's this all about?" asked the duke.

Galina ignored him, instead looking at the Orc. "Have they agreed to the warmaster's conditions?"

"Warmaster?" said Duke Alain. "I know nothing of this!"

Shaluhk shrugged. "A difficult question to answer, Galina. Temple Commander Marlena is willing to place the army under the command of Lady Beverly, but the duke may have some questions. Perhaps the warmaster herself might be the best one to answer?"

"Yes, of course," replied Galina. She raised her hands, then paused. "I'm going to cast a spell. I trust there will be no objections?" When no one answered, she began drawing on her inner magic. The air cooled as a frozen archway formed in the middle of the tent. After an audible snap, the space within the arch changed to reflect a wooded scene with a woman in plate armour standing there, wearing the surcoat of Saint Agnes, the crest of her order emblazoned in gold thread. She walked through the arch.

"Allow me to introduce Temple Commander Cordelia," said Shaluhk, "regional commander of her order."

"I know that name," replied Marlena. "You served with the Temple General."

"I did," the woman replied. "Although, at the time, she was only a knight." She waited as two more sister knights stepped through. "My pardon for the delay," she added, "but we thought it best to bring some bodyguards before the warmaster makes her appearance. We weren't certain how she might be received."

Natalia Stormwind finally walked through the archway along with Beverly Fitzwilliam.

"I hope you have a plan," said the duke. "We're in a tricky situation here."

"So I've heard," replied Beverly. "Now, let's get started, shall we? Where are the legions?"

"Coming from the northwest," replied Marlena. "Temple Captain Waleed's rearguard has slowed their advance, but they won't be delayed for much longer."

"I need to see whatever maps you have of the area."

"I'll go and get them," said Johanna.

Beverly turned to the duke. "Your Grace, I mean no insult, but time is of the essence. Will you consent to place your army under my command?"

"Do you promise us a victory?" he asked.

"I have a strategy that should defeat Halvaria, but no one can guarantee the outcome, save for the Gods… or, in this case, the Saints. I promise, however, I shall do my utmost to punish the enemy for their invasion of the Petty Kingdoms."

"Then you have my consent."

Sister Johanna reappeared with an armful of rolled-up maps. Marlena picked through them, selecting one that purported to show the area around Torburg and placed it on the table. She withdrew a dagger, using it to hold down the top before she unrolled it, revealing its contents. "This," she said, "is our present location. You can see it marked here as the tournament grounds."

"Yes," replied Beverly. "I remember it from my last visit here. What I'm more interested in is the terrain to the west and south."

"You mean southeast, surely?"

"While it's entirely possible the Holy Army could march straight up the road, I doubt that's what they'll do. My experience with knights tells me they live for the charge, and for that, they need as much open terrain as possible. The road, while useful, presents a relatively narrow pathway, particularly with these woods." She pointed at the map, then looked at Natalia. "Would you concur?"

Instead of answering, the warmaster turned to the woman beside her. "What do you think, Cordelia?"

"I cannot fault your logic, General, but I'd caution you to place at least a token force to watch that road."

"I shall do as you suggest," replied Beverly. "Now, as to the deployment of our troops, let me lay out my strategy. The Armies of Reinwick and Andover will arrive by morning, and I intend to place them on your flanks, with a small group to be held in reserve. From what I recall of my previous time here, the road on which the Halvarians are approaching is constrained by a series of hills to the north and a thick forest to the south."

"That forest eases off as you get closer to Torburg," warned Marlena. "Which gives them plenty of room to manoeuvre."

"I think they'll keep as far north as possible."

"What makes you say that?"

"Two things. First, I'd say it's fairly obvious the Halvarians are in league with this Holy Army, so their strategy would be to crush us between them, a tactic my Dwarven friends would refer to as the hammer-and-anvil approach. Now, as we've already discovered, the road isn't best suited to their preferred method of attack, meaning the Cunars will favour the more open terrain to our south. Thus, the Halvarians will have to try to come from as north a position as possible."

"And your second point?" asked the duke.

"The last time we fought them, we faced a single legion; this time, we'll be facing two, if not more, and that's a lot of men to fit onto a battlefield. I suspect they'll try to intimidate us with a display of their power, meaning they'll array all those men out in the open where we can see them, which plays directly into our plans."

"It does? How?"

"Let me answer that," offered Natalia. "We'll deploy the Army of Therengia where it can be used to the greatest effect. I can't tell you precisely where at this particular moment, for it depends on the actions of the enemy, but I think it would be somewhere to the west, behind their legions."

"Won't they see you marching into position?" asked Duke Alain. "Not to sound pessimistic, but that eliminates the element of surprise, don't you think?"

"I've already consulted with Lady Beverly at great length, and she's approved the idea."

"Might you share with us how you will accomplish this?" asked Marlena.

Temple Commander Cordelia cleared her throat. "You must take it on faith, Commander. I've seen the Army of Therengia in the field and assure you they are more than capable of doing what they say. To explain how is to risk the enemy learning of our plans."

"You suspect treason?"

"Not from anyone here, in this tent, but there are more than likely Halvarian agents within the Army of Erlingen."

"They made an attempt on my life in Korvoran," said Beverly. "We suspect a group of Cunars infiltrated the duke's estate."

"That's how they like to operate," added Natalia. "We've known for some time that both the Sartellians and Stormwinds are agents of the empire, and, as such, they've hired people to report on all manner of things. It's not much of a stretch to believe they'd have agents amongst your own troops."

"How do we counter that?" asked Duke Alain.

"We don't. We feed into it. Our true strategy must remain unknown to all but those who need to know. To anyone else, we'll be forming a defensive line to repel the Halvarians. The Army of Therengia's role in all of this is to remain a surprise. Now, to facilitate all this, communication is vital. To that end, Orc shamans are standing by, along with translators where needed. Their task will be to relay orders between the upper echelons of command, a crucial task if our surprise is to work as planned. Commit too early, and we'll have wasted our opportunity: too late, and they'll be of little use."

"How do we know the right time?" asked Marlena.

"That is my decision," replied Beverly. "My cousin, Aubrey, will be by my side, ready to relay commands when needed."

"So we are to simply hold our defensive positions?"

"For now, yes, but once the battle commences, I'll relay additional orders." Beverly paused, considering her next words carefully. "The future of the Petty Kingdoms hangs in the balance; if we are to see our way through to victory, then everyone must be willing to do their part."

"You've mentioned the Army of Erlingen will hold the centre; have you any specific orders regarding its deployment?"

"I'll leave the disposition of companies in the hands of those who know them best."

Marlena looked at her counterpart. "Temple Commander Cordelia has seniority."

"I do," the woman replied, "but my part in this battle has already been decided. My companies are now members of the Army of Therengia."

"Yes," added Natalia, "and she has lent her expertise to the commander of our heavier mounted companies… Well, I suppose I could call it cavalry, although there are doubtless those who'd argue the point."

"What could possibly be heavier than Temple Knights?" asked Marlena.

"You shall see soon enough. Now, if there are no more questions, Galina and I must take care of bringing those shamans through from Therengia. Lady Beverly, you know how to find me." With that, she left.

The entire tent remained silent, everyone within overcome by the seriousness of the situation, so Marlena tried a diversion. "Sister Cordelia, might I ask how you ended up in Therengia?"

"I was stationed in the Duchy of Krieghoff when I received word I'd been promoted to Temple Captain. Carlingen was my first command, but after our order's troubles with the Antonine, we needed somewhere safe, and I ended up commanding all the sister knights in Therengia."

"So you're saying it was all Charlaine's fault?" Marlene said with a grin.

Cordelia smiled back. "I suppose that's one way of looking at it. Listen, you've likely fought in more battles than me, and as for seniority, I've always believed it's real-life experience that counts, not simply time. You served with Charlaine, didn't you?"

"I did. How did you know?"

"A little bird told me, or should I say a Dwarf?"

Marlena nodded knowingly at the reference. "I understand completely. Best not say any more on the matter."

"Come again?" said the duke. "Is there something you'd care to explain, Commander?"

"No, Your Grace. Merely a reference to an old friend."

Two days later found Beverly standing outside her tent, gazing up at the night sky. Footsteps approached from behind, and she smiled. "I wondered how long it would take you to find me."

"How did you know it was me?" asked Aldwin.

"I felt your presence."

"Really?"

"No. Aubrey told me you were looking for me."

"And where is she now?"

"Off with the shamans, ensuring they're ready for tomorrow's battle."

He put his hand around her waist and stood beside her, looking up into the stars. "It's strange to think those same lights are visible from home." He turned to face her, but she was already waiting, staring into his eyes.

"Do you ever wonder what life would be like if we'd never met?" she asked.

"No," he replied. "Why? Are you having second thoughts?"

She cracked a smile. "Never, but I often wonder what life would be like without all this constant war."

"Well, if your father hadn't spent all his time defending Bodden, I doubt you'd have become a knight, and had you not been a knight, you never would've needed armour, so we wouldn't have met."

"True. In fact, if it hadn't been for the Norland raids, your parents would still be alive. Do you remember anything about them?"

"I remember isolated images, a face here or there, but those moments are rare. I dislike conflict as much as you, but in this case, I'm thankful for it; otherwise, we wouldn't be together. Now, enough of such maudlin thoughts. If there's to be a battle tomorrow, we need to get you to bed."

"How can you sleep knowing we're about to decide the fate of the entire Continent?"

Aldwin grinned. "Who said anything about sleep?"

THIRTY-THREE

Flight

SUMMER 968 MC

Arnim crouched beside Nikki while she peered out from behind the hedge. "Any sign of them?"

"Not at the moment," she replied, "but we should remain cautious." They'd escaped from the palace but now found themselves in Victory Park, dodging from tree to bush, attempting to avoid discovery.

"This will never do," complained Janek. "The longer we stay in Varena, the more we risk the emperor being captured."

"What would you have us do?" asked Nevarus. "Walk down the middle of the street?"

"Would that be so bad, Eminence? You are dressed as a commoner. Who would even guess at your true identity?"

"Who indeed?" said Arnim. "By now, word of his escape will have reached your enemies, and it would only take one person recognizing him to ruin everything. Better to continue as we are, avoiding all possible encounters."

"I agree with Lord Arnim," said Nevarus. "Though I am dressed like one, I cannot claim to be adept at mimicking the behaviours of someone born to the lower classes."

"Agreed," said Nikki. "And for Saxnor's sake, stop calling him 'Your Eminence'—that's a dead giveaway."

"But I cannot call him Nevarus!" insisted Janek.

"Then call him 'lord' if you must, but stop treating him as the emperor, else it'll cost us our lives."

"My apologies."

"Perhaps I should adopt a pseudonym?" said Nevarus. "What about Master Neyvar? I could be a wealthy merchant visiting from Zefara?"

"Too complicated," replied Nikki. "Invent too much of a backstory, and you'll step all over yourself."

"Whatever do you mean?"

"Do you know anything about being a merchant?"

"Well… no," admitted Nevarus.

"I spent a lot of years pretending to be someone I'm not. The key to surviving is keeping your story as close to the truth as possible. Make it complicated, and you'll start volunteering too much information, which is a dead giveaway."

"I agree," added Arnim. "Now, having said that, perhaps we could concentrate on more important matters, such as how we're going to get free of the city?"

"Can't we leave by the gate?" asked Nevarus.

"You've just admitted you're incapable of passing yourself off as a commoner. Do you want to test the validity of that statement now when your life hangs in the balance?"

"No, I suppose not."

Janek fidgeted. "But if not by the gate, then how? It's not as if any of us are mages."

"I can think of a number of ways," replied Nikki, "but some require outside help. Have we anyone we can trust outside of the palace?"

"Had you asked me that a week ago, I might have said yes, but with half the emperor's guard not showing up today, I'm forced to change my response. Why? What do you have in mind?"

"That we pass ourselves off as merchants and hide the emperor in the back of a wagon."

"Would he not be seen?"

"Not if we concealed him in a barrel or crate."

"I doubt that would work," said Arnim. "Whoever stormed the palace knows Nevarus represents the greatest threat to the empire's new ruler. They'll want him dead so there can be no turning back, which means a substantial reward to anyone finding him."

"Then we shall offer more," said Nevarus.

"With all due respect, you no longer control the imperial treasury. Unless you've somehow managed to smuggle a pile of coins out under those clothes of yours?"

"I have not."

"As I thought," said Arnim. "So, smuggling him out in a barrel is out of the question; anything else in your bag of tricks, Nikki?"

"How about the wall?" she replied. "We'd need some rope, but that shouldn't be too difficult to acquire."

"That has possibilities, but access to the top of the wall would be controlled through guard towers unless you're suggesting we climb up an inner wall?"

"Even if we could," said Janek, "with everyone looking for the emperor, wouldn't they be expecting something like that?"

"You make a good point," said Nikki.

"Any other ideas?" asked Armin.

"Without any coins, we can forget about bribing our way out. We can't go through the gates or over the walls, so the only escape route left is under them."

"What in the name of the emperor are you suggesting?" Janek realized what he'd said and looked nervously at Nevarus. "Sorry, Eminence, I didn't mean to take your name in vain."

The emperor chuckled. "I'll doubtlessly hear worse before this is all over. I am curious, Lady Nicole. What did you mean by going under? Surely you're not suggesting we dig our way out?"

"This city has sewers, doesn't it?"

"Does it? I wouldn't know." He turned to Janek. "Does it?"

"Of course, Eminence. Varena is a shining example of our civilization; to suggest otherwise—"

"Enough!" said Arnim. "We get the idea."

"Janek," said Nikki. "Can you tell me more about the city?"

"What would you like to know?"

"I noticed a river from the window of our room. Does it encircle the city?"

"It flows along the eastern side, then curves before returning to a more southerly direction. I presume it eventually empties into the Shimmering Sea, but I'm no expert in such things. Why? Is that important?"

"Sewers empty somewhere, and I'd assume that would be downstream."

"Why would you think that?"

"What merchant wants a dockyard stinking of sewage?"

"Clever," said Nevarus. "This obviously isn't the first time you've dealt with such things, although I'm at a loss as to why."

"That is a discussion for another day."

"Can you find us a way out or not?" pressed Janek.

"I can certainly try, but there's always the possibility that a grate or hatch blocks the exit."

"Then we'd be trapped, wouldn't we?"

Arnim chuckled. "I have yet to see a lock that could stop Nikki. Mind you, if it's not locked and simply a sealed grate, there won't be much we can do about it. Still, it's better than hanging around here, waiting for someone to discover us."

"Where do we start?" asked Nevarus.

"By acquiring some supplies," said Nikki. "We'll need light of some sort, preferably a lantern, but a torch would do in a pinch."

"Anything else?"

"A saw might be useful to cut through steel bars, but I doubt we'll find one of those nearby; this appears to be a wealthier area of town."

"Right," said Arnim. "Let's go shopping."

"Shopping?" asked Nevarus.

"Relax," replied Nikki. "It's just an expression; what he really means is we'll go stealing."

"And that's supposed to make me feel better?"

Janek waited, his nerves on edge. He'd tried to console himself with the fact it was dark, giving him at least the illusion of concealment, but every little sound convinced him soldiers were about to run him through. Nevarus sat nearby, staring up at the stars, seemingly unfazed by the day's events. A nearby sound made the servant jump, and then Lady Nicole's voice cut through the darkness.

"It's only us," she hissed. "Here," she said, thrusting a bundle of cloth at him.

"What's this?"

"Some food we managed to acquire."

"And by acquire, you mean…"

"Stop asking questions you already know the answer to and just eat."

He unwrapped the cloth and found a small loaf of bread that appeared burned on top. He was about to complain when his stomach grumbled, reminding him it had been nearly a day since he last ate. He broke off a chunk and stuffed it in his mouth.

Arnim drew closer, holding up an unlit lantern. "I found this in a carriage house."

"And the bread?" asked Janek.

"Discarded behind a bakery."

Janek spit out his mouthful. "Are you suggesting this was on the street?"

"Not at all," Nikki replied, waiting as he resumed eating. "It was mixed in with all the other trash."

"I'm not hungry."

"Liar," said Nevarus. "Now eat, Janek, before you pass out on us." The emperor tore a piece of bread off for himself. "Did you find an entrance to the sewers?"

"We did," said Arnim. "It's just up the street. We should have no problem getting to it this time of night."

"Any signs of guards?"

"We heard some on the next street over, but their footsteps faded away."

"That's to be expected," replied Nevarus. "Varena is a large city, and even a full legion couldn't patrol every street. Perhaps the fates are with us for once?"

"I'll place my faith in our abilities," said Nikki. "I don't like to rely on fate; it has a way of coming back and biting me in the arse."

"Such language from a lady," said Janek, "not to mention a viscountess."

"I was raised on the streets of Wincaster," replied Nikki. "I'll not apologize for my past."

"Nor should you," added Arnim. "I like you just the way you are."

"Aww, thank you. That's nice of you to say."

"In the emperor's name," said Janek. "Will this endless prattling never cease?"

"Time to go," said Arnim.

"Aren't you going to light the lantern?"

"And give away our position? I think not!"

"Then why have it?"

"Bec—" Arnim started to bark out a response but appeared to have a change of heart when his features softened slightly. "I'll light this lantern once we're in the sewers. Now come. We must be well on our way before daybreak."

He led them down the alleyway and then paused, peering around the edge of the building to look left and right. "This way," he whispered, then stepped out onto the street.

Janek and Nevarus followed, with Nikki bringing up the rear. It was only a matter of a hundred or so paces before they stood over a wooden hatch built into the cobbled street.

Arnim reached down and slid his fingers through two holes, then lifted the cover off, revealing a shaft dropping into darkness, a ladder built into its side. "You first, Nikki. I'll hand you the lantern once you're down there."

Janek watched her disappear into the darkness.

Her voice wafted up to them. "It's not very deep but watch your head. The ceiling is low."

Arnim passed down the lantern, then motioned for Janek to go next. The emperor's aide moved to stand over the hatch, and an overpowering stench hit him, threatening to close off his throat. "What is that smell?"

"Freedom," came Nikki's reply. "Now get moving. We haven't got all night."

He climbed down, and when his feet hit bottom, they sank into something wet and squishy. "What am I standing in?"

"Best you don't know."

Her hand came out of the dark and pulled him forward. "Wait here, and don't move, or we'll be running into each other."

A small spark briefly lit the tunnel, then another. The third did the trick, igniting the lantern and flooding the area with a warm glow.

A rat swam past, brushing against Janek's leg, and he felt a sudden urge to scream. He clamped his hands over his mouth to suppress it, then noticed a look of amusement on Nikki's face. "What are you smiling at?"

"Nothing."

A scraping sound came from above. "That's the hatch back in place," said Arnim.

"Where is the emperor?"

"Right here," called out Nevarus, directly behind Janek, his unexpected presence causing the fellow to jump. Nikki waited until Arnim climbed down the ladder and then began leading them south, following the flow of effluent.

The sewers were a complex web of interconnecting tunnels. There was no sense of direction here or any light other than the lantern, but Nikki followed the flow, trusting it would eventually lead them to the river. Time passed slowly, and they began to feel as though they were trapped in an endless series of tunnels that ran in circles.

The smell was awful, and on two occasions, it became so bad they were forced to hold their breath. After hours of finding their way by lantern, Nikki noticed daylight bouncing off a wall.

"I think we've reached the end. There's a turn up ahead with sunlight streaming through." She hurried forward, continuing past the bend to elicit a curse.

"What's wrong?" called out Arnim.

"There's an iron grate here, with no sign of a lock."

They moved up, eager to see what she was talking about. The end of the sewer did indeed empty out into the river, but a grate of crisscrossing metal bands prevented anyone from entering or exiting the sewers. They could easily reach through, for there was a good hand span between each overlap, but someone had gone to extraordinary lengths to rivet each spot where the bands crossed.

Nikki rattled the metal, but the entire assembly appeared intact. "This is very disappointing."

"More than disappointing," said Janek. "It's a catastrophe!"

"Don't panic," replied Nevarus. "Let Arnim take a look. Perhaps he can see something we're missing."

Arnim moved up, taking his time to examine the grill. He stepped back, placing his hands on his hips, looking it over once again. "Some of the rivets are rusty; we might be able to snap them off."

"With what?" asked Janek.

Arnim pulled out the chair leg he'd tucked into his belt and used it to try and pry apart two of the bands. The grate groaned a little, but the makeshift club cracked, obviously too weak for such work. He tossed it aside with a grunt.

"Hold on," said Nikki. "You've given me an idea." She knelt in the muck, feeling beneath the shin-deep water. After a bit, she stood back up with a look of triumph. "I thought so."

"Care to explain?" said Nevarus.

"Arnim is right. Some of the rivets are very rusty, and none more so than the ones immersed in the water. I think we can pry this thing up from the bottom or at least separate two or three overlaying connections."

"What good will that do?" said Janek. "We need more room than one or two bent bars to allow us to escape."

"I can fit through a narrow opening," replied Nikki. "Then I'll go find something larger to force the rest."

"Are you certain you can do this?" asked Arnim. "It means holding your breath and submerging yourself, and we both know you don't like water."

"I don't have a problem with immersing myself; it's being in deep water, and as you can plainly see, this is less than knee deep. Now, hand me that chair leg."

Arnim retrieved his makeshift weapon and switched it for the lantern she held. Nikki manoeuvred one end below the bottom rung of the grate and then pushed up on the leg, using it like a lever. Arnim soon joined her and was rewarded with a splash as a rivet popped.

"It worked!" shouted Janek.

They repeated the process, and then Arnim grasped the metal bands and bent them upwards. "Not wide enough," he said. "We'd best try it again."

They worked away at it until the chair leg split in two. Arnim tried using the larger of the pieces, but it proved useless.

"That's it, then," declared Janek. "We're doomed."

"I'm not ready to give up quite yet," said Nikki. She knelt once more, digging down into the muck. "Give me a hand, Arnim." They both struggled and finally managed to bend another band upward.

· · ·

"Is that enough?" asked her husband.

"It will have to be," she replied as she started removing her dress.

"What are you doing?" asked Janek.

Nevarus placed his hand on his aide's shoulder. "Patience, my friend. She is removing her outer garments so they do not snag on the grate."

"Are you suggesting she's going to immerse herself in the effluent to swim under that thing?"

"That would appear to be the case."

"How disgusting."

"Better that than have your head on the end of a pike," said Nikki. Now down to her undergarments, she knelt, facing the grate and took several deep breaths. She looked up at Arnim. "I'll need help. You know what to do."

He nodded, then waited as she submerged her head, her hands out before her to guide her through the opening. Arnim waited as she struggled. Then, when he saw that her head was through, he grabbed her by the waist and tried shoving her forward.

Time seemed to drag on forever, and Janek swore Nikki must have drowned. It was such a strange scene, watching a woman halfway through a grate while raw sewage flowed around her. He imagined himself in her position, and the mere thought made him gag. He turned away lest he add vomit to the sewer's contents.

"She's through," said Arnim. "It worked."

Janek turned to see Nikki kneeling against the other side of the grate, covered in filth with a look of triumph plastered on her face. "I'll be back as soon as I can," she said and then was off, disappearing from sight.

"We must be patient," said Arnim. "It may take a while for her to find a suitable branch."

"And what makes a branch suitable?" asked Janek.

"Long enough to work as a lever, yet not so thin as to snap when we try to use it."

"Your wife is a most resourceful woman," noted Nevarus.

"And full of surprises," added Janek. "You Mercerians are nothing like I imagined you."

"I shall take that as a compliment," replied Arnim.

Nikki soon reappeared, dragging a branch longer than she was. "Here you go." She dropped it and then went off to find something suitable to act as a fulcrum, returning with a large stone. She shoved the branch under the grate, then rolled the stone beneath the branch. She put all her weight on the end to force the metal up. The first two times, nothing happened, but on the third, an audible snap came as one side of the grate broke loose from the stone wall.

"I think that's enough," said Arnim, waving Janek through. "After you."

Janek squeezed through, thankful to be under the sun once more. He moved aside as Nevarus followed, and then Arnim joined them.

"I assumed we'd follow the river," said Nikki, "but which way, upstream or down?" They both looked at Nevarus.

"South would eventually lead us to the Shimmering Sea, but north might be a better option."

"What makes you say that?"

"The most logical choice would be for me to flee south to the very borders of the empire. I doubt they'd think to look for me going deeper into Halvarian territory."

"You make a good case," said Nikki. "North, it is, unless there are any objections?"

"Not at all," replied Arnim, "although I might suggest we get to the other side of the river first. Continuing along this side will bring us close to the city walls." He paused, remembering her bundled clothes. "Oh, here. You might want this, at least till we find you something better to wear."

"My modesty thanks you."

Arnim burst out laughing. "You're anything but modest, my dear."

THIRTY-FOUR

Ascendancy

SUMMER 968 MC

The Dwarves of Ironcliff marched in a slow procession, their vard's body borne along on a litter held above their heads. All those within sight removed their helmets, a sign of respect for the ancient ruler who'd died fighting for his realm.

The Halvarian legion had been decimated, save for a few hundred who'd fled eastward. Lanaka had been eager to chase them down, but the marshal insisted they be allowed to spread word of the empire's defeat.

Gerald watched as the body of Thalgrun Stormhammer was brought from the outer city of Ironcliff through the massive doors that led into the Undermountain. It was the end of an era, an age where the Dwarves had hidden beneath the mountains of Eiddenwerthe, isolating themselves from the other races. A throat cleared, and he turned to see Herdwin beside him.

"Sorry to interrupt," said the Dwarf, "but there's something I want to ask you."

"There's no need to apologize," replied the marshal. "I always have time for my friends. Ask away."

"Well… that is… I was wondering about… Gundar's Forge. I never thought this would be so difficult."

"Has this something to do with Kasri?"

Herdwin's face brightened. "Aye, exactly. With her father gone to the Afterlife, she'll be the new vard. We've talked about it for some time, and we both agreed we would forge before she ascends the Throne. I was hoping I might convince you to witness the ceremony… of the forging, that is."

Gerald smiled. "I would be delighted, although I must admit I know nothing of what that entails."

"An officiant will oversee the ceremony itself, but it basically consists of Kasri and I melting down two objects and using the metal to forge something new."

"Ahh. Is that why it's called a forging?"

"One of the reasons. The couple involved picks the manner of the new object; sometimes, it's a small statue or something that has particular meaning to them. It's just that, with me being a smith and her a warrior, we thought metal more suitable. I came up with the idea of crossed weapons, a hammer and an axe, and she agreed—not real weapons, of course. That would take far too long."

"If only Human weddings were so simple. What would you need me to do?"

"Just witness the process. Agramath will be there as well. He's pretty much the only close family Kasri has left."

"I wasn't aware they were related."

"They're not," replied Herdwin, "but he was Thalgrun's closest friend, so he's like an uncle to her."

"Is anyone else to be present?"

"We haven't the time, so other than the officiant, no, although there will be a public announcement once the ceremony is complete."

"When is this forging to be held?"

"As soon as her father is laid to rest."

"I imagine that would be a few days," said Gerald.

"Not so. Kasri will be crowned the new vard before sunset."

"Then we'd best head there now before it's too late."

Five of them gathered in the vard's Royal Chambers. Malrun Bronzefist, the Master of Revels, oversaw the ceremony, while Agramath and Gerald watched from either side as Kasri and Herdwin exchanged vows. They then used a hammer and chisel to break down lumps of two different metals, dropping them in a small stone cup that Herdwin placed into a forge that had been set up for the occasion. The metal melted together under the extreme heat, symbolizing that their individual histories were now blended into one future.

Herdwin placed the casting mold he'd created onto the table. Using a pair of smith tongs, he pulled the stone cup from the forge and poured the liquid metal into the mold, then stood there waiting.

"It has to cool," explained Kasri. "Then we'll open it up and see what it portends."

"Portends?" asked Gerald.

"Aye," replied Malrun. "Were the resultant mixture to shatter or break, it would cast a grave shadow over this union."

"Not much chance of that," stated Herdwin. "I've been a smith far too long to make such a mistake." He sounded confident, but the sweat on his brow said otherwise.

Agramath brought out a tray with five mugs of ale and passed them around. Gerald had tasted Dwarven ale before, but this brew was exceptionally pleasant, with a hint of something sweet, and it was chilled, making it a nice relief from the heat of the forge.

Herdwin downed his in one gulp, then put on a thick pair of gloves and pried apart the casting mold. He needn't have worried, for the finished product was perfectly formed. He lifted it out, holding it out for everyone to examine the fine details. "Careful, now," he warned. "It's still hot."

"Marvellous work," said Malrun. "This union has been blessed by Gundar himself. I offer my congratulations to you both."

"Thank you, Master Malrun," replied Kasri. "Under other circumstances, I would invite you to remain awhile and visit with us, but I understand you need to prepare for my ascension."

The Master of Revels bowed. "So I do. Master Agramath, Master Gerald, I hope you will excuse me?"

"Of course," they both echoed.

"And finally, for you, Master Herdwin, I offer the hand of friendship." He held out his hand.

Herdwin shook it in a firm grip. "Thank you, Master Malrun."

"Oh, please. We can dispense with the titles in private. You are forge mate to the vard, so we'll be seeing a lot of each other. Now, you must excuse me. As Kasri indicated, I have things to attend to." With that, he left, making his way past the gold-plated warriors standing guard outside the door.

Kasri cleared her throat. "If you don't mind, there's something I'd like your opinions on."

"Would this have something to do with Herdwin's standing?" asked Agramath.

"It does."

"Kasri, your father made some sort of arrangements concerning the guilds," offered Gerald. "He told me about them before his death." He turned to the master of rock and stone. "He said Agramath knew the details."

"He did, indeed," agreed the mage. He reached into his belt and withdrew a folded note. "This is for you, Kasri. Your father asked me to wait until you were crowned, but under the circumstances, I think it best you see it now."

She took it, slowly unfolding the last words of her father. They waited as she read its contents.

Kasri smiled. "It seems my father has seen fit to remind me of the powers of a vard."

"Meaning?" said Agramath.

"You haven't read this?"

"No! It was meant as a private message for his daughter and heir. Why? What does it say?"

"That although the guilds control much in the realm of Ironcliff, only the vard has the power to create one."

"But the existing guilds cover off all the trades."

"Not quite. There are still a few occupations lacking representation, not to mention Dwarves who are waiting to be accepted into one of our guilds."

"What would this new guild be called?"

"The Guild of Independent Dwarves, and I shall make Herdwin their guild master, providing he has no objection?" She looked at her forge mate.

"What would this entail?" Herdwin asked.

"You can be involved as much or as little as you wish, and since you're the one in charge, you get to make the decisions."

"Clever," said Agramath. "In one fell stroke, you give Herdwin status and a voice to those who lack one."

"I shall charge no fees," said Herdwin, "and I will encourage our members to seek out opportunities that may clash with the other guilds."

"That is your prerogative," said Kasri. "And if the guilds complain about these independent products flooding the market in Ironcliff, then you'll sell them elsewhere."

"I'm sure Merceria would be willing to help with that," offered Gerald. "We're always looking for new trading opportunities."

"Then it's settled," said Herdwin. "I officially accept the position."

"Splendid," said Agramath. "It's about time someone put those guild masters in their place. It will also be refreshing to hear a younger voice in the council chambers for a change."

A distant horn sounded, echoing off the mountains. "The mourning period is officially over," said Kasri. "It's time for my ascension." She held out her elbow. "Come, Herdwin. We shall enter the great hall together."

"That is most unusual," said Agramath, "and far from traditional."

"Good, because that's precisely how I mean to rule. Our people have lived in the past for too long; we need to embrace the future."

. . .

Gerald watched from one side of the great hall as the procession of guild masters entered in all their finery. Behind him stood an honour guard of Mercerian rangers, with Hayley overseeing them.

He noted movement off to his right, and Albreda approached, having snuck in behind the guild masters. She took up a position directly beside him, keeping her eyes on the procession. "Impressive, isn't it?" she said. "I've never witnessed the crowning of a vard before, have you?"

"No, but that's hardly surprising, considering their long lives."

"I'm led to believe Kasri is young for a vard. I imagine she'll have centuries of wearing that crown. We'll all be dust by then, but it gives me hope that someone of her capabilities will be here, guiding her people."

"You're sounding very philosophical today," said Gerald.

"I can't help it. It's what comes of being old."

The Master of Revels' entrance caused all the attendees to lapse into silence. He strode to the front of the hall and then turned to face everyone, tapping the base of his staff to the floor three times in rapid succession.

"Bow your heads, that we may offer a prayer for Thalgrun Stormhammer, Vard of Ironcliff."

A hush fell, and then from above came the sounding of horns similar to what had announced the death of Thalgrun but more melodic this time, ending with three notes blending together to suggest a cry of anguish.

The horns quieted while the final notes echoed off the walls of the great hall, and then silence descended, stretching on for a time. Gerald noted many a Dwarf dabbing at the corners of their eyes.

The Master of Revels struck his staff two more times, breaking the spell. "We are gathered here today, in accordance with our laws, to elevate Kasri Ironheart to Vard of Ironcliff."

The horns started again, this time sounding triumphant as the doors at the far end of the great hall swung open, and a double line of the Hearth Guard entered, their gold-plated armour polished to a brilliant shine. They marched down the aisle, spreading out to form a cordon on either side before Kasri and Herdwin stepped into the room, drawing all eyes.

Her armour still bore the scratches and dents from her recent fight against the Halvarians, but no one appeared to mind. Beside her strode Herdwin in his more modest mail, and they continued, together, to the front of the hall, halting before Malrun Bronzefist.

"Kneel," commanded the Master of Revels.

Kasri did as she was asked while Herdwin stepped aside, giving everyone a clear view of the proceedings.

"Kasri Ironheart," said Malrun, "do you promise to defend and protect this realm and rule with fairness and mercy?"

"I do."

"Then, in the name of Gundar, I deem thee worthy to accept the Silver Crown." He nodded to Captain Durgan at the head of the Hearth Guard. The captain stepped forward, carrying a small cushion with a crown of silver inlaid with gems.

Malrun held it high above as he turned to face Kasri. "With this crown, I name you Kasri Ironheart, Vard of Ironcliff." He lowered it onto her head.

The crowd applauded, although, to Gerald's ears, it sounded tepid. Did the guilds really carry that much influence? He began to wonder what this might portend.

Kasri stood, then turned to face the chamber. "I am Kasri Ironheart," she said, drawing her hammer. "And I dare anyone to challenge my right as ruler of Ironcliff." The only sound in the hall was the shuffling of feet.

Finally, after an interminably long interval, the Master of Revels rapped his staff one final time. "Let it be known throughout all the known lands that we have a new vard. All praise the Vard of Ironcliff, Kasri Ironheart."

The applause sounded more heartfelt this time, and Gerald relaxed. The guild masters congratulated their new ruler, although he had a feeling it was more about trying to gain favour. He'd witnessed the same sort of thing back in Wincaster, but Anna wasn't the type of person who handed out influence on a whim. Kasri had a difficult job ahead of her, for the guilds controlled nearly every aspect of Dwarven life, so she must be careful not to offer offence.

The congratulations went on until the Hearth Guard began forcing people to the edge of the hall, clearing the centre of the room. The reason behind this wasn't apparent at first, but then, music began playing from above.

Kasri took Herdwin's hand, leading him out into the middle of the great hall, and they started dancing. After a few beats, others did likewise, and the atmosphere of the entire room changed to one of celebration. Servants entered bearing drinks, and before he knew it, Gerald had a cup in hand.

"I must say I like this," said Albreda. "Short and sweet, just the way such things should be handled. We could learn a thing or two from these people."

Gerald turned to Hayley. "You may dismiss the rangers."

"Aye, Marshal."

He waited as they mingled with the Dwarves, then returned his attention to the Druid. "We must celebrate while we can, for tomorrow, we commence the long march into Halvaria."

"Good," she replied. "It's about time we paid them back for their invasion."

"We're not seeking to conquer them," said Gerald. "Rather, to liberate them from an oppressive regime."

"A very sensible approach. Now, if you don't mind, I'm going to see if I can find something to eat. I'm absolutely famished." She drifted off into the sea of guests.

Herdwin appeared, pushing his way through the throng, heading straight for him.

"Something wrong?" asked Gerald.

"No. I'm here to ask you to come and dance with us."

"I'm afraid I'm not familiar with your customs in that regard."

Herdwin grabbed his arm, dragging him deeper into the room. "It's easy. We form a long line, holding hands with the person on either side. Once the music starts, it's a three-beat step. Two steps are light, while the third is a stomp. Then we do the same thing backwards. Don't worry. You'll get the hang of it in no time."

They reached the centre of the room where Malrun, the Master of Revels, stood at one end, his left hand grasping Kasri's while the other held his staff. Herdwin fell in next to her, then Gerald, and then Agramath. Other Dwarves joined in, forming a line that spread the length of the room.

Malrun rapped his staff two times lightly before bringing it down a third time with a little more strength. The music began anew, and the dance commenced.

It was far later than Gerald would've preferred, but the Dwarves of Ironcliff had much to celebrate. The dancing continued, on and off, for half the night, yet from what he could see, no one had left. Having said that, the dance floor was at least less energetic than it'd been at the beginning of the celebration, a sign that people were finally growing tired.

The music ended, and the dancers dispersed to either side of the great hall. Kasri whispered something to the Master of Revels, who then used his staff to draw everyone's attention. Once the room quieted down, he made a show of bowing to the vard.

"Thank you, everyone," said Kasri, "for allowing me the privilege of being your vard. My father was a great ruler, and during his reign, we saw many changes come to Ironcliff, including new friends and allies." She waited as applause broke out.

"As my first official act as vard, I am announcing the creation of a new establishment, the Guild of Independent Dwarves, which will be overseen by their guild master, Herdwin Steelarm." This announcement garnered considerable praise from the Hearth Guard, but the traditional guild masters looked less than impressed. "I trust that I can count on all of you to treat him with the dignity and respect the position deserves."

Reluctant nods greeted her remarks. Surprisingly, Garnik Hardhand, Guild Master of the Warriors Guild, moved up, the first to offer his congratulations. He shook Herdwin's hand most vigorously. "Your reputation precedes you, Master Herdwin. It's an honour to have you on the council."

"I'm surprised to hear you say that," replied the smith. "I was led to believe there were strong objections to my presence here."

"Aye, there were, but you've more than proven your mettle." He leaned in close and lowered his voice. "And between you and me, the council needs a bit of a shakeup. Some of us are so old we're gathering cobwebs. As for the objections, that was mainly the doing of the smiths guild. Don't worry. Things will calm down once the dust settles."

"The dust?"

"There's always some tension when someone joins the council, and there's bound to be some who feel a new guild reduces the influence of the rest of us, but I doubt it'll take them long to come around."

"Thank you, I think," said Herdwin.

"Don't worry," whispered Kasri. "Master Garnik is one of the good ones."

The guild master winked. "She's only saying that because she was part of the guild."

"Was?" said Herdwin.

"Yes. Now that she's the vard, she has to be impartial, or at least give the impression of being so."

"True," said Kasri, scanning the room. "I trust the army will be ready to march come morning?"

Garnik bowed. "Of course, my vard, although some might have sore heads." He grinned. "It wouldn't be the first time they've marched after a celebration, though I daresay we've never had one quite like this."

Selia Ironfist pushed her way forward. "Your pardon, Master Garnik, but other guild masters are waiting to pay their respects, and our patience will only go so far."

"Yes, of course. Your pardon." Garnik bowed, then left.

Guild Master Selia stepped up to take his place, offering a bow to Kasri. "My vard." She regarded Herdwin. "Might I ask how we address you, Herdwin?"

"I should think guild master most appropriate," said Kasri. "Don't you?"

Selia's red face belied her true feelings, but she offered no objection. "As you wish. I look forward to seeing you on council business, Guild Master. Might I enquire who will constitute the membership of this new guild?"

"Any adult Dwarf who is not presently a member of another guild, regardless of trade."

"That will play havoc with the induction of new guild members."

"Good," said Herdwin. "It's about time we shook things up a little."

Selia turned to Kasri, ready to object, but the smile on the vard's face told her all she needed to know. Selia's shoulders visibly slumped, while her face betrayed none of her disappointment. "Congratulations, my vard. I wish you a long and prosperous reign."

THIRTY-FIVE

Prelude to Battle

SUMMER 968 MC

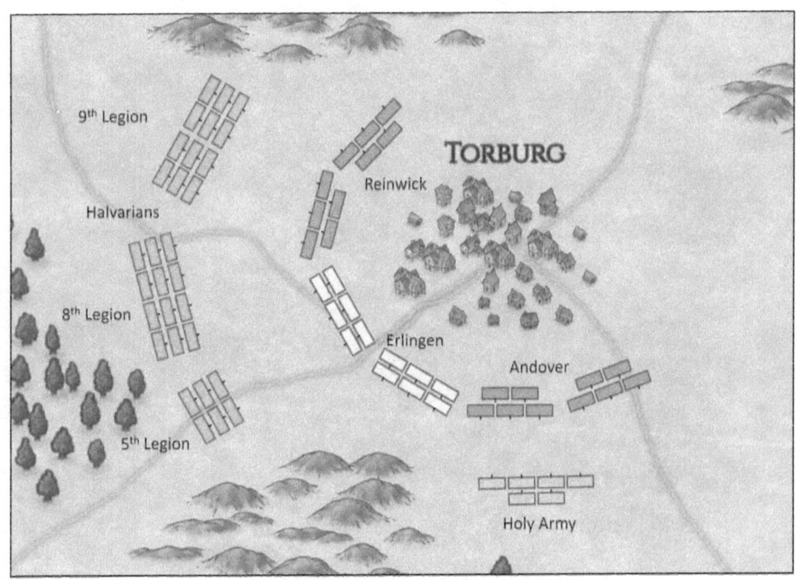

Beverly shivered as she stood on the rooftop, the morning's unseasonably cool air causing an ankle-deep fog to spread over the fields south of Torburg. The sun would soon burn it off, but for now, a sense of peace permeated the area, the enemy not yet visible in the predawn darkness.

The men were in place, prepared to do their part, but would it be enough? The Army of Reinwick, formed up northwest of Torburg, was responsible for keeping the enemy from flanking them from the north. Erlingen stood beside them in a line that bent around the city from west to southwest, while Andover guarded the south. It was, as far as such things went, a simple formation, but it allowed Beverly to shuffle companies to dangerous spots should that prove necessary.

Their numbers were encouraging. The masters of earth supplied by Therengia had spent a considerable amount of time seeking out the enemy, using owls to take advantage of their night vision.

Estimates placed the enemy at nearly seven thousand, the bulk amassed to the west, but at least half a legion had surprised them by coming up the road from Salzing to the southwest.

Her own command was just shy of that number, not including the Army of Therengia, who had yet to put in an appearance. Their role would be crucial, and their addition gave her side a slight numerical advantage.

All things considered, though, it wouldn't be numbers that won this battle; it would be the quality of the warriors, which, unfortunately, was impossible to calculate.

Had they been Mercerians, Beverly would've been confident of victory. The men of Erlingen held promise, already having defeated a legion at the Battle of the Pines, but that had cost a significant number of men, and though most had been replaced, the new recruits lacked experience.

Andover and Reinwick were unknowns. She'd travelled with them from the north, marching with them, but that wasn't the same as watching them fight.

As for the Therengians, Natalia Stormwind assured her of their battle experience, and Beverly had no reason to doubt the warmaster, particularly when Shaluhk backed up those claims.

"It's a cold morning," said Aldwin, rubbing his hands against the chill. "Are you positive it's summer? It feels more like autumn."

"It's summer, all right. Just look at the fields." She nodded to her left, where wheat blew in the wind.

"I don't imagine the farmers around here will appreciate their crops being trampled."

"That seems to be their lot in life," mused Beverly. "I wish it weren't so, but it's always the wealthy and powerful who drag kingdoms into war. The farmers just want to plant their crops and then harvest them."

"These fields will be soaked in blood by this time tomorrow. Take care that none of it is yours."

"I will. And you stay out of trouble, yourself. I want you back in Torburg, where it's at least relatively safe."

"I'll be there, helping with the wounded. They need someone strong to hold down limbs as they amputate. Not the most pleasant of tasks, but it has to be done if lives are to be saved."

"If this day brings victory, our shamans will be able to regenerate those lost limbs." Beverly was about to say more, but admitting they might lose wasn't something she could contemplate at this point. "Stay with me," she said instead, "at least for a few moments. We can watch the sunrise together."

He moved behind her, encircling her waist with his arms. Beverly laid her head back against his chest as the eastern sky lightened, hues of red and gold streaking upwards as the sun peeked over the horizon, casting long shadows. It was a glorious sight and one of the few times Beverly found herself wishing time could stand still.

Horns sounded to the west, interrupting them. The legions were moving.

"You'd best get going," said Beverly. "I'm about to become very busy." She turned and embraced him, ending it with a lingering kiss.

"Keep yourself safe." He stepped back, looking her up and down. "Just inspecting your armour," he said.

She smiled. "Like what you see?"

"I'd prefer it if I'd had a chance to knock out some of those dents, but it's who's inside that's more important. Now, I'd best get going before I become too much of a distraction."

Beverly watched him take the first few steps away, then turned to the west, where the horns were still sounding.

As the Orc mages predicted, the legions approached in three solid masses. The smaller of them, coming from the southwest, was the Fifth, the legion they'd inflicted severe losses on at the Battle of the Pines. The more immediate threat, however, was the two other full-strength legions marching directly from the west.

There was no subtlety to their approach, simply two large concentrations of warriors heading straight for the defenders. Their footmen led, supported by archers, while their cavalry massed in the back to take advantage of any breakthrough they might achieve. Beverly found herself wishing she had the Guard Cavalry here, then shook off the notion as ridiculous. She had everything she needed to claim a victory.

She closed her eyes, saying a silent prayer to Saxnor. Footsteps interrupted her, and she opened her eyes to see Aubrey coming up to join her.

"I hope I'm not interrupting?" said her cousin. "I thought, all things considered, I'd best head over before anything began. Anything to relay to the shamans?"

"Not yet. It appears they're going for a mass attack against our line in hopes of overwhelming us."

"And will that work?"

"I wish I could say no, but it's difficult to be certain. Those legions have already fought their way across half the Petty Kingdoms, and we have mostly untried warriors facing them." Beverly glanced east. "Which shaman is with the Army of Andover?"

"The Ashwalker, Vagrath."

"Contact him and ask if they can see that Holy Army."

"Will do, Cousin." Aubrey closed her eyes, drawing on her inner magic.

Beverly looked to where the northernmost legion appeared to be heading straight at the Army of Reinwick, then noticed the one below appeared intent on trying to drive a wedge between the men of Reinwick and those of Erlingen. Under other circumstances, she would've moved Erlingen farther north to counter this threat, but the presence of another legion on the southwest road precluded such a tactic. Instead, she must hope her warriors were capable of standing firm in the face of a numerically superior enemy.

"I contacted Vagrath," said Aubrey. "The Holy Army is in sight and is advancing against the men of Andover."

"Can he confirm numbers?"

Aubrey relayed the question and then waited. It was a strange situation as Beverly could only hear one side of the conversation.

From the west came a thumping noise, the telltale sound of thousands marching in unison. It rolled across the field like thunder, signalling an impending doom. Was this some strange magic, or simply her nerves playing tricks on her?

"Twelve hundred," said Aubrey, interrupting her brooding. "They have a screen of foot and bow, followed by a large mass of knights wearing grey surcoats."

"Those would be the Cunars. They're likely going to try to create a break in the line and then force their way through with their horse."

"Andover doesn't have much in the way of archers. The bulk of their army is foot."

"Send word to King Dagmar to move up his reserve. He needs his knights to plug any gaps should the enemy push through."

"Are you certain you want them to redeploy so early?" said Aubrey. "The battle is still young; wouldn't it be wise to hold them in reserve a little longer?"

"We haven't the luxury of waiting. If Andover crumbles, the enemy will flank us. Better to fill the bucket now than wait for all the water to drain out first."

"A clever turn of phrase."

"I get that from my father."

"He'd be proud of you were he here today."

"Would he?" replied Beverly. "Or would he think I'm foolish to fight with my back to the city?"

"Your father believed in you, Cousin. Don't let your own doubts question that."

"You'd think it would get easier."

"What would—battle?"

"Yes. Saxnor knows I've seen enough of it, but it never gets easy."

"Nor should it. The lives of thousands, perhaps tens of thousands, are ultimately at stake here."

"Do you think the enemy worries about that?"

"No," replied Aubrey. "They seem willing to throw away lives with reckless abandon if it fulfills their objectives. I think their only concern is that too many losses leave them without enough people to complete their conquest."

"You're right," said Beverly. "Thank you for clearing my mind."

"How did I do that?"

"By reminding me of what's at stake here."

"I'm afraid you've lost me on that one."

"Then tell me this: how do you define victory?"

"That's easy," said Aubrey. "When one side destroys the other's ability to fight..." She hesitated. "Ah, now I see where you're going. We don't need to beat them so long as we inflict enough casualties to make it untenable for them to continue their campaign."

"Precisely, although completely destroying their army would do that quite nicely."

"Well, the mages are all in position."

"And the warmaster?"

Aubrey nodded to the south. "She's out there, somewhere in those hills. I only wish there were some way to be assured they haven't been discovered."

"You could always contact Shaluhk if you wish to soothe your nerves."

"I dare not risk it, not with the enemy having mages at their disposal; the chance of discovery is too great."

"Are you suggesting mages can detect the use of magic?"

"It's a known fact, but they must be actively looking for it. It's not as if they can pass by and see the air glowing."

"Could they use their magic to disrupt your ability to talk to the shamans?"

"I'm not an expert in all types of magic, but I doubt it, not when I'm here, safely behind our troops. Were they closer, it might be a different story. Why, what are you thinking?"

"It's possible Halvarian agents could be within our ranks."

"The shamans all have bodyguards."

"Yes, but you don't, and without you, I can't coordinate anything."

"That's easy enough to rectify. I'll ride down to Temple Commander Marlena and ask to borrow a couple of Temple Knights. Unless you think they might be compromised?"

"No," replied Beverly. "Considering all they've gone through, we can reasonably assume they haven't been infiltrated. Best go get those bodyguards now, though, before the fighting begins."

"I shall do so immediately." Aubrey descended the stairs.

"I now understand the loneliness of command," Beverly said to herself, but then she heard someone approaching and craned her neck to see Krazuhk, along with another Orc she didn't recognize. "*Greetings,*" she said, slipping into their language.

"*And to you,*" replied Krazuhk. "*This is Rugg, a master of earth from the Orcs of the Stone Crushers tribe. He is here to offer assistance.*"

"*I am honoured by your presence, Master Rugg. Might I ask what the nature of this assistance would be?*"

"*The magic of the earth is powerful but draining when used on a large scale. Therefore, I think it most prudent to use one spell repetitively to affect the greatest number of recipients rather than employ my magic piecemeal.*"

"*I would agree. What spell do you think is most effective?*"

"*Defensive mound would create a series of hills upon which your warriors could defend, but perhaps a wall of earth might prove more effective.*"

"*I once saw Albreda cast a wall of thorns. Is that something you're familiar with?*"

"*I am, and it is an even better solution, as it would slow down their advance while at the same time inflicting damage.*"

"*Then that would be my preference.*"

"*Then I shall gather the other masters of earth and begin creating such a wall. Where would you like it?*"

"*In front of the men of Reinwick, for I fear they'll be the ones to bear the brunt of today's fighting.*"

"*I shall see to it at once.*" He ran off to find his fellow Stone Crushers.

"*You are well-versed in the magic of the earth,*" noted Krazuhk. "*Your time with the Meghara has been well spent.*"

"Albreda is Human, not an Orc."

"It matters little. She is a powerful wielder of magic, is she not?"

"Yes," replied Beverly. *"The most powerful in Merceria, perhaps in all of Eiddenwerthe."*

"And who taught her the magic of the earth?"

"No one. She is self-taught."

"Which supports the argument that she is the Meghara. Amongst my people, it is believed the Meghara comes to us in our time of greatest need. I can think of nothing more compelling than this war, can you?"

"But Albreda's back in Merceria, not here."

"Yet she strives to defeat the great evil threatening our way of life. Whether you choose to believe it or not, she is the Meghara reborn."

"That being the case, how is she supposed to help us?"

"That is in her hands, not ours. All we can do is concentrate on the events before us, like this battle." Krazuhk stared westward. *"The legions draw close. It will not be long before our lines converge."*

"Agreed," said Beverly, *"and then the bloodbath will begin."*

Commander-General Vorinus Moreau stared back at the messenger. "Say that again?"

"It-it is true," the fellow stammered. "A wall of thorns appeared out of nowhere."

"Plants do not appear out of thin air. There is magic at work here."

His aide, Grim, shook his head. "Impossible. That would require an Earth Mage, and the enemy has none."

"None that we know of," Moreau corrected. "Were we not informed that a tribe of Orcs was assisting them?"

"Indeed, the Ashwalkers, but they practice the art of Fire Magic, not Earth."

"Could they not do both?"

"Not on such a scale," offered the messenger. "I saw the wall of thorns for myself, and it stretches across the entire width of the Reinwick line. They either have one very powerful Earth Mage or a host of lesser ones."

"The latter would seem more likely," replied Moreau, "though it changes little. If we are to defeat this army protecting the Petty Kingdoms, we must cut our way through this obstacle."

"And how might we do that?"

"Send our provincials forward; they're armed with axes. Tell them the first man through receives an instant promotion."

"Yes, my lord." The messenger rode off with all haste.

"The first one through will likely die as he comes out the other side," said Grim.

"I'd imagine so, but how else am I to encourage them? Surely you're not suggesting they take their time and be careful?"

"No, of course not, my lord."

"Don't look so downtrodden, Grim. This plays right into our hands."

"It does? How?"

"Isn't it obvious?" Moreau waited for a response, and when none was forthcoming, he sighed. "They placed this wall of thorns here because the warriors behind it are their weakest. Once we're through that obstacle, their army will shatter like a glass window. Trust me, we'll be dining in Torburg tonight, and the war will be over."

"Shall I order our own mages up to assist, my lord?"

"That's a marvellous idea, Grim, but let's make it a request rather than a command. You know how temperamental these spellcasters can be."

Temple Commander Romanus looked on with pride. The Holy Army, the finest cavalry to ever grace the Continent, was ready to annihilate their enemy and unify all of Eiddenwerthe under the emperor's rule. The Great Dream had been long in the making, and he would be the instrument by which that dream was realized.

Once done, he would abandon the façade of a faithful member of the Church and reclaim his honour as a Sartellian. Indeed, his part in the Great Dream's completion would elevate him to a place of honour amongst the empire's elite.

"The enemy looks nervous," noted Rostyslav.

"As they should be," replied Romanus. "Few are the warriors who can withstand the might of the Cunars, and those we've assembled today form the largest Holy Army ever amassed."

"Not quite, Your Grace. The crusade of 1104 managed a larger one."

"True, but if you recall, more than half were volunteers from around the Petty Kingdoms. Our order fielded seven hundred souls, and even then, two hundred were only initiates. If we're counting only full-fledged members today, we number eight hundred Temple Knights, quite a difference."

"That is true," said Rostyslav, "though we would do well to remember the lessons from the Battle of the Wilderness."

"This situation is entirely different. There, a numerically superior enemy ambushed us, whereas here, we clearly outnumber them. I would also remind you that we face the men of Andover, a country that hasn't won a battle in decades." He paused to wipe the sweat from his brow. "You are right to be cautious, though, and I will take care to avoid falling victim to some nefarious trap."

"I hope you're right, Your Grace."

"You doubt our victory?"

"I'm as hopeful as you that we'll prevail, but I can't help feeling there's something we're not seeing."

"Go on," said Romanus. "I'm curious to hear why you might say that."

"According to Edora Sartellian, we have a numerical advantage, but it's only a slight one."

"And?"

"Given those circumstances, wouldn't it have been wiser for the enemy to withdraw north before making a stand to avoid being surrounded?"

"And give up their capital? They'd never do that, and the marshal knew it, which is how we forced them to make a stand here. Now, all we need to do is finish them off, once and for all."

The hills north of Torburg provided Edora Sartellian with an excellent view of the battle. True, the Holy Army was hidden from her by the city itself, but that mattered little in the grand scheme of things. The legions would prove victorious this day; the Temple Knights were only there to tie down the enemy and prevent them from reinforcing the thin defence facing the empire's onslaught.

And what an onslaught it would be: six thousand men formed into three large blocks! They'd slice through the enemy like fire spreading through a dry forest, consuming all in its wake. She smiled at the thought of a fire of such magnitude, seeing it as a true reflection of the magic within her.

Victory was never a guarantee, even with a numerical advantage, but she was confident her strategy would prevail. And, while the Northern Alliance's presence had not been part of her original plan, it had worked out for the better. Winning this battle would end any remaining resistance within the Petty Kingdoms, and then she could turn her attention to the more serious matter of keeping Exalor from the Gilded Throne.

She was suddenly struck by the thought that perhaps, in her absence, Exalor might've already struck, seizing the Throne for himself. She'd heard nothing from Agalix for more than a week; for all she knew, Varena could be in the midst of an uprising. Edora shook it off, concentrating on the battle about to unfold before her.

THIRTY-SIX

The Battle of Torburg

SUMMER 968 MC

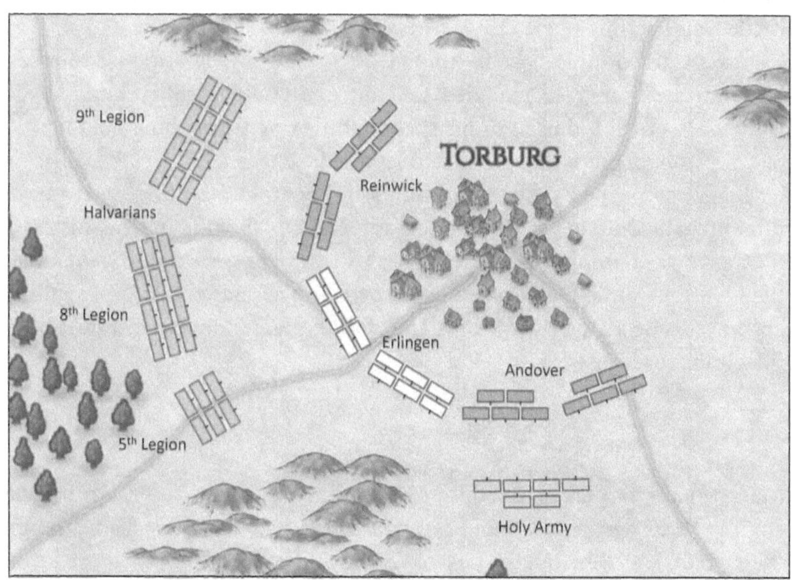

Carse Stanhome stood, the butt of his spear planted firmly into the ground to ward off danger from cavalry. The Army of Andover had maintained a blistering march to arrive in time, and his boots, like those of his comrades, had suffered. He wiggled his toes, feeling the leather separate from the sole as his blisters complained.

He glanced left and right, hoping to take inspiration from his country-men, but he only saw exhaustion and uncertainty. They were pressed men, forced into service by a king intent on becoming a military power, but were far from experienced. It didn't help that the Army of Andover had made a poor showing in the last two wars, and now they found themselves facing off against the most feared cavalry known to man: the Temple Knights of Saint Cunar.

The grey-clad army approached, led by a thin line of footmen and archers, the latter halting every ten or so steps to loose arrows and bolts. It made for a slow advance, but it only fed the terror building in the men of Andover. Behind this screening force came the Temple Knights, armour glinting in the sun, their horses kicking up a dust cloud that drifted eastward.

"This is too much," said Carse, looking down at his shaking hands as they gripped the spear. Never before had he stood in a line of battle, and now, seeing the grey-clad horde coming towards him, his chest tightened as if the very life was being squeezed out of him. He tried telling himself it was only fear, a natural enough emotion, considering they were about to fight a battle, yet that only made things worse.

He imagined himself being trampled to death by the armoured horses, his body becoming so mangled that no one could identify him. All he wanted was to rid himself of his spear and flee, yet something held him in place, a stubbornness that refused to let him lose face.

Someone pushed past him, jostling his spear, and he turned, ready to utter an oath, only to witness a green-skinned Orc moving in front of him.

Carse was dumbfounded. He'd heard the savages were around, even that they were helping, but to see one in person was incredible. The sight so entranced him that he forgot his fear and the impending doom he'd been imagining for himself.

Marag focused solely on the thin skirmish line that drew closer. Grumbling coming from her right announced that Snaga had finally pushed through the men of Andover, and the pair of Orcs could now unleash their magic on the Holy Army.

She scanned the advancing Humans, picking out one who looked like he was in charge. The man urged his fellow warriors on with a large sword, but Marag knew he would never get close enough to wield it properly. She pointed, letting loose with a streak of fire that flew across the battlefield, striking the leader in the chest, the force of the spell sending him tumbling back to the ground while those around him shied away, intent on avoiding the same fate.

The master of flame followed that spell with a ball of fire that rolled towards the enemy. The grass smoked as it passed, leaving a smear of ash in its wake, not the most powerful of spells, and had the enemy been prepared for magic, they could've easily stepped aside and avoided it altogether, but the very idea of a rolling ball of fire coming directly at them was too much to bear.

Men ran in fear, discarding their weapons in their haste to escape what they thought would be a fiery death. She risked a glance to see Snaga at work. Like her, he'd begun with a streak of fire, then used his magic to conjure a bird of flame that flew towards the enemy, leaving behind a trail of sparks and the distinctive smell of burning feathers.

The gaps in the enemy's advance widened, and then the men fled in pure panic, convinced they would all die a fiery and painful death. Behind them, the mounted Temple Knights of Saint Cunar continued, unfazed—one seemingly endless line of shining plate armour and massive horses.

"*We have done our part,*" called out Marag.

"*Agreed,*" replied Snaga, "*but will it be enough?*"

"*Only time will tell. Now, withdraw before it is too late.*"

She weaved her way back through the ranks of Andover's warriors.

Temple Commander Marlena watched the approaching men of the Fifth Legion while her command, the Army of Erlingen, stood ready to receive them. She was confident they'd hold, for the Fifth was at half strength, giving her a numerical advantage. More concerning, however, was the Eighth marching to force themselves between the men of Erlingen and Reinwick. If they succeeded, they could flood in behind the allied lines and wreak havoc.

She'd grouped her remaining Temple Knights into a strategic reserve, thinking General Fitzwilliam might have need of them. They were a mix of Agnesites, Mathewites, and even Waleed's Cunars, although the Temple Captain himself was out of the fight, a result of the wounds he'd sustained in delaying the enemy's march.

First contact came quickly, with the Fifth almost running along the road in their haste to engage. Her archers let loose with every arrow they had, thinning the ranks, but the enemy ignored their losses, maintaining their advance. They struck the Erlingen line dead centre, and the first melee of this immense battle began.

The mercenary captain, Rudolf Sturgess, watched as the Army of Erlingen was driven back by the assault. He'd been a warrior his entire life, and though his career had been filled with too many lean years, he relished the opportunity to do battle one last time. He was old, too old to be here, if truth be told, but his company, the Torburg Wolves, had finally been given the chance to win everlasting fame. Would he be up to it?

They'd been posted on the eastern flank of the Army of Erlingen, a position unlikely to see much action, which the Temple Commander had likely chosen due to the advanced years of his men.

Beside him stood Kerwain, one of his more experienced men acting as his sergeant. He'd started his career serving with a company known as the Grim Defenders but had been invalided after taking part in the Battle of Chermingen. He was a beast of a man who walked with a noticeable limp, but he was loyal, an important characteristic in the world of mercenary companies.

"Well?" said Sturgess. "What do you think? One more chance to go to the Afterlife with a sword in your hand?"

Kerwain grinned. "Is there any other way?"

"The general won't like it; we'd be breaking from our position."

"An unimportant one. If we don't stem that legion, it'll be the end of us."

Sturgess nodded his agreement. "Then let's break ranks and see if we can't render some assistance to our brothers-in-arms."

He barked out the order, and the Torburg Wolves advanced. Once past those beside them, they turned right, heading straight for the Fifth Halvarian Legion. It was ludicrous to think a single company could take on such a large group of enemy warriors, but the Torburg Wolves had a significant advantage—they intended to die gloriously in battle rather than wither away of old age. It wasn't a sentiment shared by other mercenary companies, but none of those consisted of warriors who were getting long in the tooth.

They picked up their pace, and then someone in the company let out a howl that was taken up by the others until everyone broke into a run, smashing into the flank of the Halvarian Legion.

Sturgess was with them all the way, cutting and slicing his sword with wild abandon. This was the story of his life, the epic clash where lives hung in the balance, and the spirit of battle poured through his veins like the Saints themselves possessed him.

The tip of his sword sank into someone's neck, and then he withdrew it, slicing into an arm, the blade scraping off the fellow's mail before it dug into his glove, forcing his opponent to drop his weapon. Sturgess redoubled his efforts, stabbing out yet again, striking a shield.

A spear took him in the arm, tearing through his worn mail and biting deep, but the strength raging through him was such that he ignored it. Again and again, he struck, the blood of his opponents splattering his mail.

An axe swung out, and he shifted his stance to avoid the blow. It missed his torso but sank into his thigh, cutting through mail and skin as if it were paper.

His leg went out from under him, and he glanced down as he fell, seeing only a stump remaining. Around him, the sounds of battle mingled with screams of pain, and then the ground hit him. Someone stepped on his back as they passed, driving his body into the dirt.

He turned his head, spotting his missing leg lying just out of reach and uttered his last words, "Oh, there it is. I wondered where it got to."

"It is time." Natalia Stormwind emerged from the hills southwest of Torburg and took a moment to look at her companions. "Is everybody ready?"

Galina Marwen nodded while the other seven awaited her next command, each and every one a Water Mage, some former students of the Volstrum, rescued from that place when the structure was destroyed last year, while the rest were experienced mages who'd sharpened their skills under the Warmaster of Therengia's tutelage. They strode out into the open, now behind the Fifth Legion, who was hammering the Erlingen defenders.

"This will do nicely, I think," said Natalia.

The mages spread out, leaving ten paces between them. Then, as one, they began casting. Surprisingly, Galina completed her spell first, the frozen arch forming before her as she stood with her back to the Halvarian Army. Natalia's came next, followed by the other mages in quick succession until nine frozen arches stood ready for the Army of Therengia to do its part.

The tuskers came first, giant creatures easily twice the size of the average warhorse. Upon their backs rode Orc hunters armed with long spears, ready to skewer any enemy soldier who escaped the tusks of the great beasts. Once through the gates, they headed straight for the enemy in one large herd.

The Temple Knights came next, taking time to properly form into lines, their scarlet tabards marking them as followers of Saint Agnes.

Athgar, High Thane of Therengia, stepped through, followed by his Thane Guard, the elite warriors that comprised the bulk of their footmen.

"Glad to see you could make it," said Natalia.

He grinned in reply. "I hope we're not too late?"

"Not at all; your timing, as always, is impeccable."

"Raleth," Athgar called out. "Form up the guard, archers to the rear, Orcs on the flanks, if you please." It was a standard tactic, one they'd employed on multiple occasions. The warriors continued pouring through the arches, their captains guiding them to their proper positions.

"What's our target?" asked Athgar.

"We have an opportunity," replied Natalia. "Once our cavalry cuts into the Fifth Legion, we'll use the rest of our army to drive a wedge between them and the legion to their north."

"An attack from the rear, just the sort of thing to put them ill at ease." Athgar spotted Kargen, Chieftain of the Red Hand, coming through an arch and waved him over. "I should like the masters of flame with me, if you don't mind."

"That will not be a problem," replied the Orc. "I shall take the tribe's more experienced hunters and see if we cannot find their leaders." He halted, then strung his warbow. "If they are to be found, it will be where they have a good view of the area."

"They weren't in these hills," said Natalia, "so that means they're farther north. Be careful, my friend. If you were to die, Shaluhk would never forgive me."

"Fear not. I am not yet ready to journey to the Afterlife." He grinned as he ran off, calling out his hunters by name, the group of them heading north.

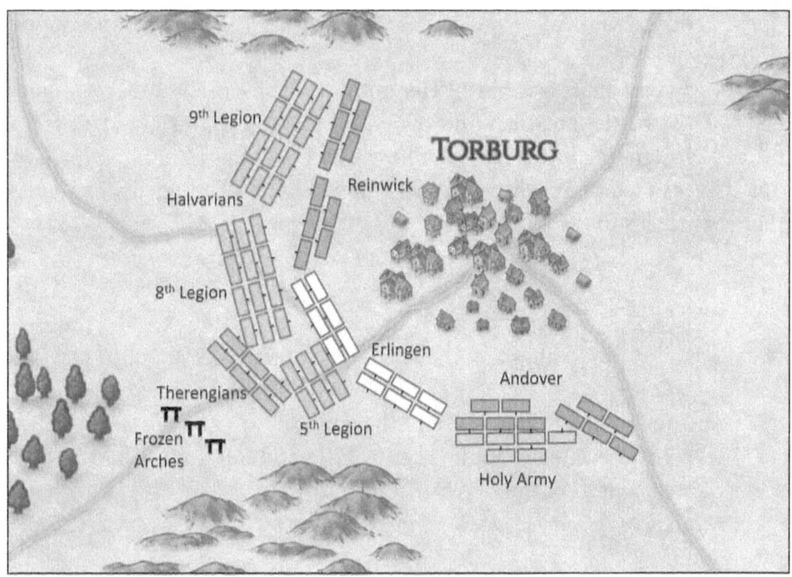

"The Therengians have arrived," said Aubrey. "I only hope they'll be up to the task; it's not as though they have large numbers."

"True," replied Beverly, "but I'm guessing the Halvarians put their best warriors out front rather than keeping them in reserve."

"What makes you think that?"

"There's no subtlety to their strategy, only a giant mass of men aimed at punching their way through, and their best chance of doing that is putting their veterans up front where they can do the most damage."

"Meaning the less-experienced warriors will be at the rear."

"Precisely."

Aubrey hesitated. "Hold on. Someone's contacting me."

Beverly waited.

"How bad is it?" asked Aubrey. The reply was inaudible to Beverly, but it clearly wasn't good news. Her cousin terminated the connection. "The Army of Andover is beginning to crumble. It's those damned Cunars; they're just too much to handle."

"Send word to Marlena. It's time to put her reserves to work, and who better to deal with the Cunars than Temple Knights?"

Once more, Aubrey drew upon her magic.

Being forced to sit and watch as the battle unfolded was frustrating, but Beverly consoled herself, knowing she was where she was needed. Her gut instinct was to ride into the fray, but doing so would take her attention away from what mattered most: directing this battle.

"It is done," said Aubrey. "The reserve is on its way. What of Reinwick? Will they hold?"

Beverly cast her gaze north. Her rooftop position allowed her a good view of the battle, but once the two sides merged into a grand melee, it proved challenging to determine who was who. "They're holding for now, but they can't take much more. Let's hope those Therengians can crack them before it's too late."

~

Natalia moved up, joining the Thane Guard as they were about to meet the enemy.

"Come to join in the fun?" asked Athgar.

"I thought the enemy might need a little softening up. Mind if I use some of my magic?"

"I'm surprised you have any strength left after holding that arch open for so long."

"Enough for one more present for our adversary." She dug deep, summoning forth the power from within her. A cold mist gathered around her and then coalesced into the icy form of a Humanoid, though it was devoid of a face or hands, its arms ending in spikes of ice.

"An ice golem," said Athgar. "A fitting tribute to your training."

She urged it forward with her mind. Used to magic, the Thane Guard parted, allowing the construct to rumble past, leaving frosty tracks in its wake.

The Halvarians reacted immediately, first with shouts of alarm, then with a slew of arrows loosed at the monstrosity, but other than a few chips of ice being knocked loose, there was no effect on the golem's steady pace.

It ripped into the flanks of the Eighth Legion, plowing its way deep into their ranks. The Thane Guard, trained to take advantage of the situation, followed along behind it, spreading out on either side and sealing the legion's doom.

~

Vorinus Moreau, Commander-General of the Ninth Halvarian Legion, looked on in dismay. He'd done his part, and his men were about to break the back of the Army of Reinwick, but his ally to the south, the Eighth, was in danger of collapsing. He considered diverting some of his men to help stem this unexpected development, but his foot were all committed to the fight. Withdrawing them now would only lead to chaos.

He'd been hoping to send his heavy cavalry forward in one last attack, certain it would break through, but now it appeared fate held something else in store for them. All he needed was to order them south to bolster the Eighth, and he would salvage the situation.

He opened his mouth to speak, but an arrow struck him from behind, cutting clean through his backplate and sinking deep into his chest. Moreau looked down in disbelief as blood oozed from his mouth, and then he toppled from the saddle, dead before he hit the ground.

His aide, Grim, tried to raise the alarm, but another arrow flew through the air and struck his horse. The beast reared up in pain, throwing his rider from the saddle, and then a group of green-skinned warriors rushed past, one stopping long enough to lift his visor up and plunge a long knife into Grim's face, finishing him off.

~

Edora Sartellian watched as her world crumbled. There'd be no Great Dream, at least not in her lifetime. She did not believe in fate or the Saints, but the one thing she'd always counted on was her superior training in the art of war. Now, all that came crashing down around her, shaking her to the core. Her mind struggled to cope with what she saw. The unthinkable had happened: she'd lost, and it was at the hand of a hastily assembled alliance, consisting of armies that only a few short years ago had been at each other's throats. How was that even possible?

One name came to mind—Beverly Fitzwilliam. The Mercerian was the cause of this; of that, she was certain. She didn't know when or how, but Edora swore to herself she would make the woman pay with her life!

A calmness descended upon her as she watched the battle with a dispassionate eye. She'd lost this war, but the enemy's casualty count was large enough that it would take them months to recover, and by then, winter would be here. They would undoubtedly march into Halvaria, but that wouldn't be until next spring at the earliest. She had time to prepare, provided she acted now to survive this.

With that, she uttered the words of power that would take her to safety. The magic built within, and then she felt the familiar tingle as a ring of fire encircled her, its warmth lending her courage.

The flames rose, blocking her view of the area, and then the air changed as she appeared in the palace, smack dab in the middle of a casting circle. The flames dropped, revealing armed guards standing with weapons at the ready. It was the last thing she ever saw.

THIRTY-SEVEN

Aftermath

Aubrey knelt by a man as he let out one final breath, and then his eyes glazed over, his head falling to the side.

"So much death," said Beverly. "It makes you wonder if it wouldn't have been more merciful to submit to the empire's rule."

"That would've doomed most of the Continent to a life of servitude. We fought today because we had to. Yes, there was a great loss of life, but that sacrifice ended the ascendancy of the Halvarian Empire."

Aldwin picked his way through the dead and wounded. "Ah, there you are," he called out. He sped up, then embraced his wife. "Glad to see you're safe."

"Likewise," replied Beverly.

"You, too, Aubrey," he added.

"I wasn't in any real danger," said the Life Mage. "All I did was use my magic to send messages." She glanced around at the bodies. "Unfortunately, that left me little strength to deal with injuries."

"The shamans are hard at work," offered Aldwin, "and will help as much as they can, but the losses were staggering, particularly on the Halvarian side. Having said that, they've chosen to concentrate on our own wounded before dealing with that of the enemy."

"That's understandable," replied Beverly. "I only wish we could do more for them." She pulled back from Aldwin to stare into his face. "Something tells me you're not here to see if I'm all right."

"The other generals are waiting to talk to you. Well, I say generals, but in actuality, it's two dukes, a king, a Temple Commander, a warmaster, and a

High Thane." He paused, looking up at the sky, his hand resting on his chin. "Let's see, did I forget anyone?"

"A chieftain, perhaps?" offered Aubrey.

"Yes, along with a shaman. How did you know?"

"The Orcs played an important part in this battle. It's only fitting they be represented when we discuss taking the campaign into Halvaria."

"Where are we to meet?" asked Beverly.

"On the crossroads southwest of the city." Aldwin offered his arm. "Shall we?"

"You go on ahead and let them know I'll be there shortly."

He bowed. "I'd be honoured to."

Aubrey waited until he left. "Are you all right, Cousin?"

"To be honest, I don't know. All this carnage has shaken me to the core. It's strange; I've seen more than my fair share of battles, but this one seemed to somehow hit me harder than most."

"That's your body reacting to the rigours of war. In those previous encounters, you were in the thick of the fighting, lashing out at the enemy and expending all your pent-up energy, while here, you were forced to play the role of a passive observer." She stepped closer, placing her hand on her cousin's shoulders. "Close your eyes and take a deep breath, letting it out slowly."

It was an odd sensation, trying to relax as her heart pounded like a horse in full gallop, but Beverly did as her cousin bid.

"Concentrate on my voice," continued Aubrey. "It might help to think of something calming."

"I'll think of Aldwin."

"No. Don't do that. We're trying to relax you, not get you all hot and bothered!"

Beverly opened her eyes to see her cousin smirking. "Very funny."

"It obviously worked. You appear much calmer now."

"That quickly?"

"Sometimes all that's needed is to focus on something singular. Think of it as clearing your mind to make room for more pleasant thoughts."

"When did you learn that trick?"

"Some time ago," replied Aubrey. "If you recall, I found my grandmother's hidden library back in Hawksburg."

"Yes. That's where you discovered her book of magic, wasn't it?"

"It was, but there was so much more, including writings about treating a whole host of maladies without the use of spells. That technique was one of those."

"Your grandmother was a wise woman. I wonder why she hid away her gift?"

"I've given that a lot of thought. Scholars have theorized that magic is passed down through the bloodline, but there have been incidents of it skipping a generation, which is likely what happened in my case. Now, much as I enjoy reminiscing, we should get going. There is a meeting you need to attend."

Beverly rolled her eyes. "Don't remind me."

"Are you up to it?"

"Yes, but I'm beginning to understand why we get grumpier as we get older."

Aubrey laughed. "Older? You're only thirty-three!"

The stench of death hung heavy in the air as the leaders of the various factions gathered around a fire.

Lord Fernando, the Duke of Reinwick, shuffled his feet. "Couldn't we have met somewhere more comfortable?"

"No," replied Beverly. "The warmaster picked this location out in the open to remind us of the sacrifice these brave warriors made today. Please sit, everyone."

"Sit? There are no chairs."

Athgar smiled. "I think she means for us to sit around the fire. It's an old Orc custom."

"An Orc custom?" said King Dagmar. "Why in the name of the Saints would we wish to do such a thing?"

Natalia Stormwind sat first. "Because it puts us all on the same level. Like it or not, Majesty, we are all equals."

"I am a king!"

"And I am the Warmaster of Therengia. Without our help or that of your other allies, this battle's outcome would've turned out significantly different. Now, I suggest you swallow your pride and sit so that we may discuss our next steps."

Dagmar grumbled something unintelligible but sat.

The Duke of Erlingen, Lord Alain, sat down, trying to hide his amusement at his colleague's discomfort. "This is a monumental victory, one that will be remembered for generations."

"Perhaps," replied Beverly, "but the war isn't over just yet." She sat, motioning for Aldwin to join her. Aubrey sat on the other side, flanked by the Orc shaman, Shaluhk.

Once everyone had joined the warmaster on the ground, Beverly continued. "As our esteemed colleague indicated, we've won a great battle, but if we are to make this victory complete, we must carry the war into the enemy's lands."

"Surely not?" said Alain. "We've taken tremendous casualties!"

"That we have, but we must press the advantage while we can. We've wiped three of the empire's legions off the face of Eiddenwerthe, but a fourth remains out there somewhere, waiting to exact revenge for their fallen comrades."

Everyone grew quiet, all eyes boring into Beverly.

Natalia broke the silence. "You have a plan?"

"I do," replied Beverly, "but it requires a tremendous amount of cooperation from all of you."

"You've beaten the empire twice," said Duke Alain. "That's all the proof I need. I shall be honoured to place my army under your command once more."

"As will I," added Lord Fernando.

"I'm not convinced," said King Dagmar. "We've defeated their invasion; surely that's enough? It will take them years to make up the losses."

"No, it won't," said the warmaster. "I don't think you appreciate how large the empire is."

"And I suppose you're going to tell me?"

"Halvaria is about the same size as the Petty Kingdoms."

"Which ones?"

"All of them combined."

Dagmar's face blanched. "Are you certain of that?"

"Absolutely."

"Then I'm in." He shifted his gaze to Beverly. "What's our next move?"

"The Marshal of Merceria has a strategy to defeat the empire, but it will take time to put into effect."

King Dagmar frowned. "The Marshal of Merceria? Hold on. We know nothing about this fellow, and you're asking us to follow his plan?"

"He's dedicated his entire life to leading men in battle."

"Yes," added Aubrey. "The Orcs call him the Grey Wolf. He has an uncanny way of outwitting the enemy."

"I can confirm that," added Shaluhk. "Kraloch has spoken of the marshal's military prowess on multiple occasions. Even now, his allies take the war to Halvaria."

"Our first step," said Beverly, "is to assess our losses and reorganize our remaining warriors into more manageable groups. The aim is that each division will be capable of fighting independently, if need be, necessitating a combination of foot, horse, and bow."

Duke Fernando shifted uncomfortably. "Shouldn't we wait until we've replaced our losses?"

"We haven't the time. Another legion is out there, and the longer we wait, the more damage they'll do."

"Are we absolutely certain of that?"

"The prisoners were most forthcoming, particularly the provincials, who were forced into service in the conquered territories."

"And where is this legion?"

"We're not entirely sure," replied Beverly. "They've been pacifying the westernmost Petty Kingdoms, so I imagine they'll be in one of the border realms, but they could just as easily have marched south into Talstadt or perhaps even Deisenbach."

"So they could be anywhere?"

"Precisely, which means our first order of business will be to send out people we can trust to seek word of them."

"Logical," said Natalia. "I doubt a legion could pass by unnoticed."

"The shamans will help," offered Shaluhk. "They can relay information the moment they discover the enemy's whereabouts."

"And once we find them?" asked Duke Alain.

"That depends on how quickly we can converge our forces. My intent is to head westward on as many parallel roads as we can, then concentrate them once the enemy is close. It means spreading out the army while on the march, but our ability to communicate over great distances allows us ample time to react."

"Providing we find them," said Fernando.

"That's where our mages come in," replied Beverly. "Several can use spells to spy out the enemy, as they demonstrated before this very battle."

"And if we are unable to locate this legion?"

"Then we'll press on into Halvarian lands, and that's where the marshal's plan comes into effect."

"Which is?" pressed King Dagmar.

"The war against the empire is to be a war of liberation, not conquest."

"Liberation? They must be punished for their unprovoked attack on us!"

"I must agree," said Fernando. "Their invasion has cost us dearly; they must be made to pay."

"The provinces of Halvaria," replied Beverly, "particularly the ones in the north, are fairly recent conquests. As such, we expect a lot of folks there will wish to throw off the shackles of the empire. If we can convince them we have their best interests at heart, it will enable us to keep our armies intact rather than being forced to garrison every city we march through."

"You make sense," said Lord Alain, "although it irks me to think we must take such an approach."

"Then let me ask you this: were it your lands under the Halvarian thumb, would you wish a foreign army to punish your people?"

"No, of course not. I concede the point."

"As do I," said Lord Fernando. "After all, it's those in charge of the empire we have cause to punish, not their provinces. Although I daresay, we'll need resources from these liberated areas if we are to feed our armies."

"Yes," replied Beverly, "and that would be easier to obtain from newly liberated realms rather than subjugated ones."

"How large an army do we march with?"

"That remains undetermined for the moment, as we're still counting our losses from today's battle."

"I think," added King Dagmar, "until we locate that missing legion, we should keep a garrison here in Erlingen."

"Agreed."

"If I might make a suggestion?" said Athgar. "What if we moved a large reserve back to Therengia, then used magic to bring them to battle, like we did today? It'd speed up our advance considerably and allow fresh troops to appear if the enemy threatened us?"

"An excellent idea," said Beverly. "We could even use them to shuffle men back and forth, allowing rotations for rest, providing your mages were up to it."

"There are some limitations," warned Natalia. "The farther we get from Therengia, the more magical strength is required to maintain the arches. Our position here stretched our capabilities to the breaking point; any farther west and we lose the majority of those mages."

"There is a solution," said Shaluhk, "but it requires us to locate more standing stones."

"That's how we arrived in the Petty Kingdoms," offered Aubrey. "Are you suggesting we tap into their energy?"

"I am. Nat-Alia has demonstrated that capability on multiple occasions, and I suspect she could teach others how."

"We should have our scouts keep an eye out for such things."

"Then that's exactly what we'll do," said Beverly. "We'll also concentrate on mapping out our route of march, which means getting our hands on whatever maps we can of the neighbouring realms and making copies for everyone."

"I have surveyors," said Lord Alain. "They've been busy creating new maps of Erlingen, but I see no reason why we shouldn't include them amongst our forces. At the very least, we could employ them to make what maps we have more accurate."

"Another excellent idea," replied Beverly, "which demonstrates how working together is for the benefit of all. Now, that brings me to another matter, one which might ruffle a few feathers. The Army of Erlingen has three very capable division commanders: Temple Commander Marlena and her two Temple Captains. I'd like the other armies to use the same command structure."

"What exactly do you mean?" said Dagmar. "Are you suggesting we place our men under the command of the Temple Knights?"

"No, merely that each division be assigned a capable, experienced commander, with a second-in-command, in case of injury or death. It's a method we've adopted in Merceria to great effect."

"There's another difference," offered Aldwin. "In Merceria, everyone, down to the lowest footman, knows what the objective is. We're going to be marching into Halvaria as liberators, and that must be made as clear as possible to everyone."

"A good point," replied Beverly, "and one I hadn't considered."

"Have we a schedule for this campaign?" asked Aldwin.

Beverly smiled as she knew full well that Aldwin was aware of all the details; he was merely prompting her for the rest of the plan. "Our priority at present is finding the last legion. The invasion of Halvaria, or rather the liberation of it, must wait until the new year. Of course, that's all subject to change. The legion may have already retreated across the border or deserted, although I doubt that's the case."

"And if they have?" said Lord Alain.

"Then we'll be in Halvarian territory come autumn. The last thing I'd like to address is the fate of Halvaria, or rather, those who rule the empire. To end their threat once and for all, we must remain united not only in military strength but in resolve to see this through to the end. If any of your kingdoms backs out or seeks a separate peace, it would be the ruin of the rest."

"What are you asking of us?" said King Dagmar.

"That we take an oath, here and now, to fight to the end and stand united when it comes to the ultimate fate of the Halvarian Empire."

Athgar stood. "Therengia agrees."

"As does Erlingen," added Lord Alain, standing like his counterpart.

Lord Fernando joined them, adding his voice. "Reinwick stands with you."

Everyone looked at King Dagmar.

"I shall abide by the majority's decision," he agreed. "Andover stands with its allies, but someone needs to give me a hand up; my legs have fallen asleep."

Lord Fernando pulled His Majesty to his feet, although it took some effort.

"It appears we stand united," said Athgar. "What's our next move?"

"I shall confer with Lady Natalia," said Beverly. "Her experience as a battle mage is most valuable. In the meantime, I'd like Aubrey to oversee our efforts to heal the wounded."

"I would defer to Shaluhk," said her cousin. "She has far more experience in battlefield medicine than I, and she's more familiar with the shamans doing the healing."

"I shall be honoured to do so," replied the Orc.

"Then it's settled," said Beverly. "Anything else anyone would like to bring up?" She waited, giving everyone a chance to speak.

After a suitable silence, Aubrey spoke. "Perhaps, Cousin, it might be appropriate to say a few words to celebrate the occasion?"

"Yes, of course. You've all done well today. I know some of you would've preferred this be the end of the fighting, but if we want to leave our children a future free from foreign oppression, we must do everything in our power to defeat the empire. Today's battle will, as Lord Alain so eloquently put it, be remembered forever, but not as the day Halvaria was destroyed. Rather, it will be seen as the turning point in the larger conflict to reclaim the freedom of the Petty Kingdoms. This war marks the greatest conflict the Petty Kingdoms, perhaps even of all Eiddenwerthe, has ever seen, but it will all be for naught if we replace one tyrant with another."

She took a moment to gather her thoughts before continuing. "We've successfully defended your homes, but must now transition from defender to aggressor. Let there be no doubt; there is plenty of fighting to come, but today's victory marks the beginning of the end of Halvaria."

THIRTY-EIGHT

Betrayal

SUMMER 968 MC

"This is madness," said Wingate. "There are soldiers everywhere!" He ducked into an alleyway, pulling Exalor along with him. The High Strategos opened his mouth to offer a rebuke, but then a trio of warriors raced past, their swords drawn and bloody.

"Perhaps you should use a spell, Your Grace? Could we not teleport?"

"And go where?" replied his master. "There's no point in going to the estate if it's been overrun. We'd be killed instantly."

"But we must do something!"

"Calm yourself. We're only a few blocks from the gatehouse. Once we're free of the city, we'll be safe." He poked his head around the corner. "I'd kill to know who's behind this."

"Those are certainly not the emperor's men."

"No, they're legionnaires, but I see nothing to indicate who's commanding them." He pulled back into the alleyway. "Keep an eye out, Wingate. I shall use my magic to determine if the way is clear." As he called forth his magic, the air shimmered, and then a slight rippling effect emerged above his head, then it quickly rose higher, becoming almost invisible.

"There," said Exalor. "I have a much better view of the area."

"Can you see the gatehouse?"

"Yes, but guards are everywhere. What's this, now?"

Wingate held his breath, expecting an answer, but Exalor offered no further details. The servant's nerves felt as if they were on fire, and even his legs, which were usually quite reliable, shook uncontrollably. A small part of him wanted to scream in frustration and flee, but unfortunately, his position as the aide to the High Strategos made him a marked man.

"Someone's coming," said Exalor. "You can relax; it's only Kelson."

Footsteps approached, and then Exalor stepped out into the street, greeting Kelson Shozarin, who was accompanied by six armed men, all experienced by the look of it. "Your Grace, you had us worried for a moment there. I trust you are well?"

"As well as can be expected, given the circumstances. Any idea who's behind this?"

"I can't say with absolute authority, but I've heard reports that Morven Rassi has been seen. You remember him?"

"Of course I remember him; how many commander-generals do you think I've dismissed for incompetence?" He was about to unleash a tirade about the fellow but then visibly calmed himself. "I have a hard time believing Rassi is capable of organizing something this complex. He must be working with someone."

"The Sartellians, perhaps?"

"Moving these men into the city unopposed would take somebody with considerable experience and influence."

"The Marshal of the South?"

"That would be my guess," replied Exalor. "The question is, what can we do about it?"

"Nothing until you are safe, Your Grace. I recommend we take you back to the estate as quickly as possible."

"That will prove difficult unless you're suggesting this trouble is limited to the confines of the capital?"

"That has certainly been my experience."

"Keep your men alert, and I shall teleport us to safety."

Wingate heard the words of power issuing from his master, and then there came that old familiar feeling of his entire body being stretched into impossible shapes. Once that unsettling feeling abated, he realized they'd teleported to the casting circle at Exalor's estate. He immediately staggered to the side of the room, the contents of his stomach threatening to overwhelm him.

"Come," said Exalor, heading up the stairs. "We have work to do." Like most casting circles utilized by the Shozarins, this had been built in the cellar, giving it the advantage of being away from prying eyes and easy to secure should that prove necessary. And, the number of people who'd been permitted to commit the circle to memory was limited, making it even more secure.

Wingate took a deep breath, trying to settle his stomach. He wanted to remain here, in the coolness of the cellar, but with everything going on today, Exalor would be in a foul mood. He stumbled up the stairs, chasing the sound of his master's receding footsteps.

Exalor marched straight to the dining room. "Fetch my maps," he ordered. Wingate offered a perfunctory bow, then left the room, running to the office of the High Strategos.

The maps in question were easy to find, for Exalor had been planning an assault on the capital for months. How strange that it should now be someone else entirely who'd seized Varena. Wingate went to pick up the maps, but then the ceremonial dagger sitting on the desk caught his eye. The academy had given it to Exalor as a reward for being an exceptional student many years ago. Now, it beckoned to Wingate like it had been waiting here all this time just for him to take it.

He'd been living a dangerous lie, betraying his master by selling information to Kelson. How long before the inevitable discovery? His fingers wrapped around the handle without thinking, and then he grabbed what he'd come for and was back out in the hallway, the blade concealed beneath the maps.

Exalor stared out the window, barely able to keep his rage at bay. His plan had finally been ready to bear fruit only to discover someone else beat him to it. Kelson had suggested the Marshal of the South, but was he attempting to deflect the blame? Could Kelson be plotting his downfall even now? His gaze flicked to the fellow, but he saw no sign of deception.

A guard stepped into the room. "The estate is secure for now, Your Grace, but you might want to consider withdrawing to a safer place such as Zefara."

"I will not admit defeat, not after years of planning." Exalor looked at Kelson. "What do you think? Can we salvage this?"

"Doubtful, Your Grace. Once they've secured the city, it won't take them long to seek out the estates."

"I agree. How much time does that give us?"

"A day, perhaps two, if we're lucky."

The door opened, and Wingate stumbled in with an armful of maps. He deposited them on the table, then stepped back as the two Enchanters poked through them.

Exalor found a map of Varena and rolled it out, using a cup to hold down one corner. "The north gate is lost. Soldiers were crawling all over it."

"You saw it?" said Kelson.

"Only by magic. I wasn't fool enough to reveal my presence."

Exalor suddenly felt a prick in his back and then a short jab that took his breath away as a dagger tip broke through his chest. Blood welled up in his throat, and he coughed crimson all over the maps. He staggered forward, grasping the edge of the table, and half turned to see his aide staring at him in horror, blood staining his hands.

"Why?" gasped Exalor, then fell forward, dead.

"There," said Wingate. "I've done it. We're free of his plotting."

Kelson met the servant's wide-eyed gaze. "His plotting wasn't what lost us the Throne."

"Yes, but with the High Strategos dead, we can make our peace with whoever's behind this assault. After all, we removed an obstacle to their rule, didn't we?"

"Indeed you did, but we know so little about who's behind this. We can speculate all we like, but until the dust settles and someone announces that the Throne is theirs, we're still in the dark."

"But you both agreed it was the Marshal of the South. I heard you say so."

"You're a fool," said Kelson, "and by taking matters into your own hands, you've made it very difficult to continue our arrangement." Kelson waved his hand, uttering words of power, and then the door locked, and the windows latched shut of their own accord.

"Please, Your Grace. Spare me. I was only doing what I thought you wanted." Wingate stepped away until his back hit the wall. He cast about, seeking a means of escape, but with the exits locked by magic, there was no easy way out. He imagined himself jumping through the window, even going so far as to shift his feet slightly to get a running start, but then Kelson slashed out with the knife Wingate had used to kill Exalor.

Wingate grabbed his neck, blood pulsing through his fingers, dripping down his chest to soak his shirt. He slumped down the wall to fall face forward, where a widening pool of red stained the wood beneath his thrashing body.

Kelson knelt by the dying aide, his voice calm as a gentle breeze. "The problem with someone turning on their master is that their loyalty can never again be trusted. Sleep well, my friend, and go to the Underworld knowing you've served the greater good." He waited until the last spasm stopped, then turned the body over. Blank eyes stared back.

He stood up and dispelled his locking spell, then called out, "Guards! Come quick. The High Strategos has been murdered!"

Exalor's guards rushed into the room, their weapons drawn.

"I killed the assassin," said Kelson, pointing at Wingate. "His body is there, but I'm afraid I was too late to save Lord Exalor."

The guards sheathed their swords. "What now, my lord?"

"Call in the rest of the guards. We shall leave for Zefara immediately."

"And then?"

"Then, unfortunately, I shall be forced to assume the role of head of the Shozarin family."

Castimar Stormwind stepped over a body, careful not to slip on the blood. The palace was littered with dead, a tribute to the efficiency of his legions. He'd finally reached his destination—the throne room where two of his men stood outside. They pulled the double doors wide open upon noting his arrival.

He stepped inside, marvelling at the opulence held within. Unlike the rest of the palace, this room remained untouched by death, the Gilded Throne resting upon its pristine floors. As Halvaria's seat of power for more than a thousand years, only the emperor had ever sat upon it. Now, he'd join the long list of rulers who'd held sway over the largest empire in Human history. He moved closer, holding his breath in anticipation.

"You'll need this, Eminence."

Castimar wheeled about to find Morven Rassi clutching Erkinwald's Mace, the traditional symbol of imperial power. The fellow advanced, holding the weapon out to him.

"Thank you." Castimar turned back to the white marble throne, reaching out and caressing its smooth surface. Centuries ago, the entire thing had undergone a transformation, accenting it with heavy gold filigree that gave the throne its present name.

"You should sit," said Rassi. "It's time you received your reward for such a masterful campaign. No one, save for yourself, could've orchestrated this."

"True, and I couldn't have done it without you, Morven." Castimar turned, then sat, enjoying the red cushion that protected him from the cold marble. He leaned back, relishing the power that coursed through him.

"How does it feel?"

"Like I was born to claim it."

"It is your destiny, Eminence."

Castimar looked around at the empty throne room. It didn't take much effort to imagine it filled with people, all coming to pay homage to their new emperor.

"A question, if I may, Eminence?"

"Speak freely."

"By all rights, you are now the Emperor of the Halvarian Empire, and may do as you please, but might it be wise to conduct an official ceremony to mark the occasion? In the past, when a new emperor ascended to the throne, a grand celebration followed the crowning."

"You raise a good point, although I'm hesitant to have someone else crown me. It would make me appear weak."

"You could always crown yourself?"

Castimar smiled. "What a marvellous idea. I shall do precisely that, and everyone can say a prayer in my honour. Afterwards, I'll host the greatest celebration ever seen in the history of the empire. It must be spectacular, something people will talk about for generations to come!"

"It shall be as you wish, Eminence."

"You have served me well, Morven, and deserve a fitting reward. What would you ask of me?"

"I would be happy to command your Imperial Guard, Eminence."

"I will gladly grant you what you wish, but you must build them from scratch; we can't very well trust those who served my predecessor."

"How large a guard would you suggest?"

"They must be capable of taking the field of battle. To that end, I authorize you to raise a legion's worth of men. Pick the best the empire has to offer, choosing them from other legions if need be. As we take back our lands, we shall expand them, forming a new army that puts the legions of the past to shame."

"Yes, Eminence."

Castimar held the mace in his right hand while his left absently stroked the arm of the throne. "We shall usher in a new age," he said, staring down at the white stone under his fingers. "An age where the might of the empire will be unprecedented." He looked directly at Rassi. "The next few months will be busy for us. The other families won't take kindly to my new position and will try to remove me."

"That would be difficult, Eminence. The legions in the west have been hard hit, and the campaign in the Petty Kingdoms used up most of our reserves."

"That does not preclude them taking a more direct approach."

"You mean assassination?"

"Precisely," replied Castimar.

"Then I shall make the palace into a fortress."

"Have the First Legion see to that. They've been with me the longest."

"Yes, Eminence."

"And while you're at it, see if you can locate the crown, will you? It must be around here somewhere."

Vola Yarenko and Bryn Valani appeared at the door, their way blocked by two guards.

"It's all right," called out Castimar. "You can let them in."

The warriors moved aside, and Vola, the bureaucrat, straightened her dress and then strode confidently into the room. Bryn followed, making barely a sound as she walked towards the throne. They both halted before the new emperor, Vola bowing deeply while Bryn nodded her head.

"We come bearing news." Vola remained staring at the floor.

"Out with it."

"The emperor has fled, Your Grace."

"You are mistaken," said Morven, stepping towards her. "The emperor sits upon the throne… and you shall address him as Your Eminence."

"My apologies, Eminence. I was unaware you'd already claimed the title."

"Merely a misunderstanding," said Castimar, "but you were saying?"

"The emperor—that is, the previous ruler—has escaped."

"How is this possible?"

"The palace is a large structure, Eminence, and our legions lacked familiarity with its halls. As you are likely aware, there are concealed doors that lead to hidden hallways throughout the palace, and he must've made his escape by means of these. There is, however, some good news; the High Regent, Karoulus, is in our custody."

"That is excellent news, indeed, but we cannot have Nevarus wandering around the streets of Varena, not when we claim to be in control."

"Our men are scouring the city," said Morven. "It won't be long before he falls into our clutches."

The emperor leaned forward. "Anyone else unaccounted for?"

"A number of servants and the two Mercerians," replied Vola.

"Mercerians? What Mercerians?"

"They were prisoners, Eminence, taken in the campaign in the west."

"I know where Merceria is. How did they get to be in the capital in the first place?"

"I am at a loss to explain it," she replied, "but Bryn has her men interrogating the palace staff. We shall get to the bottom of this mystery, but until then, you should remain well-guarded."

"Are you suggesting they might be a threat to my well-being?"

Bryn spoke for the first time. "I've learned Arnim Caster is a resourceful man, and if reports are to be believed, his wife was instrumental in suppressing an uprising in their capital, Wincaster."

"How does that have anything to do with me?"

"The reason she's so good at breaking up riots is she knows how to start one. That alone is cause for alarm."

"Nonsense," said Morven. "If she's foolish enough to start an uprising, our legions will crush it."

Bryn frowned at the warrior. "If you are so witless to believe you can be everywhere at once, then I daresay you deserve the consequences. I, however, intend to hunt down these criminals, thus assuring the continued rule of our new emperor."

"Now, now," said Castimar. "Let's not fight amongst ourselves; that would hardly be productive. We have three legions at our disposal. The First will man the palace; the Second, the walls, which leaves the Tenth to hunt down these Mercerians, not to mention my predecessor. Once they're found, we can begin Halvaria's next great age."

Epilogue

SUMMER 968 MC

Cyric stared at Korvoran over the stern railing as the *Redoubtable* sailed north, along the coast of Reinwick, a voyage that would eventually take them to the uncharted waters to the west and then, finally, to Merceria.

This trip was unlike anything he'd ever read about, and he felt guilty accompanying it without first informing his superior, but it was a once-in-a-lifetime opportunity to be a part of history rather than reading about it.

Admiral Danica turned from the ship's wheel, allowing Captain Grace to take her place. She moved to stand beside him. "Is this your first time going to sea?"

"In these waters, yes, but I have sailed the Shimmering Sea once or twice. Is it always this rough?"

"This? Rough? No, this is a mild day. When it wants to, the Great Northern Sea can produce waves that would swamp us, but we try to avoid sailing in extreme weather whenever possible." Her gaze wandered over the ships following in their wake. "I never get tired of seeing that."

"The fleet?"

"Yes. Nine ships—that's the same number we commanded at the Battle of Lidenbach, although we've replaced some of the older vessels with these new ones." She patted the railing.

"It's a fine sight, to be sure," said Cyric, "although I do wonder if we're doing the right thing."

"You travelled with the Mercerians; you tell me."

"They are earnest in their desire to destroy the empire."

"But?"

"I have only my faith in Lady Beverly that their army is capable of taking on the Halvarians."

"And is that not enough?"

A smile crossed his lips. "Yes, I suppose it is."

<<<<>>>>

REVIEW SAVIOUR OF THE CROWN

READ THE SERIES FINALE: VICTORY OF THE CROWN

If you liked *Saviour of the Crown,* then *Ashes,* the first book in *The Frozen Flame* series awaits.

START ASHES

Cast of Characters

MAIN CHARACTERS

MERCERIA & ALLIES

Aldwin Fitzwilliam - Master smith, married to Beverly
Alric - King of Weldwyn, married to Anna, father of Braedon
Anna - Queen of Merceria, married to Alric, mother of Braedon
Arnim Caster - Viscount of Haverston, married to Nikki
Aubrey Brandon - Baroness of Hawksburg, Life Mage
Beverly Fitzwilliam - General, Baroness of Bodden, married to Alric
Gerald Matheson - Duke of Wincaster, Marshal of the Army
Hayley Chambers - Baroness of Queenston, High Ranger
Herdwin Steelarm - Dwarf smith, friend of Queen Anna
Kasri Ironheart - Dwarf warrior, daughter of Vard of Ironcliff
Krazuhk - Orc, Master of Air, Sky Singers
Nicole (Nikki) Caster - Viscountess of Haverston, married to Arnim
Owen - Knight of Erlingen
Revi Bloom - Royal Life Mage, Enchanter

THE EMPIRE OF HALVARIA

Exalor Shozarin - High Strategos, Enchanter
Janek - Servant at the Imperial Court
Nevarus - God Emperor
Wingate - Aide to Exalor

SECONDARY CHARACTERS

Dwarves

Agramath - Master of Rock and Stone, Ironcliff
Durgan - Captain, Hearthguard, Ironcliff
Garnik Hardhand - Guildmaster, Warriors Guild, Ironcliff
Gelion Brightaxe - Commander, cousin to Herdwin, Stonecastle
Golmar Hengesplitter - Engineer, Stonecastle
Khazad - Vard, Stonecastle
Malrun Bronzefist - Master of Revels, Ironcliff
Margel - Stonesmiths guild, forge mate to Gelion, Stonecastle
Murdan - Captain, arbalester company, Stonecastle
Rurik Deepdelver - Senior mining supervisor, Mining guild, Ironcliff
Selia Ironfist - Guildmaster, Mining Guild, Ironcliff
Thalgrun Stormhammer - Vard, Ironcliff
Tulfar Axehand - Dwarf, Baron of Mirstone, Weldwyn

Erlingen

Alain Heinrich - Duke of Erlingen
Augustus Strappe - Baron of Salzing
Carse Stanhome - Warrior
Deiter Heinrich (Deceased) - Duke of Erlingen
Hagan Stein - Baron of Mulsingen
Kerwain - Mercenary, Torburg Wolves
Marten Drachmann - Baron of Hutfeld
Rudolf Sturgess - Mercenary Captain, Torburg Wolves
Wulfram - Baron of Regnitz

Goblins

Flint - Tinker, Stonewall Enclave
Glisnak - Chieftain, Stonewall Enclave
Grazuk - Wolf Rider, Stonewall Enclave
Quickpaw - Mountain wolf, mount of Grazuk, Stonewall Enclave
Snarlak (Deceased) - Chieftain, Crag Enclave
Tarzil - Goblin, Wolf rider, Stonewall Enclave
Virdu - Bender, Stonewall Enclave

Halvaria

Agalix Sartellian - Inner Council, Fire Mage
Bastien Lambert - Commander-General, 7th Legion
Bryn Valani - Head of powerful criminal organization
Cadmus Aldmeyer - Air Mage
Cassius - Captain, Garrison of Edgefield

Castimar Stormwind - Marshal of the South, Water Mage
Edora Sartellian - Inner Council, Fire Mage
Egreth Blackthorne - Earth Mage
Enelle Sartellian - High Purifier, Fire Mage
Erkinwald (Deceased) - First emperor of Halvaria
Fadra Stormwind - Inner Council, Water Mage
Freya Stormwind - Inner Council, Water Mage
Grafford Sartellian - Fire Mage
Grim - Aide to Commander-General Vorinus Moreau
Hamath Nordin (Deceased) - Commander-General, 5th Legion
Heliot - Guard in the employ of Kelson Shozarin
Joachim Battista - Commander-General, 5th Legion
Idraxa Shozarin - Acting Marshal of the North, Enchanter
Karoulus - High Regent, Heir to the Crown of Halvaria
Kelson Shozarin - High Sentinel, Enchanter
Kestia Stormwind - Inner Council, Water Mage
Kyre Banburn - Commander, Garrison of Edgefield
Marfor - Sergeant, 5th Halvarian Legion, Aide to Joachim Battista
Morven Rassi - Former Legion Commander
Murias Stormwind - Inner Council, Water Mage
Olynia Sartellian - Fire Mage
Praxar Shozarin - Marshal of the Empire, Enchanter
Stalgrun Sartellian (Deceased) - Marshal of the North, Fire Mage
Umberto Rakert - Commander-General, 8th Legion
Vola Yarenko - Senior Bureaucrat, Varena
Voltana Stormwind - Volstrum survivor, Water Mage
Vorinus Moreau - Commander-General, 9th Legion

MERCERIA

Albreda - Mistress of the Whitewood, Earth Mage
Aldus Hearn - Earth Mage
Andronicus (Deceased) - Royal Life Mage
Arandil Greycloak - Elven ruler of the Darkwood, Fire Mage/Enchanter
Braedon Gerald - Prince of Merceria, Son of Anna & Alric
Donald Harper - Royal guard, Wincaster
Durwin - Earth Mage
Edwina - Former princess of Weldwyn, Air Mage
Evard Brenton - Royal guard, Wincaster
Heward 'The Axe' Manton - Baron of Redridge, Knight of the Hound
Kiren-Jool - Kurathian Enchanter
Lanaka - Kurathian cavalry commander, Earl of Tewsbury

Lightning - Beverly's Mercerian Charger
Lily - Saurian
Preston Wright - Baron of Wickfield, Knight, married to Sophie Wright
Richard 'Fitz' Fitzwilliam(Deceased) - Baron of Bodden, Beverly's father
Shalariel - Elf, Earth Mage, Mistress of Thorolandrin, The Darkwood
Storm - Kurathian Mastiff, Queen Anna's pet
Tog - Troll, Earl of Trollden, Leader of the Trolls

NORLAND

Bronwyn - Queen of Norland
Calder - Earl of Greendale
Waverly - Earl of Marston

ORCS

Andurak - Wolf Clan
Ghodrug - Chieftain, Black Ravens, Norland
Gorath - Deputy High Ranger, Black Arrows, Merceria
Gurza - Hunter, Black Arrows, Merceria
Kargen - Chieftain, Orcs of the Red Hand, Therengia
Kharzug - Shaman, Black Ravens, Norland
Kraloch - Shaman, Black Arrows, Merceria
Kurghal - Shaman, Black Arrows, Urgon's sister, Merceria
Laruhk - Hunter, Orcs of the Red Hand, Brother to Shaluhk, Therengia
Marag - Master of Flame, Ashwalkers, Reinwick
Meghara - Mythical mages of ancient Orc origin
Rugal - Chieftain, Ashwalkers, Reinwick
Rugg - Master of Earth, Stone Crushers, Therengia
Rulahk - Shaman, Black Ravens, Norland
Shaluhk - Shaman, Orcs of the Red Hand, Therengia
Snaga - Master of Flame, Ashwalkers, Reinwick
Urgon - Chieftain, Black Arrows, Merceria
Vagrath - Shaman, Ashwalkers, Reinwick

REINWICK

Enid - Servant to the duke
Erhald Marwen - Captain
Fernando Brondecker - Duke of Reinwick
Galina Marwen - Water Mage
Kurlan Stratmeyer - Baron of Blunden

THERENGIA

Athgar - High Thane, bondmate to Natalia, Fire Mage
Natalia Stormwind - Warmaster, bondmate to Athgar, Water Mage

The Twelve Clans (Clanholdings)
Althea - Princess, Dungannon
Brogar Hammerhand - Bodyguard to Princess Althea, Mirstone
Haldrim - Dwarf, Captain, Dragon Company
Lochlan - Clan chief, Dungannon

The Fighting Orders
Charlaine - Temple General, Saint Agnes
Cordelia - Temple Commander, Saint Agnes, Therengia
Cyric - Temple Knight, Saint Mathew
Danica - Admiral, Temple Commander, Temple Fleet
Giselle - Temple Captain, Saint Agnes, Deisenbach
Grace - Temple Captain, Saint Agnes, *Redoubtable*
Johanna - Temple Knight, Saint Agnes
Marius - Former Temple General, Formerly Saint Cunar
Marlena - Temple Captain/Commander, Saint Agnes
Nicolas - Temple Knight, Formerly Saint Cunar
Petra - Temple Captain, Saint Agnes, Erlingen
Roland - Temple Commander, Saint Mathew
Romanus - Temple Commander, Saint Cunar
Rostyslav - Aide to Temple Commander Romanus, Saint Cunar
Vitaly - Temple Captain, Saint Mathew, Erlingen
Waleed - Temple Captain, Formerly Saint Cunar

Weldwyn
Aegryth Malthunen - Earth Mage
Beric Canning - Earl of Southport
Darvin Fairhand - Captain, Army of Weldwyn
Ekthyn Ramark - Life Mage
Elgin Warford - Earl of Riversend
Gretchen Harwell - Enchanter
Leofric (Deceased) - King, Weldwyn, Father of Alric
Osbourne Megantis - Fire Mage, Weldwyn

Others
Dagmar - King of Andover
Delsaran - Elf bard, the Darkwood
Gervais - Knight of Valour, Andover

Gwalinor - Elf, Life Mage
Harnen Runell - Captain, Merchant ship *Swift*
Kenworth - Knight of Valour, Andover
Lorenzo - Advisor to King of Andover
Ludwig Altenburg - King, Hadenfeld
Marakhova Stormwind (Deceased) - Matriarch, Water Mage
Red Wizard (Deceased) - Sartellian agent, Sunset Peaks
Talivardas - Primus, Church of the Saints
Zivka - Captain, *Illustrious*, Temple Fleet

PLACES

Halvaria

Calabria - Coast of the Shimmering Sea, absorbed by Halvaria
Dun-Galdrim - Dwarf city destroyed by Halvaria
Edgefield - City near the pass to Stonecastle
Herani - The Holy City, birthplace of humanity
Varena - Capital of Halvaria
Victory Park - Varena
Zefara - Port city on the west coast of Halvaria

Merceria

Bodden - Town, Barony
Colbridge - City
Erssa Saka'am - Saurian city/temple
Haverston - Village, Viscountcy
Hawksburg - Town, Barony
Queenston - Town, Barony
Redridge - Village, Barony
Tewsbury - City, Earldom
The Whitewood - Great forest, northwest region
Thorolandrin - Elf city, The Darkwood
Trollden - Town, southern coast
Uxley - Village, Royal estate, west of Wincaster
Wincaster - Capital City

The Realms of Eiddenwerthe

Andover - Kingdom, north of Erlingen
Angvil - Duchy, west of Erlingen
Ardosa - Kingdom, known as the heart of the Petty Kingdoms
Arnsfeld - Kingdom, adjacent to Halvaria
Carlingen - Kingdom, northeast continent

Corassus - City State, Southern coast
Deisenbach - Kingdom, northwest of Hadenfeld
Erlingen - Duchy, south of Andover
Galoran - Kingdom, east of Hadenfeld
Gotfeld - Kingdom, east of Hadenfeld
Hadenfeld - Kingdom, bordering Deisenbach
Ilea - Kingdom, South Coast
Krieghoff - Duchy, eastern portion of continent
Lubenstahl - Kingdom
Ostrova - Kingdom, eastern Petty Kingdom
Reinwick - Duchy, Northern Coast
Rudor - Kingdom, adjacent to Halvaria
Ruzhina - Kingdom, Northeast of the Petty Kingdoms
Talstadt - Kingdom, adjacent to Stormtop Mountains
Therengia - Realm east of the Petty Kingdoms
Ulrichen - Kingdom, southeast of Erlingen
Zowenbruch - Kingdom, bordering Deisenbach

WELDWYN

Bramwitch - Coastal city, southeast Weldwyn
Loranguard - Earldom, City
Mirstone - Dwarf Mine, Barony
Southport - Major port city, southeast Weldwyn
Summersgate - Capital

CITIES, TOWNS, AND VILLAGES OF PETTY KINGDOMS

Anshlag - City, Erlingen
Antonine - City State governing the Church of the Saints
Chermingen - City, Erlingen
Galmund - City, Erlingen
Grozen - Town, Erlingen
Karslev - Capital, Ruzhina
Korvoran - Capital, Reinwick
Legenfeldt - Town, Andover
Lidenbach - Capital, Arnsfeld
Lieswell - Village, Erlingen
Mulsingen - Village, Erlingen
Salzing - City, Duchy of Erlingen
The Five Sisters - Group of islands, Reinwick
Thornwood - Forest, Reinwick
Torburg - Capital, Erlingen

Zienholtz - Capital, Andover
Zurkirk - Village, Erlingen

OTHER LOCATIONS
Crag - Goblin Enclave, Sunset Peaks
Darkwood - Elven Realm, between Merceria and Stonecastle
Drakewell - Clanholding
Great Northern Sea - Sea north of the Petty Kingdoms
Halvaria - Large Empire to the east of Merceria
Haven's Rest - Roadside Inn, Erlingen
Holdcross - Town, Norland
Ironcliff - Dwarven Stronghold, Kingdom
Kharzun's Folly - Great bridge across a ravine, Stonecastle
Korascajan – Sartellian Magical academy
Lost King - Tavern, Ebenhof
Norland - Kingdom north of Merceria
Ravensview - Orc stronghold, formerly city of Norland
Runewald - Village, Therengia
Sea of Storms - Sea west of Halvaria and South of Merceria
Shimmering Sea - Sea south of the Petty Kingdoms
Singing Crow - Inn, Norland
Stonecastle - Dwarven Stronghold, Kingdom
Stonewall - Goblin Enclave, formerly Dwarf mine of Tor-Maldrin
Sunset Peaks - Mountain range, western border of the Clanholdings
The Gap - Between the Thunder Mountains and the Grey Peaks
The Oaken Cudgel - Tavern, Varena, Halvaria
Volstrum - Stormwind magical academy, Ruzhina

BATTLES
Battle of Alantra (954 MC/1096 SR) - Allied fleet defeats Halvaria
Battle of Chermingen (953 MC/1095 SR) - Duchy of Erlingen defeats Andover
Battle of Ebenhof (966 MC/1108 SR) - Duchy of Reinwick defeats Andover
Battle of Lidenbach (961MC/1103 SR) - Temple Fleet defeats Halvarian fleet
Battle of Temple Bay (956 MC/1098 SR) - Church defeats Halvarian in Reinwick waters
Battle of the Pines (968 MC/1110 SR) - Erlingen defeats a Halvarian legion

Battle of the Standing Stones (962 MC/1104 SR) - Therengia defeats Holy Army

Battle of the Wilderness - Alternate name for Battle of the Standing Stones

Siege of Riversend (961 MC/1103 SR) - Weldwyn defeats Kurathian seaborne invasion

THE LEGIONS OF HALVARIA

1st - Southern Frontier, Castimar's legion

2nd - Southern Frontier, Castimar's legion

3rd - Attacking Stonecastle

4th - Attacking Trollden

5th - Attacking the Petty Kingdoms

6th - Facing Ilea

7th - Attacking Ironcliff

8th - Attacking the Petty Kingdoms

9th - Attacking the Petty Kingdoms

10th - Southern Frontier, Castimar's legion

11th - Attacking the Petty Kingdoms

12th - Facing Ilea

GODS

Gundar - God of the Earth, Creator of Dwarves

Saxnor - God of Strength, Patron god of Merceria

SAINTS

Anges - Protector of women

Cunar - The Warrior

Mathew - Protector of the sick poor

Ragnar - Hunter of Necromancers

Augustine – Guardian of Holy Relics

ORC TRIBES

Ashwalkers - Reinwick

Black Arrow - Merceria

Black Ravens - Norland

Red Hand - Therengia

Sky Singers - Deisenbach

Stone Crushers - Therengia

SHIPS

Fearless - Warship, Temple Fleet
Furious - Flagship, Temple Fleet
Illustrious - Warship, Temple Fleet
Invincible - Warship, lost at the Battle of Lidenbach
Majestic - Halvarian Warship, destroyed
Redoubtable - Warship, Temple Fleet
Sprite - Courier ship, Temple Fleet
Swift - Merchant ship
Valiant - Single masted warship, Temple Fleet
Valour - Single masted warship, Temple Fleet
Vigilant - Single masted warship, Temple Fleet

OTHER THINGS

Afterlife - Where spirits go after death
Baroshka - Repository of magical knowledge at the Volstrum
Bender - Goblin healer
Captain-General - Leader of a Halvarian Cohort
Cohort - A subdivision of a Halvarian Legion, 600 men
Commander-General - Leader of a Halvarian Legion
Firepowder - Black powder explosives
Forest Warden - Elite Elvish warriors
Great Dream - Halvarian goal to conquer the entire Continent
Grey Wardens - Elite mounted Elven troops from the Darkwood
Grim Defenders - Mercenary Company
Grunt - Goblin hunter armed with spear
Hearth Guard - Elite Dwarven warriors, Ironcliff
Hide of the Drake - Defensive formation- interlocked shields, spears out
High Strategos - Highest military rank in Halvaria
Knights of the Golden Chalice - Order of Knighthood, Reinwick
Knights of the Sceptre - Order of Knighthood, Erlingen
Knights of Valour - Order of Knighthood, Andover
Lobber - Goblin hunter armed with ranged weapons
Marshal - Highest military rank in most kingdoms
Mountain Wolf - Large wolf native to the Sunset Peaks
Nature's Fury - Beverly's hammer, imbued with the power of the earth
Northern Alliance - Military alliance: Reinwick and Andover
Old Kingdom - Name given to ancient kingdom of Therengia
Outer City - Part of Dwarven city outside the mountain
Primus - Leader of the Church of the Saints
Runt - Young Goblin
Saurians - Lizard-like race

The Five Hundred - Temple Knights of Saint Agnes
The Gilded Throne - The Throne of Halvaria
The Great War - War between the Elves & Orcs 2000 years ago
Tinker - Goblin smith
Torburg Wolves - Mercenary company
Under-mountain - Part of Dwarven city beneath a mountain
Underworld - Where spirits go instead of the Afterlife
Vard - Dwarven Ruler
Wolf Rider - Goblin riding a Mountain Wolf

A Few Words from Paul

Saviour of the Crown details the turning point in the war when the realms of Eiddenwerthe finally come together to defeat the Halvarian invasion of the Petty Kingdoms. Central to this story is Beverly, who unites the realms of Reinwick, Andover, and Erlingen just in time to face off against the enemy in the largest single battle in all of Eiddenwerthe.

Guaranteeing victory is the arrival of the Army of Therengia, a realm that has become a major power on the Continent. They have their own origin story, which is told in one of my other series, The Frozen Flame. Those who have read those books will be happy to see Natalia and Athgar still have a role to play in the fate of the Petty Kingdoms, as do their Orc friends, Shaluhk and Kargen.

Just as important is the breaking of the siege of Ironcliff, allowing the Army of Merceria and their Dwarven allies to march into the empire's lands.

There is, of course, much more! Halvaria is fractured, its ruling elite in disarray as the empire's enemies prepare to take the war to the enemy. More battles will follow, with Beverly, Gerald, and some surprises having the biggest influence on events—events that will have far-reaching consequences for future generations.

The series will conclude in Heir to the Crown, Book 15, Victory of the Crown.

A lot of work went into the creation of this book, and all would have been for naught had it not been for the efforts of my wife, Carol Bennett. Her work in editing, cover design, and promotion has been instrumental in preparing the final manuscript for publication. I would also like to thank Christie Bennett, Stephanie Sandrock, and Amanda Bennett for their encouragement and support, along with Brad Aitken, Stephen Brown, and the late Jeffrey Parker for their contributions.

As always, my BETA team has provided valuable feedback, so thank you to (Rachel Deibler, Michael Rhew, Phyllis Simpson, Don Hinckley, Charles Mohapel, Debbie Reeves, Susan Young, Joanna Smith, Lisa Hanika, Keven Hutchison, Brad Williams, Barbara Raue, Charles Mohapel, Kari Fredlund, Jan Weinmann, Lia Diana Elliot Braddi, John Henniger, Steve Filson.

Finally, I must thank you, my readers, for your interest in my books, for without you, I would never have been able to continue this series.

The adventures in Eiddenwerthe will continue.

About the Author

Paul J Bennett (b. 1961) emigrated from England to Canada in 1967. His father served in the British Royal Navy, and his mother worked for the BBC in London. As a young man, Paul followed in his father's footsteps, joining the Canadian Armed Forces in 1983. He is married to Carol Bennett and has three daughters who are all creative in their own right.

Paul's interest in writing started in his teen years when he discovered the roleplaying game, Dungeons & Dragons (D & D). What attracted him to this new hobby was the creativity it required; the need to create realms, worlds and adventures that pulled the gamers into his stories.

In his 30's, Paul started to dabble in designing his own roleplaying system, using the Peninsular War in Portugal as his backdrop. His regular gaming group were willing victims, er, participants in helping to playtest this new system. A few years later, he added additional settings to his game, including Science Fiction, Post-Apocalyptic, World War II, and the all-important Fantasy Realm where his stories take place.

The beginnings of his first book 'Servant to the Crown' originated over five years ago when he began running a new fantasy campaign. For the world that the Kingdom of Merceria is in, he ran his adventures like a TV show, with seasons that each had twelve episodes, and an overarching plot. When the campaign ended, he knew all the characters, what they had to accomplish, what needed to happen to move the plot along, and it was this that inspired to sit down to write his first novel.

Paul now has four series based in his fantasy world of Eiddenwerthe, and is looking forward to sharing many more books with his readers over the coming years.